DEFY THE DEVIL

Sara Woods
DEFY THE DEVIL

How is't with you?
What, man! defy the devil:
Consider he is an enemy to mankind.
Twelfth Night, Act III, scene iv

St. Martin's Press
New York

Library of Congress Cataloging in Publication Data

Woods, Sara, pseud.
    Defy the devil.

    I. Title.
PR6073.063D44   1984   823'.914   84-13253
ISBN 0-312-19121-9

First published in Great Britain by Macmillan London Ltd.

First U.S. Edition

10 9 8 7 6 5 4 3 2 1

Any work of fiction whose characters were of uniform excellence could rightly be condemned – by that fact if by no other – as being incredibly dull. Therefore no excuse can be considered necessary for the villainy or folly of the people appearing in this book. It seems extremely unlikely that any one of them should resemble a real person, alive or dead. Any such resemblance is completely unintentional and without malice.

S. W.

HILARY TERM, 1975

Tuesday, 11th March

I

'I have no doubt,' said Sir Nicholas Harding severely, 'that I have Geoffrey to thank for persuading you to mix yourself up in this misguided enterprise.' The meeting was being held in his room in chambers – the chambers in the Inner Temple of which he was head – and Geoffrey Horton, who had enjoyed for some years now the privilege of being regarded by counsel as a member of his family, which only meant that the older man felt free to be as critical of his actions as he chose, looked deprecating. Antony Maitland, however, to whom the remark had been addressed, was not to be so easily confounded.

'No, really, Uncle Nick,' he protested. 'He offered me the brief and I accepted it. What's wrong with that?'

'In the circumstances, everything,' Sir Nicholas told him. 'If Mallory had known the full facts, which I very much doubt –'

'Well, sir, I admit –'

'Precisely.' An incautious opening and Sir Nicholas pounced on it immediately. 'Geoffrey, as I suspected, very improperly approached you first and Willett, by some devious method of his own, persuaded Mallory that the matter was a suitable one.' Old Mr Mallory was Sir Nicholas's clerk, and since his nephew was in his chambers the acceptance or refusal of a brief was strictly within Mallory's province. However, Maitland had a staunch ally in Willett, now second-in-command in the clerk's office, who over the years had developed his own methods of circumventing his superior's intentions.

'Well,' said Antony again, and exchanged a look, half-humorous, half-despairing, with his friend and instructing solicitor. 'At least,' he added, suddenly inspired, 'it's nothing that will take me out of town.'

'I suppose you expect me to be thankful for that,' said Sir Nicholas disagreeably, 'and in any other instance you might be

7

right. But as you very well know I have always made it a rule never to accept a case involving a plea of insanity.'

'You defended Paul Herron.'

'That was many years ago, and in any case he wasn't mad.'

'You didn't know that when you accepted the brief from Bellerby,' his nephew reminded him.

'No, it was a piece of imbecility into which I allowed you to persuade me. And see where it led!' said Sir Nicholas.

'To your quarrelling violently with Paul's grandfather, who should have been paying for his defence, and tearing up a brief in his presence that had nothing whatever to do with the case, merely to persuade him that you meant what you said.' Maitland had a smile for the memory, but his uncle obviously found no comfort in it.

'That was not what I meant,' he said repressively. 'When Bellerby felt himself unable to continue to act, Paul Herron engaged Geoffrey as his solicitor, and that was our first meeting with him. And if that had never happened he wouldn't now be offering you this extremely unsuitable case.'

'You can carry it even further if you like.' Maitland showed no sign of being moved by his uncle's arguments. 'He'd never have met Joan Bellerby and married her, or been around to back me up on a dozen occasions when the going was sticky. Think about last October, when he turned up an absolutely vital witness . . . and that was in *my* defence, let me remind you, not on behalf of a client.'

'I prefer not to do anything of the sort,' said Sir Nicholas with a slight shudder. 'I agree that we are both indebted to him' – Geoffrey made an incoherent disclaimer – 'but as this matter is in no way a personal one –'

At this point Maitland decided that his uncle had been allowed enough latitude. 'Nobody's asking *you* to take the case, Uncle Nick. We only want your opinion on the possible value of this defence our client's parents – or rather his adoptive parents – have suggested. Multiple personality disorder,' he added persuasively. 'Not insanity as it's generally understood.'

'I suppose you're about to tell me that you find the matter . . . intriguing,' said Sir Nicholas distastefully. 'If it amuses you to have a client who thinks he's a dozen people rolled into one –'

'Not a dozen, sir, only three. And the suggestion, as I said, came from his family, not from him.'

'Does that make it any better?' inquired Sir Nicholas of the room at large. 'However,' he added, with one of his abrupt changes of mood to which both the younger men were well accustomed, 'I suppose you'd better tell me what you know about the matter, though I cannot conceive that my advice will be of the slightest use to you. To begin with, what is your client's story?'

'I haven't seen him yet, Uncle Nick.'

'I presume that Geoffrey has, and is capable of speaking for himself.' Sir Nicholas's mood had slipped rapidly back into austerity.

'I know this much,' Antony assured him, 'the question opens up some interesting fields for speculation.'

'A psychiatrist—'

'Yes, I'm afraid it will come to that. It's the legal aspect we want to talk about, not the medical one.'

'Very well then.' Sir Nicholas sat back in his chair and disposed himself to listen. 'You had better tell us, Geoffrey, but kindly begin at the beginning, and don't be infected by this unfortunate habit of Antony's of jumping *in media res*.' _into the_

'It won't take very long,' said Geoffrey encouragingly. _middle_
'Simon Winthrop is now twenty-seven and was orphaned _of a_
twenty years ago. He's accused of murdering his grandfather.' _thing_

'And did he?' Sir Nicholas asked, obviously anxious to get to the heart of the matter.

'Three witnesses say he did.'

'Eye witnesses?'

'Near enough. One is the housekeeper, who caught a glimpse of him leaving the house on the night of the murder and went straight to her employer's study where she found him dead. Stabbed,' he added for good measure. 'She'd seen the old man alive not much more than an hour before, and as the police and the doctors were on the spot so promptly the time of death was fairly confidently established as having taken place not more than a few minutes before she found him dead at nine o'clock.'

'You mentioned three witnesses.'

'The other two were neighbours, who saw Winthrop leaving the house and later identified him in a police line-up. The time tallied exactly with the housekeeper's; they had an appointment and therefore noticed exactly when they left their own house next door.'

'Just a moment, Geoffrey. You mentioned, or rather Antony did, this man Winthrop's adoptive parents. Would it not have been more natural for him to join his grandfather on his parents' death?'

'I can see I shall have to explain the family to you,' said Geoffrey rather ruefully. 'The old man, the deceased, is Thomas Wilmot.'

'I know that name.'

'Of course you do, Uncle Nick,' said Antony impatiently. 'It may not be much in your line, but he was one of the foremost portrait painters of his day, and you've often heard Clare speak of him.'

'Oh *that* Wilmot,' said Sir Nicholas. 'I had an idea he was dead.'

'He is. We've just been telling you—'

'Some time ago,' said Sir Nicholas with exaggerated patience.

'He was apparently rather an odd man.' Geoffrey thought it prudent to ignore the interruption and took up the tale again. 'His will, for instance. He'd no sons of his own, but he excluded his two daughters in favour of their heirs male. That's where Winthrop's motive comes in. And he quite cheerfully agreed to Simon's adoption by a couple called Norman and Sylvia Patmore, who'd been friends of the boy's parents, according to Mrs Patmore saying he couldn't be bothered to have a child that age about the house.'

'You mentioned another daughter.'

'Yes, but she and her husband had emigrated to Canada two years before the Winthrops died in a motor crash. Mrs Patmore thinks they were still finding things rather difficult, I take it she meant financially, but in any case they also wrote giving their consent to the adoption.'

'I see. Am I to take it then that your client stands to inherit one half of Mr Wilmot's residual estate?'

'That's right.'

'And was Thomas Wilmot's wealth equal to his reputation?'

'I don't know how much he made from his painting, but he was certainly a very wealthy man.'

'Motive and opportunity,' said Sir Nicholas thoughtfully. 'I can't see that your client has a leg to stand on.'

There was a brief pause, perhaps out of respect for the fact that Sir Nicholas had permitted himself a colloquialism, a thing quite unknown until his marriage some years before. He and his nephew were both tall men, but otherwise – except for a brief, elusive likeness of expression which a keen observer might note – as unlike as could be. Sir Nicholas was more heavily built, and his hair was so fair that what silver there was in it was hardly noticeable. He had, besides, an authoritative manner of which he was quite unconscious, and sufficient pretentions to good looks to merit the adjective handsome when any of his cases caught the attention of the newspapers. Maitland, on the other hand, had dark, rather springy hair, except when it had been flattened for hours under his wig; a preference for the casual, except insofar as his profession necessitated decorum; a sense of humour that had sometimes earned him enemies; and a sensitivity that had more than once got him into trouble.

As for the third member of the party, Geoffrey Horton was a few inches shorter and a few years younger than his friend, with a cheerful disposition that was often masked by his sense of propriety where his clients' affairs were concerned.

'What has Winthrop to say for himself?' inquired Sir Nicholas, when neither of his companions seemed to be going to give him any further information.

'He says he didn't do it.'

'What is his explanation of the fact that three people have identified him, one of whom probably knows him well?'

'Just that they must be mistaken. And for an alibi,' said Geoffrey bitterly, 'he offers me the old story of having been for a walk that evening . . . alone. And not, of course, meeting anyone he knew.'

'Does he live by himself?'

'Yes, he has a flat, if you can identify it by that name. The attic of a house in Chelsea which has been altered to make a studio. Not self-contained, of course.'

'Are you telling me he's another artist?'

'Yes, but not in the same class as his grandfather, though I suppose there's no telling how he might develop given the chance. I like his stuff,' said Geoffrey, 'but I don't consider myself a judge.'

'Still, he makes a living?'

'He stretches his income by doing some commercial art on a freelance basis. That's another point against him, I'm afraid, or you could even say two points. First, he despises what he is

11

doing in that line, and secondly he grudges every moment not spent in doing the kind of work he likes.'

'And what is that?'

'I don't know the technical term, but he paints things as they are,' said Geoffrey, rather as though he were apologizing for some nameless crime. 'I believe there's a sort of return to that sort of thing after all the Impressionists and Post-Impressionists and so on. At least—'

'You're getting ahead of the story, Geoffrey,' said Antony, not particularly interested in this aspect of the affair.

'So I am. Thomas Wilmot was murdered ten days ago, on Saturday, the first of March, to be exact. Of course the housekeeper, Mrs Barham, gave her story to the police straight away, and they were waiting on Simon Winthrop's doorstep when he got back from his walk. They took him in for questioning right away, but being an utter fool he didn't call me until later, said he didn't think there was any need to be represented. And when they rounded up the neighbours he went into the identification parade like a lamb. Once that was over they didn't waste any more time in making the arrest.'

'Were you his solicitor before?'

'I don't suppose he'd ever needed one, certainly not one in my line of country. But Bernard looked after his parents' affairs and that's how I came into it.' (Bernard Stanley was Geoffrey's partner, and looked after what might be called the family side of the practice.)

'So then you went and interviewed him. What did you make of him yourself?'

'I think if I hadn't known most of this before I'd ever met him I'd have said he was a likeable chap. As it was . . . something about his denials didn't ring true. He told me where he'd been on this hypothetical walk, but I got a definite impression that he was making it up as he went along, and that the only thing that really concerned him was to bring himself to the point where the police saw him coming along the road. I told you they were waiting for him. So there we were, without a defence except what you'd call stout denial, Antony.'

'Not me, Bertie Wooster.'

'Well, you see my trouble. I went to the Magistrate's Court hearing on the Monday myself, because it was quite obvious he'd be committed for trial and you were taken up with that

Causing an Affray business, Antony. Besides, I wanted time to make up my mind what best to do with a hopeless situation. But then I talked to his parents . . . I needn't keep adding the word adoptive, need I? I thought at first it was just the old story, they couldn't believe he'd do a thing like that. But there was the evidence, so they'd both been racking their brains for something that would provide an excuse. And they came up with this multiple personality disorder business.'

'I've heard stories, of course,' said Sir Nicholas, 'and never really believed them. Some novelist, letting his imagination run riot.'

'I gather some doctors recognise it, while others are as sceptical as I imagine we all are. But what the Patmores told me was interesting, and as Antony's case finished rather more quickly than we expected I thought he might find it so too. And we both felt your advice would be useful on how such a thing might be regarded in law. There doesn't seem to be any precedent in this country.'

'I imagine there is none.'

'Not that I can find anyway.'

'And as it is just the sort of thing that every newspaper reporter in the country would fall upon with screams of delight, I imagine we should have heard from that source if from no other if there had been any previous case,' said Sir Nicholas. 'However, you'd better tell me what put this idea into – what was their name? – the Patmores' heads.'

'It started when they went round to his studio to pack up some clothes for him, and they went back at Mrs Patmore's instigation to do some tidying up. They were very familiar with his paintings, of course, there were a number of them about the place which they thought they'd better take home with them to keep them safe, and at the right temperature, whatever that is. Winthrop's so far successful that he sells a good deal of what he does but not for very high prices. So the Patmores started looking around to see if there was anything else they should remove, and were startled to find three other paintings in a completely different style put away in a cupboard.'

'He must have friends in the artistic community. Presumably that's the obvious answer, that he was keeping them for a friend.'

13

'The trouble with that idea is that they bore his signature, which is quite a distinctive one.'

'Well, even if he painted them,' said Sir Nicholas rather impatiently, 'that's hardly proof that some other personality inhabited him while he did so.'

'Not by itself. Except that the Patmores insisted that they were like nothing their son could ever have brought himself to perpetrate. Mrs Patmore described them as horrible, and Mr Patmore, who seems to me a very level-headed sort of man, called them evil.'

'You've seen them, I presume. What would you call them, Geoffrey?'

'I'd agree with Mr Patmore.'

'Pornography?'

'Not exactly. This is awfully difficult, it's rather like trying to describe a sound. All I can say is that when I looked at them I could imagine all the devils in hell rioting across the canvas.'

Sir Nicholas exchanged a look with his nephew. This from Horton, who for all his excellent qualities could never be described as imaginative. 'What does your client say about it?' Sir Nicholas asked.

'He denies all knowledge of them. And certainly he never stored them for a friend.'

'But if they were in the rather restricted quarters you have described, surely he must have known they were there.'

'He says not. And the Patmores told me they were leaning face to the wall at the back of a cupboard. If he really painted them while some other personality had him in its grip he might have taken them for his own work without ever looking at them again.'

'This is getting complicated. You're telling me he may have changed from one personality to another. The Simon Winthrop his parents know, who does, I gather from what you've told me, quite ordinary paintings, into a man capable of far from orthodox work. Wouldn't he have been aware of that?'

'Not necessarily, as I understand it.' Horton looked rather helplessly at Maitland, who took up the explanation obligingly.

'We've been reading it up, Uncle Nick,' he said. 'If we grant for a moment the premise that this disorder exists, it's sometimes true that a person suffering from it is quite aware of the fact, but there are also cases on record where each personality

14

has its own memory, and no knowledge at all of the others.'

'But is it really seriously regarded by the medical profession?'

'According to my reading the condition was first identified by an Italian physician as long ago as 1791. Some psychiatrists, of course, are complete Doubting Thomases, and I don't blame them. They think that people who display these symptoms are faking them, though they admit that they do it rather ingeniously. Others think there's no faking involved, but believe this turning into another personality or personalities to be a human defence mechanism, rather like amnesia. And still others believe that a great many cases are never diagnosed at all, that there are far more than we know about. And the odd thing is that Geoffrey took two of the paintings to Julian Verlaine, who as you know is an expert in such things, one of Winthrop's usual work, and one of the hidden ones. And Verlaine swears they were painted by different hands in spite of the signatures.'

'In that case –'

'No, Uncle Nick, that's where you're wrong. If he really escaped from one personality to another it would be a completely different person doing the painting.'

'Good God!' said Sir Nicholas blankly.

'You may well say so, but I'm not finished yet. Simon Winthrop was – is, I suppose – engaged to be married.'

'Does he deny that too?'

'No, nothing like that. His fiancée's name is Madeleine Rexford, and a few days after Winthrop was arrested a girl she didn't know came to see her. Miss Rexford says she's sure this girl meant well, which I think is charitable of her as what she had to say was so upsetting. Her name was Bertha Harvey, by the way. She said Winthrop had seduced a girl called Antonia Dryden, her room-mate, for whom he later arranged an abortion from which she died. Geoffrey says our client denies that too.'

'Would you expect him to do anything else?'

'No, but what both his parents and his fiancée say is that the whole thing is quite out of character. Naturally Miss Rexford would think so, but Mrs Patmore said two things that made Geoffrey think twice about it. One was that Simon was very fond of children and had a horror of abortion, and the other that she had never known him not to stand by the result of his actions. She says if he'd got this girl with child he would have stood by her and married her no matter what the consequences.'

'Perhaps this Dryden girl didn't want to marry him.'

'That's not what her room-mate says. Anyway, Uncle Nick, that's the second point.'

'But one of you mentioned that there were three. Three other personalities besides the one his family and friends knew.'

'Yes, well, according to the Patmores the third is the one who committed the murder. They say that now they know he had two other personalities besides the one they were familiar with, it must have been in yet another that he killed his grandfather.'

'What did they tell you of his ordinary persona?'

'That he's a quiet chap, wrapped up in his work, wrapped up in Madeleine – they were going to be married about a month from now. I'm not asking you whether you believe all this, Uncle Nick, I'm asking you what the legal position would be if we trotted it out as a defence. And before we go any further I'd better tell you that it has been tried once in the States and rejected by the court there.'

'Did they think it an insufficient defence, I wonder, or merely feel that the prisoner had invented the whole story with a view of getting away with an insanity plea?'

'I don't know that, Uncle Nick. I'm sure that's what the Patmores are doing, trying to make the best of a bad job, but to my mind the question of insanity wouldn't necessarily arise.'

'In order to answer your question I must assume for the moment that you are able to persuade the court that your client is in fact suffering from this multiple personality disorder you talk of, which I must tell you, Antony, I think is very unlikely.'

'Yes, sir, I admit that. Let's suppose for the moment that it's true and that we can demonstrate it.'

'You're not thinking, I hope, that you could base his defence on automatism. That, may I remind you, applies generally to a physical rather than a mental condition.'

'I understand that, sir.' He was treating his uncle with unusual circumspection today, knowing how much the discussion must be offending him. Sir Nicholas's dislike of anything involving the abnormal was well known.

'Then – still making the assumption I spoke of – he could be said, I suppose, to be suffering from an insane delusion, but unless it was a delusion that would entitle him to kill his grandfather, I don't think that would be admitted either. We

16

must, however, remember that *actus non facit reum nisi mens sit rea*, and if in fact he suffers from this rather unusual condition–'

'Yes, Uncle Nick, that's all very well, but supposing Simon Winthrop–the one everyone's been familiar with for years–is innocent but another of his personalities is guilty?'

'I very much doubt that the court will be willing to believe in four distinct personalities . . . I think four was the number we'd reached, wasn't it? If he himself made the claim . . . but you tell us, Geoffrey, that he doesn't.'

'No, but I haven't put to him yet the conclusions that his family have drawn; and as we've said it's perfectly possible, according to the people who believe in this condition, that no one personality has knowledge of the others.'

'In that case there must be some gaps in his memory,' Sir Nicholas pointed out.

'Quite considerable gaps I should think, considering the activities he's supposed to have indulged in.'

'Precisely. I think the only thing you can do is to see him again, together I should suggest, and perhaps between the two of you you can come to some conclusion as to his state of mind.'

'I want Antony to see him, of course,' said Geoffrey. 'He's better at that sort of thing than I am.'

'More imaginative,' said Sir Nicholas, and it was obvious that the description was not intended as a compliment to his nephew. 'If in the course of your inquiry you come to the conclusion that he is . . . let us say not normal, the very best you could do for him, I imagine, would be to get him declared unfit to plead, and detained during Her Majesty's pleasure. If you go to court with an insanity plea, which is what it would amount to, the result in the long run might be just the same. Or the jury might reject the idea altogether as new-fangled nonsense. And don't remind me again, Antony, that the first case was identified some time in the eighteenth century. That isn't going to help at all.'

'I suppose not, Uncle Nick.' Maitland sounded depressed. 'If we could call it schizophrenia it would be easier; everyone's heard of that and think they know what it means, but none of the definitions of the different kinds of schizophrenia are anything like this.'

'In that case,' said Sir Nicholas, chilly again, 'I cannot think why you brought the matter up. We'll talk again when you have a little further information,' he added, relenting, and glanced at his watch as he spoke. 'When are you thinking of visiting the prison?'

'This afternoon,' said Geoffrey, for some reason again sounding rather apologetic.

'I knew it!'

'Well, sir, if the chap really is mad –' Maitland didn't attempt to complete the sentence.

'I can see that nothing I can say will persuade you of the folly of accepting a case with such abnormal undertones. However, in the meantime, there is nothing I hope that will prevent either of you from joining me in an early lunch. But I think, don't you,' he added, getting up and coming round the desk, 'that we will banish your Mr Winthrop from our thoughts and our conversation while we have our meal.'

Neither of his companions had any objection to make to that. Maitland was already dreading the coming interview and prison visiting wasn't his idea of a really jolly afternoon, so he was glad enough of an excuse to dismiss the matter from his thoughts so far as he was able to do so. As for Geoffrey, he was anxious to know his friend's opinion, but there was no hurry. As Sir Nicholas had obviously realised, once Maitland had encountered his new client he would be committed, and Horton was quite content to wait on the event.

II

Simon Winthrop was a fair-haired young man, unusually fair, in fact. He was of about Geoffrey's height, though rather more slightly built. Certainly, Maitland thought, the first impression he made was a good one. His blue eyes had a direct look, and if his chin argued a certain obstinacy, the rest of his features were regular enough and he might even be categorized as good-looking.

He came into the interview room a little hesitantly, and had a wary look for his counsel when Geoffrey performed the introduction. There was a strained look about him that Maitland didn't quite like, a bad witness probably. But that was a snap judgement, and must wait for confirmation or refutation. Antony took the chair at the side of the table furthest from the door, mastering his own preference which would have been to have wandered around the room while he asked his questions. But that might prove distracting, and until he knew the other man better . . .

'I'm afraid you're going to find this a bit of a bore, Mr Winthrop,' he said. 'You've already told your story to Mr Horton, and now I want it again from the beginning.'

That brought a silence. Winthrop too had seated himself and now glanced uncertainly at Geoffrey, who had taken a chair on his left. His eyes lingered on his solicitor while he answered the other man's question slowly. 'Mr Horton must have told you that there is no story, except that I didn't kill my grandfather.'

'Well, that's a beginning anyway,' said Maitland encouragingly. 'Let's go over the prosecution's case point by point and see what answers we can come up with.' He glanced at Horton. 'Where shall we begin, Geoffrey?'

'The motive,' Geoffrey suggested.

The weakest part of the case . . . or was it? Only time would tell. 'Very well, Mr Winthrop, what about it?' Maitland asked.

'I didn't want Grandfather's money,' said Winthrop quickly.

'The question remains, however, could you be said to have needed it?'

'If you put it that way I can only answer, yes. But I thought –'

'You thought I was supposed to be on your side. I can assure you, Mr Winthrop – and Mr Horton will confirm this if you don't believe me – to be on your side means that I must know the very worst that the prosecution can come up with. We don't know yet who'll be taking the case – it's very unlikely to get into court before the Easter recess – but whoever has it in hand that's something you'll be asked, and I imagine he'll have a pretty good idea of your financial circumstances to face you with if you attempt a denial. In any case we have the jury to think of, and most people have been pressed for money at some time in their life. They might take some convincing that the same thing didn't apply to you.' He paused there, but as his client didn't reply immediately he went on after a moment, 'There's also the little matter of your being on oath. I don't know how important that is to you.'

For some reason Winthrop flushed. 'As a matter of fact,' he said, 'I do take it seriously. But is there any need for me to give evidence?'

'That's something I can't answer yet, but if all we're going to

19

have to offer is your denial of guilt I imagine the court will want to hear it from your own lips.'

'And that means questions,' said Winthrop, obviously not relishing the thought.

'A lot of questions, I'm afraid. Don't think I don't sympathize with your dislike of having to answer them,' Maitland assured him. 'I hate explanations myself. But I really don't see how we're going to get away without any answers at all.'

'Of course you're right but . . . you don't understand,' said Winthrop despairingly.

'Tell me then,' Maitland invited.

'I'm hard up, I have been ever since I struck out on my own.'

'That's nothing to be ashamed of.'

For the first time a flicker of amusement showed in the prisoner's face. 'I suppose I'd better start one of those explanations you spoke of,' he said. 'You know my parents were killed in an accident when I was seven. There wasn't any insurance, and there was apparently no one else involved whom I could claim against. Norman and Sylvia adopted me –'

'The Patmores,' Geoffrey put in, in answer to Maitland's inquiring look.

'– and they've been endlessly good to me. I used to call them aunt and uncle, they'd been friends of my parents they told me, but gradually we dropped that. I know Norman would have liked me to follow in his footsteps, but I seem to have inherited an artistic tendency from my grandfather, and I just couldn't see myself going into banking.'

'Was your leaving home the result of a disagreement?'

'No, nothing like that. Neither of them tried to press me in any way, though I think Sylvia too would have liked what she felt was a more respectable profession. But there was nowhere at home for me to work, and even if there had been I couldn't see myself filling up their house with pictures, disordering their existence altogether. I got a job with an advertising firm, and they seemed to like the stuff I turned out. Anyway before too long I could afford a small place of my own, and there was a little to spare for paint and canvas. Occasionally I sold a picture, that helped too, and it happened more often as time went on. I think myself there'll be a return to realism before long, not just reproducing things like a colour photograph but . . . oh well, that doesn't matter. Meanwhile things have been pretty precarious . . . financially, I mean.'

'And I understand you're being married in a month's time,' said Maitland in an expressionless tone.

'Yes, I am. I should say, I was going to be. And if you want to know how I intended to manage, I went to see my old firm, the one I was with when I first left home, and they seemed glad enough to have me back as soon as they had a vacancy. So I was going to start work there, nine to five, as soon as we got back from our honeymoon.'

'I rather get the impression that the idea didn't please you much.'

'No, it didn't, but if it was a choice between that and not marrying Madeleine . . . but I expect that doesn't matter either now.'

'Then we come to the point, did you know about your grandfather's will?'

'Oh yes, he told me about it on my twenty-first birthday, that was six years ago. He said I'd inherit half his property, the half that would have come to my mother if he hadn't had this thing about not approving of women inheriting. I know it's an old-fashioned idea, but he thought it was the man's business to be the breadwinner, and as soon as his daughters were married he'd no further responsibility for them financially. He knew my Aunt Celia had one son as well, so that was fair enough and the other half would go to him. It may be a bit of a muddle because I know Sylvia hadn't heard from my aunt for years. She may have kept in touch with Grandfather, but if so he never told me.'

'Half his estate is not an inconsiderable fortune, I believe.'

'That's what I understand too. Don't misunderstand me, Mr Maitland, I'm not saying I wasn't glad to be one of his heirs, I'm not saying the money wouldn't have been useful, but I wouldn't have wanted to get it that way. He was an old man but quite healthy, and I think in his own way he enjoyed his life.'

'What was your relationship with your grandfather, Mr Winthrop?'

'He didn't care much for children, though Sylvia used to take me to see him regularly when I was too young to go by myself. Lately I've seen a fair amount of him. I'd go to dinner about once a month, I suppose, always a rather ceremonial occasion. We never quarrelled, if that's what you're getting at, and he'd even come round to my place sometimes and give rather grudging

21

approval of the work I was doing. His own fame was as a portrait painter, you know. He used to call my style facile, by which I think he meant I should be trying my hand at something more difficult.'

'If you visited him so frequently you must have known his housekeeper quite well.'

'Mrs Barham? Yes, of course I did. She and her husband, Charlie, who acted as Grandfather's chauffeur and did any odd jobs that needed doing about the place. They'd been with him for ever, since my grandmother's death I think, which was before I was born, according to Sylvia.'

'A devoted couple,' Maitland asked.

'To each other, yes, I should say so.'

'I meant to Mr Wilmot.'

'I suppose that's true too.' Simon Winthrop sounded doubtful, however. 'They're old-fashioned enough not to think domestic service is anything to be ashamed of, and both of them saw that everything was done exactly to his liking. But he was an autocratic old boy, he wouldn't have stood for anything else, so I suppose you could say it was just that they knew when they were on to a good thing. And the same thing might be said from Grandfather's point of view. He paid them very well but I expect he realized how difficult it would have been to replace them. He wasn't by any means a miser, but not one to waste his money.'

'As you dined so regularly with Mr Wilmot and knew Mrs Barham quite well, it follows that she must have known you quite well by sight.'

'Of course she did. That's why I can't understand –' He broke off, looking from one of his companions to the other. 'I always thought she rather liked me,' he said.

'What is it that you can't understand, Mr Winthrop?'

'Why she should lie about seeing me that night. I wasn't there, I've told Mr Horton that already.'

'Her exact words,' said Geoffrey, 'were that she caught a glimpse of you.'

'Yes, but knowing me so well how could she have been mistaken? She wasn't in any doubt herself that it was me she saw. I could tell that from the way she spoke in the Magistrate's Court. And you saw the kind of person she is, Mr Horton, not malicious, the last person in the world you'd think would tell a lie about a thing like that. And yet she couldn't have been mistaken, she must be lying.'

'When you went to your grandfather's house what was the ordinary course of events. For instance, who let you in?'

'I told you my visits were mostly . . . I suppose you could say rather formal. I'd be expected, and Charlie would come to the door.'

'He hasn't said anything about seeing you that night. What exactly did Mrs Barham say, Geoffrey?'

'That she came into the hall just as Mr Winthrop was letting himself out of the front door,' said Geoffrey. 'She didn't see him full face, but she knows him so well she was quite sure there was no possibility that she was mistaken.'

'That's a thought. How do the Barhams stand under Mr Wilmot's will?'

'He bought them an annuity a few years ago when he reached his eightieth birthday. The understanding was that they would stay with him as long as he needed them. A gentleman's agreement only, nothing in writing, but you see they abided by it. And actually it was to their advantage to do so, because as long as they were receiving their salary as well they could put away the whole income from the annuity.'

'Thank you, Geoffrey.' If they had been alone Antony would have added, 'You always know everything', in a gently satirical tone, but as it was he turned straight back to their client. 'You don't think then, Mr Winthrop, that either of them would have felt any cause of resentment towards you for benefiting in a more generous way?'

'No, I don't. I've always thought they were quite content with their lot, and though I haven't seen either of them since it happened, except when Mrs Barham was giving her evidence, I'm quite sure they'll be upset by Grandfather's death.'

'But still you say Mrs Barham is lying about seeing you?'

'Yes, though I can hardly believe it. But it's difficult to see how she could have been mistaken. The hall is very brightly lit. I think Grandfather's eyesight was failing, though he never admitted it, because he always insisted lately on rather more highly powered bulbs than most people consider necessary.' He hesitated and then threw his hands out in a rather despairing gesture. 'It doesn't make sense, any of it,' he said. 'I realize everything I say contradicts itself, but I can't help that. I

23

just don't understand.'

'There are also Mr Wilmot's next door neighbours, Mr and Mrs Alford,' Geoffrey reminded him.

'You told me their full names but I've forgotten them,' Maitland admitted.

'Cecil and Adela.' As if it mattered at this stage, Horton's tone added, but then he wondered with some surprise whether the interruption had been deliberate, to give Simon Winthrop time to recollect himself. Which wouldn't be like Antony: if his sympathies were aroused he was far more likely to attempt to disguise the fact by speaking sharply to his client.

'Yes, of course,' said Maitland meaninglessly. 'Mr and Mrs Cecil Alford. Do you know them, Mr Winthrop?'

'I never met them. When I dined with Grandfather it was always alone. He wasn't exactly a recluse, but he preferred old friends, people of his own generation, and so many of them had died and he didn't seem inclined to make new friends to take their place. I saw the Alfords at the Magistrate's Court. They'd be round about forty I should imagine – do you agree with that, Mr Horton? – not the sort of people he'd have been interested in knowing in any case.'

'I see. Do you agree with that estimate, Geoffrey?'

'As far as age goes, yes, though I'd put Mrs Alford as several years younger than her husband. But they both said quite definitely that though they knew Mr Wilmot had a grandson who visited him fairly regularly it was only through gossip between their charwoman and the one Mrs Barham employed. They'd never noticed him entering or leaving the house . . . until that night.'

'Was the identification parade properly conducted?'

'From what Mr Winthrop tells me, yes. Besides the investigating officer is your old friend, Chief Inspector Conway, Antony. Yes, I know,' he added in answer to Maitland's grimace, 'you don't like the fellow. But I've never heard that he was sloppy about things like that, or unfair either according to his lights.'

'I agree with you there, but identification's a tricky business.' He turned again to their client. 'I suppose there's a convenient street light just outside your grandfather's house,' he said, making the words a question.

Winthrop looked a little startled. 'As a matter of fact there is,'

24

he said. Whoever it was, the Alfords must have seen him quite clearly, and even less than Mrs Barham had they reason to be lying. But they'd picked him out without any hesitation. 'Do you think – I know it sounds unlikely – but do you think someone could have shown them a photograph of me and paid them to say they'd seen me that night?'

'That's an expensive neighbourhood they're living in.'

'That doesn't always follow. They might be living beyond their means.'

Antony smiled at him. 'It will have to be looked into certainly,' he said, 'but I'd be raising your hopes falsely, Mr Winthrop, if I told you I thought anything would come of that idea. If I can succeed in raising a doubt in the mind of even one of these witnesses when I cross-examine them . . . but meanwhile you say your grandfather's circle of acquaintances was somewhat restricted nowadays. Can you think of anyone with a motive for killing him?'

'No, I can't.' For the first time Winthrop smiled himself. 'Only the rather facetious one, that someone didn't like the portrait he'd painted of them. But it must be at least five years since he accepted any commissions in that line.'

Maitland returned the smile. 'I should very much like the chance of bringing that up before the court,' he said, 'but I'm afraid, like you, I think it's rather a forlorn hope. By the way, Geoffrey, what time is Mr Winthrop alleged to have left Mr Wilmot's house? I really haven't had time to study my brief yet,' he added apologetically.

Geoffrey thought, but did not say, nor will you till the last moment, if then. Nor did he remind his friend that the matter had been gone into when they talked to Sir Nicholas that morning. Aloud he replied, 'Mrs Barham says she's sure it was nine because she looked at the hall clock.'

'Did she say what she was doing in the hall at that time?'

'No, and I didn't ask her. It was obvious that a committal was inevitable, and I thought it best to hold our fire.'

'Yes, certainly. Did the Alfords agree with that time.'

'They did, and explained that they were going to some neighbours for after dinner drinks. And for the moment,' Geoffrey added, 'that takes care of the police case against Mr Winthrop. But you remember, Antony, that a couple of matters have come up on which we need his opinion.'

25

'I haven't forgotten. But as you had these matters at first hand, Geoffrey—'

'As you like.' Privately, Geoffrey was wondering how long it would be before his friend took over the questioning, even though it promised to be an awkward business. 'You'll remember, Mr Winthrop, that you handed me the keys of your studio and asked me to give them to Mrs Patmore so that she could pack you a bag, and arrange for the removal of your private things and paintings to a safer place.'

'Yes, of course I remember that.' But Winthrop, though he'd been speaking easily, sounded suddenly wary. 'Sylvia didn't mind, did she? I can't imagine her minding doing that for me. Unless of course . . . oh my God, are you telling me that she and Norman really think I killed the old man?'

'They say,' said Geoffrey carefully, 'that any such action would be completely against your nature.'

'Well, thank goodness for that anyway.' He paused again, looking rather closely at his solicitor. 'That last sentence of yours sounded as if you were about to add, "but",' he remarked.

'They have come up with a theory, and I think I should stress, Mr Winthrop, that it is out of concern and affection for you that they have done so. Have you ever heard of multiple personality disorder?'

'Multiple—? You mean split-personality, schizophrenia?'

'Not exactly, though I think most people confuse the two. It's a matter about which there's a good deal of controversy, but—'

'But it's sheer nonsense!' Winthrop interrupted without ceremony. 'I lived with them since I was seven until about five years ago. They can't think I've changed so much in that time. And—whatever you mean by this disorder you've mentioned, I'm not mad!'

'They are trying,' said Geoffrey, who was clearly getting moment by moment further out of his depth, 'to explain something which otherwise would be to them quite inexplicable.'

'Then they do think I killed him.' Winthrop turned helplessly to Maitland, who came abruptly to his feet, his chair scraping across the wooden floor with an ugly jarring sound.

'Bear with us for a little, Mr Winthrop,' he said. 'If you'll be patient I'll try to explain to you exactly what is meant by the term multiple personality disorder. I'm sorry it's such a clumsy one, but it seems to be the accepted medical way of describing it.'

'I know,' said Winthrop. 'At least, I think I do.' He leaned back slightly in his chair, his hands limp on the table in front of him and a look of utter despair on his face. 'Dr Jekyll and Mr Hyde,' he said.

'I suppose the answer to that is, yes and no,' said Maitland. 'There's no funny business involved in the change, though some doctors – I rather think the majority of them, in this country at any rate – feel that the whole thing is put on for some obscure purpose by the patient. Others speak of "human defence mechanism", and feel that the switching of personalities may be a useful escape from an embarrassing situation. Rather like amnesia. In fact, losing time, as they describe it, is one of the most frequent symptoms.

'There are, I understand – you see I've been doing my homework, Geoffrey – distinct physiological differences between the alternate personalities, habits alter and so sometimes do speech patterns and the range of the person's voice.'

'You're trying to tell me that I . . . that Sylvia and Norman think that I . . . it couldn't happen without my knowing.'

'On the contrary, each personality may have its own memory, and no knowledge of the others. Some doctors feel that the state can be treated by introducing the personalities to each other. What I'm trying to get over is that a perfectly normal, pleasant person might have another side to him, sadistic, or hostile, or perhaps promiscuous.' He stopped there and went to the window and back again before he continued. 'This must be horribly confusing to you, Mr Winthrop, and I'm sorry for it. The matter has been raised and in fairness to yourself we have to go into it. So will you reserve your protests and do your best to put us straight on one or two matters.'

'I –' Simon Winthrop's hands were clenched into fists now. 'I appreciate your trying to put this as delicately as you can, Mr Maitland, but something that was said makes me realise that Sylvia and Norman . . . and that I find hard to believe.'

'They're trying to explain something that is otherwise hard for them . . . inexplicable, as Mr Horton said.'

'You'd better tell me.' He glanced from Maitland to Geoffrey. 'Is this "something", Mr Horton, about some girl I'd never heard of, and whether I'd ever done any paintings in a different

27

style than my usual one?'

'Yes. You know that Mr and Mrs Patmore went back to your studio to move your paintings.'

'But what have they to do with what's happened, or my studio either for that matter?'

Maitland took up the tale again. 'Your family and friends are all familiar with your work in – in a certain style,' he said. 'Some others signed with your name but completely different both in subject and composition were found in a cupboard. You told Mr Horton you knew nothing of them.'

'Which cupboard?' The words came sharply.

'The one, I understand, where you keep your painting paraphernalia, spare canvasses and so on, when it's not in use,' Geoffrey put in.

'I usually stuck my stuff round the walls,' said Winthrop. 'I expect you'd think the whole place was an awful mess, but it's convenient for the few people who are interested in my work, and besides – you'll think this is a sort of vanity – I like to remind myself that I'm not exclusively a commercial artist.'

'That seems very understandable. Did you ever notice these other paintings leaning against the wall at the back of the cupboard? How many of them were there, Geoffrey?'

'Three, and all facing the wall, I'm told.'

'I might not have noticed them. I open the door and grab what I want and very rarely need to turn the light on. But how could they be there? I'd never have put anything I'd done, in my own style or another, away and forgotten about it.'

'That's the puzzle that Mr and Mrs Patmore were trying to solve,' Antony told him. 'At first – I'm quoting Mr Horton because I haven't seen them yet – they disliked what they saw intensely, but thought you'd been trying your hand at a different style. It wasn't until another point came up that Mr Horton thought of showing an example of each to an expert. His opinion was that the same person couldn't have painted what we'll call your own work and these three hidden ones.'

'And all this about – what was it you called it? – multiple personality disorder. Am I supposed to have painted them and forgotten all about it?'

'The possibility has been suggested,' Maitland said cautiously.

'What were they like?'

Maitland fumbled in his pocket and produced a rather

28

battered-looking envelope. The words he'd scribbled on the back were almost indecipherable, even to him, but he remembered their drift well enough. 'It was as if all the devils in hell were rioting across the canvas,' he said.

'I don't understand,' said Winthrop hopelessly. For the moment he seemed beyond protest.

'Neither did your . . . will it confuse you if I call them your parents?'

'No, of course not, I always looked on Sylvia and Norman like that.'

'I'll tell you something else that came to their knowledge, that they mentioned to Mr Horton, and which prompted him to take the paintings to an expert. So we must go back a little to the time when they were still puzzling about the differences. Miss Rexford went to see them.'

'Madeleine? What's odd about that? They always got on well together, and perhaps they were able to comfort each other a little.'

'I think a better way of putting it would be that what she told them only added to the confusion,' Maitland told him.

'I'm beginning to realize that Sylvia and Norman believe I killed my grandfather,' said Winthrop rather bitterly, 'but surely Madeleine . . . I'd have thought she knows what I'm really like even better than they do.'

'I haven't met Miss Rexford—' Maitland began.

'I have,' said Geoffrey. 'We met almost immediately after your arrest, and I assure you, Mr Winthrop, she told me quite clearly that nothing would convince her that you'd done such a thing. But that was before—'

'Before what? For heaven's sake tell me and don't beat about the bush.'

'Before a girl called Bertha Harvey went to see her,' said Horton, his eyes fixed on his client's face. Winthrop stared at him.

'Bertha Harvey. I've never heard of her,' he said. 'Is she the girl you mentioned to me, Mr Horton?'

'Not exactly. According to her you'd never met, but she had heard of you from the girl she shared a flat with, Antonia Dryden.'

Again there was only a blank look. 'I've never heard of her either,' said Simon Winthrop.

29

'She died three months ago as the result of an abortion.'

'But what in hell's name could that have to do with me?'

'You're confusing Mr Winthrop, Geoffrey,' said Antony quietly. Winthrop turned to him eagerly. 'I don't like the story, any more than you do, but it won't get any better if we hesitate to tell him. Miss Harvey, Mr Winthrop, went to see your fiancée after she heard of your arrest, because she said she thought it would comfort her to know what an escape she'd had in not marrying you. And while we're about it, you say Mr Horton mentioned both these matters to you. You seem to have taken it pretty calmly.'

Winthrop spread his hands in a gesture that seemed to disclaim responsibility. 'There were so many questions,' he said, 'and I didn't understand the half of them. And I was so bewildered.'

'That's very understandable. Shall we get back to Bertha Harvey?'

'I tell you I don't know the girl. What on earth could she mean?'

'She said her friend Antonia Dryden had known you for months, and sometimes entertained you at the flat when she knew the Harvey girl would be out. She became pregnant and as she was very much in love with you I gather she hoped that eventually you'd be married. And when you told her there was no question of that she was frantic, because her family is well-known and old-fashioned about these things, but later she told Miss Harvey you'd promised to help her.'

'But this is all lies too.'

'Hear me out, Mr Winthrop. I told you you'd have to be patient. The help was in the form of getting her something to take and it certainly caused an abortion, but also resulted in her death. I can't remember off-hand what the substance was, but it all came out at the inquest, and I understand that there is practically no drug or combination of drugs that will cause an abortion without endangering the life of the mother if taken orally.'

'I'm not a murderer. I'll have to say again I've never heard of either of these women. In any case, even if I wanted to get hold of something to cause an abortion I wouldn't know how to set about it.'

'The thing is – I'm not saying I endorse the view – that one of your other personalities might have known.'

'But I . . . oh, I've heard of this so-called split personality business, but I can't believe that Sylvia and Norman would suggest in all seriousness that it applies to me. I don't remember ever having seriously thought about it, but I think if I had I'd have believed like those doctors you spoke of that it was all a fake. In any case, this girl who died, if there'd been an inquest why didn't all this come out? I mean, if the other girl believed that I was responsible surely she'd have said so. Wouldn't it have been a crime?'

'Quite a serious one. But apparently she talked the matter over with the dead girl's father, who felt that to bring an accusation of that sort would only invite more publicity, which was something he wanted very much to play down. And as it was very much hearsay evidence they decided to say nothing about it.'

'Anyone could have used my name, but why should they?' Winthrop seemed to be trying to puzzle it out. 'You're not going to tell me this Antonia had a photograph of me that the other girl produced when she talked to Madeleine. I tell you again I never heard of either of them.'

Maitland regarded him in silence for a moment. 'The description that Bertha Harvey gave Miss Rexford fits you well enough,' he said, 'but I don't consider that as anything approaching proof. Your question as to why anyone should have used your name is to my mind a more cogent one.'

'Yes, I suppose –' Winthrop seemed unable to complete his sentence. 'Let's get this straight,' he pleaded. 'Sylvia and Norman, and Madeleine for all I know, think that besides being myself I have three other sides to my character which I carefully keep hidden. A chap who goes round seducing people and then murders them rather than take the consequences of what he's done –'

'There's no suggestion that Antonia Dryden's death was intended. Only that of the child she carried.'

'Well, that's just as bad. And besides *that* chap, another artist who paints in a quite different style from mine, one which from what you say I gather I should find distasteful; and a third – or fourth, however you look at it – so vicious that he'd murder a perfectly harmless old man to get a half-share of his money. Is that what they think?'

'I think you must realize, Mr Winthrop, that the evidence against you in the murder case is very strong. If it had been only that I'm sure your parents and your fiancée would have gone on believing in you in spite of anything that might have been said. When the other things came up . . . what they're doing now is to try to reconcile what they've been told with the man they know and are fond of.'

'You can wrap it up as much as you like, they'd rather think me mad than guilty. Well, perhaps I am.'

'We brought up the matter, Mr Winthrop, to get your reaction to the suggestion. You deny having painted those hidden pictures, you deny having known Antonia Dryden, and you tell us you didn't murder your grandfather. There are two courses open to you, and we should be failing in our duty if we didn't put them both to you as clearly as we can. A straight Not Guilty plea, in which case neither of these two other matters need be brought up at all.'

'Unless this Bertha Harvey goes to the police.'

'Your morals have nothing to do with the case, unless we choose to make them so. I think I should have said there are three possible pleas, but we have consulted with my uncle, Sir Nicholas Harding, who is more experienced than either of us, and he agreed that a plea of automatism would have very little chance of success.'

'What is automatism?'

'To put it as simply as possible it implies some failure of the mind *not* due to disease, and in theory could also lead to a straight acquittal, though both Mr Horton and I agree with my uncle that it wouldn't be accepted in your case. As for this multiple personality disorder, if the court believed us we might get away with insanity, in which case no doubt some appropriate treatment would be recommended and I'm afraid your freedom would be curtailed until the doctors were satisfied with your condition. You must remember, however, that in that case the prosecution as well as ourselves would be calling for medical evidence, and no doubt their psychiatrist would disagree completely with ours.'

There was a long pause. 'And if I opt for a straight Not Guilty plea – ?' said Simon Winthrop at last.

'The first thing would be to ask you to amplify your account of what you were doing on the night of your grandfather's death.' Maitland replied.

'I don't know.'

'I beg your pardon.'

'I don't know! I have these mental blackouts, I've had them as long as I can remember. Sometimes I find myself walking down the street, or in a shop, or on a bus even, and haven't the faintest idea of how I got there.'

'How long has this been going on?'

'I told you. As long as I remember.'

'But surely Mr and Mrs Patmore at least—?'

'I always managed to keep it from them. I thought they'd think what you're thinking now, that I'm not fit to be out alone.'

'How long do these—did you call them blackouts—last?'

'Perhaps only a few minutes, sometimes for several hours. I do assure you I had no knowledge of these things you've been telling me, but you must be right about them. I didn't kill Grandfather, yet some part of me must have done. It wouldn't be right to plead Not Guilty in that case, would it?'

For a moment and very unusually for him, Maitland was almost bereft of words by this sudden capitulation. 'Would you be willing to see a doctor?' he asked.

'Of course, I want to. Is there anything that can be done?'

'I think for the moment our best plan will be to wait and see what the doctor says.' He paused, quite frankly not knowing how to continue. 'Be as open as you can with him,' he advised, 'and we'll talk again after we've had his report.'

It cannot be said that either Antony or Geoffrey was particularly happy when they got back to the street again. They were moving towards the car when Maitland said rather abruptly, 'It's no good your going out of your way to take me home.'

'Of course I will.' Geoffrey asked no direct question, but perhaps the slight note of impatience in his voice did it for him. In any case Maitland smiled at him.

'I'm only trying to save you trouble,' he said, rather as if this were a matter for apology. 'What you could do is take me to the nearest bus stop. I want to think.'

'I suppose you mean you're beginning to believe this—this farrago of lies,' said Geoffrey sourly.

'That's a nice word. I don't think I've ever heard it used

before,' said Maitland absently. And then, rather irritably, 'I don't know what I think yet.'

'Don't you?' asked Geoffrey sceptically.

'If our client is laying a foundation for a plea of Not Guilty by reason of insanity, which seems to be what you're implying, why didn't he tell you about these memory blackouts before?'

'I suppose he thought the information would sound more effective dragged out of him this way.'

'Well . . . perhaps. But he wasn't to know his adopted parents would come up with this theory, they wouldn't have done it just on the evidence of the paintings, and he couldn't have known that Bertha Harvey would turn up with her story.'

'All the same—'

'All the same, you don't believe a word of it,' said Maitland, and smiled again. 'I don't know that I do myself but at least it must be looked into as a possible line of defence.' They were in the car by now but Horton made no attempt to start the engine.

'How do you propose we should set about that?' he demanded.

'The obvious place is with the doctor. Dr Macintyre, don't you think?'

'He's not a man to equivocate about his opinions,' Geoffrey warned him.

'That's what we want, isn't it? Will you arrange it, Geoffrey? But I'd very much like to see him myself after he's talked to Winthrop.'

'You don't need to tell me that,' said Horton, slightly less grumpily. 'And don't forget you'll want to talk to the Patmores, I suppose.'

'Yes, and to Madeleine Rexford. And I daresay to Bertha Harvey too.'

'I don't see how that will help.'

'You never know,' said Maitland vaguely. 'However, it may not come to that.'

'How are you placed for the next few days?'

'A couple of conferences tomorrow and some papers to go through, but nothing urgent. Nothing that will take me to court this week, anyway.'

'All right, I'll do what I can. If I call you at chambers in the morning—'

'That will do excellently. Now what about that bus stop?'

'I don't so much mind you thinking,' said Geoffrey, rather with the air of one making a great concession, 'so long as you don't come up with some half-cocked idea.'

'If the chap suffers from occasional amnesia –'

'That is a plea that juries are just not receptive to,' Geoffrey pointed out. 'But I daresay,' he added more hopefully, 'when you've talked to Dr Macintyre you'll feel differently about it.' On which more optimistic note he leaned forward to turn the ignition key.

III

In spite of the comparatively early hour at which they had left the prison, Maitland was later than usual getting home. Later certainly than Gibbs, Sir Nicholas's aged retainer, felt he should be on a night when he was entertaining his uncle and aunt.

In addition to Antony's professional connection with his uncle he and his wife Jenny had occupied for many years now an anything-but-self-contained flat devised from the two top floors of Sir Nicholas's house in Kempenfeldt Square. Sir Nicholas's marriage to Miss Vera Langhorne, barrister-at-law, had been comparatively recent, but it had changed none of the traditions between the two households that had grown up over the years. One of these was that Sir Nicholas, and now he and his wife, dined with the Maitlands every Tuesday evening when Mrs Stokes, his housekeeper, took herself, rain or shine, to the cinema.

Vera, naturally, who had looked after herself for many years, would have been quite capable of providing sustenance for both of them, but though Sir Nicholas's small staff, who had done exactly as they liked for years, had taken very kindly to her coming, this, everyone felt, would have been carrying things a little too far. Antony had been known to reproach his new aunt with the fact that her arrival had made it quite certain that Gibbs would never retire, an end towards which they had all been striving for years. As it was, the old man did exactly as much or as little work as he pleased, and very much enjoyed playing the martyr, and among his more annoying habits was one of hovering at the back of the hall at a time when he expected his employer or his employer's nephew to be returning from chambers. Tonight his, 'Sir Nicholas and Lady Harding joined Mrs Maitland some time ago,' was too familiar to cause Antony any anxiety, in spite of the distinct note of reproof that it held. He said, 'Thanks, Gibbs,' rather absently, and went up the stairs as though he were tired.

Jenny came to the hall to meet him, a thing she rarely did when they had visitors unless she had some special information to impart, and as this evening she came from the kitchen it was impossible for him to tell whether their meeting was accidental or not. She had what he always called her serene look, which made it practically certain that their encounter was fortuitous. 'Uncle Nick's been telling us,' she said. 'I don't think he's awfully pleased about this latest client of yours, Antony, but I think it all sounds quite fascinating.' She had been used for years to listening to legal shop with a good deal of enjoyment. Vera's arrival had if anything intensified the frequency of such discussions and the Maitlands sometimes speculated between themselves whether she didn't miss her own years at the Bar, though they were both quite positive that she had never regretted for a moment abandoning it for marriage.

Antony bent to kiss his wife. 'I don't think, love, that the word fascinating is quite the *mot juste*,' he said, and watched her grey eyes cloud with sudden anxiety. 'Nothing to worry about,' he insisted. 'This mood of Uncle Nick's is only routine, you know that. He can't be happy without something to grumble about.'

'I don't care about that,' said Jenny undutifully, 'only I thought for a moment –'

'Nothing . . . truly. Come and get me a drink, love, and I'll tell you the rest of the story.'

It was a good thing that he had come in prepared to do so, because it was quite obvious that between the three of them there was no chance at all of escape. Sir Nicholas, stretched out in his favourite chair – one of the two wing chairs that flanked the hearth – raised a hand in languid greeting; Vera, a tall, rather heavily built woman with thick hair that nobody – certainly not the hairdresser she now visited occasionally – had ever succeeded in controlling, twisted round to smile at him as he crossed the big, rather shabby room. 'Nicholas has been whetting our appetites,' she told him. 'We're all agog to hear what your newest client is like.'

'A nice chap,' said Antony, with intent to annoy not her, but his uncle. He took up his position on the hearth-rug a little to the side of the fire, where he could lean his left shoulder against the high mantel. He then stood silent, apparently absorbed in contemplation of Jenny's action in filling his glass.

Sir Nicholas sat up. 'I suppose it would be too much to ask you,' he said severely, 'to tell us to which of his personalities you refer.'

'I've only seen one of them myself.' He accepted the glass of sherry, and placed it near the clock. 'I suppose you'll tell me I'm guessing if I assume it's the one most of his friends and relations are familiar with.'

'He didn't—'

'He didn't change into a werewolf before my eyes, if that's what you mean, Vera,' Maitland told her, smiling. 'He says he didn't paint the other pictures, which of course we could only describe to him; he denies any knowledge of Antonia Dryden—'

'Which, considering the outcome of that episode, was only to be expected,' Sir Nicholas put in.

'Yes, I agree, but he might be telling the truth for all that,' said Maitland mildly. 'Equally, of course, he denies having anything to do with Thomas Wilmot's death. At least he did until—' He broke off there, looking from one to the other of his companions. 'It's rather complicated,' he admitted.

'And you're making it no less so,' his uncle told him with some asperity. 'For heaven's sake, boy, you ought to know by now how to give us a connected narrative. From the beginning,' he added.

'Yes, Uncle Nick. You can thank Vera for planting me squarely into the middle of it by asking questions. What I was going to say was that he became visibly more and more agitated as one revelation after another was made to him (he doesn't seem to have realized the implication of Geoffrey's questions before) and finally when I asked him about the night of the murder, and where he had been while it was going on, he admitted that he couldn't remember. He then said he'd been subject to fits of forgetfulness—no, that's not a strong enough way of putting it—to blackouts of memory sometimes lasting for several hours for as long as he could remember.'

'Amnesia is not a good defence,' said Sir Nicholas. But he was leaning back in his chair again by now and sipping his drink.

'No, sir, I know it, and if I didn't Geoffrey has already pointed it out. He thinks – Geoffrey, I mean – that Winthrop was laying the foundation for a plea of insanity, but I've been thinking and thinking and I just don't see it that way.'

'You're telling us you believe all this nonsense . . . that there are at least four different personalities inhabiting his body, some of which only manifest themselves occasionally.'

'No, I'm not telling you that either. Don't scowl at me,' Antony pleaded. 'Geoffrey's just as annoyed with me as you are because I can't give him a straight answer. But there is one thing. Everything that Winthrop said – or sometimes didn't say – tends to make me believe that he's no personal recollection of his childhood before he lived with the Patmores, though he didn't say so right out. And that might mean that he's telling the truth about the blackouts.'

'Or it might mean something quite different.'

'So it might. Oh well, who lives may learn . . . or perhaps not,' he added doubtfully. 'Anyway, Geoffrey's arranging for Dr Macintyre to see our client. I may be a bit clearer in my mind after I've talked to him.'

'That, if I may say so, is a consummation devoutly to be wished,' said his uncle. But after that he allowed the subject to drop and nothing else was said about Simon Winthrop and his affairs that evening, even when the visitors had left and Antony and Jenny were alone together. A time for confidences, but she knew, as well as if he had spoken the thought aloud, that he didn't want to be reminded of the prison and of a man who, innocent or guilty, was shut in with no hope, for the moment at least, of getting out.

Wednesday, 12th March

I

Geoffrey was as good as his word, phoning soon after Antony had arrived in chambers to say that he had arranged for Dr Macintyre to see their client that morning, and that he and the doctor would come to the Inner Temple to report the results of the interview immediately after lunch, if that would fit in with the conferences Maitland had arranged. Antony's immediate reaction was to invite them both for lunch, and after a little discussion it was agreed that they should meet at Astroff's at one o'clock. Geoffrey didn't think they could get back from Brixton before that, but as Maitland's afternoon conference was not until three-forty their talk would not be in any way rushed.

Sir Nicholas declined the invitation to make one of the party, saying that he had a previous engagement with his friend Bruce Halloran. 'But I shall be interested to hear your conclusions after you've talked to Macintyre,' he said, though this was a reminder his nephew could well have done without. 'I have the greatest faith in *his* good sense,' Sir Nicholas added, the unspoken corollary being, 'That's more than I can say of yours.'

So Maitland went to the restaurant alone and arrived only just before his guests. He had known Dr Macintyre for some time, though they hadn't had occasion to meet recently. The doctor was a down-to-earth Scot of his uncle's generation, a tall, bony man who either by accident or design had never lost his boyhood pattern of speech. Antony was privately of the opinion that this added to his credibility as a witness in some way, though that was of little use unless his opinion happened to coincide with the interests of the defence.

Geoffrey, uncharacteristically, was looking a trifle harassed, but that was probably nothing that a stiff drink wouldn't put right. Bill, the waiter who served the table that was always reserved for them until it became obvious that no one from

39

chambers was going in that day, was waiting for orders. Until he returned (he was always a fast worker, so that Antony had sometimes voiced the opinion that he had some sort of a hold over the barman) nobody attempted anything but greetings, a few comments on the clemency of the weather, and inquiries on the doctor's part as to Jenny's well-being. But as soon as they were alone again and Dr Macintyre was able to pick up his glass and swirl the contents thoughtfully preparatory to tasting them, he looked up at his host and said in an abrupt way, 'Well now, Maitland, this is a fine kettle of fish.'

'You've seen Simon Winthrop?' asked Antony, not very sensibly in the circumstances.

'What d'ye think Mr Horton and I have been doing all this time?' asked Macintyre, almost as irascibly as Sir Nicholas might have done. 'Ye ken fine what we've been doing and why we're here.'

'Aye,' said Maitland, whose unconscious habit of mimicry had got him into trouble more than once. On this occasion though the slight note of mockery was intentional; he knew perfectly well that though the doctor's accent was unmistakable his choice of words had been quite deliberate.

'You'll be wanting to know then what I thought of the young man.'

'Aye,' said Antony again. 'Unless either of you is terribly hungry and would rather talk after we've had our meal.'

'What I have to tell you will hardly delay us,' said Macintyre with a sort of grim satisfaction. 'You know as well as I do there's no way on earth I could swear he's telling the truth.'

'I think what worries me more is, could he be?' On the whole he was glad that the doctor had reverted to plain English.

'That he's been suffering from lapses of memory since he was a boy, yes, of course that could be true.'

'But you don't believe it?'

'I didn't say that. It could be true,' Macintyre repeated.

'I remember that once in a similar situation you talked about a retreat from reality.'

'That's as good a way as any of putting it, but if we're both thinking about the same case it was actually in no way similar. Your client then had lost his memory completely, didn't even know who he was. There was no suggestion that he was suffering from what it has become fashionable to call multiple personality disorder.'

'Well, what do you think about that suggestion?'

'There have been what seemed to be well-attested cases,' said Macintyre slowly, 'though I think I would have said that the doctors who reported them were the victims of some clever trickery.'

Maitland pounced on that. 'You would have said, Doctor?' he asked.

'Until this morning,' Macintyre amplified. 'I've read the matter up, of course, out of interest, and re-read what little information there is on the subject last night after Mr Horton phoned me. And what seems to be generally referred to as "losing time" appears to be one of the most frequent symptoms. I know that some of my professional brethren are quite convinced, quite sincerely convinced, and I have to admit that, if it is possible, switching personalities would be a useful escape from an unpleasant situation. The fact that Mr Winthrop insists that he has no knowledge of what happened during these blackouts of his is not inconsistent with the suggestion his friends have made, and my reading tells me that there have been occasions when people suspected of this condition have found things among their belongings of which they had no previous knowledge.'

'You mean in the same way as the paintings were found in the studio, but Winthrop disclaimed all knowledge of them?'

'Yes. I should be very much interested, by the way, to see those for myself; not that I think, being a complete amateur, I should find myself convinced by them one way or the other, but they might tell me something about the man who painted them if they're as impressive as Mr Horton says.'

'This business about the abortion—'

'Raises more questions than it answers. I should say that Mr Winthrop—the Mr Winthrop I met, and who, I believe, is the same as the one you have met—is rather a well-behaved young man, I'd almost say old-fashioned, either naturally so or as the result of his upbringing. If the latter, it's possible that his repressed desires break out in the form of another personality or personalities of which he professes—truthfully or not—to have no knowledge.'

'Everything you say is . . . well, at least, not inconsistent with what we've been told.'

41

'Not inconsistent, no. But there's one big difficulty.'

'What is that, Doctor?'

'In all the cases, or alleged cases, of which I have read this disorder has been the result of physical or, even more often, sexual abuse during the childhood of the subject. I spoke about this to Mr Winthrop at some length, and he assures me that nothing of the kind ever happened to him.'

'But that doesn't rule out the possibility altogether,' Antony protested.

'No, indeed. He's certainly a very disturbed young man, but quite frankly I'm unable to decide whether that is his normal condition or the result of the conversation you and Mr Horton had with him yesterday.'

'We had to find out what he had to say about these suggestions,' said Maitland defensively.

'I can quite see that. Why are you so concerned to prove the matter one way or the other?'

'I wondered at first, though now I can see it was stupid, whether a plea of Not Guilty could be justified if another personality of the real Simon Winthrop had committed the murder. I don't know any more than you do, Doctor, whether he's telling us the truth about his condition, but it seems we are going to have to build our case on an insanity plea.'

'Amnesia? No recollection of the night in question? The most I could say is that it's quite possible, and though the prosecution will certainly bring evidence in refutation it would be scarcely more convincing than mine.'

'That isn't the point, Doctor. The point is that juries won't accept amnesia as a defence. If we could get across this other thing, this rather – what was Jenny's word? – fascinating idea, the jury might be more willing to find him Not Guilty by reason of insanity. And that brings up another question. Is this condition, if it exists, subject to treatment?'

'I shouldn't like to undertake it myself,' said Dr Macintyre frankly, 'but many of the people who believe in it completely would tell you that a cure can be made, though possibly only after many years of therapy.'

'There's no medication?'

'So far as I know there isn't. The most recommended treatment seems to be the fusing of the personalities . . . introducing them to one another, as it were.'

42

'How on earth – ?'

'In the case of your client, who professes to remember nothing of the other people who sometimes control his actions, it would be a matter of getting him to recognize what is happening and learn to suppress the undesirable sides of his nature,' said Dr Macintyre rather doubtfully. He smiled suddenly and finished his Scotch. 'You'll be thinking, Maitland, that I'm giving you a poor return for the luncheon you're going to provide me with in a moment.'

Antony was too absorbed even to give voice to a disclaimer. 'At least you can tell me, Doctor, what you suggest we should do.'

'I think you'll have to see the people who came up with these stories and find out what they have to say. Who knows, you may be able to convince me. As I said, at the moment I can see points in favour of the theory, and one big mark against it. But that may be all cleared up when you've talked to your client's parents.'

'I had a feeling when I was talking to him that he remembered nothing of his life before he went to live with the Patmores.'

'Then it seems very likely they'll be able to help you,' said Macintyre briskly, but he obviously wasn't interested in theorizing until he had the facts. Which was sensible, no doubt, but Maitland, for one, was not feeling particularly sensible just then.

However, he yielded to the inevitable, and signalled to Bill so that they could order their lunch. Dr Macintyre did full justice to the meal, though neither of his companions, for one reason or another, seemed that day to be particularly hungry.

II

Before they parted Geoffrey asked about the afternoon conference, was told that it was unlikely to last very long, and admitted that he had made an arrangement to visit the Patmores any time after five-thirty. 'Give me a call when your people go and I'll come round and pick you up,' he promised.

The Patmores lived in Streatham, in what had once obviously been a fashionable neighbourhood. Their house and grounds were beautifully maintained, the neighbouring ones had a sort of shabby elegance of their own, and the overgrown gardens were not without attraction. As the two lawyers waited on the doorstep, Antony thought that perhaps the fact that they had not moved away told him something already about the character of the people they had come to see.

The man who admitted them was obviously, in more senses than one, a solid citizen. He had dark hair, receding now at the temples, and a pleasant welcome for them both. He led the way almost immediately into a room at the right of the hall, a large room with windows that must have cost a fortune to curtain. There was nothing modern about it except a pile of books still in their jackets on the side table, and it seemed obvious that it had been furnished for comfort rather than for beauty. When Sylvia Patmore got up from her chair by the fire it was obvious that she was a little taller than her husband, a thin woman with fair hair and a worried expression.

'You remember Mr Horton, dear,' her husband was saying. 'And Mr Maitland, who is Simon's counsel, has been kind enough to come and see us too.'

She barely gave him time to complete the introductions. Her eyes were fixed on Antony's face. 'I hope, Mr Maitland, that this means you're taking what we told Mr Horton about Simon seriously. Have you seen him?'

'Yes, I saw him yesterday afternoon. We both did.' He paused there, wondering what he could add by way of reassurance. 'You're going to ask me next how he is,' he said, and smiled at her. 'In health, perfectly well, but I'm not going to lie to you about his feelings. The charge itself creates an unpleasant situation for him, but I'm afraid the information we had to give him yesterday was not exactly of a consoling nature.'

She looked at him for a moment in silence, and then turned to seat herself again. 'Please make yourselves comfortable,' she said, 'and then we can talk. I'd hoped, you see –' She made no attempt to finish the sentence, but looked up at her husband rather helplessly.

'I think perhaps a drink would be in order,' said Norman Patmore briskly. 'It's a little early, but in the circumstances –' He too left his sentence uncompleted. 'A sherry for you, my dear. And what can I get for you gentlemen?'

There was a silence while their host attended to their needs, somehow even on such a short acquaintance not an uncomfortable one. 'Will you tell us about your talk with Simon?' said Mr Patmore as he seated himself at last.

'Very willingly, but will you tell me first how you came to this conclusion about his state of mind? You're not a doctor by any chance . . . either of you?' he added, realising belatedly that the profession might as easily be embraced by the woman as by the man.

Mr Patmore shook his head. 'Nothing like that. In a way you can say my profession is the same as yours; that is, I qualified as a solicitor but I've never worked except in the legal department at Bramley's Bank. So in that sense I'm narrow-minded, more a banker than a lawyer by now. As for my wife, we're both old-fashioned enough to think a woman's place is in the home. At least . . . I don't think you have ever felt frustrated, have you, my dear?' he added, turning to her with a smile.

'Not in the slightest. We've never been fortunate enough to have children of our own, Mr Maitland,' she explained, 'but for the last twenty years there's been Simon. I know he left home a few years back, but he's none the less our son for that.'

'No, I understand. But you were going to tell me –'

'How we reached that rather bizarre conclusion.' Norman Patmore took up the tale. 'We knew Simon, you see, the real Simon. It was a shock to hear about his grandfather's death but we didn't know Thomas Wilmot very well, and when Simon was arrested we felt, as any parents would, I think, in the same situation, that the police had made some ghastly mistake. But then there were these identifications. We don't know the neighbours, of course, but we both realize that quite genuine mistakes can be made, and often have been made in fact. But the housekeeper, Mrs Barham . . . Simon's often spoken of her with quite a degree of affection. He visited his grandfather regularly, and knew her well, so that even if she didn't come face to face with him it's hard to see how she could have been mistaken, but I can't think of any conceivable reason why she should have said she'd seen him out of malice. She doesn't sound like that kind of a person at all.'

'And that shook your faith in your son?' It was obvious that both the Patmores preferred this way of referring to Simon Winthrop.

Mr Patmore glanced at his wife, and this time it was she who answered. 'Not exactly,' she said. 'It certainly made us realize that it wasn't going to be too easy to prove his innocence, but Simon . . . he's not a violent person, just the opposite in fact. And though Mr Horton explained to us about Mr Wilmot's will, and Simon was certainly in need of money with marriage in prospect because he didn't want to go back to a full time job, still–' She hesitated and then fell back on the phrase her husband had used, 'We knew him, you see.'

At least, thought Maitland, they haven't said, 'He wouldn't do a thing like that,' but it seems to amount to the same thing. 'So what happened then?' he prompted. 'I know you've told this to Mr Horton already, but it does help to get things at first hand.'

'I'd already packed some things for him, toilet articles, a change of underwear, things like that,' said Mrs Patmore, 'but then I thought about his paintings and said we ought to bring them here, it would be safer than leaving them in the studio. So we went back together, and that was when we found those – those horrible things.'

'Did you bring them here with you?'

'Yes. I admit I'd have preferred not to bring them into the house, just seeing them would give me nightmares. But we didn't think Simon had painted them, we thought he was just storing them for a friend, so we felt a certain obligation. But we couldn't understand why they had Simon's signature.'

'Did you tell anybody else about them?'

'Only Madeleine . . . Madeleine Rexford, Simon's fiancée. And, of course, Mr Horton showed one of them to a Mr Verlaine.'

'Julian Verlaine.'

'Yes, do you know him?'

'I've encountered him,' said Maitland. 'I'm sure any opinion he gave you would be a sound one.'

'Yes, Mr Horton told us that he looked at Simon's own work and at one of these things, and he said the same hand couldn't possibly have done them. But that was later. We hadn't really thought anything about it until Madeleine came to see us. And what she had to say . . . well, it was even more unbelievable than the rest of it if that were possible.'

'We've forgotten to tell Mr Maitland one thing, my dear,' Norman Patmore put in. 'Madeleine had already told us that she had an engagement with Simon that evening, to meet him for dinner. The evening of Thomas Wilmot's death, I mean. But he never turned up, and Mr Horton tells us he was out walking. It seems very strange, because he's devoted to Madeleine.'

'We'll come to all that in a moment,' Maitland assured him. 'Will you first tell me what Miss Rexford said to you?'

'She's a very self-contained person, you know.' Sylvia Patmore took up the tale. 'Not given to going off into hysterics over even quite serious matters, but that evening . . . well, I knew at once it was something dreadful, something even more dreadful to her than Simon's arrest.'

'Forgive me for interrupting you, Mrs Patmore, but had her feelings about that been the same as yours?'

'Oh yes, just the same. We'd talked and talked about it and we couldn't come to any conclusion except the one we mentioned to you, that there'd been some dreadful mistake. And we all realized by now that that was unlikely in the face of Mrs Barham's evidence, but still we believed it was what must have happened. Only that evening, it was the first time we'd ever seen Madeleine cry–do you remember, Norman?–but that wasn't until later. At first she tried to sound normal, asked how we were, that kind of thing. But of course it was obvious she was upset so I asked her right out and then she said in a hard voice quite unlike herself, "I'm beginning to think I never knew Simon at all." And then it all came out that this girl called Bertha Harvey had been to see her.'

'Don't distress yourself, Sylvia,' Patmore interrupted her. 'I can tell Mr Maitland anything he feels he needs to know. It isn't a pretty story, even if no one we knew was involved in it.'

'I shall be seeing Miss Rexford, no need to go into it again for the moment,' Maitland told him. 'It was this story then that led you to question the meaning of what you had heard before.'

'Yes, because you see I think Sylvia and I know Simon even better than Madeleine does, though she's a dear girl and they are very much in love. I'm not saying he hasn't had friends before of the opposite sex, he's a perfectly normal young man, but what I *am* sure is that if any difficulties arose he would face up to them, not take what some people may think of as the easy way out.'

'You mean if he'd found the girl was pregnant he'd have married her?'

'That's exactly what I do mean.'

'In spite of being engaged, and in love–as we must suppose–

47

with Miss Rexford?'

'In spite of that. And what I'm quite sure of, Mr Maitland, is that he – the Simon we know – would never have suggested an abortion, let alone procured the means for it. It would be completely against everything he's been brought up to believe in.'

'And did believe in,' Sylvia Patmore put in.

'I see. So that was when you began to cast about for an explanation of all these things?'

'Don't you think that was natural? We talked about it for so long that it was too late for Madeleine to go back to her flat and she had to stay the night. And . . . you see we were very vague about this business of multiple personalities, except that there have been cases known, but when once it occurred to us it seemed obvious that there were four completely different sides to the same person. Didn't it, Sylvia?'

'It's the only explanation, Mr Maitland,' Mrs Patmore agreed. 'We've known Simon all his life and there's never been any trace of violence in him or viciousness, or avarice, or any of the other things it seemed we had to begin to believe about him.' She broke off there, fumbling for a handkerchief, and after a moment her husband went on.

'Having come to this conclusion it seemed to us that perhaps it would be the makings of a defence, and that if Simon could be treated for what was wrong instead of just being put into prison perhaps some day–' He stopped there, getting to his feet, and crossed the room to sit on the arm of his wife's chair and put an arm round her shoulders. 'You must forgive Mrs Patmore,' he said more formally than he had previously spoken. 'There isn't really a bright side to the situation, we're just trying to make the best of it we can.'

'I'm sorry, believe me, to have to make you think about it all over again. I wouldn't if it weren't necessary.'

'But we want to know what Simon said,' said Sylvia Patmore. She had put up a hand to cover her husband's, and now she twisted to look up at him. 'I'm all right, Norman,' she said, 'really I am. I want to know whatever there is to know, even if it's not all favourable.'

'I'm afraid there's nothing conclusive I can tell you at the moment, Mrs Patmore. Mr Horton will have informed you already that your son had instructed him to plead Not Guilty.'

'Yes, he told us that. Are you trying to tell me that he's changed his mind?'

'It isn't quite so simple. We put these matters to him, the ones you've just been discussing with us, and he denies all knowledge of them. But he was visibly shaken by what we told him, and at last, when I pressed him for details of what he was doing the night of his grandfather's death, he admitted that he had no memory at all of where he had been. He went on to say that these blackouts had been occurring . . . I think the phrase he used was "as long as I remember". Sometimes they would last for only a few seconds, and sometimes he'd lose several hours. He said he'd always tried to cover them up. I think he must have felt that people would think there was something very odd about him if he admitted what was happening. Had you any idea about those lost hours, either of you?'

'No idea in the world,' said Sylvia. 'At least . . . did you know anything about it, Norman?'

'No, I didn't. Can you tell us, Mr Maitland, had he spoken to a doctor about this – this illness?'

'Not, I think, until Dr Macintyre saw your son this morning at our suggestion. Later we had a long conversation about him.'

'What did the doctor think?'

'He had to admit that this is something outside his experience, but from his reading he could confirm that these blackouts would fit in very well with what you have come to believe, as it seems that in a number of the cases of this sort that have been reported one personality is quite unaware that the others exist. But this, you know, is a long way from proving that this condition exists in Mr Winthrop's case. A good many doctors – perhaps the majority of them – are doubtful whether it exists at all. And there's one particular stumbling block. I didn't press your son for details of his life before he came to live with you because he seemed disinclined to speak of it. So I thought it would be better, perhaps, to get the information I needed during the course of our talk today.'

'It wouldn't have helped you if you had pressed him on the matter,' said Mrs Patmore, smiling rather sadly. 'We can give you the details, of course, but Simon seems to have completely forgotten the matter, for which we can only be thankful. But I don't quite understand what you mean about a stumbling block.'

49

'That where this disorder has been known or has been believed to exist the cause in almost every case can be traced back to childhood. Mr Winthrop assures us that his was extremely happy.'

'I think you mean something more than you're saying, Mr Maitland,' said Norman Patmore shrewdly. 'When you say that the cause can go back to childhood you mean to some particularly traumatic experience, don't you? Perhaps to the subject being abused in some way.'

Maitland glanced at Sylvia Patmore but she returned his gaze steadily. 'The terms physical or sexual abuse have been used,' he said, 'but I understand – did Macintyre tell us this, Geoffrey, or was it the result of your initial researches? – that women are more subject to this particular condition than men.'

'And you're remembering that the Jesuits say, "Give us a child until he's seven years old and his character will be formed." Seven is exactly the age Simon was when we adopted him. So you've been wondering about his parents, and what horrors went on in his home before that time.'

'Something of the sort,' Maitland told him.

'Well, I'm sorry to disappoint you if knowing that they were monsters of depravity would have helped our case in some way,' said Mr Patmore, 'but Rosalie and Peter Winthrop were our closest friends, pleasant, ordinary people, rather like Simon in fact, except that his grandfather's artistic ability seems to have skipped a generation and surfaced in him. Peter and I were at school together. Our families lived quite near to each other, so even when he went straight into the bank as a junior – did I tell you he was with Bramley's too? – and I went to do my articles we saw a good deal of each other. We all met at the local tennis club, and fortunately Rosalie and Sylvia became as close friends as Peter and I already were. We married within a few months of each other, so when I say we knew Peter all his life that's exactly true. It has been a small grief to us – the only one until now that Simon ever caused us – that since he came to live with us the subject of his parents has been more or less a forbidden one. He seems to have forgotten the circumstances of their death and all that went before it, and we felt it better to stay away from the subject entirely rather than risk reminding him. If he'd ever asked questions of course we should have told him – we never concealed the fact that he was adopted – but he never did. We saw to it that he visited his grandfather regularly right from the beginning, but we'd warned Mr Wilmot and although he was in some ways a cross-grained man I think he was willing enough to forget the matter himself. After all Rosalie was his daughter, and though he affected to despise women the memory must have been a painful one.'

'The circumstances of their death,' Antony repeated. 'You're making me curious, Mr Patmore.'

'Nothing, unfortunately, that is very unusual today,' Norman answered. 'Their car left the road, hit a tree, and burst into flames. Nobody ever discovered exactly what had happened. If there had been any mechanical fault the fire had been fierce enough and had burnt long enough to hide it. The question of drink was raised, of course, but I know enough of Peter to be perfectly certain that if he was driving on the highway he was stone cold sober. The most likely thing seems to me to be that he was forced off the road by another car whose driver had indulged too freely, but there was no proving that. But the dreadful part was, so far as Simon was concerned, that he was in the back of the car at the time of the crash.'

'But obviously he survived.'

'We shall never know whether he was thrown clear, or whether he managed to open the door himself. It was a well-travelled stretch of road and it can't have been long before several other cars arrived on the scene. Even so the fire had taken well hold by then, and Simon was discovered tugging at the front door on the passenger's side. His hands were badly burned and he'd been unable to get it open. Some of the passers-by pulled him away, of course, somebody else called the fire brigade and an ambulance. The others, I'm sure, did what they could, but it was only too obvious that Rosalie and Peter were already dead.'

'Obvious to Simon too, perhaps.'

'I'm afraid so. He was taken to the nearest hospital and his burns treated. There are some scars on the palms of his hands still but thank heavens they've never hindered him using them. He couldn't tell them who he was or who the car belonged to so it was quite a while before we learned what had happened. By then, of course, the only thing we could do was to take Simon home with us. I told you Thomas Wilmot was a strange

51

man in many ways, he'd no objection to our adopting the boy. And as his only other relative was Rosalie's sister in Canada, who also made no objection, the thing was arranged fairly quickly. But to this day he's never spoken of what happened, or of his life before the accident, and whether he's really forgotten or just doesn't want to remember I don't know. We've respected his silence. It seemed the only thing to do.'

'Yes, I can understand that.' He turned to the woman. 'I'm afraid going over all this must have distressed you, Mrs Patmore, but if it's any consolation you gave Simon a very happy home. That's what he tells us, isn't it, Geoffrey? And I've no reason to disbelieve him.'

'But do you think this would explain what's happened now as far as the doctors are concerned?' she asked anxiously.

'Not being a doctor I can't answer that exactly, I'm afraid, and in any case if we come to believe that your son is indeed suffering from this multiple personality disorder and wish in consequence to change his plea to Not Guilty by reason of insanity the onus of proof will be on us. The law considers a man sane until it's proved otherwise, which is not always so easy to do. But to the lay mind this story certainly makes it easier to believe that the experience your son went through may have had a very devastating effect on him. I wish I could give you more comfort than that, but we're only starting to work on the case and there's a lot to be done yet.'

'Yes, I understand. No false hopes.' She eyed him for a long moment, noting the seriousness of his look though there were lines about his eyes that made her all at once certain that laughter came easily to him; his mouth too held its own contradiction. A humorous man, she thought, but one too with a streak of sensitivity in his make-up, too strong, perhaps, for a profession that brought him into constant contact with other people's troubles. 'Is there anything else we can tell you?' she asked.

'Not really, I think. You've been very frank, very helpful, even I'm sure at some pain to yourselves. Now that Mr Wilmot is dead you are then Simon's only relations?'

'Except for Rosalie's sister, Celia, who went to Canada with her husband two years before the accident. I did hear her husband Bob Camden had died there but we never knew him very well and I lost touch with Celia years ago. They had one boy a little older than Simon.'

'Incidentally,' said Norman Patmore, 'he seems to have forgotten all about the Camdens too, as well as everything else about his early life. Sylvia did speak to our doctor and he talked about retrograde amnesia, and thought it would wear off in time.'

'Then there's just one thing more. Did you ever notice these memory blackouts that he speaks of?'

'That's a difficult question. It didn't really occur to me until you mentioned it, but there were times when he went off by himself and didn't seem to be inclined to talk about where he'd been when he came home. I think you must be right and if that is what was happening he was ashamed of the fact somehow.'

'That would be very natural.' Maitland drank the last of his sherry, which was rather too sweet for his taste, and got to his feet. 'You've been very patient with us.' He turned and smiled at Geoffrey. 'Perhaps I should have said with me,' he added. 'My only excuse is that we really had to know these things. Mr Horton will be in touch with you again, of course, when we have reached a decision as to what line the defence will take. But I can't add, don't worry,' he told Geoffrey when they were in the street again, their farewells said. 'It'd just be adding insult to injury. They're a nice couple and deserve better of life.'

'I agree with you *there*,' said Geoffrey, stressing the last word in what can only be called a marked manner.

'You may do so with a clear conscience,' Antony told him, 'because it's the only thing I've made up my mind about in this whole messy business. And tonight you *can* take me home,' he said, getting into the car and subsiding into the passenger's seat. 'And if you'd like a drink when we get there, or even to stay to dinner to take away the taste of Mrs Patmore's sherry,' he added, 'you know Jenny always provides enough for an army so you'll be quite welcome.'

'Joan will be expecting me,' said Geoffrey, 'and unless I'm very much mistaken Sir Nicholas will be waiting to cross-examine you about the doctor's opinion. So I think on the whole—'

'Coward,' said Antony without malice. 'This is one evening when I could very happily forget our unfortunate client's affairs myself, so don't think I blame you. And perhaps, after all, I'll be able to sneak upstairs unregarded.' But he spoke without very much optimism.

III

Which was just as well, as he wasn't, of course, to be able to discard all thought of Simon Winthrop's affairs as easily as that. When he let himself into the hall at Kempenfeldt Square the study door was open, a good enough hint that Sir Nicholas wanted a report, so that it didn't need Gibbs's additional, 'Sir Nicholas intimated that he would like a word with you, Mr Maitland,' to take Antony in that direction instead of towards the stairs. Jenny was there too, which meant that the plot had been carefully laid and he wasn't going to get away without a blow-by-blow account of everything that concerned the client in whose affairs his family were now taking an interest.

'If you want me to talk,' he said disagreeably as soon as he had greeted them, 'I shall need a drink first.'

'Help yourself, my dear boy.' Sir Nicholas waved a languid hand, and raised his eyebrows a little when he saw that his nephew chose Scotch rather than his usual preprandial sherry. 'We should not, of course, dream of hurrying you,' he added in his most velvet tones, which really meant, as Antony well knew, that his patience was not inexhaustible.

So he crossed the room and seated himself on the sofa beside his wife. Vera took one look at him and said with some compunction, 'After dinner will do, if you'd rather.' She had learned some time since that when Antony was tired, or when his shoulder was giving him more pain than usual, any reference to the fact was tacitly avoided by the family. 'You're dining with us, so there's no hurry about it.'

It was Maitland's turn to raise an eyebrow in a rather comical look of surprise. 'How did you persuade Mrs Stokes to that departure from custom?' he asked.

'Have my methods,' Vera assured him blandly.

'For which we are all grateful.' He glanced round to make sure that the door was firmly shut. 'I suppose you couldn't add to your magic by persuading Gibbs it's time he retired.'

'Seems to be beyond me,' said Vera. 'But I told him if Roger came this evening to say you were with us, so that's all arranged.'

'Oh most competent of women!' said Antony and raised his glass to her in a sort of mock salute. 'I think after that you deserve to have your curiosity assuaged immediately, even if Jenny and Uncle Nick have done nothing to deserve it.'

'Well you see, Antony,' said Jenny, 'we can't help being interested because it is rather . . . different.'

'You can say that again.'

'Thing is,' said Vera, 'what did the doctor say?'

He took a moment to think about it, and gave them a clear enough account of Dr Macintyre's views. 'And Geoffrey and I have just been to see the Patmores,' he added, 'which is why I'm so late.' He closed his eyes for a moment and when he opened them again he stared straight into the fire, not looking at any of his companions. 'It was, I think, one of the most unpleasant interviews I ever remember,' he said, 'but I'd better tell you about it because it could be held to explain Dr Macintyre's reservations about the usual cause of this kind of phenomenon.' He went on conscientiously to recount what he had been told, leaving nothing out. Sir Nicholas, for once in his life, heard him in silence, but as soon as he concluded he had a comment to make.

'Am I to understand, Antony, that this has convinced you that the theory these good people have come up with is true?'

'It hasn't convinced me of anything. It would explain the amnesia though and the recurrent blackouts to which Simon Winthrop has admitted. I'm inclined to believe him about that, though I don't know what it means.'

'Amnesia,' said his uncle flatly, 'is not a defence that a jury is likely to accept.'

'The Podola case isn't an exact parallel, if that's what you're thinking of.'

'No, but you must admit that it set a pattern of scepticism in these matters. And I've been giving some thought to the matter, Antony, as I'm sure you have yourself. Not Guilty by reason of insanity is a special verdict, and would only be given in very exceptional circumstances, as I've no doubt any judge would explain to the jury in the clearest of terms.'

'I know that, Uncle Nick.' He sounded weary now, as though the account he had given had taken the last of his strength.

'Furthermore,' Sir Nicholas went on relentlessly, 'you can't

55

call expert evidence to prove insanity without laying some foundation for it. I hardly think that to tell the court that your client, while engaged to another woman, had seduced and discarded a young girl would influence them in his favour. And that, you know, is what it would amount to.'

'Agree with Nicholas,' said Vera gruffly. 'Not possible.'

'I've thought of all that, and so, I'm sure, has Geoffrey. In any case he doesn't believe a word of this multiple personality business, in Winthrop's case or in any other. But supposing it's true.'

'I agree with Geoffrey. It may be possible to engender a certain amount of sympathy for your client by relating this very unpleasant childhood experience, but that can hardly be taken as excusing the cold-blooded murder of an old man for gain.'

'Supposing it's true,' said Maitland again. 'He has no recollection of any of the events we told him about yesterday, but I know that by the time we left him he was beginning to think he really had killed Thomas Wilmot.'

'Do you really think you can persuade the court that though the real Simon Winthrop is rather a nice sort of man he has other personalities of which he knows nothing that go about doing all these unpleasant things?'

'On what we've got now, no. I doubt that we shall get any further on that line anyway. All I'm saying is—'

'I know, suppose it's true.' Whatever patience Sir Nicholas had started the interview with seemed to be wearing thin, or perhaps he was getting hungry. 'There seem to me to be three courses open to you. You can ask for a special verdict and see the case thrown out of court; you can plead Not Guilty, with nothing whatever to back up your story except your client's insistence that he has suffered from amnesia for a long time, and had a mental blackout on that particular night. If you couldn't shake the identity witnesses you could suggest that he'd gone to see Wilmot and found him already dead, though the medical evidence seems to be against you on that point, and it seems unlikely that he'd have then forgotten all about it.'

'His parents—his adoptive parents—would give evidence as to the accident that killed Rosalie and Peter Winthrop, and say that there had been occasions while he lived with them when he went out alone and seemed unwilling to explain where he'd been when he got back.'

56

'Do you really think that would be enough?'

'No, sir, I don't.'

'Very well, then, the alternative is a straight Guilty plea which would save everyone a lot of bother.'

'I have to agree with you, Uncle Nick, I think the results will be the same whatever we do. What's troubling me is that if he really does need some sort of therapy a span in prison won't do him any good at all.'

'You're half way to believing this extraordinary theory,' said Sir Nicholas accusingly.

'No. No, I'm not. But I don't think we can just watch him going down for the third time without at least putting out a hand to try to save him.'

'I'm warning you, Antony, if you attempt to substantiate this plea you may do more harm than good.'

'That's what worries me.' He glanced up at the clock and said apologetically, 'Mrs Stokes will be ready to murder the lot of us, Vera. I've done my best to assuage your curiosity but now I think you'd better leave me to worry over the problem alone.'

'And that's just what he will be doing,' Sir Nicholas complained to his wife later that evening when they were alone. 'Why the devil he always has to get involved with clients with whom he sympathizes I simply cannot think.'

'At least in this case he doesn't seem to be in any doubt about the man's guilt,' said Vera. 'Look on the bright side, Nicholas. With the murderer in prison there can't be any physical danger, and there'll be no more trouble with the police now that Chief Superintendent Briggs has retired.'

Sir Nicholas smiled at her. 'If Antony were here I feel sure he would commend you for being a little ray of sunshine,' he said. 'Those two particular problems may not exist, and one of them at least won't recur. As for the way he's made, I ought to be used to it by this time, and in any case there's nothing to be done about that.'

Thursday, 13th March

I

Geoffrey had arranged for them to see Madeleine Rexford at her flat the following morning. She worked as a doctor's receptionist, but had managed to arrange for one of her colleagues to take over her duties that morning. Her flat was within walking distance of Kempenfeldt Square, so Horton – also by arrangement – came to breakfast with the Maitlands and by arriving at an early hour was able to find a parking space. Most of the houses in the Square were now offices of one kind or another, so that Sir Nicholas occasionally remarked that they were fortunate in that no vandals had yet proposed pulling them down and putting up a glass and concrete monstrosity in the interests of progress. Oddly enough a small number of families, all on the north side of the square, had stuck grimly to their residences, and though some of the original owners had passed on, these houses all belonged to the same families as Antony remembered from the time he first came to live with his uncle at the age of thirteen.

They kept determinedly off their client's affairs during the meal, and afterwards set out on foot for Miss Rexford's flat. 'Though what good you think all this is going to do for us,' said Geoffrey, 'I simply can't imagine.' A small enough grumble for which Maitland was ready enough to forgive him considering the way he knew the solicitor felt about this matter.

The block of apartments looked imposing, but Madeleine's proved to be a sort of lowest common denominator, what is generally known as a studio apartment, although the description has nothing to do with its being used for artistic purposes. A single room, a divan bed neatly made up with a bright red cover and a generous scattering of cushions.

Maitland's first impression of Madeleine Rexford was that

58

the description he'd already heard of her, that she was a very self-contained person, was almost uncanny in its accuracy. She was, of course, expecting them, and greeted them pleasantly but coolly. She was a tall girl and slender with dark curly hair, and she was wearing a beltless brown dress that didn't suit her at all (it reminded Antony in fact of the colourless garments Vera had been used to affect before her marriage) but which had at least the advantage of not clashing with anything in her rather colourfully furnished room. She offered coffee, which was the last thing either of them needed, having drunk their fill at breakfast-time; but Geoffrey immediately accepted for both of them for which his companion was on the whole glad. A relaxed witness was likely to be more talkative and the mere sharing of refreshment might help in that direction. Perhaps Madeleine too had thought it might make matters easier; she disappeared for only a moment before returning with a tray. When they were all supplied she didn't attempt to speak, but sat looking at Horton, who had introduced himself and his companion, expectantly.

'You know why we're here, Miss Rexford,' Geoffrey began.

'Because you're Simon's lawyers. You're his solicitor, and Mr – Mr Maitland is his counsel. I've got that right, haven't I?'

'Quite right. I meant really . . . it's about the matter you discussed recently with Mr and Mrs Patmore.'

'Yes, I know. I've wondered since if I should have come directly to you about it, Mr Horton.'

Before Geoffrey could speak, Antony interrupted with a question of his own. 'Does that mean you felt from the beginning that it would be helpful to Mr Winthrop's defence?' he asked.

'You know I . . . it's so difficult to explain.' As she spoke she moved her hands in a wide, almost despairing gesture, so that Maitland realised very forcibly that the composure he had noted was very hard held.

'Perhaps, Miss Rexford, it would help if you told us the story from the beginning,' he suggested.

'What was the beginning?'

'From your first meeting with Simon Winthrop, say.'

'I . . . I'm not very used to talking about my own feelings, Mr Maitland.'

Antony smiled at her. 'I can see that, but talking to us is . . . oh, like talking to your doctor. Anything that isn't relevant just goes in at one ear and out at the other. But it is quite important that we understand, isn't it, Geoffrey?' And then thought that perhaps the question was unfair, knowing his friend's real feelings.

'Very important,' Horton agreed. Long experience had led him to realise that this interview was no longer under his control, a fact for which he was sincerely grateful. He leaned back in his chair and prepared to enjoy his coffee, which was good and strong and after all not unwelcome.

Madeleine's colour was a little heightened as she went on. 'I met Simon about a year ago at a party a friend was giving. I don't know exactly how he felt, of course, but I'm afraid I've got to use the cliché love at first sight for my own feelings. But he was certainly attracted to me because we drifted together immediately, and he took me home and we've been seeing each other regularly ever since. In fact we were engaged six weeks after we met and I wanted to get married as soon as it could be arranged, because if I went on working we could have managed quite well. But Simon insisted he must get some kind of a regular job first. His paintings are really good, you know, and I'd rather he'd have gone on as he was because perhaps he might make a name for himself more quickly that way. His parents felt that way too, and I know Norman had offered a thousand times to give him an allowance so that he wouldn't have to worry even about the freelance commercial art that he was doing when we met. They're really good people. They're paying for his defence, but of course you know that.'

Antony nodded, which seemed all the answer that was called for. 'All right, Miss Rexford, you became engaged approximately ten months ago, Simon had now found a job, and you were going to be married in a month's time.'

'Yes, that's how it was.'

'Have you ever noticed anything strange in his behaviour, anything you couldn't quite understand?'

'You mean a sign of one of these other personalities Norman and Sylvia have become so convinced of? No, I haven't. Whenever I've seen him it's been the Simon I know best. But –' She hesitated.

'But what, Miss Rexford?'

'There have been occasions when he hasn't met me when he said he would, or when I've gone to his studio by arrangement and found he wasn't there. He always gave me an explanation afterwards, but sometimes I didn't find it very convincing. And that's what happened the night his grandfather was killed. Simon was going to call for me and take me out to dinner . . . only he never came.'

'And then?'

'The next thing I heard was that Mr Wilmot was dead and Simon had been arrested.'

'What did you think, Miss Rexford? Did the question of amnesia, for instance, ever occur to you?'

'Not at that stage. I'd come to a sort of compromise with myself that there were times when Simon felt he must be alone, and that the excuses he made were because he thought he might hurt me by telling me so. But I knew – I thought I knew – that he could never have done a thing like that. Not in cold blood, and particularly not because he wanted to inherit. Mr Wilmot is – was an old man, and Simon knew perfectly well that one of these days there'd be some money. It wasn't immediately important, I can testify to that. Can't you make that point in court, Mr Maitland?'

'I could, of course. At least . . . at the moment neither Mr Horton nor I is quite sure what line the defence will take.' He avoided Geoffrey's eyes as he spoke. 'And I'm afraid even if I did, it would be negated to a certain extent by the fact that Thomas Wilmot was well-known to be a very healthy man and might have lived for years. In view of your impending marriage which had already been delayed for longer than either of you wanted . . . I think you see how it might look to the jury, don't you?'

'Yes, I do see that.' She sounded a little cast down, but went on determinedly. 'I was telling you how I felt. I knew Simon, and money wasn't important to him, not in itself, but only so far as it prevented him from feeling he was sponging off other people. So I felt, just as Norman and Sylvia told me they felt, that a dreadful mistake had been made but it was bound to be discovered sooner or later who had really murdered Mr Wilmot.'

'In spite of the evidence of identification.'

'That was a facer, I admit. Not so much the neighbours, the

61

Alfords I think they're called, but Mrs Barham who I knew must know Simon very well by sight. He often spoke of her and I think he was fond of her, and I always supposed that she must be fond of him as well. But then this girl, Bertha Harvey, came to see me, and the whole world seemed to be turned upside down.'

'I know this must be distressing for you, Miss Rexford, but I'm afraid we should like your own account of what was said.'

That brought a faint, unamused smile. 'Yes, I gathered as much,' she said. 'The funny thing is that even now I can't make up my mind whether she told me out of spite or out of kindness. But I don't suppose it matters really. She certainly made no bones about telling me, but she said it was because she thought I might find it comforting to know that I'd had a lucky escape when Simon was arrested.'

'Had she met him herself?'

'No, but Antonia Dryden, the girl she shared a flat with, had talked about him. She'd apparently been seeing him for about six months and they must have become intimate quite quickly, because about two months before Antonia died Bertha had noticed she seemed rather preoccupied, and eventually she admitted that she'd been to a doctor, not using her own name, and he confirmed that she was pregnant.'

'How did Antonia feel about that?'

'In despair by the time Bertha talked to her. She'd already told Simon, and he told her there was no way he could support a wife, let alone a family, and they'd have to do something about it. And then later she told Bertha that Simon had got something for her that would do the trick, she meant, get rid of the baby. Only it killed her too.'

'And what was your reaction to this story?'

'What do you think it was? At first I absolutely refused to believe it. I'm afraid I was rather rude to the girl. Then she said, why should anybody else be using his name? And she said she could see I didn't believe her, and would it convince me if she told me what Antonia's Simon Winthrop was like? And I didn't say yes or no, but just asked her to tell me, and the description fitted Simon well enough.'

'As it would have fitted several thousand other men in the London area no doubt.'

'There aren't so many people with hair as fair as that. But

62

what was really awful, Mr Maitland, was the fact that Antonia having described him so closely must have meant that she loved him so much she just had to talk about him.'

'You have his photograph on the top of the bookcase there.'

'You mean Bertha might have been lying to me? You can't tell from that photograph how tall he is, or the colour of his eyes.'

'No, you can't, and I've no opinion yet about Miss Harvey's story, not until I've talked to her myself. I think you're telling us – aren't you? – that at this stage she'd convinced you.'

'Yes, I–I think so. I've heard it said a hundred times that you can never really know about other people . . . what they're like. And there was no reason why this girl should have been lying, or why Antonia should have been lying. I just didn't know what to do but I had to talk to someone so at last I went to Norman and Sylvia.'

'I gather you get on well with your future in-laws.'

'No one can help it; I think they're the kindest people. And of course I knew it would upset them but I had to talk to someone,' she said again. 'And then they told me about the paintings, the other paintings, the ones I've never seen. Sylvia wouldn't let Norman show me. And we talked and talked, and somehow out of it all this theory about having more than one personality emerged. That's why I said, Mr Horton, perhaps I should have come to you instead of upsetting them, you might have thought of it for yourself. And even now –'

'Even now you don't know whether to believe it,' Maitland finished for her when she left the sentence uncompleted.

'It would explain a great many things,' she said with an air of apology.

'Such as?'

'Simon – the real Simon – couldn't possibly have done all these things.'

This time Maitland permitted himself a glance in Horton's direction, an appeal for sympathy perhaps. 'He couldn't have done a thing like that' is perhaps the most common phrase a lawyer with a criminal practice hears in the course of his profession. 'I think that's about all we need from you for the mmoment,' he said, and drank the rest of his coffee, quite cold by now. 'Mr Horton will be in touch with you, of course, though I can't see at this stage that, whatever we decide to do, we shall need your evidence.'

'I wish I could help,' she said, following his example and getting to her feet. 'The trouble is, whatever happens now I don't see any prospect of a happy ending.'

'The trouble is, she's quite right about that,' said Antony rather violently as they went down in the lift together. 'I suppose you realize that, whatever she says, she's still in love with him.'

'Then the sooner she gets over it the better,' said Geoffrey prosaically. 'Not that I'm not sympathetic, but we both know by now it's most often the innocent bystanders who get hurt in these cases. And if you're beginning to get ideas into your head, Antony, about proving this wretched chap had a multiple personality you may as well forget it. Even if it was true – which I can't believe – it wouldn't work.'

'So Uncle Nick was at pains to point out to me last night,' said Antony. 'Not that I hadn't realised it already.' He glanced at his watch. 'Too early for lunch,' he said, 'and Bertha Harvey, you told me, wouldn't see us before this evening.'

'She obviously isn't particularly concerned for Winthrop's welfare,' said Geoffrey dryly. 'I suppose she doesn't see any reason to give up a day's work to help his defence.'

'No, why should she? Will you come back to chambers with me, or do you want to go straight to the office?'

'The latter, I think. I want to get hold of the keys to Winthrop's studio since you said you'd like a sight of it.'

'Yes, I think it would be a good idea, don't you?'

'I think the whole thing's hopeless since you ask me,' said Geoffrey frankly. 'But I suppose nothing less will satisfy you.'

Maitland smiled at his disgruntled tone. 'Nothing less,' he affirmed. 'All right then, what time does Miss Harvey get home?'

'She said she could be sure of being in at about a quarter to six,' Horton told him. 'I'll ring up when I'm leaving the office, and pick you up as usual at the top of Middle Temple Lane.'

'Thank you.' They were out in the street by now and walking back towards Kempenfeldt Square. 'I ought also to thank you,' Antony added formally, 'for giving up so much of your time to a matter you're convinced is hopeless.' But he added, smiling, 'and if you're in touch with Chief Inspector Conway about the keys take care he doesn't bite you in the ankle when he knows you've briefed me.'

II

But he himself was to be in touch with the police before he
expected. Willett was waiting when he got back to chambers
with a message from Superintendent Sykes asking if Mr
Maitland would telephone him as soon as he got in. The reason
for this demand turned out to be that the detective wanted to
know if his old friend was free for lunch, and as he was they
arranged to meet at a restaurant they had patronized before, a
sort of half-way house between the Inner Temple and New
Scotland Yard. It cannot be said that Antony got much work
done in the interval before he had to leave for the rendezvous.
Sykes's voice had been as bland as ever, the invitation might
have been no more than it seemed, a chance for two men to get
together who always had plenty to discuss and whose work kept
them both very busy a good deal of the time. But he couldn't
help the feeling that there was something beyond that in the air,
and was glad when the time came to push aside the papers that
he ought to have been working on and leave chambers to look
for a taxi.

Superintendent Sykes was one of the people who had changed
very little over the years. He was a solidly built man of placid
disposition who thought before he spoke and was never,
whatever the circumstances, to be startled into incautious action.
It was a long time since he and Maitland had first met, and
sometimes it had been as allies and sometimes as adversaries,
but each considered himself in some degree indebted to the
other and as both were conscientious men each considered his
own obligation the greater.

Sykes had arrived already and organised a table strategically
placed in a corner where he could survey the whole room and
make sure that no one came within earshot. They exchanged
greetings and punctilious inquiries about the health and well-
being of each of their families, a ceremony which the Superintendent never on any account neglected. It was some weeks
since they had seen each other, and as usual there were a number
of subjects for discussion. It wasn't until their meal had been
cleared away and their coffee served that Maitland, watching his
companion stirring his own cup carefully to dissolve the five

65

lumps of sugar he knew it contained, leaned back in his chair and demanded, 'Out with it, Superintendent. I'm glad to see you, that goes without saying, but I can't help a nasty feeling there was some ulterior motive behind your sudden desire for my company.'

Sykes smiled at him in his sedate way. 'What other reason could I have?' he asked, but it was obvious that the reply was intended to be provoking rather than informative.

'I can't think . . . now.' They both knew what he meant by that. About five months earlier the long feud between Maitland and Chief Superintendent Briggs had come to a head. It had been conducted with extreme bitterness on the detective's part but with no more than an instinctive dislike on Antony's and he had often reproached himself since for not taking the matter more seriously. He had been warned often enough, both by his family and by his present companion, but had suffered from a complete inability to see where the other man's distrust of him would lead.

The Chief Superintendent was retired now, and Sir Edwin Fairclough, at that time the Assistant Commissioner (Crime) at New Scotland Yard, had been at pains to express to Maitland the Force's gratitude that no charges had been laid in the matter. But as far as Antony was concerned the incident was over, though he still sometimes – that being his nature – continued to blame himself for the whole thing. If somehow he could have got on to terms with Briggs the detective would not have felt at last that his activities must be stopped at any cost. Still, it was one worry the less for his long-suffering family, and for that he was truly grateful.

All the same . . . 'You've been kinder to me in the past than perhaps I deserve, Superintendent,' he said, 'in the way of issuing warnings when you felt my actions might be open to misconstruction, but though there are members of the Force with whom I'm not on the best of terms' – Chief Inspector Conway came immediately into his mind – 'there's no one now who's willing to believe I'd commit any crime in the calendar to protect a client.' He paused, watching the other man's expression. 'Or is there?' he inquired, and his tone had sharpened.

Sykes did not give him a direct reply. 'This latest client of yours, Simon Winthrop,' he said – being a member of the murder squad himself he was apt to disregard lesser crimes – 'I

66

understand you had a psychiatrist to see him.'

'How the d–devil did you know that?'

'Mr Maitland, you know as well as I do the formalities that have to be observed in these cases. It came to my ears by chance, and Chief Inspector Conway, who is the investigating officer as I'm sure you know, very naturally wondered about it. There's been no suggestion at all that Winthrop might not be perfectly normal.'

'You can tell Conway to go to hell,' said Antony more amiably. 'You know as well as I do, Superintendent, to repeat your own phrase, that even if I knew at this stage what I was going to do I shouldn't tell him . . . or even you. If my cross-examination of his witnesses makes counsel for the prosecution think that's what I have in mind, it's open to him to call evidence in refutation.'

'It won't do a bit of good, lad, for us to sit here exchanging information that we both know perfectly well,' said Sykes, who had this much in common with Dr Macintyre; his Yorkshire accent had lingered, and he reverted to the local idiom only when it suited him. In this case Antony took it as a gesture of friendship, which instead of being a comfort made him extremely nervous and also a little angry, a fact that Sykes recognised as soon as he spoke.

'All r–right then, let's get it out into the open. You're warning me of s–something, but for the life of me I can't make out what it is. Not, surely, that Conway's got as large a b–bee buzzing in his bonnet as Briggs had.'

'No, not that. Chief Inspector Conway,' said Sykes carefully, 'is not one of your greatest admirers, largely because he has reason to be grateful to you–'

'What reason, for goodness' sake?'

'His promotion was delayed beyond what he felt was reasonable,' said Sykes, 'and as he has you to thank for his elevation to his present rank naturally he resents the fact.'

'But I had nothing to do with it!'

'That case you worked on together–'

'I remember, of course, but I'd no idea . . . well, if that was really the cause of his promotion no wonder he doesn't like me. Gratitude is a perfectly damnable emotion but I didn't know you had it in you to be so cynical. And I still don't know what you're getting at.'

'You've succeeded in confusing the issue, Mr Maitland,' said Sykes rather severely, 'as you so often do. Conway has really nothing to do with the case.'

'You said he was the investigating officer.'

'My last remark was intended metaphorically,' said Sykes, in almost as dampening a tone as Sir Nicholas might have used. 'All I was trying to tell you when I started is that it's well-known at the Yard that you're taking a special interest in the Winthrop case, and our new A.C. –'

'Wait a bit! I knew Sir Edwin had retired, but I don't know a thing about this new chap.'

'Sir Alfred Godalming. In his case the title isn't hereditary. He's our new Assistant Commissioner (Crime) and judging from this and that I'd say he's taking a more than usual interest in your activities.'

'For heaven's sake he can't think Briggs was right about all that s-stuff he tried to pin on to me last year!'

'No, he knows the truth of that but I can't say it endears you to him.'

'I d–don't understand.'

'I'd better tell you a little bit about his background. He was Chief Constable of Westhampton, succeeding Colonel Wycherley whom I believe you once told me you had met. Before that he was chief of the C.I.D. in one of the smaller towns in that county, and took note of your operations on the West Midland circuit on four or five occasions.'

'But Vera was involved in all those c-cases, and Uncle Nick too in s-some of them. He couldn't possibly have thought there was anything wrong.'

'No, but . . . I'm guessing, Mr Maitland, which is a thing I'm not particularly apt to do, but what I think is that they aroused his interest in you, and also he heard that stupid remark that started going the rounds at about the time you first went down to Chedcombe. The man who never loses a case.'

'I'm glad you said stupid. It's nonsense and you know it. What's more, this Sir Alfred of yours must know it too.' He had the slight stammer under control now, but Sykes realized that his temper was hard held.

'Yes, of course he does, but he's always taken an interest in murder and it happens that he knew Briggs quite well. He thought him a very valuable officer, in which I'm bound to say he was right, except that when the Chief Superintendent got an idea into his head there was no budging it.'

'He was a pig-headed old bastard,' said Antony flatly.

'That too,' Sykes agreed. It occurred to him fleetingly that this was something like holding a conversation with a ticking bomb. 'Now I can't pretend to know exactly what was in Sir Alfred's mind – as I said, he's perfectly well aware that Briggs went off the rails and tried to frame you – but I've a sneaking suspicion that at the back of his mind he thinks it was partly your fault.' He saw Antony close his eyes for a moment and said in a concerned tone, 'That disturbs you more than it should, Mr Maitland.'

Antony opened his eyes again but he did not meet the other man's worried look. 'If you want to know, Sykes, I've been blaming myself ever since it happened. You warned me, and Uncle Nick and Vera warned me, but I still wouldn't see where that obsession of his was leading him. I thought, I said so often enough, that as long as I kept on the right side of the law – which I had every intention of doing – everything would be all right. But he got to within a few months of retiring age and he thought that somehow or other I had to be stopped so he set about it in the only way at his disposal. I should have made it my business to convince him long since that those suspicions of his were all nonsense.'

'And how would you have set about that?'

'I don't know,' said Antony helplessly.

'No, I'm quite sure you don't, and nor does anybody else. You've nothing whatever to blame yourself with and perhaps I shouldn't have brought the subject up again.'

'I'm glad you did. What exactly *are* you trying to tell me, Superintendent? That this Sir Alfred of yours thinks I ought to have seen what was coming and taken steps to stop it, or that he thinks Briggs was right about me all along? I've lost count of the things he was ready to accuse me of, but you know them as well as I do.'

'The answer to that, Mr Maitland, is that I just don't know. But you can't be involved in my kind of work for long without getting a sort of sixth sense about what's going on, as I know quite well you do in the case of some of your clients.' Antony made a deprecating gesture. He had a profound distrust of instinct, at least on his own part. 'All I can say is,' Sykes was continuing, 'that he'll cause trouble if you give him half a chance.'

'And you think this Winthrop case might provide it? Good Lord, Sykes, you talked about a sixth sense, I only wish I had one where this chap's concerned.'

'You're finding the case difficult?'

'Damnably so.' But there was nothing more to be said between them on that particular subject and they both knew it. 'I wonder how many times I've said to you, Superintendent, that I'm grateful to you. I am, more than I can say. But at least,' Antony added, with an attempt at humour, 'you're not going to tell me this other chap is going to go round the bend too.'

'No, I don't think so. I just want you to watch your step, that's all. We could adapt the old saying and put it that the law must not only be kept, it must be seen to be kept. And as there seems to be some hint of the unusual in the preparation of the defence in Winthrop's case I thought it as well to bring the matter up.'

'Unusual is the word, and I wish I could tell you about it.' They left the matter there, and parted about ten minutes later, each to go his own way. Antony, who wasn't in the mood to face the documents on his desk again, walked back to chambers, wrestling as he went with the problem of whether he should tell Uncle Nick what Sykes had said. Sir Nicholas wouldn't be pleased if he found out later, and if the new A.C.'s animosity was being talked of openly at Scotland Yard it wouldn't be long before it reached the legal grapevine and Sir Nicholas's close friend Bruce Halloran would certainly hear of it. He could make a clean breast of it now or he could wait and see what developed.

And then there was Jenny . . .

III

As usual the rendezvous with Geoffrey went without a hitch. He wasn't the most dexterous driver of Maitland's acquaintance but knowing what the late afternoon traffic would be like he had allowed himself plenty of time, being a reliable sort of man, and particularly conscientious where his professional duties were concerned. This meeting with Bertha Harvey definitely came under that heading, and he was inclined to think that it might be

70

even more unpleasant than the ones that had gone before.

When he had enlisted Antony's help in Simon Winthrop's defence it had been with two ideas in mind: first that the oddness of the suggested defence would intrigue his friend so much that it was hardly fair to keep him out of it, and secondly because he had hoped that Maitland's ingenuity would have provided good arguments to convince the Patmores that the idea they had come up with was a poor one. He should have known, of course, he told himself ruefully now, that once Antony got his teeth into a matter he was unlikely to let go until he had resolved the problem one way or another. But it was too late to think of that now, and perhaps, when all possible steps had been taken, he and Sir Nicholas between them would be able to persuade Winthrop's counsel to take a reasonable line of defence.

Bertha Harvey had a two bedroom apartment in what Antony thought must have been one of the first blocks of flats ever to be built, three floors only, and two flats to a floor. It was in Earl's Court, and though the exterior of the building was shabby it was pleasant enough inside, and still more pleasant when Miss Harvey let them in to her own place. The furnishings were modern and there wasn't a comfortable chair to be seen (which Antony privately thought was natural enough in a place that had been shared by two women) but it was light and clean—perhaps a little aggressively clean—and, though it lacked the riot of colour with which Madeleine Rexford had surrounded herself, it was cheerful enough. Bertha herself was a short, rather square girl with a snub nose, an amiable expression and straight mouse-coloured hair. She barely waited for Geoffrey to introduce them and express his gratitude that she would see them before she said rather belligerently, 'I can't think why you want to. What I have to tell you won't help that horrible man you're working for.' Perhaps the look of amiability was a delusion after all.

'I daresay not directly,' said Geoffrey smoothly, leaving her to make what she could of that. 'We should be grateful, however, if you'd tell us exactly what you told Miss Madeleine Rexford. A story at second-hand is not quite so satisfactory.'

'I talked to Mr Dryden—Antonia's father—after I'd spoken to you, Mr Horton. He said there'd be no harm in seeing you, he'd promised to do so himself. You wouldn't be anxious to spread the story about, and it might make you realise the sort of man you're dealing with. But you'd better sit down,' she added, 'both of you. It won't take long, but I can't think with you towering over me like that.'

They sat down obediently and she took what was obviously her usual chair. 'Exactly what do you want to know?' she demanded.

Maitland felt it was time to take a hand. 'Everything,' he said simply.

'But–'

'Start with how long you knew Miss Dryden,' Horton suggested.

'I suppose for about a year before she died.'

'And when was that?' That was Maitland again.

'Three months ago. Well, at the beginning of December. And how we met was because I put in an advertisement for someone to share the flat, which I shall have to be doing again only the rent's paid until quarter-day and Mr Dryden didn't want any refund. I had a few answers, of course, but Antonia was the nicest of them. And if I must be frank with you the fact that her family were obviously well-off was quite a help. I can manage my half of the rent all right, and the living expenses, but if you team up with someone who gets into difficulties it can be awkward.'

'Yes, I can imagine that. And Miss Dryden, you say, came of a wealthy family?'

'You'd only to look at her,' said Bertha, 'though later I came to understand they were an old family and rather proud of their position too. But her clothes . . . well it was obvious they cost the earth, and her haircut was quite evidently expensive too, and I was sure she had a regular manicure. Professional, I mean. I wouldn't want you to think that was the only thing that impressed me, she was a nice person, I could tell that straight away, and . . . as a matter of fact I miss her terribly.' This was said in a defiant tone, as though any sort of emotion was to be deprecated, but her eyes filled with tears as she spoke and Antony began to think that his first impression of her had been the right one after all.

'Forgive me, Miss Harvey, this must be very distressing for you. You met Miss Dryden and liked her and she came to live here quite soon after that I suppose.'

'Yes, within a few days. She'd been living with her family in

Midhurst – or rather near Midhurst – and doing some volunteer work at the local hospital. But she was twenty-five and she said to me, making a joke of it, that she didn't want to be an old maid. That wasn't what she meant really, I just think she found it rather dull at home. So she persuaded her father – her mother died a few years ago – that if she shared a flat with another girl she'd be perfectly all right in London, and if he'd give her an allowance for the first few months she was sure she could find a job. I've a sort of feeling Mr Dryden found it difficult to refuse her anything that she really set her mind on, and anyway that's how it was arranged.'

'And did she find a job, even without any qualifications?'

'Yes she did, as hostess at a restaurant on the Brompton Road. Mr Dryden didn't like that a bit, and he came up to town to make sure it was a proper sort of place for her to be. But even he couldn't find fault with it; all she did was show people to their tables. Of course there's more to it than that, making sure one waitress doesn't get all the work and another none, but that wasn't the point. It's intensely respectable, the sort of place people take their grandchildren to on their birthdays. I think it puzzled Mr Dryden a bit, because of course he's never eaten anywhere where there wasn't a *maitre d'*. But he said if she'd really set her heart on doing it he'd go on with her allowance because the pay wasn't all that good. So that was how it was left.'

'Then she stayed with that job?'

'Yes, right up to the end. At first I introduced her to a few people, sometimes we'd double date, and then perhaps she'd go out with the man for a time or two, but she didn't seem to be keen on any of them. Then one evening she came home from work – it wasn't terribly late because they closed at ten – and told me she'd met this marvellous man and they were going out to dinner together on her first free evening.'

'I suppose, Miss Harvey, you don't happen to remember the date, either of this conversation or of that appointment?'

'No, I'm afraid not. Only that it was about five or six months after she came to live here.'

'Did you ever meet this man?'

'No, I told Miss Rexford that, but later Antonia described him to me, she couldn't stop talking about him, and Miss Rexford seemed to recognize the description.'

'It would fit a great many men.'

'Yes, but Antonia had spoken of him so often by name. Mostly just Simon, of course, but I knew his surname too. Why should she have lied to me about that?'

'I'm sure she didn't. But the man might have lied to her.'

'I don't see the point of that either. Besides, there were other things. She told me his address, and Miss Rexford recognized that too. And that he was an artist and did some commercial work as well as freelance.' She paused for a moment, frowning. 'Don't you think it would be too much of a coincidence if he'd just hit on that name and description accidentally, and then the person it fitted got into trouble over a murder?'

'Coincidences happen.' Though he mistrusted them himself and there was very little conviction in his tone. 'Did you know, did your friend Antonia tell you, that she and this man had become intimate?'

'I knew he'd been here quite often when I was out. Not just when she was free in the evening, but her days off weren't usually at the weekend so there was plenty of opportunity. I didn't know, but I suppose I guessed what was going on.'

'Was there any talk of marriage between them?'

'In a way. At least I know Antonia wanted it, she made no secret of that, but she told me Simon said he couldn't afford it and he wouldn't live on her money.' She paused again, looking from one to the other of her companions as though weighing up their capacity for discretion. 'If you want to know it all, I think that's why she let herself get pregnant,' she said. 'She'd have liked to live with him and I don't know whether she'd have cared very much herself whether there was a legal tie or not, but her family would have minded dreadfully.'

'I see. Miss Rexford said you told her that your friend was rather worried for a month or so before she admitted to you that she was pregnant.'

'Yes, but I think that was because she was wondering whether her plan would succeed.'

'But it didn't?'

'Obviously not. She was crying too much when she told me what had happened when she broke it to Simon for me to understand very well what excuses he made; all that was clear was there was going to be no wedding. So then Antonia was really frantic because of having to tell her father, and when

74

Simon told her he could give her something to fix things she jumped at the chance. She took it one night when I was out and when I came home–' She broke off, and for a moment seemed to be fighting against the memory. 'It was horrible!' she said at last with a shudder. 'I called the doctor at once but of course it was too late by then.'

'And what happened after that?'

'I realise that he had to tell the police, there were questions and questions. But first, when they'd taken her away and before I knew she was going to die, I telephoned her father. I'd only met him once, and it was terribly awkward. I just told him over the telephone that she'd been taken ill and could he come at once, but when he did come of course I had to break the whole thing to him.'

'How did he take it?'

She stared at him for a moment. 'Do you know, I don't really know,' she said. 'He . . . oh, I know he was terribly grieved, but I couldn't help thinking that he might feel–what's the old phrase?–that death was better than dishonour.'

'It must have been very difficult for you, Miss Harvey.'

'It was, because I'm quite sure he thought I was what I'm sure he'd call a fallen woman too. Of course his opinion doesn't matter, but his attitude was so remote and unsympathetic.'

'I'm a little puzzled about what happened after that, Miss Harvey. There must have been an inquest into your friend's death.'

'Yes, there was.'

'Weren't you asked questions about the man? After all he'd given her a drug that killed her.'

'I just said that Antonia had told me there was someone but I never met him. You see, Mr Dryden and I had talked it out, he knew there'd have to be some publicity, but if the man had been named and there had been further inquiries it would all have been so much worse. I'd never met Simon, that was perfectly true, and besides it was only my word against his if he denied the whole thing. So there really wasn't any point in saying any more.'

'No, I see.' He thought he saw also that Mr Dryden must be a fairly formidable personality. 'What prompted you to go to see Miss Rexford, Miss Harvey?'

'Not spite, if that's what you're thinking,' she said quickly. 'I read about the murder, which was pretty horrible even when it was only someone I'd known at second hand who'd done it. But then it said he'd been engaged to this girl Madeleine Rexford, and I realised he was even more duplicitous than I thought. If that is a word,' she added doubtfully. 'But I knew if it had been me I'd be thinking it was all a mistake, and probably that was what she felt too, and when he went to prison it would be simply terrible for her if she was still in love with him. So perhaps if I told her he wasn't quite the kind of person she thought he was it might help. I didn't know if what I'd done was the best thing, I don't know now. But I still don't see,' she added, harking back to her original theme, 'what good all this information can do you.'

'Perhaps none at all, Miss Harvey, but we're grateful just the same.' Maitland got to his feet as he spoke, and Geoffrey followed his example with alacrity. 'We won't take up any more of your time,' Antony went on, moving towards the door, but then he stopped. 'Is that Antonia Dryden?' he asked, glancing at the photograph that stood on a table at the side of the room.

'Yes, it is. I've wanted to throw it away because quite truthfully I don't like remembering what happened, but every time I've been going to do it I felt like a traitor so it's still there.'

'I can understand that, but the past is the past, Miss Harvey, and when you get someone else to share this place with you I think you'd be advised to put it away at least.'

'Yes, when that happens I will.'

'She was a beautiful girl.' He was staring down at the photograph as though trying to imprint it on his memory, but he thought as he spoke that pretty would have been a better word. Enchanting, yes, but there was more than a hint of weakness too. Not the strong-minded girl that Bertha Harvey had seemed to describe, unless Mr Dryden was more easily twisted around her little finger than seemed likely. He turned back to his hostess, and both he and Horton expressed their gratitude again.

'And thank goodness that's over,' said Geoffrey as they reached the street.

'I wonder if it is,' said Maitland rather absently, but Horton was feeling that enough time had been spent that day on Simon Winthrop's affairs and didn't challenge the remark. He drove off alone a few minutes later, leaving Antony looking for a taxi to take him home.

IV

The study door was closed when he got in, but even if it had been open he'd had every intention of ignoring the fact. He said 'Good evening' to Gibbs, received a rather sour greeting in return, and went up the stairs still debating the question of how much, if anything, he should tell Jenny about his talk with Sykes.

In a way the question answered itself as soon as he had let himself in at his own front door. He heard the murmur of voices from the living-room, Jenny's unmistakable tones, and a deeper voice that he knew immediately for their friend Roger Farrell's. Jenny turned to smile at him as he went in. 'Meg had to go to the theatre early, so Roger's here to dinner. Isn't that nice?' Roger and Meg Farrell were their closest friends, and as Meg (Margaret Hamilton) was a very successful actress her husband often spent his evenings at Kempenfeldt Square after he had taken her to the theatre.

'Very nice,' Antony agreed. 'We haven't seen you for a day or two, Roger. How's the play going, and how are all the little stocks and shares?' Roger, it is perhaps unnecessary to add, was a stockbroker.

'Up and down as usual,' said Farrell, answering the last part of the question first. 'As for the play, it's doing only too well. I expect,' he added despondently, 'it will run for ever.' But he was watching his friend rather closely as he spoke, obviously aware that something was in the wind, so that Antony realized immediately that his own attempt at light-heartedness had not been too successful as a camouflage.

It occurred to him again, as it had done perhaps a hundred times in the course of their acquaintance, that Roger's character would have made a good study for anybody interested in paradox. He was by temperament a man of action, who, with a change of attire from the usual trappings of his calling, could have modelled any day for an artist wishing to draw a typical pirate. Nor was he a man who generally went unnoticed; any room he entered would very soon show distinct signs of his presence. But at the same time he could, when he felt the need, efface himself, and he had a sensitivity to other people's feelings

77

that Maitland, not given to displaying his emotions, might have found both inconvenient and annoying in someone he liked less well.

'Jenny's been telling me all about your latest client,' said Roger as Antony helped himself to sherry and came to stand near the fire. 'Have you made up your mind about him yet?'

Maitland had a smile for that. 'I'm sorry I didn't get in earlier if it would have saved you one of Jenny's explanations,' he said. Jenny pulled a face at him, but she had been teased for so long about her lack of lucidity that his remark was no more than she. had expected.

'I'm sure Roger understands perfectly well,' she said with dignity, but then she smiled too. 'At least he should by now, he cross-examined me just as closely as you or Uncle Nick might have done.'

'You can only be talking about Simon Winthrop,' said Maitland resignedly. 'I'd better tell you what happened today.' He did so in as few words as possible, omitting all mention of his luncheon with Sykes, and when he had finished Jenny jumped to her feet.

'I've got a feeling something ghastly may be happening in the kitchen,' she said, and departed at something very near a run.

Roger picked up his glass, regarded the contents for a moment, and then looked up at his friend over the rim. 'What's the matter with you two?' he asked. 'First you come in looking like a cat with its fur rubbed the wrong way, and now Jenny dashes off. She never has crises in the kitchen.'

'She doesn't like all this talk of abortion,' Antony told him. 'All these years, and she's never really got over losing the baby. If we could have had another . . . but Dr Prescott said from the beginning there wasn't any hope of that.'

'Girls are different today,' said Roger. 'Tougher.'

'I don't know about this one . . . Antonia Dryden. It's been the most damnable day, Roger.'

'That much is obvious,' said Roger, in a fair imitation of Sir Nicholas's manner.

'According to Bertha Harvey, Antonia's friend, who is a tough cookie if I'm not mistaken –' He broke off and grinned. 'There, I've used that expression,' he said. 'I was saving it up for Uncle Nick's edification.'

'Never mind about that,' said Roger impatiently. 'What were

you going to tell me?'

'Only that she thought Antonia had got pregnant quite deliberately to force Winthrop into marriage. It may have started that way for all I know, but reading between the lines I'm pretty sure she didn't want to lose the baby. All this women's lib business . . . do you remember Chesterton's poem, Roger?'

'I've read some of them, but I can't think which one you mean.'

'The one where he was enumerating all the things he'd like to do if he were a heathen. Not that he mentioned abortion, of course, it wasn't the kind of thing people talked about then, let alone wrote poems about. But he finished each verse, after he'd said all the dreadful things he'd like to do, with a few lines that began *But Higgins is a heathen*, and went on to say how little advantage he took of the fact.'

'Yes, I do remember that one,' said Roger, 'and I think I know the verse you mean as well. *But Higgins is a heathen, and to lecture rooms is forced, where his aunts, who are not married, demand to be divorced.*'

'As Meg isn't here I shall say, precisely. You also obviously know why that came into my mind.'

'Because all the women agitating for freedom of choice are the ones who are least likely to need it,' said Roger. 'But I don't think, Antony, that sympathy for Antonia Dryden was everything that was on your mind when you came in.'

'No, damn you, it wasn't,' said Maitland without animosity. 'I'd better tell you about it, I suppose, and then you can tell me what to do. You know we thought all that business with Briggs was over.'

'And it isn't?' Roger was startled. 'It must be,' he insisted.

'In a way that's true, but you might say his ghost is walking,' said Antony carefully.

'For heaven's sake man, don't talk in riddles!'

'All right then. I had lunch with Sykes today.' He went on to give Farrell the gist of the conversation. 'It doesn't worry me too much,' he concluded – which was obviously a lie – 'except that it may make our friendship with Sykes awkward. But it will worry Jenny, and as for Uncle Nick he'll go straight up the wall. He always blamed me for the bad feeling between Briggs and me –'

'Or said he did,' Roger interrupted.

79

'He meant it all right,' said Antony, unconvinced. 'And he'll just think this is my fault too.'

'If you're thinking of keeping this new stumbling block to yourself it's a good thing I'm here tonight,' said Roger without any hesitation at all. 'To begin with, you must know by now that Jenny can face anything as long as she doesn't feel you're keeping things from her.'

'Yes, I do know, but –'

'There are no buts about it,' said Roger firmly. 'It is also a fact that she's not going to get *really* worried unless your physical safety is threatened in some way, having a good deal of faith in your ingenuity to deal with things like this, a faith which Meg and I share and with good reason. I don't suppose this Sir Alfred whatever-his-name-is is going to come after you with a battle-axe. As for Uncle Nick –'

'Don't lecture me, Roger.'

Roger smiled. 'It's for your own good,' he insisted. 'You'll tell Uncle Nick and Vera what's happened for two reasons. The first and most important is that they'll be hurt if you don't, because they're bound to find out sooner or later. And the second I should have thought was obvious if you'd taken a moment to think about it. Superintendent Sykes telephoned you in chambers, didn't he?'

'What a fool I am. Of course everyone knows I had lunch with him and Uncle Nick will want to know why,' said Antony in a rather hollow tone. 'All right, Roger, you win. Will you have another glass of sherry?'

'I've had my ration, but I'll pour you another if you like,' said Roger, getting up obligingly. 'While you're drinking it I'll go and see if there's anything Jenny wants carrying through, during which interval you can put the situation you've just described to me into a few well chosen words so as not to scare her into fits when you tell her.'

Friday, 14th March

I

By chance Horace Dryden was in town for a few days, and Geoffrey had been able to arrange a meeting with him at his hotel at ten-thirty. The hotel was central and convenient and Horace Dryden joined them in the lounge after they had been waiting only a few minutes. The room was almost deserted at that hour of the morning. He led them to a table near the window and waved away impatiently the waiter who appeared to inquire if morning coffee would be welcome.

Maitland's first thought was that whoever Antonia Dryden had taken after it hadn't been her father. He was a dried up little man, who from his expression might just have bitten into some extremely bitter fruit. He dealt with Geoffrey's introductions and explanations as shortly as he had done with the waiter. 'Yes, yes, you told me all that when you spoke to me on the phone. But there's nothing I can tell you, nothing.'

'In that case, Mr Dryden,' said Maitland mildly, 'I can't quite see why you agreed to see us, or why you advised Miss Harvey to do so.'

'Can't see any harm in it, won't do you any good to rake up a scandal.' His speech was as elliptical as Vera's very frequently was, but unlike his aunt's it caused Antony no amusement. 'I'm not a vindictive man, Mr Maitland, but it won't give me any sorrow to see this fellow Winthrop get his deserts. All the same, prefer to tell you what you want to know myself than have you asking questions all round. Don't know what your idea is or what makes you think the story may be helpful, but better hear it from me than anyone else.'

Antony didn't attempt to enlighten him. 'We spoke to Miss Harvey yesterday,' he said.

'Fool of a girl but means well,' said Dryden. 'Now you must understand I knew nothing of the affair until Antonia was ill, dying in fact, so there's not much I can tell you.'

'You had agreed though, approximately a year before, to your daughter coming to live in London.'

'Agreed? Practically threw the girl out of the house.'

For once in his life Maitland's next question didn't come smoothly. He glanced rather helplessly at Geoffrey, who obligingly came back into the conversation. 'Do you mean she'd done something to offend you, Mr Dryden?'

Horace Dryden turned on him almost as if there was something unfair about his intervention. 'Don't put words into my mouth, young man,' he ordered. 'The girl was moping about at home, should have been married long since but she never seemed to fancy any of the men she met. Thought it was time for her to stand on her own feet and told her so.'

'And you approved of the job she found?'

'Seemed a respectable enough place and it made a beginning, didn't it? If you want the truth Antonia hadn't the brains for anything better.'

That brought Maitland back into the talk again. 'We understood from Miss Harvey, sir, that Miss Dryden had no training for any kind of employment.'

'Went to a good school, couldn't get a university entrance. She wouldn't have needed any training if she'd settled down to get married like a normal girl.'

'Did you see her often during the year she was away from home?'

'Come up to town about once a month on business,' said Horace Dryden. He didn't specify what the business was, and neither Maitland nor Horton felt it politic to inquire. 'Saw her then, of course. Took her out to dinner, once or twice to a theatre, that sort of thing.'

'What impression did you get of her state of mind during that time?'

'Nothing particular. Should I have done?'

If this irritating little man thought that noticing other people's feelings was in some way beneath him perhaps a little flattery would help. 'A man of your discernment, Mr Dryden,' said Antony dulcetly. 'After all, you must have known your daughter far better than anybody else did.'

'Well, I suppose . . . seemed to find town life a bit strange at first, but then she settled down. Tell you the truth the last few times I saw her I was congratulating myself on my decision.' He paused, and for the first time Maitland felt a stab of sympathy, which wasn't decreased when the older man went on, 'Seemed happy, seemed in a kind of glow. More alive, if you get my meaning. Shows how wrong you can be.'

'I think perhaps you weren't mistaken, Mr Dryden,' said Antony gently.

But Horace Dryden had had enough of sentiment. 'Perhaps not,' he said. 'Only makes what that fellow did to her worse, doesn't it?'

'Did she ever speak to you of him?'

'Deceitful little minx,' said Dryden incredibly. This time Maitland was not deceived however. 'Let me think, when she went out it was all what she called double-dating with that Harvey girl and some friends of hers. Never had any idea there was anyone special, in fact I'd have been pleased if there was so long as it was all above board and she introduced me to the chap. As it was I came up to town when Miss Harvey sent for me, knowing Antonia had been taken ill but nothing more. What the girl had to tell me came as a complete shock.'

'I'm sorry to ask you to re-live such unpleasant memories, Mr Dryden.'

'Unpleasant fiddlesticks! Man's a rotter and it's better that you know it.'

'When you came to town you went straight to the flat your daughter shared with Bertha Harvey?'

'Yes, of course. I heard Miss Harvey's tale before I went to the hospital, and by then Antonia was dead. I went straight back and put the fear of God into that girl. There'd be an inquest later to get into the papers, but no good making more of a sensation than there was already.'

'By introducing the man's name, you mean?'

'That's right.'

'He had committed a very serious offence, and in view of your daughter's death might even have been indicted for manslaughter.'

'I'll be frank with you, Mr Maitland,' Usually this phrase put Antony on his guard, but this time he felt that Dryden meant exactly what he said. 'I'd have been glad enough to see the man punished, but what had we against him? Hearsay evidence, and second-hand at that.'

83

'You're right, of course.'

'I didn't leave it there, I made some inquiries of my own through a private inquiry agency. But they couldn't find anything even to show Winthrop had known Antonia. And perhaps that isn't surprising. Antonia, poor girl, would know she was doing wrong, and insist on the affair being carried on with discretion.'

'Yes, and I think that is evident too in the fact that Bertha Harvey never met the man concerned.'

'Well, you've got the whole story. What do you think of this precious client of yours now?'

Maitland got to his feet. 'It seems unfair,' he said, 'that when you've answered all our questions so kindly we should have to refuse to discuss that. But I'm sure when you think about it you'll see our predicament.'

'Professional ethics, eh? Does you credit I suppose. All the same, best you should know the truth.' He escorted them himself to the door of the hotel, and his goodbyes were far more amiable than his greetings had been.

'What next?' asked Geoffrey as they walked away. And then, 'The things you talk me into.'

Maitland ignored this. 'Do you need to go back to the office?' he asked.

'No, there's nothing on my plate that Bernard won't look after for me.' He meant that his partner, Bernard Stanley, preferred not to deal with criminal matters. 'And I thought – I don't know what you're up to, Antony, you must see it's hopeless – but I thought that as long as you insist on going on with this we'd better get it over.'

'That might have been put more gracefully,' Maitland pointed out. 'All the same, I'm grateful. Did you manage to get hold of the keys of Winthrop's studio?'

'I did. Not without a certain amount of argument from Conway. After all the murderer's home is not exactly part of the *res gestae*.'

'No, but it should hardly be out of bounds to the defence either. However, Geoffrey, I've got something to tell you about that. I had lunch with Sykes yesterday.'

'You didn't tell me when we went to see Bertha Harvey.'

'No, I still had some thinking to do. I'm not trying to be mysterious, Geoffrey, but we can't talk about it here. Let's go

84

and have a look at the studio, and then we can get some lunch and talk things over.'

'All right then.' Geoffrey was beginning to look nervous. 'I thought we'd got Briggs out of our hair—'

'It's nothing to worry about, believe me,' said Maitland. 'Except perhaps for its effect on Uncle Nick,' he added with belated honesty. And with that Geoffrey for the moment had to be content.

II

Simon Winthrop's studio was much what Maitland had expected, an airy, comfortable, untidy place that several weeks of being unoccupied had done nothing to improve. The first thing that caught his eye was an easel at the far end of the room with a canvas propped up on it. He made for it straight away and saw a half-finished landscape, less than half-finished perhaps, the completed portion showing trees overhanging a stream, and the stream itself being half in sunlight and half in shade. For the rest there was a roughly sketched-in outline but even in its present state it conveyed to him a notion of serenity. The word bothered him, because it was the one he always applied mentally to Jenny. He became aware of Geoffrey at his elbow. 'Clare always says painting water is the most difficult thing of all,' he remarked.

'I expect there's a sketchbook around,' said Horton. 'He must have been working from something.' But they found nothing of the sort and came to the conclusion that if it had ever existed, it must have been moved by the Patmores with the rest of Winthrop's paintings. 'It somehow didn't occur to me when we were with them to ask if I could see them,' said Maitland. 'I wish now I had, I'd like to have had a look at them.'

'I expect this gives you a fair idea of his normal style,' said Geoffrey. 'I like it,' he added, 'as I think I told you. I mean, it's the sort of thing you could live with.'

Antony grinned at him. 'You're as much of a Philistine about art as I am,' he said. 'All the same, I know what you mean, and I could almost forgive the friends and loving relations of the man who painted that for saying "he couldn't have done such a thing" when faced with an accusation of murder against him.'

'I never thought to hear you say that under any circumstances,' said Geoffrey. 'I thought it came at the top of the list of things you hate.'

'It does. What about the other paintings, Geoffrey? Didn't you tell me Mrs Patmore had sent them back here, didn't like having them in the house?'

'Probably the ones over there, facing the wall.'

'Then let's have a look at them.'

Geoffrey obliged by turning the canvasses round and propping them against the wall so that they could be studied at leisure. For a moment neither of them spoke. Then, 'You wouldn't say what you did just now about the man who painted those,' said Horton.

'No, I wouldn't, I . . . Mr Patmore obviously is an imaginative man, I mean there's nothing you can pick out exactly in the way of a subject, and yet his description of them was rather horribly apt. There's something unmistakably evil about them.'

'I'm not surprised Mrs Patmore wouldn't let her husband keep them at home,' said Horton. 'All the same, they've got Winthrop's signature clearly enough.'

'But the experts say they weren't painted by the same man. And anyone capable of painting like that could copy a signature, I suppose.'

'Damn all experts!' said Geoffrey cheerfully. If Maitland's last remark seemed to contradict what he had previously been maintaining he made no comment. 'But I've been thinking . . . you know I don't go along with this multiple personality nonsense, not that it would do us the slightest good if we both believed in it absolutely. But what happened to Winthrop as a child could have had a tremendous effect on him. These things may have been a means of getting . . . of getting some sort of agony out of his system.'

'He says he's no recollection of painting them,' Maitland reminded him.

'Yes, but that was just jumping on the bandwagon when we told him what the Patmores thought. He wouldn't realize that it was completely unprovable, and that even if we could prove it, it wouldn't do him very much good.'

'No, I see.' Antony sounded depressed. 'Turn those things round again, Geoffrey, there's a good chap. I can't bear the sight of them.'

'Well, you would come,' said Geoffrey, but he complied with

the request readily enough. 'Was that all you wanted to see?'

'No.' He sounded vague again. 'I thought we might just have a look round.'

'What for, for heaven's sake?'

'There might be something that enlightened us a little as to Simon Winthrop's character . . . don't you think?'

'Since you ask me, I should think it very unlikely. However, as I'm quite sure you mean to have your own way –' He stood looking around him at the disordered room. 'Where the hell do you want to start?'

'What about that little bureau over there?'

'If you think the police will have left anything worth looking at. They'd be bound to go through his things for evidence as to his financial situation, and he must have kept some sort of books, however rudimentary, because he's a self-employed person.'

'So I suppose but . . . bear with me, Geoffrey. I've got a feeling something might turn up.'

Horton sighed elaborately and came over to his side. 'A love letter or two from Antonia Dryden,' he said. 'A diary perhaps, with notes of places they met. Antony, you must be sick of hearing this, but even if you could find some proof – and remember Horace Dryden tried – what good would it do us?'

'That's not what I'm looking for, though I admit we might find something of the sort. It's just that I've got this feeling –'

'So you said before,' said Geoffrey rather sourly. 'What feeling, for heaven's sake?'

'Suppose some more personalities turn up.'

'I think you're mad,' said Geoffrey with conviction. 'In any case, the situation would remain unchanged.' Then he grinned. 'Let's get it over with,' he suggested. 'I want my lunch.'

'I won't be long.' Maitland glanced round the room again. 'Unless he hid something under his mattress, or under the chair cushions, or in a book – in any of which cases the police would have been on to him like a shot – there's nowhere to look besides this.' He turned back towards the bureau again. 'I say, Geoffrey, do you notice something?'

'It looks like a perfectly ordinary bureau to me.'

'Yes but . . . it's very slightly dusty, but not with quite such a thick layer as the rest of the room has acquired.'

'You gave me the answer to that yourself. There was nowhere else for the police to look so they looked here, and Conway being a tidy soul probably felt it necessary to remove the fingerprints and so forth that they'd left behind them.'

'I suppose so.' Maitland's depression seemed to have deepened. 'But do you have to trample on every idea I come up with?' he asked in an aggrieved tone.

'Only because I'm not sure what kind of a wild goose you're chasing at the moment,' said Geoffrey. 'But if you must, get on with it. The next people to be in here are likely to be removal men when the Patmores get round to emptying the place, so that they won't complain if you leave things a bit untidy.'

Antony started by pulling out one drawer after another and finding them all empty. He then pulled back the flap of the desk, exposing the writing surface and the usual row of pigeon-holes. 'I'm quite sure you're right, Geoffrey,' he said. 'The police will have moved anything that might be of interest.' In spite of that he began systematically to remove the remaining papers and glance at them, giving a running commentary as he went. 'A receipt from a firm of suppliers of artists' materials; a receipt for the rent, for electricity, from the gas board. No bank statements, the police would take those along with any account books, I suppose. You'll be hearing about that from them in time. It'll be interesting to know how much a painting like the one over there, for instance, will fetch. And how much he made from his forays into the commercial market. He seems to have been a methodical sort of chap; this side is all business, or things connected with the sheer business of keeping alive. If there are any personal papers . . . ah, here we are!'

'Have you found something?' asked Geoffrey, when the silence had stretched out for several minutes.

'Wait a bit! There's a diary, but nothing interesting in it. Just a few notes of appointments and at a guess, Geoffrey, I'd say it was only appointments he wasn't particularly interested in, and might need a jolt to his memory to enable him to keep.'

'How do you mean?'

'Well, you said he visited his grandfather about once a month, and that's recorded meticulously. And there are a few notations that a sketch is required by such and such a date by one of the advertising agencies. That kind of thing. Not a word about

Madeleine Rexford or about the occasions when he visited his parents. And certainly nothing about Antonia Dryden. There's an address book too and that's just as dull. Obviously Conway didn't think it worth impounding. Madeleine's telephone number is in there, and the Patmores; perhaps he was one of those people who have difficulty in remembering figures. But nothing for Antonia either under her Christian or surname, or even under the comparative anonimity of initials. No correspondence, but then when you come to think of it why should there be when he's lived all his life in the London area and it's so easy to pick up the telephone? Except this one thing, Geoffrey, and I'd like to know what you think of it.' He held out a sheet of paper, good quality writing paper, but without either an embossed or a written address. The handwriting was uneven, and the short message started abruptly:

Mr Winthrop,
I'm sorry I can't meet the payment that was agreed between us this month but I will do so without fail in February and make up the missing amount as soon as I can. If you wish to talk the matter over I suggest we meet at the King's Head on neutral ground as you might say, but I'm sorry to say I shall be empty-handed.

M.B.

'I don't see anything in that,' said Geoffrey, handing it back. 'He sold a picture on the H.P., I suppose, something like that.'

'I daresay somebody might be so anxious to acquire a particular painting he'd be willing to go into hock for it,' said Maitland doubtfully, 'but it doesn't sound likely to me. Besides there's a sort of desperation about the letter, not as though M.B. was writing to someone he liked and knew would understand his temporary embarrassment.'

'There's a pub called the King's Head just round the corner from here,' said Geoffrey, declining to comment on this surmise.

'That's convenient, but even so it sounds fishy to me. If M.B. owed Winthrop money, because he'd made him a loan or because he'd sold him a picture, why shouldn't that be mentioned? I wonder if, by any chance, the payments were usually made at the King's Head.'

'It's far more likely the chap just sent him a cheque.'

'Don't be such a spoilsport. If you want to know what it sounds like to me, Geoffrey, it sounds like blackmail, and I think we've found the fourth – or is it the fifth? – personality.'

'You only say that because you were expecting something of the sort,' said Geoffrey. 'I don't believe it's true, and as I've said a hundred times if it were it wouldn't help us.'

'I know your opinion,' said Maitland, suddenly impatient, 'and I know Uncle Nick's opinion and I know what Vera thinks. Probably Jenny does too, though she hasn't said so. But I'm going to have my own way about this. I'm sorry, Geoffrey. Vera's told me – since she married Uncle Nick and I've got to know her better – that sometimes when she called me in on a case she felt as if she'd conjured up the devil. You may be feeling that way too, but I can't help it. I'll deal with this my own way or not at all.'

'I've often felt like that too,' Geoffrey confirmed, but he smiled as he spoke. 'You know as well as I do, Antony, that I'll follow your lead as I have done many times before, even though I'm sure this time you're wrong.'

'Thank you. I can't see anything else that might be helpful.' He looked around vaguely, and his eye alighted on a pile of newspapers lying on the seat of one of the armchairs. 'Somebody was interested enough to cut something out of one of them,' he said, picking up a clipping from the top of the heap. 'Three dead in blazing car,' he read. 'Cheerful!'

'Friends of Winthrop's,' Horton suggested. 'Something to remind him to write a note of condolence.'

'Very likely. I wonder if anybody would object if I pocketed the letter, and perhaps this as well. I'll tell the Patmores that I have them, that should make it all right. And I want to talk to them again, but perhaps the telephone would do, and I want to talk to Macintyre; the telephone will probably do for that too. And I'll have to talk to our client again. After all, when we explain the position to him he may not want to follow my advice. I don't like this business, Geoffrey, I don't like it one little bit.'

'I can't say I'm particularly enamoured of it myself,' Horton told him. 'What about that lunch you promised me,' he added more briskly, 'and an explanation of whatever it was that Sykes had to tell you?'

III

At Maitland's suggestion they lunched at the King's Head, which was certainly convenient for the studio. A pleasant place, old-fashioned in a way that didn't look contrived, and with red velvet curtains which, when lighting-up time came, must make it look so attractive as to be practically impossible to pass. The pub lunch was good too and the draught bitter excellent.

'Now!' said Geoffrey, when they were comfortably settled with their meal spread out before them.

Maitland obliged with a brief account of his talk with Sykes. 'I don't see that it makes any difference,' he concluded, 'except that people are inclined to take their lead from the head of whatever establishment they work for . . . in this case members of the C.I.D. from this chap Sir Alfred Godalming. Which may lead to a certain amount of obstructive tactics on their part, but the rules are clear enough, they can't get round them, so even if you go on briefing me I don't think it will be more than a mild annoyance.'

'You said that about Briggs's attitude,' Geoffrey reminded him. 'What does Sir Nicholas say?'

'I went down last night to tell him and Vera. She's upset, more upset than I could have believed possible, and you know I don't like hurting people. Uncle Nick was just plain angry, so angry I don't think he took time to think out the possibilities of the situation. He says – as he always has done – that my relations with the police are my own fault because I got off on the wrong foot with Briggs in the beginning. And he may be right for all I know, but Sykes was in on that first case too and over the years we've become good friends. I've a number of kindnesses to thank him for, not least this last warning, but as I say I don't really think that the fact Sir Alfred disapproves of me will make much difference.'

'I shouldn't be too sure about that.'

'How can it?'

'You have to admit, Antony, that your ways are inclined to be unconventional.'

'I only do what I think is best for my client.'

'Yes, I know, but if you make the wrong decision –'

'Everybody makes mistakes sometimes.'

'I'd be happier if I knew what your intentions were in this case,' said Horton in a worried tone.

'I'll tell you as soon as I'm sure myself.'

'You see,' Geoffrey went on as though his friend hadn't spoken, 'the A.C. will have the ear of the Bar Council, and if he's ill-disposed—'

'You're making my blood run cold.' Maitland's tone was so light as to be almost flippant.

'You may think it's funny, Antony, I don't. There have been times in the past when if things had gone wrong—'

'But they didn't. In any case, if it turns out I've advised Winthrop wrongly nobody can do anything about it, to me or to you. Unless, I suppose, we were suspected of selling the pass, but as it's a criminal case, not a civil one, that hardly arises.'

'You're right, of course, but if you're off on one of your damned crusades—'

'I'm sorry, Geoffrey, really I am. Look here, will you come to lunch tomorrow, and arrange for us to see Winthrop during the afternoon, if you can?'

'I can certainly arrange that, but you always lunch with Sir Nicholas and Vera on Saturdays.'

'I'll square it with Vera. You know you're always welcome at their board. Then we can have a council of war. I'll know what I want to do by then.'

'Very well. It's a pity though,' said Geoffrey sighing. 'Mrs Stokes is almost as good a cook as Jenny is, and the food will probably turn to ashes in my mouth.'

IV

Maitland went back to chambers, and did his best to concentrate on one or two matters that Willett told him had become urgent. He didn't want to ring the Patmores until Norman got home, but at half-past five he asked Hill to try their number and found he was in luck. They were both in, and when Sylvia heard who it was she said immediately, 'I'll tell Norman to get on the other phone.' This suited Maitland down to the ground, and he waited quite willingly until he heard the second receiver lifted and Patmore's voice greeting him.

'I'm sorry to trouble you both again,' he said when the other man had finished speaking, 'especially when you were both so patient with my questions before.'

'Nonsense! We were grateful for your interest' – Patmore was obviously not to be outdone in politeness – 'and now, as you can imagine, we're eager for news.'

'I'm afraid that isn't the purpose of my call exactly. A few more questions,' said Maitland apologetically.

'Anything we can tell you, of course. But I did gather you were going to look into our idea a bit further. For instance, have you seen Madeleine?'

'Indeed we have.'

'She's a nice girl, isn't she?' Sylvia Patmore broke in. 'And she'd tell you just what we did, that Simon would never –'

'She's obviously very much in love with him,' Antony interrupted before the offending phrase could be completed. 'And she's quite willing to give evidence if Mr Horton decides to call her. But – forgive me – I do understand your anxiety, but I feel it would be better if we discuss the whole matter later when we've made up our minds how best to deal with it.' He could almost hear Geoffrey's voice saying bitterly, When *you*'ve decided, but they had been sparring on those lines for so many years now that he'd have known there was no malice in it.

'Just as you wish, Mr Maitland,' said Patmore before his wife could protest. 'Except perhaps for one question. Have you discovered anything to disprove our theory?'

'Nothing at all.' He might have added that it would have been as difficult to disprove as to prove, but if his rather evasive answer would satisfy them for the time being all the better. 'My questions are very simple. Mr Horton and I visited your son's studio this morning, and I was wondering . . . when you went there to pack his things, and later to move his paintings, did either of you touch the desk?'

'I didn't,' said Sylvia Patmore. 'I'd have left it to Norman anyway, but –'

'There was no need for me to do so either,' Patmore broke in. 'The police had been there already, of course, and told me they'd cleared all the drawers, where apparently he kept his record books. Simon always said you had to be awfully careful when you were self-employed, though I think his natural inclination would have been to shove everything into a drawer and forget

93

about it. And they . . . it was a man called Chief Inspector Conway, as far as I remember, whom my wife took rather a dislike to –'

'He was a cold man,' said Mrs Patmore.

'He can't help it,' said Antony, feeling in some obscure way that an apology was called for.

'At least he had the kindness to sort out the unpaid bills and hand them over to me for payment,' said Patmore. 'Later, of course . . . I'm afraid things may take rather a lot of sorting out if the case goes badly, but we won't think of that just yet.'

'I took the liberty myself of removing one short letter,' said Antony, and hurried on before they could ask him about it. 'Do the initials M.B. mean anything to you?'

'I can't think of any of Simon's friends with those initials,' said Norman Patmore. 'Can you, my dear?'

'No, I can't. Was it a letter from a friend?'

'That wasn't evident. Did your son ever mention to you that he'd sold a picture and not been paid for it immediately. Or that he'd made a loan to anyone who was paying him back in monthly instalments?'

'The answer is, No, to both those questions. Unless . . . Sylvia?'

'No. He might have sold a picture that way without telling us, thinking that to get the money eventually was better than nothing, but though he's a very generous person any loan he made couldn't have been more than five pounds to the end of the month, something like that. His income wouldn't allow it, and he never would let us help him.'

'I see. Well that leaves just one more question. You mentioned to me that your son had relations in Canada.'

'Celia, yes. But I'm afraid we've lost touch with her,' said Sylvia Patmore. 'You know how it is when people are so far away, and we'd never known her really well, not the way we knew Rosalie.'

'She was married, you said.'

'Yes, to Bob Camden. Robert, I suppose, but he was always called Bob. And their son was called Robert too. There couldn't have been any other children after they left England. I think she'd have mentioned that.'

'Can you give me Mrs Camden's address?'

'How on earth could she help? They went abroad two years

94

before the accident that killed Rosalie and Peter. Simon would
have been about five years old at that time so she couldn't tell
you anything about him.'

'All the same I should like the address if possible.'

'Mr Wilmot's lawyer – ?'

'Doesn't know it.' (It was odd, actually, that he hadn't been in
touch with the Patmores. Perhaps he was that *rara avis*, a
solicitor who was capable of feeling embarrassment.) 'If they
exchanged letters, Mr Wilmot doesn't seem to have kept any of
them.'

'Well, I don't know. Celia and I used to exchange Christmas
cards,' said Mrs Patmore, 'and of course there was a lot of
correspondence about our adopting Simon, but after that it was
just a card, and perhaps a note written on it at Christmas. About
ten years ago, I can't remember exactly, she put in a note that
said quite baldly that her husband was dead. And though I went
on sending cards to the same address for a few years we never
heard from her again.'

'Ten years is a long time for someone to stay in the same
place, especially in North America. But if you could find that
old address, we might be able to trace her.'

'I'm afraid I don't keep my Christmas card list up to date very
well,' said Mrs Patmore. 'I just cross out people who have died
or dropped out of the picture as Celia did, and change other
people's addresses when they move somewhere else. I expect I
can find it for you. Do you mind holding on?'

'I'll hold on all night if it will help,' said Maitland, and then
regretted the remark as it could only have raised their curiosity
still further. Norman Patmore, for all his obvious good
intentions, did allow himself a question or two while they were
waiting, which Maitland answered as well as he could without
really telling the other man anything.

At last Sylvia Patmore came back. 'I found it,' she said, still in
a rather doubtful tone. 'She lived in Shelburne, Nova Scotia.
Have you a pencil, Mr Maitland?'

'Yes, I'm still in chambers.' An unnecessary piece of
information, but perhaps he felt some explanation was needed of
so extraordinary a fact.

'Good.' She dictated the brief address. 'I remember she told
me once it was a very small town down the south shore,
whatever that means. But you know it's quite likely she moved

95

after her husband died.'

'We'll just have to hope for the best,' Maitland assured her. 'If it's such a small place somebody may know where she went.'

'Yes, but I wish I could see how that might help Simon.'

'Mrs Patmore, please don't get your hopes up. Mr Horton and I are doing our best, really we are, but it wouldn't be fair to let you think these questions have any particular significance. I'm just fishing in the dark. But if I might make a suggestion, I think Mr Wilmot's solicitor would appreciate this information too.'

'Well, of course, if you say so,' she told him doubtfully, 'I'll speak to him as soon as I can.'

After that the conversation didn't continue very long. Norman Patmore obviously was sensitive to Antony's discomfort, and interrupted his wife's questions gently with the remark, 'We mustn't ask Mr Maitland for information he can't give us, my dear.' Antony rang off thankfully, and without giving himself time to think picked up the phone again and asked Hill to get him Superintendent Sykes at Scotland Yard. 'If he hasn't gone home already,' he added doubtfully, glancing at his watch.

But he was in luck. 'You just caught me as I was leaving, Mr Maitland,' said Sykes's voice placidly in his ear a moment later. 'Mrs Maitland is well I trust and—'

'They've none of them dropped dead since we talked yesterday,' said Antony rather impatiently, and immediately regretted having spoken.

The Superintendent, however, was not a man to take offence where he was sure none was intended. 'You sound in a hurry,' he said, 'and perhaps rather worried. What can I do for you now?'

'Something off the record. If you can manage it without running into trouble.'

'I shouldn't worry about that. Even Assistant Commissioners aren't infallible, and what the mind doesn't know,' said Sykes placidly and without any pretensions to originality, 'the heart needn't grieve over. And there's this much to be said for having the pleasure of your acquaintance, Mr Maitland, it prevents life from getting dull.'

'I don't think you'll find this assignment particularly enlivening,' Antony assured him. 'There's a woman who used to live in

96

Shelburne, Nova Scotia, but the address I have is ten years out of date. Her husband's name was Robert Camden, generally known as Bob, and he died at about that time so it does seem likely that she may have moved. Her name is Celia. I don't know anything about Shelburne, but I'm told it's a small place down the south shore. I haven't a map handy but—'

'The Halifax police will tell me who to get in touch with.' It would take more than this to shake the Superintendent's placidity. 'There may be a Chief of Police in—Shelburne did you say?—otherwise I think it would be the R.C.M.P. But I'll find out, don't you worry. What is it you want to know?'

Maitland was mentally thanking heaven for somebody who didn't ask a thousand questions about his motives. 'If possible I'd like her present address and telephone number,' he said. 'I know she has one son called Robert after his father who must be about thirty now. It would be helpful to know where he is too.'

'At least we can ask.'

'It's a long shot, Superintendent, and I can't really tell you what else I want to know, but any scraps of information might turn out to be relevant. And I think that they're four hours behind us in time so—'

'So you'd like me to get the request off straight away?' Sykes's voice definitely held a note of amusement. 'All right, Mr Maitland, I'll do what I can for you. Can you give me her last known address?'

'Yes, I've got it here. I'm more than grateful,' he added when Sykes had written it down. 'It's the sort of thing that could cause endless delays if I had to deal with it myself.'

'I think you'd better save your gratitude until we see if I can do anything,' said Sykes prosaically. And then, in an obvious attempt at the reassurance he seemed to feel the other man needed, 'Don't worry, lad. It'll all be the same in a hundred years.'

So it will, said Maitland to himself as he replaced the receiver, but somehow he didn't find the thought very comforting. He consulted his watch again. With any luck Dr Macintyre would be home by now, and though interrupting his before dinner drink would not be a popular move, perhaps in the end it might be forgiven. Hill was still waiting patiently to see if anything more was needed of him. 'Just get me Dr Macintyre on the phone,' Antony asked, 'and then cut along home. I'll see

97

everything is locked up.'

'Mr Willett is still here, Mr Maitland,' said Hill in the apologetic way that Antony was sure he would have used even if he were reporting that the recipient of the information had just won a million pounds.

'Is he though?' He thought for a moment. John Willett was now next to old Mr Mallory in seniority in the clerks' office, and his devotion to the interests of his employer's nephew was well known, and frequently very useful. 'Ask him to wait until I've finished this telephone call,' Antony said. 'I'll come out then and have a word with him.'

Dr Macintyre, in spite of Maitland's qualms, was his usual laconic self. 'You again, Maitland?' he asked. 'Don't tell me you're still harping on this multiple personality business?'

'You said yourself, Doctor, that certain members of your profession consider it a distinct possibility.'

'Well, I suppose you know your own business best,' said Macintyre rather doubtfully.

'I'm not so sure that I do.' Antony sounded rueful. 'All the same—'

'What can I do for you now?' That had been Sykes's question too. He seemed to be putting a great many people to a great deal of trouble.

'I can answer the main objection you raised to the Patmores' theory.' He explained about the accident that had killed Rosalie and Peter Winthrop, and Simon's part in it. 'I should say myself,' he concluded, 'that would be a bad enough experience to explain any number of later aberrations.'

'A bad business,' said Macintyre slowly. 'He didn't tell me about it, or you either, I gather.'

'No, Mr and Mrs Patmore did. He seemed to them to have forgotten the whole episode, and not even to remember his previous life with his parents. I think I mentioned that that struck me too when I talked to him. At any rate he never mentioned any of it, and they felt it best not to bring the matter up. I don't know that I blame them.'

'Neither do I, but it might have been better to refer him to a psychiatrist at that time.' The doctor laughed, a sharp sound—more like a bark really—that made Maitland move the receiver quickly away from his ear. 'Don't think I've known you all these years without realising what you think of my profession,' Macintyre said. 'But we have our uses, you know, we have our uses.'

It seemed better to leave that remark unanswered. 'There's just one other small point, that Winthrop had a date with Madeleine Rexford, the girl he's engaged to, on the night his grandfather was murdered, and didn't keep it. It had happened before, apparently, so she wasn't especially surprised when he didn't turn up. She said that previously he had always given her a rather weak explanation and she'd come to the conclusion that he was one of those people who just had to be alone sometimes, and if she loved him enough to marry him – as she did – it was simply something she'd have to learn to live with.'

'It fits in with Winthrop's story of the recurring attacks of amnesia, which in turn could quite well follow the incident you describe about his parents' death. I should say myself the blackouts probably occurred when something happened that threatened to make him remember. He'd just retreat from reality until the threat had passed.'

'But equally this – what did you call it? – human defence mechanism might have sent him off into another personality altogether?'

'So the people who believe in it say. I think I've conveyed to you already that I'm sceptical about it. Are you trying to tell me you're going to call on me to expound this unlikely theory to the court?'

'No, Doctor, in fact I think it's very unlikely . . . well, perhaps if we get to the stage of having to explain that our client doesn't remember anything about the night his grandfather was murdered you might be able to say that wasn't impossible, perhaps even that it was quite likely, considering all that had gone before.'

'I think I might do that without straining my conscience. Hysterical amnesia is a reasonable hypothesis in the circumstances. What are you going to do, Maitland? Plead Not Guilty in order to have a chance of putting the extenuating circumstances before the court?'

'Whatever I do, whatever Geoffrey and I decide,' said Maitland, though he knew well enough already that whatever line they took the responsibility would be his, 'we shall have to get our client's agreement first. Can I leave it there for now? One of us will be in touch.'

'I'd like to know what's really in your mind,' grumbled Macintyre, 'but I suppose I can't force you to tell me. All right, we'll leave it there, just don't worry yourself into a mental breakdown, that's all,' he added in a disagreeable tone which Antony realized well enough was intended to disguise a sympathy Macintyre knew would be unwelcome.

'Thank you, Doctor . . . for everything,' said Maitland, and replaced the receiver carefully. He took a few moments to put the papers on his desk into some sort of order, and then went down the corridor to the clerk's office.

Willett, who had been in chambers almost all his working life, was a cheerful individual of whom it was said that he never walked anywhere if it was possible to run. He was also, as Maitland had realized for some years now, something of a psychologist, having his own rather devious methods of getting his own way when old Mr Mallory, if told the full facts of the situation, would have gone stubbornly in the opposite direction. He jumped to his feet when Antony went in but didn't immediately speak.

'What's all this, Willett?' Maitland inquired. 'Why aren't you at home with your loving family?'

'Wife's away, Mr Maitland, and the kids with her. Rotten time of year for the country, but it seems her mother wasn't feeling quite the thing.'

Antony seated himself on the corner of one of the desks, Mr Mallory's as it happened. 'In that case it seems it would have been better to leave the children with you,' he said, still on an inquiring note.

'You don't know my mother-in-law,' said Willett cheerfully. 'Says she's dying. Well, that happens three or four times a year, so we don't take all that much notice. Still, Betty always goes along because there'll be a time some day when she isn't crying wolf. But there'd be nothing but complaints if she didn't take the youngsters, the old lady wanting to see her grandchildren for the last time, that sort of thing.'

'I see. Well that explains why you're in no hurry to get home, but I'd have thought there'd be more amusing places to be than in this office after the week's work is finished.'

'Well, you see, Mr Maitland, it's like this.' Willett was suddenly very much in earnest. 'What with you seeming to be worried, and Chief Inspector – sorry, Superintendent Sykes –

100

telephoning you yesterday, and then Sir Nicholas being fit to be tied all day today . . . well, it just crossed my mind there might be something I could do to help.'

It came as no surprise to Antony to realize that the clerks knew as much of what went on in chambers as he did himself, probably more if the truth were known. 'That's extraordinarily good of you,' he said. 'As a matter of fact –'

'There *is* something,' said Willett eagerly.

'I wouldn't have dreamed of asking you if Mrs Willett was at home, but how would you like to go on a pub crawl? Well, only one pub actually, it's called the King's Head and it's –'

'Just round the corner from that Mr Winthrop's studio,' said Willett.

'How the devil did you know that?' This time he was genuinely surprised, though there was no annoyance in his tone.

'Not far from where I live either,' said Willett, 'so when you took his case on I was naturally interested.'

'Are you known there?'

'Does that make any difference?' asked Willett anxiously. 'It's our favourite place, Betty's and mine, and we probably go there once or twice a week when her sister can come in and sit with the children.'

'It's just perfect,' said Maitland. 'Here you are this weekend a grass-widower, so what's more natural than that you should go round to one of your favourite haunts and be in a mood for conversation? One thing I want to know is whether Simon Winthrop is an *habitué*.' He paused, looking rather startled. 'I hadn't thought of that, perhaps you've met him there yourself.'

'Not to know it,' said Willett. 'No reason why I should. I've seen his picture in the papers, mind, but you couldn't recognize anyone from that.'

'No, you're right. Do you think you could find that out then?'

'Easy enough if he's known there. I can ask the landlord to have a pint with me, and he's a talkative chap, nothing he likes better than a good gossip. And of course with this chap being in the news –'

'Yes, I can see it helps, but I'm afraid that's not quite all. If he does go to the King's Head, does he go alone, or does he perhaps meet friends? And I'm particularly interested in a man – though come to think of it I suppose it might be a woman – whose initials are M.B. Is he or she known there? That'll be tricky,

Willett, because you can't ask right out. But if you can keep the landlord in conversation long enough–'

'Consider it done, Mr Maitland.' Willett was obviously delighted with his assignment. 'If I pretend to remember a name and stumble over it a bit, ten to one he'd put me right. If he knows the chap, that is.'

'Yes, I'm afraid it's all very vague, but you've obviously got the idea and I can safely leave it to you.' Antony got up from the corner of the desk, and was amused to note that Willett immediately moved to straighten the items he had disordered. 'I don't think in all the circumstances we'll raid the petty cash to cover your expenses,' he added, feeling for his wallet. The two men smiled at each other over a shared memory; they had first met when Willett was office boy to a solicitor of Maitland's acquaintance, and had got into trouble over his failure to make his records balance.

'That's all right, Mr Maitland,' the clerk said quickly. 'It'll be something to amuse me, what with Betty away and all.'

'All the same you'll be working out of hours and should really be demanding overtime,' said Antony, and smiled again. 'Besides, plying witnesses with liquor comes expensive.'

Willett took the proffered note and eyed it with some respect. 'Are you expecting me to get us both plastered?' he asked. And then, 'When do you want me to report?'

'Tomorrow morning will do if you haven't got too bad a headache,' said Antony, entering into the spirit of the conversation. 'As far as I know at the moment I shall be at home all the morning. And Willett–'

'Yes, Mr Maitland?'

'It's an interesting case, rather weird really. I'll tell you all about it later, if I ever get to the bottom of it myself,' he promised.

V

Luckily, from Maitland's point of view, Sir Nicholas and Vera were dining that evening with friends, and were already upstairs dressing when he arrived home. No questions, therefore, which at this stage would be an embarrassment. He confined himself to one glass of sherry, didn't allow Jenny to linger over dinner, and was relieved when Roger arrived just as they were clearing things away. He had just two requests for his friend.

'Can you find something out for me about a chap called Cecil Alford?' he demanded.

'I've never heard of him. Who is he?' Roger relieved Jenny of the tray – the last time Antony had tried to help in this way he had dropped the whole thing ignominiously – and departed towards the kitchen with Maitland following.

'He's the Chairman of the Board of the Imperial Insurance Company, though I don't suppose that occupies all his time. But it should be a beginning at least.'

'And why . . . wait a bit, haven't I heard that name before?'

'He and his wife live next door to where Thomas Wilmot did –'

'And are witnesses to the fact that your client was seen leaving the house a few minutes before the man was found dead,' said Roger triumphantly. 'What exactly do you want to know?'

'His financial position, also I suppose that of his wife, who I believe is called Adela. She may have money of her own.'

'I don't see –'

'You don't need to.' Then he relented. 'I'm sorry, Roger, I've got something on my mind.'

'This Winthrop business?'

'Yes, of course. And to answer your question, I want to know whether the Alfords would have been amenable to a bribe.'

'I didn't know the truth of their statement was in question,' said Roger bluntly, putting down the tray on the kitchen table.

'I don't think it is, I'd just like to be sure.'

'How urgent is it?'

'Not really urgent at all. I know it's the weekend.'

'That makes no difference. There are one or two people I can talk to, and if it'll put your mind at rest . . . tomorrow morning might be better though.'

'Yes, tomorrow morning, of course. I've got a job for you tonight.'

'What now?' asked Roger, smiling.

'To take Jenny to the pictures, if there's anything worth seeing. Or just for a drive. I saw some daffodils out the other day,' he added vaguely, perhaps by way of inducement.

'You only seem to be operating on one cylinder, Antony,' Roger told him. 'Daffodils won't be much good to us at this

103

time of night. However, I'll take Jenny out with pleasure, and if nothing else appeals to us I daresay the management of the Cornmarket will let us use one of their boxes. At least we'll be warm there.' The Cornmarket was the theatre in which Meg was playing.

'That would be fine,' said Antony, obviously not having heard a word of all this. Then he roused himself from his abstraction. 'I've explained to Jenny already, more or less,' he said. 'It's just that I want to think, and if I go down to the study, which is empty because Uncle Nick and Vera are out, Gibbs will be in and out to make up the fire, or make sure I'm not drinking the best brandy, or any other excuse he can think of. So –'

'No need to say any more,' Roger assured him. They went into the hall together and met Jenny coming from the bedroom, already buttoned into her winter coat. 'Do you think you can bear seeing *Othello* again, Jenny, because I've a feeling that's where we're going to end up?' He thought also that one of the bars at the theatre might prove a useful haven. Jenny's eyes met his with her usual candour, but she had a worried look.

Antony kissed her and said, 'Sorry to turn you out of the house, love,' but he had already opened his briefcase and spread his papers across the dining-room table by the time the front door closed behind them.

Saturday, 15th March

I

Antony slept later than usual the following morning, and Jenny, who had come home to find him still hard at work and gone to bed without disturbing him, got up quietly and did nothing to rouse him. But at about nine o'clock the phone rang and Willett's voice greeted her. 'Is he in, Mrs Maitland?'

'Yes, but—'

'He's busy. I don't want to disturb him, but he did ask me to let him know. I thought if I called fairly early—'

'That's all right, Mr Willett. My husband told me you might call. I'll fetch him to the phone.'

A few minutes later Maitland, still in his dressing-gown and a little tousled and bleary-eyed, was sitting at the writing-table with the receiver to his ear. The thought crossed his mind vaguely that when, if ever, telephones had visual as well as verbal abilities it wouldn't all be pure gain. 'I hope you haven't got a hangover, Willett,' he said.

'What do you take me for, Mr Maitland?' Willett was indignant. 'A few rounds of beer, well, I'm not saying it wasn't enjoyable, but nothing to do any harm.'

'No, I'm sure, but I shouldn't like to feel I'd set you on the path to perdition. Is this call to report success or failure?'

'Well, it all depends what you mean by success,' said Willett cautiously. 'Kenmore, that's the landlord, knows your Mr Winthrop all right, and once I'd told him my sad story about Betty and the kids being away he was only too ready to settle down with a pint of his own for a good chat. Well, naturally it caused a bit of a stir there . . . someone you know being arrested for murder. Who'd ever have thought he'd do such a thing? You know the kind of thing they say, Mr Maitland.'

'I do indeed.'

'Well, as I said, he was a regular, and sometimes he had a girl

105

with him,' Willett volunteered.

'Always the same girl?' asked Maitland quickly.

'That's what Mr Kenmore said. A tall girl with dark curly hair. Do you know who that'd be, Mr Maitland?'

'His fiancée, Madeleine Rexford, from the sound of it. Did he ever go in alone, or in the company of another man?'

'Alone occasionally. You must understand, Mr Maitland, that Mr Kenmore thought him a quiet sort of chap, and didn't take too much notice of him until after he read about his arrest. That was when he grew really interested.'

'I can imagine it. He went in alone, you say, but did he remain alone?'

'When I said he was quiet I didn't mean he was unfriendly. Talk to anybody, he would, from what Mr Kenmore told me. It was just that he was more inclined to get into conversation with just one man, when he was alone, rather than join a group.'

'So when he went to the pub by himself you're telling me his conversations were confined to other men. He wouldn't pick up a girl who was there on her own too, for instance?'

'Not from what I was told. I know he didn't drink very much. But there was one thing that puzzled Mr Kenmore. Always when he went in Mr Winthrop would greet him by name, seeing him so regularly. But just once in a while he wouldn't do that, he'd come in quietly and sit down in a corner by himself. Give his order to the barman, and not a word for anyone else. And then he'd leave just the way he came. On other occasions he'd arrive without a word to anyone, as I've just described, but then some time later be just his usual self. Does that make sense to you, Mr Maitland?'

'A good deal of sense, Willett. It's part of the story I promised to tell you later. These people he talked to, were they all casual encounters? Or was there anybody he met regularly, say once every month?'

'Not that Mr Kenmore ever noticed. I don't mean he never talked to the same person twice, but not on a regular basis as you might say.'

'I see. Were you able to get any information about M.B.?'

'That was a difficult one, Mr Maitland. Took me all the evening it did.' Willett sounded pleased with himself, and Antony could imagine him grinning at the telephone. 'I went at it round about like, not until we'd been talking about this and

106

that and everything else for quite a long time. Then I said there was this chap Betty and I had met sometimes, did he still come in, it was some time since we'd seen him? Trouble was I couldn't remember the name right. And I sort of stuttered on the letter B as though the name was on the tip of my tongue, and Mr Kenmore said, Mark Benson, just like that. And of course I said that was the one I meant, though of course I didn't know if it was. But what else could I do?'

'And had he been in lately?'

'Not for a week or two, and he was another who mostly had a girl with him, and Mr Kenmore didn't notice much about who he talked to when he was alone, though he wasn't surprised when I told him Betty and I had known him, which was just as well. And he hadn't noticed him talking to Mr Winthrop . . . I didn't exactly ask him that, but I sort of gathered it. But it reminded Mr Kenmore of one rather odd thing he'd noticed, on one of what he called Mr Winthrop's unsociable evenings.'

'What was that?' In spite of himself Maitland sounded eager and Willett answered rather quickly, obviously afraid of having raised false hopes.

'Nothing much, Mr Maitland. Just that on those evenings he'd sit alone not talking to anyone, but on one particular occasion a man went up to him, spoke for a moment, and Mr Winthrop got up looking delighted and shook him by the hand and then they settled down together and had a good talk. And that was one of the nights when Mr Winthrop still didn't seem to know Mr Kenmore when he left, though he was always very polite.'

'Which of them left first?'

'The stranger, it seems. That's a funny thing, Mr Maitland –'

'That wasn't the only time they met?'

'That was what I was going to tell you. Mr Kenmore saw this other man again a couple of times . . . no, he must have meant more often than that. He'd come in quite early and sit nursing his drink, and if Mr Winthrop didn't arrive he'd go away without exchanging a word with anybody. If Mr Winthrop came in as he usually did with a word for Mr Kenmore and a request for the usual the other man would make no move to join him, and neither of them gave any sign of recognizing the other. But on the one occasion when he was in one of his morose moods – Mr Winthrop that is – the other man joined him, and his

107

presence seemed to cheer him up a lot.'

Antony leaned back in his chair. 'Heaven and earth!' he said weakly, and heard Willett's voice, urgent in his ear.

'Are you all right, Mr Maitland?'

Antony spoke more directly into the telephone. 'Quite all right, Willett,' he said. 'A bit flummoxed, that's all.'

'It doesn't make sense to me,' said Willett frankly.

'No, but . . . well perhaps it doesn't to me either yet.' Things seemed to be moving a little too fast for him. 'The trouble is,' he said to Jenny when he had expressed his gratitude and made his farewells, 'this brings me face to face with that decision I told you I had to make.'

'And Uncle Nick isn't going to like it?' said Jenny sympathetically.

'Uncle Nick is going to kick like a horse,' said Antony with irreverent frankness. 'I don't like to let you in for all this, love, but I'm afraid our luncheon engagement today isn't going to be a very pleasant one.'

That Saturday luncheon, another very rarely broken tradition, was one of the occasions when Gibbs, probably warned by some sixth sense that his presence was unwelcome to at least some of the party, insisted on serving them himself. So it wasn't until they were back in the study with their coffee that they were able to turn to the subject that was in all their minds.

'At least,' said Sir Nicholas blandly, as though the subject had been already broached, 'I imagine that Geoffrey's presence – welcome as it is – means you have something to say to me, Antony, about the Winthrop affair.'

'Yes, sir, I have. It seemed a good opportunity –'

'I further gather,' said his uncle, steam-rollering over him without compunction, 'that it is something I shall not like.'

'I don't know why you should think that, Uncle Nick.'

'Jenny's rather guilty expression, my dear boy. Can you deny it?'

Maitland took a moment to glance at his wife. 'Perhaps you would like her to explain,' he suggested.

'Heaven forbid! However, as you seem disinclined to come to the subject, Antony, perhaps Geoffrey –'

'I don't think it would be fair to ask that of him. Geoffrey's conclusions are not quite the same as mine.'

'You are leading, I suppose, to a disclosure of how you intend to advise your client to plead,' said Sir Nicholas. 'We have already discussed the possibility of basing the defence on the fact that your client is suffering from this so-called multiple personality disorder, and I trust you agree with me that this is an impossibility.'

'Yes, I do, Uncle Nick.'

'To plead Guilty –'

'I've told you –'

'Yes, Antony, let me finish. To plead Guilty is one possibility, which I gather does not appeal to you, which only leaves a plea of Not Guilty, which will have the advantage of allowing you the opportunity of bringing out such extenuating circumstances as you can. I have discussed this matter thoroughly with Vera, who agrees with me wholeheartedly, and I have no doubt that Geoffrey realizes the impossibility of any other course of action as well as we do.'

'I'm sorry for Winthrop, Sir Nicholas,' said Geoffrey rather doggedly, 'and for myself I favour the latter course of action.'

'Well, Antony?'

'I should agree with Geoffrey, sir, if those were the only two courses open to us. But there is a third.'

'You just agreed with me –' He broke off, looking round the assembly in a rather distraught way. 'You all heard him,' he said. 'He agreed with me that there is no possibility of persuading the court that this multiple personality business was to be taken seriously, however firmly he may believe in it himself.'

'But I don't,' Maitland told him.

'I thought –' Geoffrey started, but then changed the course of his sentence. 'I admit you never actually said so.'

'Thank you,' said Antony, with just a trace of irony in his tone. 'That being disposed of, Uncle Nick, will you listen to my third possibility? I meant a straight Not Guilty plea, nothing to do with extenuating circumstances, nothing to do with insanity. Not Guilty, just like that.'

'You must be insane,' said Sir Nicholas despairingly.

'I was afraid you'd say that. But you see, as I told you, I don't believe in this multiple personality disorder any more than you do. At least, there may be cases, but I don't think Simon Winthrop is one of them.'

'You'd better explain yourself,' he said, tight-lipped.

'I want to.' Which was rather far from the truth, but he accepted the necessity. 'What I do believe about him is that he's suffered from recurrent fits of amnesia since the accident that killed his parents. It seems quite natural to me that he should try to hide these attacks, thinking they set him apart, made him different from other people. Dr Macintyre assures me that this is quite a reasonable possibility, so I see no reason to doubt Winthrop's word that he has no recollection of what happened on the night his grandfather was murdered.'

'The witnesses—'

'We'll come to them presently. At the moment let's just assume that their evidence is accurate in every respect, that Winthrop did kill his grandfather, and that he cooked up the amnesia story as a cover. We must also assume that he hoped to visit Thomas Wilmot's house unobserved, but there's one big point against all these suppositions. He had an appointment with Madeleine Rexford that night. Would he have made it, knowing he wouldn't keep it, knowing she'd wonder about his absence and make his story of taking a walk during the relevant period an obvious lie? I don't think so.'

'If you've no better reason than that to offer us—' Sir Nicholas stopped there, apparently at a loss for words. 'I think you've taken leave of your senses,' he said again.

'You said you'd hear me out, Uncle Nick, and I'm going to hold you to that. Let me tell you first what Geoffrey and I found when we searched Winthrop's studio.'

'The second set of paintings, I presume. Didn't you say the Patmores had returned them there?'

'Yes, and they were just as unpleasant as I'd been told, but they don't prove anything except that they were done by a person of some artistic ability, who had access to Winthrop's flat. I don't think he'd ever kept many private papers, and the police have made a pretty clean sweep of things, looking for evidence that he was in need of money I presume. There were some unpaid bills, Mr Patmore told me, and they'd very properly been handed over to him for payment. We found only one item of personal correspondence that I thought needed explaining . . . a note addressed rather abruptly to Mr Winthrop without any more polite salutation. The writer owed him money, and was apparently in the habit of paying him a monthly sum on account. He said that month it would be impossible, but he'd make the amount up later, and if Winthrop wanted to talk about it he suggested a meeting at the King's Head, which is a pub close by. The note was signed M.B. Geoffrey thought that perhaps Simon had sold a painting on the instalment system, or made a loan to somebody, though his family assure me that his finances were never in a state to enable him to do that, except for some insignificant amount. I thought the tone of the letter sounded more as if M.B. was paying blackmail, but Geoffrey doesn't agree with me.'

'I'm glad at least one of you retains some vestiges of sanity,' said Sir Nicholas, with what was obviously quite spurious cordiality. 'Antony, on the other hand, seems to be getting back to this multiple personality idea. The blackmailer was the fifth personality, was he?'

'No sir, that's not what I'm trying to say, though it did occur to me that evidence of some further wrong-doing on Winthrop's part might turn up. But let's think about these personalities for a moment. There was Simon Winthrop, the one everyone knew, a rather quiet, ordinary young man except for his artistic talent. There was also the blackmailer, the painter of extremely unpleasant pictures, the murderer, and the seducer.'

'Who also succeeded in killing the girl he had seduced,' Sir Nicholas reminded him.

'Yes, that's true, but think about it for a moment.'

'We've been doing nothing else for the last half hour,' said his uncle testily.

'I talked to the girl's father,' Antony went on, ignoring the interruption. 'He'd wanted the matter hushed up as far as possible, though he'd have been glad to see the man concerned punished if anything could have been proved against him. He got a firm of private inquiry agents on to it, but they couldn't turn anything up, or find anyone who'd ever seen Antonia Dryden with our client. Do you think it's natural that no one had ever seen them together, that Antonia had never introduced him to the girl she shared the flat with, that Bertha Harvey had never surprised them there together? It argues an extraordinary degree of caution on the man's part.'

'Natural enough, since he was already seeing Madeleine Rexford and was actually engaged to her.'

'Yes perhaps, but along with everything else . . . there was

111

too much evidence turning up altogether that Simon Winthrop was a thoroughly bad character.'

'Unless I'm very much mistaken, Antony, you're trying to tell us that you believe your client is innocent, and that someone else killed Thomas Wilmot and attempted to frame him for it by proving that he had not one personality but five.'

'No, Uncle Nick, I'm not saying that at all. Nobody could have thought up such a fantastic plot, and I don't believe they did. I think the idea was to discredit him in advance of a perfectly straightforward frame for murder.'

'But he was seen and identified.'

'Evidence of identification is the most unreliable in the world.'

'The jury won't think the housekeeper's evidence unreliable.'

'No, I'm afraid not. But let me tell you two more things, neither of which Geoffrey is familiar with yet. The first is that Willett went round to the King's Head last night at my instigation.'

'What on earth could you hope to learn from that?'

'One thing and another. I was in luck, because it's not far from where he lives, and he and his wife are in the habit of going there from time to time. So with Mrs Willett away there was a good excuse for him to have a quiet drink and a chat with the landlord. Simon Winthrop's arrest has caused a sensation as you can imagine, as he was in the habit of visiting the King's Head too. Sometimes he had a girl who sounds like Madeleine Rexford with him; I shall have to ask her about that. But when he was alone there were what I might call three kinds of visits. One when he was perfectly normal, went in and greeted the landlord by name, talked to some of the other regulars, nothing out of the way. Other times he'd go in and take a seat in the corner, not greeting anyone, and stay like that the whole time he was there. Or he might go in, in that unfriendly way, and suddenly change during the evening and talk to the landlord just as usual. On one of the—I think Willett called it the nights when he was morose—a man who was a stranger to the landlord came in, went over to the table where Winthrop was sitting alone, was greeted with apparent enthusiasm and stayed and talked with him for some time.'

'Are you trying to tell us that this was M.B.?' asked Sir Nicholas suspiciously.

'Far from it, Uncle Nick. This stranger made several other

112

visits to the pub, and his actions were rather peculiar. If Simon Winthrop came in in his usual manner neither of them would give any sign of knowing the other. On one occasion, however, when Winthrop came in without a word to anyone, the stranger joined him, and seemed, in the landlord's words, to cheer him up.'

'That is an odd story, but hardly relevant,' said Sir Nicholas coldly.

'Don't you think so, sir? Wait till I tell you the rest. Willett managed to get a possible name for M.B., Mark Benson, but I haven't had time to check it yet. Just bear it in mind for future reference. The other thing that Geoffrey doesn't know about is that I spoke to the Patmores again yesterday, and Mrs Patmore was able to give me the most recent address she had of Simon Winthrop's aunt in Nova Scotia.'

'No really, Antony, this is too much. You told us before this woman had been abroad for twenty years. How could she know anything of her nephew's recent behaviour?'

'You're forgetting Thomas Wilmot's will, Uncle Nick. Winthrop's aunt, whose name is Celia Camden, had a son Robert, about three years his cousin's senior, who inherits equally with Simon.'

'If he can be found,' Geoffrey reminded him.

'Yes, of course, you're right. But Robert Camden's motive is at least equal to Simon's, there is every chance that Thomas Wilmot's artistic ability, which seems to have skipped a generation, should have surfaced again in him, and there is also the possibility that he is sufficiently like his cousin to have been mistaken for him, even by Mrs Barham, who says – remember? – that she only got a glimpse of him. There are still inquiries to be made, but that is what I shall attempt to prove, and that's why I shall recommend to Simon Winthrop that he plead Not Guilty without any qualification at all. Provided, of course, that Camden can be found. But if I'm right and he wants to get hold of his grandfather's money – all of it, because by framing Simon he ensures that *he* can't inherit – my guess is that he won't be far to seek.'

'You must be out of your mind,' said Sir Nicholas, who was beginning to sound to his nephew like a gramophone record that had got stuck in one groove. 'Any chance of obtaining the court's sympathy –'

'You needn't remind me, Uncle Nick.' Maitland sounded suddenly very tired. 'We may have to fall back on that, but I don't like injustice, and I think if Simon were sent to prison, or even somewhere where he could be treated for what I think is a non-existent condition, it would be the greatest injustice in the world. Don't you see I've got to at least try?'

'I see you're in great danger of doing both yourself and your client a disservice,' said Sir Nicholas. 'You're proposing, unless I mistake you, to bring out in court all the evidence you can of Winthrop's alleged crimes, in order to prove that someone else is deliberately trying to have him convicted of murder.'

'Painting unpleasant pictures is hardly a crime,' Maitland pointed out. 'And unless I can find Robert Camden–'

'Both those comments are irrelevant. What's to prevent the jury from believing the evidence with which you so obligingly provide them about the unpleasant sides to your client's character? And when he's found guilty with no extenuating circumstances because of bad advice from you, who is to explain your actions when the press get hold of the story?'

'You're thinking that because the new A.C. is hostile–'

'Sir Alfred Godalming, precisely,' said Sir Nicholas.

'Geoffrey had the idea he might drop a hint to the Bar Council, but as we all know there's nothing they could do.'

'Far more likely to talk to some journalist,' said Vera.

'And you know what that could lead to,' her husband added. 'The trouble about bad publicity is that you've no means of answering it. I tell you frankly, Antony, you're putting yourself in jeopardy as well as your client. Perhaps that's your right, but you've no excuse for playing games with his safety.'

'It's his safety I'm trying to ensure. What you're telling me, Uncle Nick, is that you don't believe a word I've told you. You believe he's guilty?'

'As I'm sure everyone else in this room does, with the possible exception of Jenny. Vera?'

'I'm afraid I must agree with you, Nicholas.'

'Geoffrey?'

'I've already told Antony what I think. I agree with you, Sir Nicholas.'

'And if Antony persists in this – this folly?'

'I shall do my best not to let him down.'

'Then there's nothing more to be said. If you won't listen

to me, Antony —'

'Won't you understand, sir? I can't!'

'You said there were still some inquiries to be made.'

'Yes. The most important thing, naturally, is to find out where Robert Camden is.'

'And if you find that he's still in Canada, or in Australia perhaps?'

Antony smiled soberly. 'Uncle Nick, bear with me. If I find positive proof that he's in either of those places I shall begin to wonder what acquaintances he has over here.'

'There's one thing even your ingenuity may find it difficult to explain. If this man Camden, or anyone else, was trying to discredit your client, how is it that the police know nothing of it? Geoffrey would surely have heard by now, or if he hasn't yet heard from the prosecution I imagine Superintendent Sykes would have told you.'

'I think the identifications were a lucky break for the real criminal, one he couldn't have foreseen. With Simon under arrest and an apparently watertight case against him there was no need to risk communicating with the police, which I imagine would have been done by an anonymous letter or telephone call.'

'And if Winthrop had spent the evening with the girl he's engaged to, as apparently he planned?'

'Give me a chance, Uncle Nick, I expect that was provided for, but I don't know how.'

'It seems to me quite an important point.'

'I know it is. I don't like this any better than you do, Uncle Nick, but unless something happens to change my mind drastically I mean to go ahead until I'm convinced it's hopeless.'

'You can't get up in court and accuse this man.'

'I can do my best to make him incriminate himself. So let's leave it there for the moment, shall we?'

'So long as you are not under the impression that either Vera or I agree with what you are doing,' said his uncle frostily.

'Don't worry, sir, you've made yourself perfectly plain,' Antony told him. He finished his coffee and got to his feet. 'Forgive me, Vera, Geoffrey and I are going to see our client and I think it's about time we left.' He stretched out his left hand to pull Jenny to her feet. 'As there's not a chance of our getting into court before the Easter recess we shall have plenty of time to argue,' he added, and from his tone it was impossible to tell whether he found some comfort in this. But the truth was that his spirits were at an even lower ebb than that to which the prospect of prison visiting usually brought them.

II

Geoffrey was silent as they drove out to Brixton. Perhaps he felt that his friend had suffered enough already without adding his reproaches, and Antony was content enough with the arrangement. Only when he stopped the car at the nearest point he could find to the prison did Horton say, looking straight ahead of him and obviously avoiding his companion's eye, 'This chap Mark Benson, do you want me to trace him?'

'I suppose there are dozens of people with that name in the phone book, but it might not be too difficult to find out if any of the ones who live near the King's Head frequent that pub.'

'That's what I was thinking. It still wouldn't be proof that he was the M.B. who wrote the letter.'

'I realize that.'

'Well, do you want to talk to him?'

'No. No, I don't think so. Look here, Geoffrey, we're taking a chance – all right then, *I* am if you prefer it – and it's damned unlikely to come off. Let's go the whole hog.'

'You mean *sub poena* him without talking to him first?'

'That's exactly what I do mean, provided, of course, we have a pretty good idea that he wrote the letter we found. But leave it for a while. I mean, unless we can trace this Robert Camden – '

'All that guff you gave Sir Nicholas about blackening our client's name in order to clear him, will have to be scrapped,' said Geoffrey, turning for the first time to meet Maitland's eye. 'Antony, you know I'll go along with whatever you say but are you sure it's wise? I mean – '

'You mean, I think, that however it turns out Simon Winthrop won't be much worse off. He might as well be hanged for a sheep as a lamb.'

'That's exactly what I do mean, but only the beginning. What sort of a label do you suppose the press will tie on you?'

'They'll say I bungled the whole affair, and in fairness, Geoffrey, they'll be right.'

'That's all very well, but *you* can't write to *The Times* explaining your motives.'

'You may as well save your breath, Geoffrey, at least until we know if we can find Camden. This may all be beside the point.'

'So it may. But you're going to try to get our client's permission here and now to go ahead on these lines, aren't you? Why not wait at least until you know – ?'

'Because I don't want him to go on any longer thinking he's a dangerous lunatic,' said Antony. He opened the car door and put one foot out on to the pavement, 'Let's get it over with, Geoffrey,' he said over his shoulder. 'I may be raising false hopes, but I know if it were me I'd rather face the prospect of imprisonment than think I was mad. And that's saying something.'

He got out of the car and slammed the door with rather more force than was necessary. Geoffrey followed his example but not without misgivings. For one thing he had a pretty good idea exactly what the prospect of being behind bars would do to his friend, and if Maitland was sufficiently worked up about Simon Winthrop's plight to forget that fact for the moment his judgement perhaps was rather less reliable than usual.

It was obvious at once to the two lawyers that Simon Winthrop was doing his best to behave normally, and equally obvious that his inward disquiet was very great indeed. After greeting them he turned to Maitland. 'I didn't expect to see you again just yet,' he said. 'Not until the trial in fact.'

'I came,' said Antony briskly, 'because I'd reached two decisions. Shall we sit down while I explain them to you?'

'Very well.' He took the chair he'd occupied before, and looked from one to the other of his companions. 'You said you'd reached certain decisions, Mr Maitland. Does that mean that Mr Horton doesn't agree with you?'

'It means that he hasn't yet decided whether the course of action I'm recommending is a wise one,' said Antony quickly. 'That's what I want to discuss with you, before this meeting's over. But first I wanted to tell you – '

'Yes, these two decisions of yours.'

'I think perhaps you'll forgive me if I say first of all that the suggestions made in this case are most unusual, and that the decision as to how best deal with the matter has been a very difficult one. That was in the beginning when I accepted the

117

prosecution's version of the evidence. I may as well start by telling you that I no longer do that.'

That led to a moment's dead silence. 'But I told you,' said Simon at last. 'I told you I've no idea where I was that night, and about all the other mental blackouts I've had. And if I've been doing these other things that I knew nothing about, what possible reason do you have for deciding that I didn't murder Grandfather as well?'

'To begin with there's this multiple personality business,' Antony told him. Forgetting the good intentions with which he had started the interview he got up and began to walk back and forth across the narrow room. 'There are apparently doctors who believe in it, and doctors who disbelieve, and on the whole I find myself on the side of the latter, though I don't pretend to *know*. We have the evidence of your character from the people who know you best, but that is something that no lawyer is ever going to take into consideration; on the other hand, it did occur to me from my first talk with your parents that altogether too much evidence was cropping up that tended to blacken your character. Another point is that though I understand quite stringent inquiries were made at the time no one has ever been found to say that you and Antonia Dryden were seen together. You remember who Antonia Dryden was?'

'The girl I'm supposed to have seduced and then killed by getting her something to induce an abortion.'

'Exactly. That was another point that seemed odd to me. Then I talked to Dr Macintyre again, giving him more particulars of your childhood than you were able to yourself.'

'I don't understand.'

'That also is something we shall come to in a moment. In the circumstances he tells me that what he refers to as hysterical amnesia is quite natural, awkward perhaps, but something that once you've come to understand your family and friends will be able to take care of between them.' He was embroidering freely on what the doctor had said, but after all it was mostly common sense and might provide some reassurance. 'In fact,' he went on, 'it's quite possible it might disappear altogether, once you have admitted to yourself the reason, have allowed yourself to remember – I'm using layman's terms – something that your mind has always rejected as intolerable.'

'If what you're telling me is true –'

'As far as anyone can be sure about anything I'm telling you the truth now.'

'Then . . . but somebody signed my name to those pictures . . . somebody gave my name to Antonia Dryden . . . somebody, who three independent witnesses have identified as myself, killed my grandfather. Are you trying to tell me that all this was done deliberately so that I should be thought to be mad?'

Antony said, as he said to his uncle, 'Nothing like that. I think somebody planned to murder your grandfather, and did his best to blacken your name in advance so that people would have no difficulty in believing this last iniquity of you.'

'That person . . . no, I don't believe it. I can't see why anyone should hate me like that.'

'That isn't what I'm suggesting. You're not the only person with a motive for murdering your grandfather. I don't think you were framed because someone dislikes you, but at least partly in self-defence.'

Geoffrey, sitting on the sidelines, was beginning to find a certain wry humour in the situation. Maitland had stopped his pacing and was standing behind the chair he had taken first, gripping the back of it so that his knuckles stood out white. He was now by far the most emotionally disturbed person in the room. Just for the moment Simon Winthrop had forgotten the seriousness of his own situation in the sheer interest of an idea that had obviously never occurred to him before. 'I know Grandfather could be an awkward old so-and-so,' he said slowly, thinking it out, 'and he wasn't a young man and – I suppose famous wouldn't be too big a word for him. He must have had enemies, people who were jealous of him, but in the last few years he was almost a recluse. Why should anybody have waited until now to kill him?'

'You're familiar enough with the motive that will be adduced against you, Mr Winthrop.'

'Yes, of course, I inherit half his money. I mean I shall if – if you get me off.'

'There's a corollary to that. Haven't you thought about the cousin who inherits the other half of his fortune.'

'Robert Camden. Grandfather mentioned him when he told me how he'd left his money, and Mr Horton mentioned that no one knows where he is. But I don't suppose he'll stay lost once he hears about all this,' he added.

'No, I don't suppose so either. Think for a moment about the person I'm suggesting really killed Thomas Wilmot. Unless he was a homicidal maniac he'd have a motive. He'd have some skill as a painter, and somehow he must have got hold of a key to your studio.'

'You mean he planted the paintings there?'

'If I'm right it has to follow, doesn't it?'

'But nobody else had the key, not even Madeleine.'

'Your landlord, perhaps?'

'No, he hasn't.'

'He might not tell you.'

'I think he would have done. You see, once when I was away my sink overflowed and starting dripping into the apartment below. He didn't know where I was, so he had to get a locksmith to force the door. If he'd had a key he'd never have done that.'

'However, I suspect a new lock was probably put on after that. He might have thought it wise to keep one key for himself.'

'Yes, I suppose that would have been sensible.'

'Well now, let's see what else we know about this hypothetical person. He gave your name when he got to know Antonia Dryden, and he was at least personable enough to have her fall for him pretty hard. Also he conducted the whole affair with extreme caution, so that no one ever saw them together who could say later on that you weren't the man.'

'The caution might have applied to me too.'

'Not if you were conducting the affair while you were having one of your memory blackouts. I'm assuming for the moment you're telling me the truth about that. Why should you have taken such unnatural care?'

'Do you think he meant to kill her?'

'I don't know. It depends on how much he knows about drugs and their application in cases like this. I'm told that it's extremely unlikely that an orally induced abortion will be safe for the woman concerned, and I think perhaps he knew that. In fact, now I come to think about it I'm sure he must have done, because though Bertha Harvey could say Antonia had told her you were the man concerned she'd never seen you, whereas if Antonia had still been alive she'd have denied it.'

120

'There's still those people who say they saw me. And Mrs Barham.'

'That's my last point. The man we're talking about must be sufficiently like you to have led to their mistake. You must have read about cases of mistaken identity, there've been dozens of them,' said Maitland, waving a hand in a wide, all-encompassing gesture. 'Have you seen pictures of Adolf Beck and the man for whom he was twice mistaken. I assure you a superficial likeness would have been sufficient.'

'Well, I'll admit that I don't suppose the person the Alfords saw was a black man five feet tall,' said Simon rather reluctantly. 'But what's worrying me is Mrs Barham.'

'She only got a glimpse of you. Her own words,' said Maitland.

'All the same she knows me very well by sight.'

'If she saw a man of about your height, of your colouring, who moved perhaps as you do, that would be reason enough for her to believe as she did,' Antony assured him. 'Don't you see where all these points take us . . . to this long-lost cousin you spoke of. Just as you did he may have inherited your grandfather's facility with a paintbrush, there's a good chance he resembles you in appearance, and he inherits the other half of Mr Wilmot's money.'

'I didn't even know I had any relations· of my own until Grandfather mentioned him, and as I didn't remember him at all I didn't take much notice. Norman and Sylvia never told me.'

'How much do you remember about your childhood? Your early childhood, I mean.'

'I don't really think I remember anything before living with Norman and Sylvia. They came to see me in hospital –'

'Is that the first thing you remember?'

'Not quite. There was a doctor and some nurses. I didn't understand where I was or even who I was, and they seemed to be trying to reassure me, but I couldn't make out what they meant. Then Norman and Sylvia came. I didn't even know who they were, but they were kind and said I mustn't worry about anything but I should live with them. Later they told me my real parents had been killed in a motor accident, and I understood I was adopted, and I've always looked on them as my father and mother as I don't remember anybody else.'

'Didn't you ask questions?'

121

'I used to puzzle about it sometimes. But when I formulated some query to put to them something always seemed to stop me. And very often, following one of those blank spots in memory, when I'd come back home for instance and find it was much later than I thought, Sylvia would ask me where I'd been and I used to make up something to tell her because I was afraid of being thought different from other people. You say now I was trying to forget something intolerable. What was it?'

'I think I'll leave it to the doctor to tell you that, and talk over the whole situation with you. He'll do it much better than I can. Did Mr and Mrs Patmore never talk about your relations in Canada?'

'No. If there was something awful in my background –'

'Nothing that you could help, Simon. Just something very sad, that a child of seven couldn't be expected to take in his stride. I expect your parents, your adopted parents, thought the memory of it would upset you. I know they warned Mr Wilmot not to talk to you about the past.'

'I suppose they must have done because he never did. Sylvia used to take me on a formal visit about once a month when I was a child, and then later on I'd go by myself and in the last year or two we had a rather formal dinner together. That was once a month too, regularly on the first Sunday. I think I told you that when you were here before.'

'Well, you told me about these fits of amnesia that have occurred from time to time. When you woke up from them were you always in the same place?'

'No, I might be walking down the street, or going up the stairs to the studio. That must mean that even when I couldn't remember who I was I had some subconscious idea where I lived.'

'That seems reasonable.'

'Yes, because quite a few times when it happened I was in the King's Head when I woke up . . . that's a pub quite near where I live. I used to take Madeleine there sometimes, and sometimes go alone when she was busy.'

'You know the landlord there?'

'Yes, his name's Kenmore. And I know quite a few of the regulars by sight, whom I'd have a casual conversation with, particularly when I was alone.'

'Do you know anybody there with the initials M.B.?'

'No. It wouldn't fit the landlord, and the barmen I just knew as Bill and Stan. What has M.B. got to do with it?'

'There was a letter – well, no more than a note really – in the bureau in your studio signed with those initials.'

'I can't understand that. I don't think I know anyone that fits, except Mrs Barham whose first name I think is Mary. Could it have been from her?'

'It implied that the writer owed you money, that he or she was paying by instalments, but couldn't manage to provide anything that month.'

'But nobody owes me anything. Good lord, I hardly had enough to live on, let alone being able to lend anyone money.'

'So I gathered. Mr Horton suggested that you might have sold a painting to someone who couldn't pay you the full sum at once.'

'No, that never happened either.'

'The writer offered to meet you in the King's Head if you wanted to talk the matter over. He seemed rather nervous over the results of missing one month's payment.'

'I can't understand it at all.'

'And you don't remember seeing such a letter among your other correspondence.'

'No, I don't, and as a matter of fact I've never written many letters or got many either. Not since I used to write home from boarding-school. I mean all the people I was in communication with live quite near, and it was much easier to pick up the telephone.'

Antony couldn't resist a glance at Geoffrey at this echo of his own words. 'We're trying to trace M.B.,' he said. 'There was no envelope with the letter, so we've no proof it was addressed to your studio, though it started "Mr Winthrop", rather abruptly. What I think is that it's part of this blackening your character business and that it'll turn out that you – or someone using your name – was blackmailing this person or threatening him in some way. But that's guesswork so far. It may help or it may not. And that brings me, Mr Winthrop, to the second point I mentioned at the beginning of this talk. Do you remember?'

'Yes,' said Simon rather doubtfully.

'I want your permission to deal with the case as I think fit.'

'But of course!'

'No, it isn't quite as easy as that. You see, Mr Winthrop –'

'You called me Simon a moment ago. That feels more comfortable.'

'You may not wish to be on such intimate terms with me when you hear what I have to say,' said Antony, smiling slightly. 'You see, Simon, I can't promise anything except that we'll try to get you acquitted. I won't hide it from you either that that's going to be difficult. The exact way we set about it will depend on circumstances, and it may be that we can offer no more than your denial, and Dr Macintyre's evidence to back up your story of not knowing where you were the night Thomas Wilmot died. But even if we succeed it will still leave you with a large black mark against your name in the public's mind, unless we can at the same time prove who really did it.'

'That sounds reasonable. I don't see why I should take offence at that.'

'Wait a bit! The police know nothing yet about these attempts to blacken your character, though I think there'd have been an anonymous letter or letters by now if it hadn't been for those very positive identifications that were made. Those couldn't have been foreseen. If they do hear that would suit me down to the ground, because I should be in a position to cross-examine the people concerned. If not . . . well, first I want you to plead Not Guilty. I really believe that's true or I wouldn't be suggesting it. And then I want your permission to call evidence for the defence of all these alleged misdeeds of yours, because I think it's the only chance we have of getting at the guilty party. If we fail, you'll be considered a murderer and a pretty bad hat in other ways besides. Do you think it's worth the gamble?' His hands were still clasped tightly on the back of the chair in front of him. 'I'm asking you to trust me,' he said, and Geoffrey, who knew him very well indeed, realized at once how much that request had cost him.

Simon Winthrop was staring at him. 'I do, of course,' he said, 'and if I'm in prison it won't much matter what people think of me, will it? But what about you? Couldn't some complaint be made against you for giving me the wrong advice?'

Maitland smiled at him. 'You couldn't sue me,' he said.

'That wasn't what was in my mind,' said Simon rather sharply.

'No, I know it wasn't. Professionally, no. There'd be no question of my being disbarred. Though the press might have a field day—'

'They certainly would. And there'd be no way you could answer them.'

'That's right, Simon, you're better informed than I expected. I was going to say it would all blow over in time.'

'Still, it doesn't seem fair to you.'

'Then let's put it another way. It won't do me any good professionally to lose the case for want of trying.' Geoffrey's eyes opened rather wide at this statement. It was obvious which course he would have preferred, but fortunately he held his peace, even when Simon turned to him.

'Should I be doing the right thing, Mr Horton?'

'I think you should take Mr Maitland's advice,' said Geoffrey slowly. 'As he told you the chance is a faint one, and neither of us wants to raise false hopes. But it exists, and unless some positive evidence turns up that this cousin of yours couldn't have been in England at the time I think we should take it.'

'All right then.' Winthrop was still uneasy, and it cannot be said that either of his lawyers, after they had left their client and were driving back to town, showed any particular evidence of high spirits.

III

That day Geoffrey took his passenger back to Kempenfeldt Square, but declined an invitation to have tea with the Maitlands, for which Antony for once was glad. He could have recited without prompting all the things he knew Geoffrey wanted to say to him, but just at the moment he was glad enough to postpone hearing them.

He was not however to be allowed to forget Simon Winthrop's affairs altogether just yet. Jenny met him in the hall, which might just mean that they had a visitor of whose arrival she wished to warn him, or might, as it proved in this instance, indicate that she had a message to deliver that she found agitating. 'Inspector Sykes phoned,' she said, and for once Antony didn't correct the downgrading of the detective's rank. 'He says Mrs Camden is still living at the same address and I've written down the telephone number, only she isn't Mrs Camden now, she's Mrs Burton. She has only one son, the Robert

125

Camden the Patmores told you about, and he left Shelburne about five years ago to work in Halifax, Nova Scotia. They think he's been back for holidays, but don't know when the last time was.'

All this had come out at top speed. 'My dearest love, stop and take a deep breath,' Antony advised her. 'I'm glad to know Sykes is doing his stuff, but we've a few weeks' grace before the trial so there's no desperate hurry.'

'No, of course not, only I haven't told you the most important bit. Mrs Burton says she doesn't know where her son is.'

'You said in Halifax, Nova Scotia.'

'That's where he went when he left home. He was working as an insurance salesman and about eighteen months ago he wrote to her to say his firm had moved him to their Head Office in Montreal. But he never let her know his new address. That's funny, Antony, don't you think? I mean, in view of what you believe.'

'Very funny. Did you get the name of the company?'

'Yes, I wrote that down too. Are you going to call them? I expect the overseas operator can find you the number.'

'Yes, I'll do that, but I think from chambers on Monday. In the afternoon, I suppose, we're quite a few hours ahead of them in time. And I won't disturb Sykes again this afternoon with my gratitude either, because I'm quite sure you expressed my thanks very adequately.'

'I did my best. I even remembered his proper title,' said Jenny proudly. 'But there was another message too, and this isn't quite such an encouraging one.'

'Something else from Sykes?'

'No, I didn't mean that, I meant that Roger had phoned as well. He had been asking that friend of his – well I think he was a friend of his father's, really, wasn't he? – anyway the one who knows everything.'

'Mr Tremlett,' said Antony without hesitation.

'Yes, that's the one. He says he knows Cecil Alford very well by reputation, and there's no doubt at all that his financial position is sound. Roger didn't ask him outright of course but he thinks you can take it there'd be no question of him being open to a bribe.'

'That's the answer I expected, and it isn't really disappointing because if someone had paid him and his wife to make the identification I don't see how we'd ever prove it.'

'Well, Roger said he'd give you the details when he and Meg come to tea tomorrow. He's got something on tonight, a dinner in the City, I think.'

'I hope you warned him, love, to wait until Uncle Nick and Vera have left before he brings the subject up. I don't suppose for a moment we've heard the last of the matter yet, but as long as we can let sleeping dogs lie we may as well do so.'

'I don't think it's really respectful to refer to Uncle Nick as a sleeping dog,' said Jenny reflectively. 'But he is horribly angry, isn't he? I'm afraid it's partly because this Assistant Commissioner, whatever his name is, seems to be taking up where Chief Superintendent Briggs left off.'

'It was your idea to tell him, Jenny,' Antony reminded her. 'Yours and Roger's.'

'Yes, of course, because he was bound to find out sooner or later and then he'd be even angrier,' said Jenny. 'You're always telling me I'm not logical,' she added with dignity, 'but even I can see that.'

'Well, love, there's nothing to worry about. Sir Alfred isn't likely to carry the feud as far as Briggs did – heaven and earth! I've never even met the man – so as long as I stick to the paths of righteousness –'

'This case could cause trouble,' said Jenny flatly.

'The press could do that perfectly well without his intervention,' Maitland pointed out. 'Uncle Nick's quite right in one way, though, it won't help matters if he stirs the pot a little.' They were still standing in the hall, and he put up his left hand now to tilt her chin so that she was looking directly into his eyes. 'Tell me honestly, Jenny love, which would you rather I did? What I think is right, or what I think is expedient?'

'What you think is right, of course. You didn't have to ask me that.'

'No,' he said and smiled at her. 'There's no turning back now. One way or the other – I mean whether we find Robert Camden or not – I'm committed to Simon Winthrop's defence. But I meant it when I told you all those years ago that I'd give up criminal practice if you asked me.'

'I'd never ask you that.' He wasn't touching her now, but her eyes were still fixed on his face and perhaps what she saw there prompted her next remark. 'If you did that, Antony, it would be the cruellest thing you could do to me.'

127

He was looking down at her with an understanding not unmixed with amusement. 'I won't,' he promised, 'as you seem to feel so strongly about it. And now let's go into the kitchen and make some tea. Somehow or other I don't think I ate very much at lunch time.' But he added as she turned to go ahead of him, 'I'm not just being stubborn about this, love, whatever Uncle Nick thinks. I really believe that one of the two courses I've outlined is the only fair way of dealing with the matter.'

'What did Mr Winthrop say when you told him you didn't believe he killed his grandfather?'

'It took him a little time to take it in. I think all his life he's been terrified of these lapses of memory, but I'm hoping Dr Macintyre can explain to him that considering what happened to him when his parents died, they're perfectly natural. And I suppose in one way he was relieved by what I told him, though you do understand – don't you? – that I couldn't really give him any hope. The trouble is, love – you'll understand this if nobody else does – I had to ask him to trust me, and he said he did.'

'You won't let him down,' said Jenny, sounding more confident than she felt. She had lived long enough in a law-oriented household, which it had always been even before Vera's arrival made it more so, to realise without any further explanation the difficulties that lay ahead.

128

Monday, 17th March

I

It cannot be said that the intervening Sunday was one of the most pleasant Maitland had ever spent. As was customary, Roger and Meg came round in the afternoon to share the pleasant ritual of Sunday tea and then stay on for dinner, that being in general Meg's only free evening. Sir Nicholas and Vera, as was also customary, came to tea as well, though it was their habit to attend a concert later and then dine out. But far from leaving the subject alone as Antony had hoped, his uncle insisted on a detailed description of the talk he and Geoffrey had had with their client the previous day.

Antony told him, and added Sykes's message for good measure, so by that time there was no point in delaying Roger's small contribution to the subject. Sir Nicholas was in one of his more caustic moods, and after he and Vera had gone Meg demanded her <u>meed</u> of information, saying – probably with truth – 'You can always explain things so much more clearly than Roger can, darling.'

Maitland ignored the blandishment, and gave her a pretty bald account of what had been happening, after which she annoyed him still further by giving him a wide, innocent look and saying, 'But of course, you'll get him off, darling, you're so clever.' Which, as she had probably intended, had at least the effect of distracting him from more serious preoccupations.

Altogether, though, not a good day.

The first thing Maitland did on Monday morning was to set Hill on to finding out the Montreal telephone number of the insurance company that Robert Camden worked for. In doing so he came up with the information that though there was four hours difference in time between London and Halifax, Montreal was in a different time zone and another hour behind. It seemed to Antony, therefore, that if he started with Mrs Burton at about

129

half-past two, and tried somewhere in the region of three o'clock for the insurance company he'd stand a fair chance of both finding Celia Burton at home and getting the information he wanted about her son.

Before he could start anything else Geoffrey phoned to say that he had located, via the telephone book, a couple of men named Mark Benson who lived within easy walking distance of the King's Head. He was putting Cobbold's (the firm of private inquiry agents he generally used) on to finding out which of the two frequented that particular hostelry; and, if they could come up with that bit of information, to try to find out something about him. He didn't sound optimistic, but neither did he sound as though he found counsel's ideas particularly unreasonable.

Antony responded with an invitation to lunch – 'We can talk things over at leisure then' – because he realized there was nothing to gain by putting matters off any further. Geoffrey agreed, adding the information that it would be just as well to get on with the matter, as he'd learned that the case of Regina *versus* Winthrop would be one of the first to be heard when the new term started in April. They arranged to meet at Astroff's at twelve-thirty, and Antony was just pulling the pile of papers that represented the first of the tasks he had allotted himself that day towards him when the telephone rang again and Hill announced with his customary diffidence, 'Dr Macintyre would like to speak to you, Mr Maitland.'

A moment later he heard the doctor's unmistakable voice. 'Well now, Doctor,' he said, 'I didn't expect to hear from you again so soon.'

'I decided it would be a kindness to go and see the young man again yesterday,' Macintyre told him. 'Didn't Mr Horton mention it to you?'

'I expect he forgot. We were . . . well, there were a lot of discussions going on.'

The doctor chuckled. 'Aye, so I gathered,' he said. 'But I understand you yourself told young Winthrop that it would be better if I described to him the accident that killed his parents, and his own part in it. I think perhaps for once in your life you were right in that decision, certainly he seemed . . . more at ease with himself when at last he understood what I was telling him. If it's a genuine case of hysterical amnesia, which I'm inclined to believe myself, and which I understand you have also come to

130

accept, now that the matter is out in the open it should make all the difference to him.'

'You mean there won't be any further reason for him to retreat from reality when his memory of that event starts to surface?'

'I can think of other ways of putting it, but perhaps that'll do well enough. But there's some doubt as to what line you'll be taking at the trial from what Mr Horton says. Will you be needing me?'

'We shall be pleading Not Guilty. Not just so that I shall have the chance of telling a sob story to the jury, but because I really think it's correct in this instance. Those were our first instructions from our client, you know, before all this confusion arose about multiple personality disorder. What did Winthrop have to say about that?'

'Unless he's a better actor than I take him for he believes your version of things completely. And if my opinions are of any interest to you, Maitland, I'd say he's a very truthful young man.'

'That's comforting, that you agree with me, I mean. You know,' he added, speaking with some difficulty, 'I told my uncle, and I told Geoffrey, that I was absolutely certain, but just occasionally I wonder. Who am I to judge after all?'

'Have I ever known you when you weren't troubled by doubts?' asked Macintyre rhetorically. 'That's your nature, and I'd almost say your weakness. But at least your judgement, if it errs at all, does so on the side of charity.'

Antony was completely silent for a moment. For some reason that was just about the most unexpected thing the doctor could have said to him. 'I didn't get round to telling you that we shall need your help when the case comes on,' he said, when at last he recovered his power of speech, 'one way or another. What defence we put on depends on whether we can trace a certain gentleman, but if we put Winthrop into the witness box to say he remembers nothing of what happened that night we shall need you to explain why.'

'That, I think, should be well within my capabilities,' said Macintyre dryly. 'If you need me in the meantime Mr Horton will let me know. And don't go worrying yourself into fits about this business,' he added in an admonitory tone. 'It strikes me that, one way and another, there's quite enough trouble brewing without that.'

After the doctor rang off, Maitland was allowed to work in peace until it was time for him to leave for Astroff's to meet Geoffrey. His uncle had mentioned the afternoon before that he was lunching that day with another of his legal brethren, so he was comfortably sure that they were safe from interruption. 'You didn't tell me you'd talked to Dr Macintyre again,' he said, as soon as they had seated themselves and given their order.

'I thought you'd had enough of the subject,' said Geoffrey, 'but when I thought it over I came to the conclusion that it was a case of the sooner the better. I think it was a good idea of yours to leave Macintyre to break the news to Winthrop, and you know, Antony, I'm beginning to feel you may be right about him after all.'

Maitland stared at him for a moment. 'Don't tell me I put up such a good argument that it even convinced you,' he said.

'It wasn't convincing at all,' said Geoffrey. Maitland had had occasion to complain before of the pleasures, and otherwise, of having a candid friend. 'The thing is I thought from the beginning that Winthrop was humbugging us, but I've seen more of him by now than the jury ever will and I'm beginning to think he's telling the truth as he sees it. Of course, it's still possible that he murdered his grandfather and then forgot all about it.'

'Thanks for the reminder.'

It was Geoffrey's turn to look at his friend rather sharply. 'Second thoughts?' he asked.

'Not exactly,' said Antony, who combined a preference for telling the truth with an extreme dislike of exposing his own emotions. He was still wondering what had made him speak so frankly to Dr Macintyre earlier in the day. 'No,' he added more firmly, 'I think we should go ahead as planned. I haven't been able to talk to Canada yet, of course, because of the time difference, but I'll report to you as soon as I've done so. In the meantime . . . well, no, I don't mean that exactly, whenever you say it's convenient for you.'

'If there's one thing,' said Horton thoughtfully, 'that makes me more nervous than another it's when you become polite.'

'All right then, there are two things I want you to put in hand.'

'Only two?'

'Well, I suppose . . . the other things concern the ordinary preparation of the case.'

'Or in this instance, two cases,' Geoffrey reminded him. 'As you said, the line we take will depend on how things turn out.'

'Two cases then. Warning the witnesses who may be needed, you know all that side of it better than I do.'

'Talking to the Patmores, I suppose,' said Geoffrey in rather a dreary tone. 'I might have known you'd delegate that to me.'

'Your job, don't you think?'

Geoffrey made no direct response to that. 'And Horace Dryden too, I shouldn't wonder,' he said.

'As Uncle Nick would say, "precisely". Could you talk to the landlord of the King's Head too. Kenmore, Willett said his name was. Confirm Willett's story about the way Winthrop behaved there on various occasions—not that it needs confirming, but we've got to get it at first hand. And also talk to him about this man who only spoke to Simon when he was obviously in one of his amnesia fits.'

'Without mentioning M.B. in any way, of course. I've already scheduled a visit to Mr Kenmore for this afternoon,' said Geoffrey. 'If I go in just before closing time he'll see me as soon as he's shut up shop.'

'I might have known it! I suppose you've already thought of the other thing for yourself.'

'Perhaps, perhaps not. But before we go on to that, there's one very awkward point about the second man you're interested in, and it applies whether he was Robert Camden or not. How did he know that Winthrop suffered from these occasional fits of amnesia?'

'It must have been obvious after the first time he spoke to him.'

'That won't do. If you're right about it being the cousin, he wouldn't want Simon to know he was in London, to remember having seen him.'

Maitland frowned. 'You're right, of course, and I admit it never occurred to me. There must be some explanation.'

'Winthrop himself says he was ashamed of the occasions when he lost his memory and never told anyone about them,' said Geoffrey, rubbing it in.

'No.' Antony sounded doubtful. 'But Madeleine Rexford told us he'd several times omitted to keep engagements they'd made, and the Patmores too were aware of times when he didn't want to explain where he'd been. If one of them had mentioned his forgetfulness to a friend, particularly to someone who knew of his background, they might have deduced the rest.'

'I should think Miss Rexford would have been more likely than the Patmores to have mentioned it casually, making a joke of it perhaps. But to another girl, not to a man.'

'Well, we shall have to ask her.'

'We can't,' said Geoffrey. 'That's something else I forgot to tell you. The prosecution are calling her.'

'Do you think they've got wind of this multiple personality business and think we're going to try to trade on it?'

'No, I don't think that at all, and for the simple reason that they're not calling a psychiatrist, only the usual medical evidence. But they've got Winthrop's records, if you remember, and know all about his financial situation. I expect they just want Miss Rexford to confirm the engagement, and that the wedding was being put off until he got himself a regular job. A little bit of emphasis on the motive, that's all.'

'Then I shall have to ask her in court, which doesn't leave us with much time if she gives us an affirmative answer. However, that can't be helped. This other point, Geoffrey.'

'You want me to ask the landlord – there are getting to be too many landlords in this business, we'd better refer to Kenmore as the publican in future. Which is all right, I suppose,' he added doubtfully, 'so long as we remember not to refer to the other one as the sinner.'

'You're quite right, of course. I mean the owner of the house where Simon had his studio. It shouldn't be difficult to find out who he is, even though I forgot to ask our client when we saw him.'

'Don't worry, I asked him yesterday. The man's name is Ridley, he's a retired ship's engineer, owns the house, and lives on the ground floor himself. You want me to ask him about the keys, if he kept one for himself when the lock was changed, and whether anybody else has had access to it.'

'If you're going to add mind-reading to your other accomplishments, life will be hardly worth living,' Maitland grumbled. But secretly he was relieved at the change in Geoffrey's attitude, it was one complication the less, though his long association with the solicitor should have warned him that it was likely to take place. Geoffrey was one of the what-can't-be-cured-must-be-endured school, and though he might kick like a mule in the beginning when he disagreed with Maitland's theories, whether he came to accept them or not there was never any doubt that he would co-operate to the full.

Perhaps this was in Antony's mind when he went on, 'Derek tells me you've offered him the other brief.' Derek Stringer was also a member of Sir Nicholas's chambers, and preferred the security of the connection he had built up for himself while practising at the junior bar to the hazards of taking silk. Where his leader went he would follow without question, and generally – unlike Horton – without expressing any opinion as to the rights and wrongs of the matter, a fact of which Geoffrey was only too aware, and which had undoubtedly influenced his choice.

'I thought you'd feel safe with him,' he said sympathetically. 'You've enough arguments on your hands as it is.'

Antony raised his glass to him in silent appreciation, and after that they got on with the serious business of selecting their meal.

II

When the time came to make his transatlantic calls Maitland was surprised at the ease with which they went through, and at the clarity of the line. Perhaps because he hadn't expected to do so he got through without any difficulty to Shelburne, and heard an unmistakably English voice announce itself as Celia Burton. It hadn't occurred to him that a little over twenty-two years' absence wouldn't have changed the way she spoke.

'You don't know me, Mrs Burton,' he said, 'and I must apologize for intruding on you like this. My name is Maitland, I'm a barrister, and I've been briefed to defend your nephew, Simon Winthrop, on a rather serious charge.'

'I've heard about that,' she said rather sharply, 'from the lawyer. He killed my father.' (So Mrs Patmore had wasted no time in following his advice, and the solicitor still less.)

'Forgive me, Mrs Burton, but there is – shall we say? – a great deal of doubt about that.'

'Well, I can't help you, I haven't seen him since he was five years old. But Sylvia Patmore told me he'd gone a bit queer after

Rosalie and Peter died, he was in the car when they were killed, you know, so I daresay you can make up some excuse for him that way.'

'Mrs Patmore told me he seemed to have lost his memory,' said Antony cautiously. He didn't want to offend Mrs Burton in case she hung up on him. 'He couldn't remember the accident, or anything that had gone before. She and her husband thought it better not to force him to remember, at least that's what she told me.'

'That's it, near enough,' said Celia Burton. 'Not that it matters too much to me, being so far away, but Simon was a nice enough little boy, and I daresay you can make up some tale to satisfy people that it wasn't altogether his fault.'

'That isn't what I want to do. He's pleading Not Guilty, and I'm quite in agreement with that.'

'You know your own business best, I suppose,' she said, rather grudgingly. 'But if that's the case, what do you want from me? I tell you, I haven't been home since we left in fifty-three. We've had no money to throw away on plane trips, and I don't know if you've heard that my first husband died ten years ago. Things are different now, Wayne – my second husband – being a doctor. But he's a local man and doesn't seem to have much interest in travel.'

'Yes, I'd heard of Mr Camden's death and I'm sorry, as I am about your father's. You see, Mrs Burton, what was in my mind was that your son, Robert, might have gone home to England, even for a short visit, and got to know his cousin while he was there. And called on his grandfather too, that would be only natural. He might be able to help me more than anybody else about the relationship between them, between Simon and Mr Wilmot, I mean. And if your father had made any enemies he might have been more willing to confide in the elder of his grandsons than in the younger one.' He knew as he spoke that the argument was a weak one, but he couldn't think of anything better.

'Robert's never been to England . . . as far as I know,' she added doubtfully.

'You don't sound too sure about that, Mrs Burton. If I could get in touch with him –'

'Well, you can't through me. He went to Montreal eighteen months ago, and I've not heard from him since.'

'But you know the company he worked for. Couldn't you have got in touch with him through them?'

'If he didn't want to tell me where he was I wouldn't demean myself by doing that.'

'Forgive me, Mrs Burton,' said Antony again, though he wasn't quite sure what he was apologizing for. 'Had you had some sort of a quarrel?'

'Never a wrong word between us. And if you're thinking he didn't get on with his step-father, you're wrong. They spent all the time they could together and I think if I'd married Wayne sooner Robert might have gone into medicine too.'

'I see.'

'And if you want to know, Mr – Maitland did you say your name was? – I did go to the police when no word came at Christmas. But they said there hadn't been an accident reported or anything like that, and a grown man . . . I suppose I shouldn't say they just weren't interested, obviously they thought he'd his own reasons for not getting in touch, but anyway they told me there was nothing they could do.'

'I see. You say your son worked as an insurance agent. He didn't inherit his grandfather's talent then?'

'Always sketching when he was a kid. All nonsense, I told him, he'd never make a living that way.'

'You say Mr Wilmot's solicitor got in touch with you.'

'Certainly he did, it was only right. I was a bit annoyed at first he hadn't done it sooner, but apparently Dad didn't keep any of my letters so he didn't know where I was until Sylvia Patmore thought to tell him. Robert was one of Dad's heirs, as he told me himself years ago. Which I don't think was right, Mr Maitland, a woman can have as much trouble making ends meet as a man can. But Dad wouldn't see it that way, and of course Robert agreed with him, which was natural as it was to his benefit.'

'Is your son married?'

'Not unless he met someone after he left Halifax.'

One complication the less . . . or was it? 'Did you correspond with Mr Wilmot until he died?'

'We kept in touch. A card at Christmas and a letter on my birthday. Not much news, but then he was getting an old man and I daresay he didn't get about very much.'

'I think Mrs Patmore was sorry when she didn't hear from you again after the note you sent her when your husband died.'

'To tell you the truth it didn't seem worth the bother. What was there in England for me now? I've never thought of going back.'

'Your father –' Maitland ventured.

'I wrote to him now and then, as I told you, that was only my duty. But he didn't care for girls, Mr Maitland. I used to think sometimes it was a judgement on him just having the two, Rosalie and me. And Robert wrote, I suppose, and probably heard from him; at least he said he wrote sometimes when I asked him, but I was never one to pry into his correspondence.'

'Then I must thank you for your patience in answering my questions, Mrs Burton, and not detain you any longer. There is one last thing, though. If you hear from your son, would you mind letting me know?'

'If you think it'll do any good you can give me your address if you like.' He did so, slowly and carefully, but wondered at the same time whether she was even writing it down. 'Of course, I'm sorry Simon's in trouble,' she said when he had finished. 'He was a nice boy as I remember, a bit young to play with Robert, of course. But it all seems a long way away and a long time ago, and Dad was an old man, he couldn't have lived much longer anyway. Whatever happens it won't make much difference to us over here.'

Maitland sat and stared at the phone for a long time after he had replaced the receiver. An odd woman, was she naturally devoid of all filial affection, or had life dealt with her too hardly? After a while he said aloud, 'I don't suppose I shall ever know,' pulled the telephone towards him again and rummaged in his desk for the piece of paper with the Montreal telephone number written on it. When he found it he asked Hill to give him an outside line.

The Montreal number was also easy to get, after a short argument with the operator because he wanted to make it a personal call to the personnel manager, and she wanted a name to amplify the description. He suspected that if he had persisted he would have got his way, but quite unreasonably his talk with Mrs Burton had depressed him and he was too impatient to suffer the delay. 'Just get me the number then,' he said resignedly.

'It'll cost you less that way,' the operator assured him, willing to offer consolation after she had got her own way. And added gratuitously, 'It'll sound like the engaged signal, so don't be put off by that.'

'Thank you,' said Maitland quietly, slightly ashamed, as he always was, when he came even close to losing his temper.

When the phone was answered it was in French, and he replied absent-mindedly in the same language. He had stayed once in Montreal with an aunt of Jenny's and having a good ear had quickly accustomed himself to the slight distortions that had crept in to their way of speech since the first settlers landed.

He soon realized that he couldn't have made a better move. 'You are calling from London?' the voice at the other end said cordially when he had explained himself. 'But Monsieur surely is French.'

'No, but I have the good fortune to know your language well.' Perhaps it would have been better to agree with her, but on the whole he thought not. On reflection his name would have been bound to betray him. It didn't seem to matter, the mere fact that he was speaking her own language and not attempting to slide away immediately into the English tongue was enough to ensure her co-operation, and the slight delay engendered while she complimented him on his proficiency was well worth the extra money the call would cost. 'I'll see if M'sieur Dumouriez is in his office,' she said at last. 'A call from England! He must certainly make time to talk to you.'

Monsieur Dumouriez sounded a little harassed, but relaxed slightly as the conversation proceeded. As a matter of policy Antony stuck firmly to French. He had read enough about the present situation in Canada to realize that it would be only too easy to put a foot wrong. 'I need not delay you long, M'sieur,' he said. 'I only want to get in touch with a man called Robert Camden, whom I understand is employed by your company.'

'Camden? Camden? Another Englishman?'

'He was born in England, but lived since he was a boy in Nova Scotia. I have been told he worked in your branch in Halifax in that province, and was transferred to your head office about eighteen months ago.'

'I must look at my files, M'sieur. You will wait?'

'As long as you like,' Maitland assured him.

As it turned out it wasn't very long. 'Ah yes, I remember now,' said Monsieur Dumouriez, and Antony would hear the rustle of paper, presumably as he consulted the file. 'He came to us certainly, but left after six months.'

'May I ask, M'sieur, whether he left of his own accord, or was he by any chance dismissed?'

'Of his own accord, but I remember him well now that I look

139

at the file, and I cannot say we were sorry to see him go. If I may explain,' said Monsieur Dumouriez, who seemed in no hurry now to terminate the conversation.

'I should be obliged if you would do so.'

'M'sieur Camden had enough French to be officially bilingual, though I must say he spoke it vilely. Do you know Montreal at all?'

'I have visited there once.'

'Then you may know that there are districts which are almost entirely English-speaking, among them an area where many wealthy people live. We find it more satisfactory to use men whose first language is English as salesmen in these places. There is sadly a good deal of ill-feeling here and not all of it one-sided as you will see in a moment.'

'So that was why Robert Camden was transferred from Nova Scotia. You were able to employ him because he was officially bilingual, but what you needed was someone whose native tongue was English?'

'That is it exactly, M'sieur. He was not, of course, the only one of our employees in that position. And at first all seemed to be well. M'sieur Camden is an intelligent man, the reports we received of his work were good, but then we began to hear things that disturbed me.'

'Would it be asking too much, M'sieur–?'

'You are curious,' said Dumouriez. 'Québec is–Québec, M'sieur. We have our own ways, and we mean to keep them. It is sad, but some English resent our attitude, some even who have lived here for many generations. Many firms have left, many individuals have left . . . perhaps in this way the problem will at last solve itself,' he added more cheerfully.

'Perhaps it will,' said Maitland cautiously, not quite sure where all this was leading.

'But there are many English families who are good neigh-bours, who resent criticism of *la Belle Provence* which has given them a home for many years. It was from some such families that the complaints I mentioned came. Friendliness is a great asset in this business, to discuss people's financial needs, to try to arrange what is best for them, and then perhaps a glass of wine, a cup of tea.' This last was said with a questioning inflection, so that Antony realized it was intended as a small joke.

'Certainly a cup of tea,' he agreed gravely.

140

'Ah, we understand one another.' Dumouriez seemed to find the thought gratifying. 'And of course when the business is over and a social occasion begins ideas are exchanged. And to some of these families, the ones I call good neighbours, M'sieur Camden has made remarks that are not altogether kind. I don't know if you are familiar with Nova Scotia, M'sieur.'

'I've never been there.'

'It is not an island, though there is only one way in by road, across the Tantramar Marshes. So perhaps it is not surprising that the people are insular in their ways. I have been working there for a while – though we are talking my own language, M'sieur, I am fairly proficient in yours – and I have noticed that whenever one of them speaks of a French man or a French woman they use also the adjective "stupid". It is something like that that M'sieur Camden has been saying to our good English friends here.'

'That was very discourteous of him.' And stupid too, thought Antony. In his opinion, whether you liked or disliked the French as a nation, that was the very last description that fitted them. 'These complaints you received – '

'You are going to ask me if they led to his leaving, and that is true. He was warned several times, and on the last occasion I spoke to him myself. He told me quite openly that he was unhappy here, disliked the atmosphere, had made no friends at all. I said that was a pity because, apart from this one fault, his work was good, but he must remember where he was living and behave accordingly. At that he lost his temper, he said, "You French! *Vous n'êtes même pas bon pour décharger du fumier.*" As that is a colloquialism, perhaps I should translate it for you, M'sieur.'

'You're not fit to shovel muck,' said Antony readily.

'Muck?' Dumouriez seemed to be savouring the word. 'That is perhaps the same as dirt?'

'The same, but more so,' Antony explained.

'Then you understand, I am angry too. But before I can say anything he tells me he will go straight back to his desk and write out his resignation. I told him in the circumstances the month's notice will not be necessary, he is free to go at once, but he says it will be more convenient, give him time to think what to do next. You may be sure, he tells me, I shall not stay in Montreal, but find somewhere fit to live. That is not the last time I saw him, but the last conversation I had with him.'

'I can see you're not in sympathy with Camden, and I can't say I blame you,' said Antony. 'He sounds a thoroughly unpleasant person. But what I'm afraid you're going to tell me next is that he left no forwarding address, that you don't know where he went after he left there.'

'That is exactly so, M'sieur. I should not be surprised if he shook the dust from his shoes when he left this building for the last time.' Monsieur Dumouriez was not above indulging in a flight of fancy.

'And you say he had made no friends there who would be likely to know where he went?'

'I think not, but if you like I will ask around, M'sieur, and cable you the information if I discover anything. But if you don't hear from me within, say, a week . . . would that be too long?'

'That would be excellent, and I'm more than obliged to you.'

'I can, however'—the Frenchman sounded triumphant—'give you his address while he was here and the telephone number. Madame Bouchier. So I'm afraid you will have to use your French again, if you speak to her.' He dictated for a moment. 'I can give no assurance that she can help you, but certainly she is the most likely person to be able to do so.'

The conversation concluded after that with an exchange of compliments that took quite five minutes. For once Maitland didn't grudge the time. He had learned nothing really to the point, but he had a feeling that he and Monsieur Dumouriez would have got on well together, and he was genuinely grateful that the other man hadn't snubbed him. When you got right down to it, his questions must have seemed an impertinence.

By contrast his conversation with Madame Bouchier took only a few minutes. Monsieur Camden, whom she remembered only because most of the guests who stayed with her were Québecois, had had a bedroom in her house for six months, but got his meals elsewhere. He paid weekly, and hadn't informed her that he was leaving until a week before he actually did so. Neither she nor her daughters had ever had any conversation with him—he is *tête d'épingle*, that man—and he had left no forwarding address. In spite of what could only be regarded as a disappointment Maitland was smiling as he replaced the receiver. Monsieur Dumouriez had said Robert Camden was intelligent, while his landlady referred to him as a pinhead. It

142

seemed probable that she and her family spoke no English, and that Camden had felt no need to put himself out to speak French on their behalf.

Geoffrey phoned just before he left chambers to say that he had spoken to Mr Kenmore, who confirmed everything that Willett had said and wouldn't mind giving evidence though he had obviously no idea why he should be asked to do so. He'd be in touch again if Cobbold's came up with anything, and of course after he'd talked to Mr Ridley, Simon Winthrop's landlord.

Antony responded with an account of his various transatlantic telephone conversations, which seemed to cause Geoffrey some amusement though he was careful to express disappointment at the result. 'If he's responsible for all the things that have been happening,' he pointed out, 'he must have been in this country for at least six months; probably longer, because it's unlikely he picked up Antonia just as he was getting off the plane.'

'I thought of that. It's time enough to have established a residence, but the Robert Camdens in the phone book had all lived in the same place for years. Willett did some phoning for me, and that was the result. And it seems to me unlikely that he was living out of town, if he was carrying on an affair with Antonia.'

'It's beginning to look as if we shall have to fall back on Plan B,' said Geoffrey.

'Which is doomed to failure,' said Antony rather morosely. 'Something might come through from M'sieur Dumouriez,' he added more hopefully, 'or even from Mrs Burton, though she didn't sound as though she particularly wanted to be helpful. Let's see, there's not much more than a week until the end of term, and you say the case will be high on the list after Easter.'

'Not later than the tenth or eleventh of April, I should think,' said Geoffrey. 'And, by the way, it's on Conroy's list, and Halloran will be leading the prosecution.'

Maitland groaned. 'If you're doing your best to drive me to suicide, Geoffrey –'

'You said yourself there wasn't much hope anyway,' Horton pointed out.

'No but . . . you know what Halloran is. The biggest gossip in the business, and particularly fond of letting Uncle Nick know if ever I put a foot wrong.'

'He also collects information like a–like a sort of vacuum cleaner,' said Geoffrey, 'so you can be sure Sir Nicholas would hear all there was to hear anyway. Still you know, I don't think Halloran's being unkind, I think he's actually rather fond of you and hopes Sir Nicholas will be able to bring some influence to bear in getting you to observe a little more moderation.'

Antony grinned. 'He ought to know better by now,' he remarked, 'and if he's fond of me he certainly knows how to disguise it. However, I'll take your word for it. As for Conroy–'

'He's very fair.'

'Justice untempered by humanity,' said Maitland firmly. 'He's got this craze for order, everything has to be done just so, and he won't give me an inch of latitude unless he can't see any way around it.'

'In that case it's probably just as well you won't be acting on Plan A,' said Geoffrey. He may have meant this to be consoling, but his friend didn't find it so and chose to disregard it.

'There's just one thing we've got to remember,' he said. 'If Robert Camden killed his grandfather it was so that he could successfully frame Simon. Therefore he's got to show up sooner or later, or it would all be for nothing.'

When they closed the conversation a few minutes later it was Geoffrey's turn to feel depressed. He wanted the best for their client, but he didn't think they could accomplish anything either way. And as far as he was concerned what he called Plan B was the more likely to keep Antony out of trouble.

III

It was getting late by then but Sir Nicholas had not left chambers. They went home together, therefore, by cab, and when Sir Nicholas had preceded him into the house he walked straight to the study door and held it open invitingly. But when Antony had recounted his progress–or lack of it–his mood became noticeably more genial. 'I still don't agree with this alternate plan of yours–'

'Geoffrey calls it Plan B,' Maitland interrupted him.

'–but at least it has two points in its favour.' He paused there, possibly for dramatic effect, and Vera–looking up and smiling at Antony – chose to complete his thought for him.

'Wouldn't attract so much attention from the press,' she said bluntly. 'And when it goes wrong nobody can blame you.'

No use going on with the subject, no use explaining that he wanted desperately to catch up with Robert Camden. Not to prove to them that he was right, but to prove it, if possible, to himself. He was committed now, and – worst of all – Simon Winthrop had agreed to trust him. And if he was wrong, if his client had been playing all along some devious game of his own . . . . it didn't bear thinking of, but for all that he could act decisively enough on occasion the doubts would come back. He didn't realize that they were doubts of himself rather than of his client.

'Am I supposed to find that thought comforting?' he asked Vera, a bitterness that he very rarely allowed to tinge his voice when he was speaking to her for once very evident.

'Think you should,' said Vera seriously.

He smiled at her again and got to his feet. 'I'll try,' he promised.

Sir Nicholas, still in his mellow mood, offered a drink but Antony declined. 'It's getting late,' he said, 'and Jenny will be wondering where I am.'

For once Gibbs had no comments to make as he went through the hall. By the time he reached his own front door Antony was aware of his tiredness, and of the fact that his shoulder was hurting damnably. For some reason the characteristic squeak that the door gave as he pushed it open was reassuring. It was only when you came to think of it that you wondered why Jenny, with her passion for turning the place upside down in the interests of improving it, had never attacked that squeak with an oil can. But here she was coming out of the living-room and as usual just the sight of her raised his spirits, which were badly in need of it.

'Antony,' she said, not giving him time to greet her, 'do you realise it's nearly Easter and we have almost two weeks to ourselves?'

He was shrugging off his coat and when he had succeeded in doing so threw it untidily on to a chair. 'Of course I realize it, love,' he assured her. 'I have to get back to chambers a couple of days early, because Geoffrey says that case of ours is coming on early. But even so –' He bent to kiss her, not attempting to complete the sentence.

'Roger's here,' she said, 'and he's got the most marvellous idea.'

'Here already?' said Antony, urging her into the living-room with his left arm round her shoulders. 'I didn't know we'd started taking in boarders.'

Roger took this in the spirit in which it was meant. 'Meg had to go to the theatre early again,' he said, 'so Jenny took pity on me.'

'That's good. At least, I'm sorry you've seen so little of Meg lately. What's this marvellous idea anyway?'

'I'll get you a drink, Antony,' Jenny offered, making for the writing-table where the tray was already in place.

'Thank you, love.' For once he didn't take up his stance on the rug, in front of the fire, but sank into the wing chair to the left of the hearth. Roger was already occupying the one that, when Sir Nicholas was present, was reserved for him.

'It's about the Easter holidays, as I expect you gathered from what Jenny said,' Roger told him. 'Mrs Mott is getting the cottage at Grunning's Hole ready for us and laying in some supplies. I thought you two might like to come down for a while.'

'I gather Jenny approves,' said Antony, smiling. 'Thank you, love,' he added as she put down a glass at his side.

'I do, very emphatically,' said Jenny. 'If we stay here Mr Mallory will be fixing up conferences for you almost every day, and everyone needs a change sometimes.'

'So they do. Are you coming down, Roger?'

'Yes, for as long as you can manage. That's why I thought it was such a good idea. I've a few chores to do, getting the *Windsong* ready for the summer, but they won't take up too much of my time.'

Antony was staring at him. 'What about Meg?' he asked in a surprised tone.

'I'm not thinking of deserting her, if that's what's on your mind,' said Roger, amused. 'The play's coming off at the end of this week, Saturday night will be the last performance.'

'I thought it was doing so well.'

'So it was, but you know Jon Kellaway's appendix blew up all of a sudden, or whatever it is appendixes do. They tried to carry on with the understudy, but Jon's taking longer to recover than they expected. There were some complications, I think.'

'I'm sorry about that.'

'Oh, so am I,' said Roger cheerfully. 'On the other hand –'

'You'll have Meg to yourself for a while,' said Antony, exchanging a smile with Jenny.

'Yes, it'll be worth all the time she's spent on extra rehearsing, trying to get the understudy into shape, which I understand is pretty hopeless. And the beauty of it is, because the closing's so unexpected she hasn't got anything else lined up immediately.'

'If appendicitis were infectious I should suspect you of spreading a few germs around. Anyway, this invitation of yours, are you sure you wouldn't like to have her really to yourself for a while?'

'I can't think of anything nicer than having you two with us,' said Roger, and obviously meant it. 'Besides, Meg may be playing the role of housewife for a few months anyway. Don't tell her, will you, but I hope it works out that way.'

'Then we'll come with the greatest of pleasure,' Antony told him. 'Where's the calendar, Jenny? Let's start making plans.'

As regards Simon Winthrop's affairs only two things of note occurred during the rest of the term, both contained in reports from Geoffrey. The first was that he had seen Mr Ridley, the owner of the house where Simon had his studio. He was a big man living alone in a place where everything was ship-shape . . . so tidy in fact as to be almost painful, or so Geoffrey said. He had indeed kept an extra key when the lock was changed after the flooding of his tenant's kitchen on the first floor. Not that he'd a word to say against Mr Winthrop, who'd always been straight with him, and considering he was an artist had kept the place in pretty good order. But accidents would happen and he thought it as well to be prepared.

'So I asked him,' said Geoffrey, 'where he kept the key, and whether anybody else could have had access to it. To which he shook his head. "Except for the time Mr Winthrop forgot his own key," he said, "and asked me to leave mine on the ledge over his door so that he could let himself in".'

'It must have been in one of his fits of forgetfulness,' said Maitland. 'He told us he didn't think anyone else had a key. No, that won't do,' he corrected himself. 'If he was in a state of amnesia he wouldn't know where he lived.'

'That's right, so of course I asked Mr Ridley a bit more about it. It turned out it wasn't Winthrop himself who phoned, but some girl or other with a message from him.'

'Ho *ho!*'

'Now don't go getting ideas into your head,' said Geoffrey hastily. 'All the same,' he admitted, 'it is a bit odd. Winthrop didn't return the key immediately, and after a couple of days Mr Ridley was going to ask him about it, but then he found it pushed through his letter box. He never asked Winthrop about it, said it didn't seem worthwhile.'

'Had he ever noticed any oddness in his tenant's behaviour?'

'No, but come to think of it there's no reason why he should.

Apparently Winthrop walked past him in the street one day, but Mr Ridley just thought it'd be the sort of thing any artist might do . . . walk along with his head in the clouds, thinking about his work and never noticing anything or anybody around him.'

'Yes, I see.'

'I asked the Patmores after all, just in case they'd ever mentioned Winthrop's forgetfulness to any of their friends, but they were both quite sure they hadn't. We can't find out unless you ask her in court whether Madeleine Rexford ever did, but even so, why should this woman want to get hold of the key, and what good would it do Camden?'

'He could get a duplicate made. If I'm right about him, Geoffrey, he was here long enough to acquire at least one girl friend. Perhaps he had two strings to his bow.'

'Both under Winthrop's name?'

'Maybe, maybe not. I just can't answer that question, Geoffrey.'

'Well, it doesn't get us much further on,' said Horton. 'Except to put still more ideas into your head,' he added disagreeably. 'Concentrate on Plan B, there's a good chap.'

'That's what Uncle Nick says, and I can see I shall probably have to.' He closed the conversation then, and it was some days later when Geoffrey rang up to arrange a luncheon date, so that he could show him Cobbold's report.

'I'm beginning to think you've got second sight or something,' he said by way of greeting as they settled themselves at the corner table. Not at Astroff's today, because Sir Nicholas was likely to be there and Antony was emulating Brer Rabbit in his dealings with his uncle at the moment, at least as far as Simon Winthrop's affairs were concerned.

'You mean they've come up with something?' asked Maitland eagerly.

'Something, yes. I don't see how it will help, but something.'

'Tell me then.'

'You can read it for yourself.'

'I will, of course I will. But tell me first.'

'All right. They identified the Mark Benson who frequents the King's Head, and made a few inquiries about him. It seems he's a bookkeeper, and recently lost his wife, who'd been ill for a long time. *Not* the girl he used to take to the pub with him apparently, so if it was a fully-fledged affair and he'd any feeling for his wife he'd have been a good subject for blackmail – wouldn't he? – while she was still alive. Which is what you suggested when you first saw that note.'

'If there was any way of Camden knowing what he'd been up to.'

'Yes, that's the point isn't it? Look here, Antony, what do you think his plan actually was? Blackening Winthrop's character wouldn't do any good unless somebody, preferably the police, knew about it.'

'We went into all this before.'

'Yes, but not in detail. I'd like to get it perfectly straight in my mind.'

'That three people identified Simon as the man they'd seen was a bit of luck for the murderer, something the murderer couldn't possibly have foreseen, so he made use of Winthrop's name in a number of ways, in activities which he thought would make the police look twice at him. The motive would have ensured at least a degree of interest in him, remember. The out-of-character paintings they must know about, but of course they don't prove anything, except perhaps that Simon's character is not quite as straightforward as everyone believed. Camden couldn't know that Antonia Dryden's father insisted on hushing the whole thing up and persuaded Bertha Harvey to fall in with his wishes.'

'Just a minute! What if they *had* talked at the inquest?'

'All the better. No proof which would have put Simon out of circulation, but lots of suspicion. Benson obviously wouldn't incriminate himself by talking, but I think an anonymous letter or two: Ask Horace Dryden who was responsible for his daughter's death? Ask Mark Benson what he knows about Simon Winthrop? That would have made the police look at him still harder, wouldn't it? And for all we know there may be other misdemeanours that we've never heard about.'

'I think we've got quite enough to be going on with,' said Geoffrey. 'You're telling me, I think, that when the identity witnesses came along, sure that it was Simon they'd seen, Camden thought that was proof enough along with the motive and decided not to go ahead with the rest of his plan.'

'Too risky, and unnecessary into the bargain,' Maitland agreed. 'And if Sylvia Patmore hadn't come up with this crazy idea of trying to explain her son's behaviour we'd never have

heard of all this either, never questioned Simon's guilt probably.'

'And his having a blackout that very evening was just a piece
of good luck on Camden's part, something he couldn't have
foreseen. I still think we ought to come up with an explanation
for that.'

'I think I have. That newspaper cutting we found . . . it's
obvious once you think about it. Three Dead in Blazing Car. If
it had been introduced into Simon's room that evening – we're
assuming his cousin had a key, remember – wouldn't that have
been enough to set him off?'

'So that's why you wanted to keep it!'

'No, it was just . . . well, you never know what may come in
useful. I forgot all about it, didn't even remember to mention it
to the Patmores as I said I would. It was only later I realised, and
I'll bet if we ask Dr Macintyre he'll agree with me. Is it too far-
fetched for you, Geoffrey?'

'To tell you the truth,' Horton admitted, 'I'm beginning to
think that long association with you has addled my brain. I
almost,' he added with a show of reluctance, 'find myself
agreeing with you. But what we've both got to remember,
Antony, is that none of this is any good unless Robert Camden
turns up before the trial to claim his inheritance.'

EASTER RECESS, 1975

Thursday, 27th March to Monday, 7th April

I

The interlude at Grunning's Hole was as pleasant as they had expected, and they all returned to town on the Sunday after Easter, the sixth of April. Maitland was in chambers early enough the following morning to satisfy even old Mr Mallory, and was met with a message that Superintendent Sykes was anxious to get in touch with him immediately.

'Get him for me straight away then, will you, Hill?' said Antony and went off down the corridor to his own room. It was rather gloomy, even on sunny days, and he had no time to do more than switch on the desk light when the phone rang to announce that the Superintendent was on the line. Antony said, 'Thank you, Hill, put him right through,' grimaced at the piles of documents that had accumulated during his absence, and settled back in his chair to see what the detective had to say.

Sykes inevitably began with the usual inquiries as to the family's health and, having been reassured on this point and assured Antony in turn that Mrs Sykes was well, continued smoothly, 'I understand you and Mrs Maitland have been out of town.'

'You've been trying to get in touch with me? Has anything happened?' Maitland asked sharply.

'Nothing urgent enough to disturb your holiday. You remember the inquiry I put through for you as to the whereabouts of a woman called Celia Camden?'

'Of course I remember!'

'I was able to give you her address and new name and telephone number,' Sykes went on, nothing if not deliberate. 'You never told me, of course, whether anything came of your inquiries, as I understand it was a confidential matter concerning one of your clients. But were you able to get the information you needed about her son?'

'Why should you think it was Robert Camden I was interested in?'

'The Winthrop case, Mr Maitland. It has come to my knowledge that he and your client are cousins.'

'You mean you were curious and made it your business to find out,' said Maitland. But the sharpness had gone from his voice, now he sounded merely amused. 'Well, I suppose you can't be a good detective unless you're inquisitive, so I'll forgive you.'

'That's magnanimous of you, Mr Maitland, but you didn't answer my question.'

'Whether I located Robert Camden? No, I wasn't successful.'

'Well, if you're still interested I may be able to help you,' said Sykes. 'I had a message through official channels. It seems this Shelburne is a small place, where everyone knows everyone else's business, much as in a village here. After rather a long silence Mrs Burton heard from her son. He'd decided he might have a better chance of making a good living over here – though what put that idea into his head I can't imagine – and arrived in England just before Easter, March the twenty-fifth to be exact.'

'The information reached there rather quickly, didn't it? When we write to Peter and Nan they always say our letters take an age to get there.'

'He sent her a cable, a night letter actually, which I believe is cheaper. What he wanted was her advice as to whether he should go to see his grandfather.'

'But –'

'You don't sound as if you found the information entirely to your liking, Mr Maitland. Shall I go on?'

'Is there more?'

'A little more. He gave her a *poste restante* address, and as those night letters are delivered by the post office she replied in the same way, telling him of Thomas Wilmot's murder, and of his cousin's arrest. At this point I admit the curiosity you spoke of got the better of me. I made a few inquiries at the post office, found that he was no longer using their facilities but had left an address to which letters could be forwarded. He's staying at an hotel in Knightsbridge,' said Sykes, and named it. 'From which we may infer, I think, that he had visited his grandfather's solicitor as soon as he heard of the murder, and been given perhaps an advance on his inheritance.'

156

'I agree, that's an expensive place as far as I know. But if he only arrived on the twenty-fifth of last month—'

'That's one piece of information you can rely on, Mr Maitland. Travelling on a Canadian passport there was naturally a record of his arrival . . . he came by plane from Toronto. Things have changed, you know, since we joined the E.E.C., it's the Commonwealth people who have to answer all the questions coming in.'

'He could have been over here earlier and gone back again.'

'I don't know what your interest in this man is, Mr Maitland, but I'd already gathered it was considerable so I pressed my questions a little and was able to run to earth the man who talked to him in immigration. He remembered him because he said Camden was the first person who had spoken to him like a human being that day, who didn't seem to resent having to go through the rather complicated procedure, which apparently comes as something of a shock to people who were born here. He made some joking remark about this being his first visit to the old country since he left with his parents as a child, and asked how he would find things here. And the man who admitted him is positive there were no earlier stamps in the passport, and thinks—though he wasn't noticing particularly and couldn't swear to this—that it was fairly new.'

'Who was it said, *Oh God! Oh Montreal!*' asked Antony. 'That's just about put the cat among the pigeons, Superintendent.'

'I was afraid of that, but I thought you ought to know.'

'You're quite right, and I'm grateful. The only thing is, in view of the A.C.'s attitude, weren't you taking a risk having these extra inquiries made on the side?'

'I have my methods, Mr Maitland.' Sykes sounded faintly amused again. 'You can take it this is just between you and me.'

'Then, between you and me, don't you think it rather suspicious that he should have drawn attention to himself when he arrived?'

'It may be suspicious, though I think you're in danger of twisting things to suit your way of thinking, Mr Maitland. But suspicious or not it doesn't alter the facts, and my informant was very sure there'd been no previous visits.'

'A fact is a fact is a fact,' said Antony rather drearily, and after renewing his thanks rang off, picked up the phone again, and asked Hill to get Mr Horton on the line for him.

II

He made an unsolicited visit to the study when he got home that evening, and found his aunt and uncle drinking sherry. 'I looked for you at lunch time, Uncle Nick,' he said, 'but Mallory told me you weren't in today.'

'Time enough tomorrow,' said Sir Nicholas, 'I've nothing urgent on my list.' He gave his nephew a rather searching look. 'Help yourself to a drink, my dear boy,' he invited. 'I gather you've something to tell me.'

'Yes, I have, and a drink would be welcome.' He was already pouring it as he spoke.

'We're not, I presume, about to hear about your vacation with Meg and Roger.'

'Not about that,' Maitland agreed. 'Jenny will have told you all about it already, Vera,' he added.

'With exceptional clarity,' said Vera, smiling one of her grim smiles, which in the early days of their acquaintance would have frightened him to death. 'Some new case that's worrying you? Or is it the Winthrop business?'

'The latter. I heard from Sykes today . . .' He repeated what the Superintendent had told him, for once without any interruption from his uncle.

'That's a relief anyway,' said Vera when he had finished.

'In a way, I suppose it is,' said her husband thoughtfully. 'Though I can't say I'm exactly enamoured of what Geoffrey calls Plan B.'

'Don't worry, sir, we're not going to follow it.'

'What do you mean?' Perhaps something in the younger man's tone had alerted him but he sounded definitely suspicious.

'That I shall proceed exactly as I outlined to you in the beginning, with Plan A, if you'd like to put it that way.'

For a moment both his companions stared at him incredulously. 'Quite mad,' said Vera, finding her voice first.

'You'll not be surprised, Antony, when I tell you that I endorse my dear wife's opinion,' said Sir Nicholas in the gentle tone that his nephew knew only too often spelled trouble. 'To bring out quite deliberately all this evidence of misconduct on your client's part—'

'Yes, but you see, Uncle Nick, I still don't believe he did any of those things.'

Sir Nicholas didn't care to be interrupted. 'I hoped you had learned long ago that there is no point in going against the evidence,' he said. 'And in the circumstances—'

'If you mean because this Sir Alfred whatever-his-name-is has taken a dislike to me, sight unseen,' said Antony, interrupting again, which anyone could have told him was a mistake, 'we've been through all that before. Giving bad advice to a client isn't a crime, nor is it anything the Bar Council could take action on. As a matter of fact,' he added stubbornly, 'I don't believe it *is* bad advice.'

'In the circumstances you have just described to me, I must beg to disagree with you,' said Sir Nicholas coldly. 'If you will allow me to speak, Antony, I will tell you exactly why I dislike this project of yours, apart from my thinking it's misguided and unfair to Winthrop. It will turn the trial into a sensation, and your friends in the press will certainly make the most of the story, and not to your advantage. The other thing is that though, as you rightly point out, the Assistant Commissioner can take no action that will harm you, you will be confirming his opinion of you, which may have grave disadvantages in the future. Don't you see, this is all part and parcel of the suspicions that Briggs used to harbour . . . a client obviously guilty but whom you are bound and determined to get off at any cost. Even by accusing an obviously innocent man in court, a man who wasn't even in the country at the time of the murder, let alone when these episodes you say were designed to discredit your client took place.'

'I shan't accuse him openly, Uncle Nick. You know I've never done that, and never shall . . . unless I'm sure.'

'And you aren't sure in this case?' Sir Nicholas pounced on the admission.

'How can I be? I only know that if Simon Winthrop is innocent—and I haven't changed my mind about that—the man who stands to gain by both Thomas Wilmot's death *and* by Simon being found guilty of his murder, is Robert Camden.'

'But you mean to call him as a witness?'

'Yes, of course.'

'If you hope to induce him to incriminate himself on direct

159

examination,' said Sir Nicholas, 'I can only re-echo Vera's opinion. You're quite insane.'

Maitland finished his sherry and got to his feet. 'I'm sorry I've disturbed your peaceful evening,' he said, 'but I thought you ought to know what I intend. And I don't know whether I can discredit Robert Camden or not, but I do know I have to try.'

After he had gone, closing the door very softly behind him, there was another perceptible period of silence. Finally, 'I might as well have saved my breath,' said Sir Nicholas angrily. 'Whatever I say he'll go to the devil his own way.'

Vera – the unemotional Vera – heaved herself out of her chair and came to stand close to him, putting a hand on his shoulder. 'What hurts those two hurts us,' she said. 'But it won't do any good to try to persuade Antony from a course of action he thinks he ought to take.'

'But in this case . . . you'll be reminding me next of the occasions when one of his crack-brained schemes has worked,' her husband said suspiciously.

'Not this time. My opinion's exactly the same as yours, I foresee nothing but trouble and disaster. All the same –'

'I shall only make matters worse by interfering,' Sir Nicholas completed the sentence for her. 'I shouldn't say anything more, my dear, even without your excellent advice. I've often tried to induce in Antony a more reasonable frame of mind over some folly or other, but I can't say I've ever succeeded. And this time I can see it's hopeless, though in view of what Superintendent Sykes told him I can't see what he bases his optimism on.'

'Shouldn't exactly call it optimism myself,' said Vera, reverting for the moment to her elliptical manner. And then, more practically, 'Get you another sherry, Nicholas? Then we shall just have to wait and see.'

REGINA *versus* WINTHROP, 1975

THE CASE FOR THE PROSECUTION
Thursday, the first day of the trial

I

Mr Justice Conroy was a man quite confident in his own ability, and therefore took less exception to Maitland's sometimes unorthodox ways than a number of of his brothers on the bench. The judge was, though quite unconscious of the fact, an arrogant man, quite capable in his own estimation of dealing with any attempt that Counsel for the Defence might make to steer matters in favour of his client unless there was good legal precedent for his doing so. That morning, therefore, as he entered the court he was able to look forward with some complacency to what was to come.

Bruce Halloran, Q.C., who was appearing for the prosecution, was a man whose length of experience at the criminal bar almost matched Conroy's own. A big man in every sense of the word, with a booming voice that he could only modulate with difficulty, a thing he didn't attempt unless circumstances seemed to call for it urgently. With regard to this Maitland, no respecter of persons, had been heard to comment, '*I will roar you as gently as any sucking dove*'. But there was no malice in the remark; he admired Halloran's ability, and the only real complaint he could have found against the older man – not a very serious one – was that Halloran, perhaps more than anybody else, had his finger on the pulse of the legal fraternity, so that no item of gossip, however small, escaped him.

Antony, who had a weakness for choosing his own ground when there were battles to be fought, sometimes regretted the fact that his more unconventional doings were apt to come to his uncle's ears before he had a chance to recount them himself. Sir Nicholas Harding and Bruce Halloran were old friends, and for all he knew Geoffrey might have the right of it, that these communications were prompted more than anything else by a mistaken impression that some influence might be brought to bear to prevent any worse excesses on his part.

In the present instance, where he was appearing himself, any communication Halloran made to Sir Nicholas would be confined, of course, to the day's happenings, insofar as they were public property. But Maitland had a feeling that there were a few surprises awaiting his learned friend to which he wouldn't take kindly. If he had been equally confident that those surprises would lead the defence anywhere he'd have been a happier man. As it was he imitated Halloran's complacent look to the best of his ability, and perhaps only Geoffrey and Derek Stringer, sitting beside him ready to take the note, were aware of his very grave misgivings.

By now the preliminaries had been completed. Simon Winthrop had pleaded Not Guilty in a surprisingly firm tone and Counsel for the Prosecution was well into his opening address. Simon had been offered a chair and had accepted it with becoming gratitude, but paradoxically his manner was causing his counsel some alarm. A bad case of the jitters would not have helped anyone, but it was to be hoped that Winthrop's calm demeanour was not due to over-confidence in his lawyers' ability to get him off.

However, there was nothing to be done about that. Maitland leaned back and disposed himself as though for slumber. There would be nothing new to be learned from Halloran's opening address, or if there was the mere closing of his eyes wouldn't prevent him from noticing it. It was unlikely that this affectation of unconcern would have any effect on the jury, but it had become a habit, and he saw no reason to discontinue it. Remembering the first time he had appeared with Geoffrey as his instructing solicitor his lips almost twitched into a smile; Horton had genuinely thought him asleep and had prodded him from time to time to try to remedy this unsatisfactory state of affairs.

'I'm afraid you will find, members of the jury,' Halloran was saying, 'that this is a particular distressing case. Though Thomas Wilmot had lived almost as a recluse for several years many of you will know him by reputation. A famous man, one of the foremost portrait painters of our time, but latterly living quietly because, as you will hear from his housekeeper, so many friends of his own generation had pre-deceased him.

'Mrs Wilmot had been dead for many years, and they had two daughters, Rosalie and Celia. Mr Wilmot, I should explain to

164

you, was an old-fashioned man, in a way with which many of us, I am sure, will find ourselves in sympathy.' (Maitland opened an eye at that for a quick look at the jury; they were the usual nondescript lot, but in the main middle-aged at least, so he thought that Halloran's comment was not inappropriate.) 'Both his daughters had married,' Counsel for the Prosecution continued, 'and regardless of his natural affection for them he felt that from that moment their financial well-being was in the hands of their husbands. He therefore wished his not inconsiderable wealth to be passed on in the male line, which, as he had no son of his own, meant his two grandsons. His will divides his fortune equally between them. One of these young men need not concern us, he emigrated to Canada when he was eight years old. The other grandson, Simon Winthrop, stands here today accused of his grandfather's murder, an old man from whom he had never received anything but kindness. We shall show you that his motive was purely a financial one.'

And indeed the case, as Counsel for the Prosecution unfolded it, seemed to offer no room for doubt. The prisoner's wish to marry; the unsatisfactory nature of his finances; the murder weapon lying ready to hand in Thomas Wilmot's study, as he must very well have known being a regular visitor to the house; and finally and most damningly the three positive identifications of the prisoner as the man seen leaving the house a few minutes before the murdered man was found. Halloran sat down at last looking justifiably self-satisfied, the judge put down his pen and adjourned promptly for lunch.

II

Over the meal Geoffrey was inclined to re-open his arguments against Maitland's proposed course of action; Derek nodded his agreement from time to time, but made no attempt to join in the discussion. 'What Sykes told you is unanswerable,' Horton said. And then almost pleadingly, 'It isn't like you to be so stubborn, Antony.'

Maitland smiled at that. 'I was rather under the impression that you'd made that complaint about me many times,' he said.

'Well, perhaps I have. And then somehow or other you've worked things round until your way of thinking was shown to be right. But this time that's impossible.'

'The man who never loses a case,' murmured Derek, not looking at either of his companions.

'To h-hell with that bit of nonsense,' said Maitland, almost angrily. The description would have annoyed him even if it had been half way true. He turned back to Horton, but made no direct comment on what he had been saying. Instead, 'Have you issued a *sub poena* to Robert Camden?' he asked.

'I did as you asked me,' said Geoffrey, his tone disclaiming all responsibility. 'He seems pretty confused about it, as well he might be, so I've promised to go back to the office and see him after the court has adjourned this afternoon. If you've any suggestions as to what I'm to say to him –'

Antony gestured vaguely. 'I'm sure I can leave that to your own ingenuity, Geoffrey,' he said in a dulcet tone that reminded both his hearers irresistibly of Sir Nicholas. 'Meanwhile we'll proceed as planned, and since that's decided we may as well enjoy our lunch.'

Geoffrey cast a despairing glance in Derek's direction, but didn't attempt to argue any more.

The Crown's first witness was Detective Chief Inspector Conway of the Criminal Investigation Department at Scotland Yard, one of the men whose speciality was murder. Maitland's acquaintance with him went back over many years, without much love lost between them but with by now a good deal of mutual respect. The detective had a narrow face which made the squareness of his chin more noticeable, and if Antony always thought of a wasp when he saw him it may only have been because he had had some experience of the puritanical streak in Conway's nature and the acidity of his tongue. He was, of course, completely at home in his present surroundings, and Halloran took him through the preliminaries with practised speed. His evidence was given almost as quickly, from his first arrival at the scene of the crime, which the local police had left untouched for his inspection. Thomas Wilmot had been lying in the middle of the room, which, he had learned, was the deceased's study and the place where he most frequently sat, and the jewelled hilt of the dagger which had apparently killed him was still protruding from his chest. On inquiry he had found that this weapon had been presented to Mr Wilmot by a grateful client, a gentleman from the Middle East who had worn it when he sat for his portrait several years before. When she came to give evidence, Mrs Mary Barham, Mr Wilmot's housekeeper, would confirm this fact, and also that the dagger was customarily kept on a table that stood just inside the door.

'The picture that comes to mind,' Halloran interjected at this point, 'is of Thomas Wilmot crossing the room to greet the visitor, who, knowing the whereabouts of this rather dangerous ornament, snatched it up and killed him immediately.'

'My lord!' Maitland was on his feet in a moment. 'I have the greatest respect for my friend's perspicacity, but that is something quite beyond his knowledge.'

'Yes, Mr Maitland, I'm inclined to agree with you,' said Conroy. 'Perhaps you should allow your witness to continue to describe the facts of the case as he saw them, Mr Halloran.' Which was all very well, thought Antony as he resumed his place, but the old boy knows as well as I do that that idea is now firmly implanted in the collective mind of the jury.

'If your lordship pleases,' said Halloran smoothly. 'Perhaps, Chief Inspector, you will continue with your very interesting narrative.'

Conway went on with his account of the investigation, to the steps that led him to question the accused and to apply for a warrant for his arrest almost immediately. It was some time, as might have been expected, before Halloran seated himself and Maitland got up to cross-examine.

'That is all very clear, Chief Inspector,' he said, 'and I don't think I shall need to detain you very long. The thing that is puzzling me, though, since I understand that both Mrs Barham and her husband deny having let the murderer in, is how he entered the house. If Mr Wilmot himself let his visitor in, that would invalidate my learned friend's graphic picture of how the murder took place.'

'To which you yourself took exception, Mr Maitland,' the judge reminded him.

'Precisely, my lord. May I re-phrase the question?' He went on without waiting for the required permission. 'Was any evidence forthcoming to show how the killer entered the house?'

'The officer first on the spot in answer to Mr Barham's telephone call will tell the court when he gives his evidence that when he arrived the Yale lock on the front door was fixed in the open position.'

'So that the door could have been readily opened even by someone who had no key?'

'If it had been like that earlier in the evening.'

'Yes, I see. May we now move, Chief Inspector, to your examination of my client's studio?'

'That was done after his arrest, everything was perfectly in order.'

'I'm sure it was,' said Maitland cordially, 'if you're referring to the legal position. I understand that artists are not always the most tidy of people.'

'From that point of view there was nothing unusual about his quarters,' said Conway non-committally.

'You examined them thoroughly, I have no doubt. Did you look in the cupboard where he stored his painting gear when not in use?'

'Certainly we did.'

'And found some paintings there, face to the wall behind all the other paraphernalia? You might almost say hidden from view.'

Conway's expression became more austere than ever. Obviously too, he was surprised at the question. 'The majority of the prisoner's paintings were stacked round the walls of the studio,' he said, 'and they were innocuous enough. As for the three that you seem to be referring to, I am not surprised that they were kept out of sight where no chance visitor might see them. They were unpleasant in the extreme.'

'Could you perhaps describe them to us?'

'I am not an expert in art, Mr Maitland,' said Conway coldly.

'It makes no matter, I shall be introducing them into evidence myself. But even a non-expert can tell us whether they were similar in any way to the paintings admittedly done by my client that you found in open view.'

'I should say they did not resemble them, except that they were all signed in the same way.'

'Thank you, Chief Inspector. Now you have told us that you searched my client's desk and removed certain documents. His account books for instance.'

'Certainly.'

'And, as you are about to remind me, we shall be hearing evidence on their content in due course. What else did you find there?'

168

'Some receipts, an address book, and a diary with very occasional notes of appointments. These were all left in place after a note had been made of anything that might prove useful. There were also a number of unpaid bills, which at Mr Norman Patmore's request were handed to him for payment.'

'Mr Patmore is my client's adoptive father, my lord,' said Maitland turning to Conroy for a moment. Then he went back to the witness again. 'What about correspondence?' he asked.

'There was very little. That too I handed to Mr Patmore.'

'Then we may assume that there was nothing of interest to you. Nothing incriminating?'

'No, Mr Maitland, there was not.' Conway was growing impatient, and the reply came with something of a snap.

'My commiserations.' As the other man grew more impatient Maitland's urbanity increased. 'Of course it is hardly likely that even if my client had kept a diary for anything but engagements he would have made a note: March the first, murder Grandfather in the evening.'

'Mr Maitland?' Mr Justice Conroy had come to life again. 'The witness is doing his best to answer your questions clearly. There is no need to make fun of him.'

'Indeed, my lord, that was the furthest thing from my mind,' said Maitland, horrified. 'The Chief Inspector and I are old friends and he knows my ways. But you see there is something else that is puzzling here, because when I went to Mr Winthrop's studio with my instructing solicitor, Mr Horton, we found this note in the desk, which I'm sure had been thoroughly searched. I should like to introduce it into evidence, and then to ask Chief Inspector Conway if it was there when he made his search.'

There was a brief interval, but eventually the letter was in Conway's hand. 'Have you ever seen that before, Chief Inspector?' Maitland prompted him.

'Never.'

'I have said that I'm sure your search was thorough. Did you examine the desk yourself, or did one of your assistants do it?'

'I considered the matter important and conducted the search myself. In any case, the note seems innocuous enough.' His curiosity was as obvious as if he had expressed it openly.

'Perhaps you would care to read it to us,' Maitland suggested.

'*Mr Winthrop*,' Conway read obligingly enough, but not altogether hiding the scorn in his voice, '*I'm sorry I can't meet the payment that was agreed between us this month but I will do so without fail in February and make up the missing amount as soon as I can. If you wish to talk the matter over I suggest we meet at the King's Head on neutral ground as you might say, but I'm sorry to say I shall be empty-handed. M.B.'*

'We shall hear more of it later,' Maitland promised him. 'To get the matter quite clear, Chief Inspector, my client was already in custody at the time you made your search?'

'I believe I have said as much.'

'If I may interrupt for a moment, my lord, I should like to say that both Mr Horton and I are willing to swear to the finding of the note in the studio if your lordship feels it necessary.'

'I shall make a note of your offer, Mr Maitland.'

'I am obliged to your lordship.' He turned back to the detective again. 'The letter, I think, was meant for you to find, as were the pictures which you have described as unpleasant, but its introduction was mistimed and it fell into my hands instead.' From the corner of his eye he saw that Halloran was about to heave himself to his feet and added hastily, 'I quite agree with my friend, my lord. That remark was inexcusable and I withdraw it without reservation. I have only one more question for the witness. After your search of the studio, did you dust the desk?'

'Certainly not,' said Conway, affronted.

'Or did any of your men do so?'

'No, why should they?'

'I only wondered,' said Maitland innocently, 'because when Mr Horton and I made our examination one would have expected some dust to have gathered during the time the studio had been empty. Yet there was very little on the article of furniture to which we are referring, much less than on everything else.' He sat down quickly before Halloran could raise an objection, saying as he did so, 'I'm grateful to you, Chief Inspector, but I have no further questions.'

Halloran declined to re-examine. He must, Antony thought, have been puzzled by now, but he proceeded with his case just as he had obviously intended to all along. The Chief Inspector was followed by a number of police witnesses, the local men who were first on the scene, the fingerprint expert who had found no prints in Mr Wilmot's study that could not be accounted for in the way of normal use. After that there was the pathologist. The

170

weapon was introduced as an exhibit at this point, an ornate handle with a wicked-looking blade. There could be no doubt apparently that it was the instrument of Thomas Wilmot's death, and that he had died very shortly before Mrs Barham found him, a matter of minutes most likely. The blow that killed him was described as a single blow, struck upwards straight for the heart. 'You might almost say,' said Halloran, 'by someone with some knowledge of anatomy,' and paused, obviously waiting for Maitland's challenge. But counsel for the defence only smiled and shook his head at him and declined to cross-examine at all.

At this point Mr Justice Conroy obviously felt that they had gone on long enough, and adjourned until the following morning. Geoffrey went back to his office, clearly not looking forward to the coming interview, and Derek and Antony made their separate ways home. Gibbs waylaid Antony with a message from his uncle, but an account of the day's proceedings didn't detain him long.

'When you introduced M.B.'s letter into evidence,' asked Sir Nicholas when he had finished, 'I suppose that must be regarded as committing you to this insane course of action?'

'That and the paintings. Yes, I think I'm committed.'

'And you still intend to take the chance of calling him as a witness without a previous interview? Without even asking Geoffrey to see him?'

'I know what you're going to say, Uncle Nick, never ask a question unless you know the answer. That's fair enough in most cases, but here I have a feeling—' He broke off there, catching Vera's eye. 'Yes, I know,' he said apologetically. 'Feelings are just as much anathema to Uncle Nick as guesswork is. Tomorrow may be more interesting. Why don't you come to dinner, both of you, and I'll tell you what's transpired?'

'If Jenny agrees—' Vera started.

'You know Jenny'd like nothing better.'

Vera smiled her grim smile. 'And you?' she asked.

'I shall have to give an account of myself anyway,' said Antony, smiling back at her. 'It may as well be on my own ground.'

But Vera shook her head after he had left them.

'Don't think he's happy about the way things are going, Nicholas,' she said, and for once her husband replied to a remark of hers almost snappishly.

'He'd be a fool if he was,' he said.

Friday, the second day of the trial

I

The next morning started dully, in court that is, though Antony noticed with some misgivings that there were more members of the press corps present than there had been yesterday, and that all of them looked more alert. Perversely, outside the sun was shining with enough warmth to give an illusion that summer had already arrived.

Under Halloran's guidance – Maitland had a suspicion that he was as bored with this part of his case as anyone else in the room – a chartered accountant explained endlessly the very simple facts of Simon Winthrop's financial position: how many (or how few) paintings he sold and at what price, and how much he earned from the freelance commercial work he did. The rent he paid, which might be regarded to some extent as a business expense, was also gone into, and the amount of his expenditure, carefully noted down, on canvas and oils and all the other incidentals of his profession. The result, as even the dimmest jury could have seen if he had spoken for five minutes instead of fifty, was that there was obviously very little left for day to day living expenses, and Antony – he hoped – earned the court's gratitude by declining to cross-examine.

Thomas Wilmot's solicitor followed, and proved to be only slightly less verbose than the previous witness. In the circumstances, though he was named as executor, he had done nothing so far towards taking out probate, but since his late client's affairs had been in excellent order, he was able to estimate very closely the extent to which the prisoner would have, in the ordinary way, benefited from his grandfather's death. The house of course, being part of the residuary estate, would be put up for sale and you could never, as he pointed out, tell exactly how these things would go. Still, the amount he could have counted on would be close to half a million pounds, a statement which sent a sort of shudder through the jury box. It could hardly be envy of a man facing a life sentence, Maitland thought, but he was pretty sure there was some resentment mixed up in it, which could hardly do his client any good.

When his turn came, Maitland got to his feet in a leisurely way. 'Just one small matter,' he said. 'Simon Winthrop is not the only beneficiary from his grandfather's will, I believe?'

'No, indeed.'

This was going to be like drawing teeth, and the witness looked as though he found it just as painful to have to reveal facts which in the nature of things would soon be common knowledge. 'I suppose there were some minor bequests,' Antony prompted him, 'but it is the disposal of the residuary estate that interests me.'

'Mr Winthrop would have shared equally with his cousin, who is, I understand, the only son of his mother's sister.'

'What is this gentleman's name, and have you met him?'

'His name is Robert Camden, and he came to see me recently.' He paused a moment hopefully, but counsel was regarding him stonily and would obviously prod him with another question if he didn't amplify his reply. 'Mr Camden's family emigrated to Canada when he was a boy, and he only returned to this country about a fortnight ago, knowing nothing of his grandfather's death. When he tried to get in touch with Mr Wilmot he was naturally told what had happened, and equally naturally came to me for details.'

'Knowing nothing of his inheritance?'

'No, that came almost as a shock to him.'

'Still, as executor you felt it proper to advance him a sum of money for his immediate needs?'

'My lord!' said Halloran, getting up as quickly as his increasing bulk would allow, his booming voice almost drowning out the witness's rather huffy, 'I did.'

'I am sure my learned friend, Mr Maitland, would be glad to obscure the issue, but these questions have no reference to the matter that brought us here.'

'Have they not, my lord?' asked Maitland gently. 'I have no wish, of course, to waste the court's time, but in any case I have nothing further to ask the witness.'

'I'm glad to hear it,' said Conroy dryly. 'All the same, Mr Maitland, I agree with Mr Halloran that this line of questioning

174

is out of order. I should advise you to adhere more closely to the matter in hand in future.'

'I am obliged to your lordship.' Maitland's tone was a little too deferential. 'I am perhaps confused by the emphasis the prosecution has laid on the question of motive, which, as your lordship knows, is not strictly relevant either.'

'I believe I am as well aware of that as you are, Mr Maitland, and shall so instruct the jury when the time comes. Meanwhile I can only trust that you will remember what I have said.'

'Indeed, my lord, I shall.' A remark which was the literal truth, but made with certain mental reservations of which Conroy would not have approved.

Halloran, still on his feet, decided to re-examine, an exercise which achieved nothing except to remind the jury that if they set him free Simon Winthrop would find himself a rich and fortunate young man. After that Mr Justice Conroy decided on an early break for the luncheon recess. 'Though we will re-convene at one-thirty,' he added, 'as I imagine none of us is anxious to sit late just before the weekend.'

II

'Much ado about nothing,' said Stringer as they seated themselves. 'Do you think you achieved anything, Antony?' There was no malice in the question, just a straight desire for information.

'Nothing at all except to annoy old Conroy. And perhaps,' he added hopefully, 'to make Halloran wonder a little what I'm up to.'

'I should think he may well do that,' said Geoffrey. 'And your tactics are causing the vultures to gather; I expect you noticed that.' But he seemed resigned to the situation now, and didn't attempt to continue a discussion of the case. They got back to court in good time, and the first witness called by the prosecution was Madeleine Rexford.

This was one of the moments that Antony had been dreading because he thought he had a very good idea how the girl would be feeling. In a way he was grateful that the prosecution had called her and he hadn't been forced to ask Geoffrey to do so, but either way the experience would be just as bad for her.

175

At a casual glance she looked as calm and self-contained as ever. Maitland's study of her, however, was anything but casual. She was tense and it showed in the way she moved, in the way she spoke, in the quick look she allowed herself at the prisoner and the small smile that accompanied it. She took the oath in a low voice, and twice during his introductory questions Halloran had to ask her to speak a little more loudly. After that she answered him slowly and clearly, rather as if she were addressing a deaf person, and there could be no doubt that her words were clearly audible to everyone in court.

Halloran had decided on his avuncular manner, thought Maitland disrespectfully, intended partly to put the witness at her ease, and partly to induce in her a mood of confidence. 'Now, Miss Rexford, I am sure this is an unpleasant experience for you and I will try to make it as brief as possible. At the time of Thomas Wilmot's death you were engaged to be married, I believe, to Simon Winthrop?'

'I was, and I am.'

'I see. Would you mind telling the court how long you have known the accused?'

'I think a little over a year now.'

'And how long have you been engaged to him?'

'I can remember that quite clearly. He asked me to marry him on the sixth of June.'

'You had not known one another very long then?'

'No.' She stopped for a moment. 'I must have been wrong when I said a little over a year, because I remember that it was almost exactly six weeks after our first meeting that we became engaged.'

'When were you to have been married?'

She closed her eyes for a moment, and Antony had an uneasy feeling that the breaking point had come. But after a moment she answered steadily, 'Tomorrow.'

'I'm sorry to have to bring the matter up so inopportunely,' said Halloran, and Maitland took a moment to think, I was misjudging him, he really doesn't want to hurt her. 'But there is one more question I must ask you,' counsel was proceeding. 'After that rather quick engagement, why so long a delay over your marriage?'

'I didn't want the delay. I wish we hadn't waited.'

'The reluctance, then, was on the part of the accused?'

176

'Not in the way it sounds when you put it like that. It was just because he thought it was his duty to give me all kinds of things I don't really need or want. With what we both earn we could have managed perfectly well. In fact he could have spent more time on his own work, his serious work. But he said he must get a full-time job. There was a firm he'd worked for before, when he first branched out on his own and hadn't started to sell any of his paintings. They wanted him back, but they hadn't a vacancy immediately.'

'Thank you, Miss Rexford, that explains matters perfectly. Now, obviously you know Mr Winthrop very well. Do you think he wanted this full-time employment, which was bound to cut into the time he could devote to what you call his serious work?'

There was a long moment's silence before she answered. Almost as clearly as if she had said the words aloud Maitland knew she was thinking, I'm talking too much. 'I don't know. How could I know? Nobody knows what anyone else is really thinking.'

'I'm afraid, Miss Rexford, I must remind you that you are under oath to answer my questions truthfully.'

'Everything I've told you is true.'

'Except perhaps that last answer?'

'No one can tell what someone else is thinking,' she said again.

'Did Mr Winthrop never say anything to you on the subject?'

'Only that he didn't mind.'

'You believed him?'

'I think I minded more than he did. His own work was important.'

'Very well, we'll leave it there. Unless . . . Mr Maitland?'

'Yes, indeed I have some questions for Miss Rexford,' said Antony, getting up quickly. And because, since I knew she was being called by the prosecution I couldn't explain to her, and nor could Geoffrey, I shall probably hurt her even more than you have done. Unless the Patmores . . . he took what consolation he could from the thought that perhaps they had explained to her, as Geoffrey unwillingly had explained to them, the line the defence was taking.

'I, too, Miss Rexford, will not detain you long.' There was a slight wariness in her look, he thought, as she turned to face

177

him. 'My friend has gone at length into the fact of your engagement. Since you first met my client I suppose you have seen a good deal of him.'

'Oh yes, a great deal.'

'So you feel that you know him reasonably well?' He smiled at her. 'In view of what you said just now I realize you have reservations about the degree to which one person can know another, but you knew him well enough to agree to marry him. You trusted him sufficiently after – what was it? – six weeks' acquaintance to entrust your whole future to him?'

'Very willingly.'

'And you have had no reason to change your mind?'

'I haven't changed.'

'Tell me, Miss Rexford, what was your first thought when you heard of Thomas Wilmot's death and of my client's arrest?'

'I thought there'd been some dreadful mistake, I mean about what the police believed Simon had done.'

'And this instant reaction was based on what you knew of his character?'

'Yes, it was.'

'This next question is a little difficult, Miss Rexford, because I mustn't ask you to repeat what you heard from another person. But perhaps his lordship will permit me to inquire whether, after Mr Winthrop's arrest, you began to hear some strange things about him.'

Surprisingly neither the judge nor Counsel for the Prosecution intervened. 'Yes. Yes I did,' said Madeleine doubtfully. Her glance flickered for a moment towards the man in the dock, and then she was looking full at counsel again. 'Two things, to be exact,' she said, 'and both of them as impossible for Simon to have done as the murder was.'

'And what was your reaction to these stories?'

'I was confused at first, then I realised the truth of what I've just told you. Simon couldn't have killed his grandfather, and he couldn't have done . . . these other things.'

'Thank you, Miss Rexford. Like my learned friend I realise this is difficult for you. And my next question may be even more so. May I ask whether you ever, seeing as much of him as you did, noticed anything at all strange in my client's conduct?'

Her eyes were still fixed on his face and he read in them both bewilderment and the trust that he had both hoped for and

178

feared. 'Sometimes when we had arranged to meet he wouldn't turn up,' she said. 'The first few times it happened I asked him why, of course, and I got the definite impression that the question puzzled him, as though he remembered nothing at all about our arrangement. Then he'd find an excuse, not always the same one, quite frankly after the first or second time I didn't believe him. But he was still just the same . . . as loving . . . as kind . . . I made up an explanation for myself but I don't know if it was true. I decided he was one of those people who just had to be alone sometimes, and I'd just have to learn to live with it. So I never questioned him again.'

'Did they occur often, these fits of – shall we say – absent-mindedness?'

'Fairly often, but there was no regularity about them.'

'Did you ever mention them to anyone else, other than to Mr Winthrop himself on those first occasions you told us about?'

There was another pause before she answered that, while she eyed him in a bewildered way. 'I did, as a matter of fact,' she said, 'to a girl who has a flat on the same floor as mine.'

'How did that come about?'

'We were saving all we could you know, Simon and I, so mostly when we saw each other I'd make a meal at home, and then if we felt like it we'd go out afterwards. Or sometimes – usually when he had some new work to show me – Simon would get in Chinese food, or something like that. When it was my turn I used to make things as nice as I could, so that we could pretend we were eating in a good restaurant, and on that particular evening I had the table laid for two, with what was left of my mother's good china, and the candles were ready for lighting. It was getting rather late so I was wondering if Simon was coming at all when Freda knocked at the door.'

'Freda?'

'Freda Parkinson, the neighbour I spoke of. If we were both alone we would quite often have coffee together in the evening, and as she hadn't heard anyone come and she was alone herself . . . well, you can see how it was. As soon as she saw the table she said "Oh, you're expecting someone", and prepared to go. But I said no she should come in, because to tell you the truth I did feel a bit lonely and let down when that kind of thing happened, in spite of my good resolutions. And I told her I thought I was going to be alone after all, so if she hadn't eaten

179

we could share the meal.'

'And then, Miss Rexford?'

'She had eaten, I told you it was getting late, but perhaps she saw I'd welcome company so she came in after all. But I saw her looking rather curiously at the table once or twice, and at last she said, "You must have been expecting someone special, was it Simon?" because of course she knew about my engagement and I said, "Yes, but I suppose he must have had some work to finish," and when I saw she still thought it a bit odd I used the phrase you did just now and told her, making a joke of it, that he was dreadfully absent-minded.'

'You'll forgive me for pressing the point, Miss Rexford, but do you think this Miss Parkinson could have got the impression from what you told her that his forgetfulness was a frequent occurrence?'

'Yes, she could.' She paused again and he could almost see the words, I can't see why it should matter to you, quivering on her tongue. But she went on, rather, he thought, like a child reciting a poem it didn't understand. 'I can't remember our conversation word for word, but she did say, hadn't he phoned? And wasn't I worried there might have been an accident? And it was then I told her it was quite a frequent occurrence – nothing to make a fuss about.'

For some time Halloran had only too obviously been making up his mind whether to interrupt or not. Now, as Maitland said, 'Thank you, Miss Rexford, that is all I have to ask you,' counsel for the prosecution lumbered to his feet.

Madeleine hesitated, the judge looked inquiring, and Halloran said, not troubling this time to moderate his voice, 'No, my lord, thank you, I do not wish to re-examine. But I think the line my learned friend is taking requires some explanation.'

'In what way?' Maitland's tone was just a little too polite. From the corner of his eye he saw Madeleine leave the witness box, and an usher directing her to a place in the body of the court.

Mr Justice Conroy leaned forward. 'Yes, Mr Halloran, my mind has been running on much the same lines, I think, as yours. Perhaps you will explain to us, Mr Maitland.'

'With all respect, my lord, what is there to explain?'

'Are you by any chance endeavouring to lay the foundation for a plea of Not Guilty by reason of insanity? Is that the question that was in your mind, Mr Halloran?'

'It is, my lord. My learned friend is surely aware that when such an intention on the part of the defence becomes obvious in cross-examination it is the prosecution's right to call their own witnesses as to the state of mind of the accused.'

'I wonder,' said Maitland, who in a perverse sort of way was beginning to enjoy himself, 'what on earth could have got that into your mind?'

'The drift of your questions to the previous witness.' Halloran was perfectly well aware that he was being needled, but was too old a hand to allow his irritation to show. 'Your intention was sufficiently obvious for his lordship to have noticed it too.'

'I must apologize, my lord, if I've misled you.' Maitland sketched a bow in the direction of the bench. 'However, if my learned friend still entertains some doubts as to my intentions may I assure him that I should be only too happy if he were to call for a psychiatric examination of my client. I'm sure any competent man would find that he is as sane as . . . I should hesitate to say as sane as your lordship, but perhaps as my friend here, or myself.'

'Then I cannot understand the tenor of your questions,' said Conroy rather pettishly.

'If you'll have patience, my lord –'

'I can see I shall need to.' Mr Justice Conroy's tone was severe. 'Do you still wish for an adjournment while this examination is arranged, Mr Halloran?'

'If the prisoner is as sane as his counsel,' said Halloran nastily, 'it would obviously be of little use. May I proceed, your lordship?'

'Certainly, if that is your wish.'

'Then I shall call Cecil Arnold Alford.' Maitland took his seat again, and began to sketch a Viking ship doing duty as a funeral pyre on the back of his brief.

Cecil Alford turned out to be a smallish, sleek man who gave his profession as a businessman. Halloran's direct examination was short and to the point. Mr Alford had been leaving his house in company with his wife at nine o'clock on the evening of Thomas Wilmot's murder. He was sure of the time because he had consulted the clock just before they left to make sure they weren't too early. They had been invited for an after-dinner drink by some neighbours down the road. Thomas Wilmot's house was next door to his, but he scarcely knew the old gentleman except to say Good morning if they passed in the street. Nor had he ever met Mr Wilmot's grandson. That evening, however, as he and his wife were going down the steps from their front door, he saw a young, fair-haired man letting himself out of Mr Wilmot's house. A quite striking-looking young man, whom he identified now as the prisoner in the dock. Yes, there had been an identification parade previously at the police station, but he had not been shown, or seen accidentally, any photograph of Simon Winthrop before he picked him out on that occasion.

A positive, self-confident little man. Try then to shake that self-confidence a little. Antony took his time about getting to his feet, and paused for a perceptible moment before asking his first question. 'I realize, Mr Alford, that you are completely sincere in what you have told us, but according to your own evidence you cannot have seen this young man for very long.'

(Never ask a question unless you know the answer.) 'On the contrary, I observed him quite closely as he went down the steps to the street,' the witness asserted. 'If Mr Wilmot had guests in the evening they usually went to dinner and left at a later hour than nine, so I was a little surprised. I also have my share of curiosity.'

'You told my friend that you had only the barest acquaintance with Mr Wilmot.'

'Yes, but I knew a little about him from neighbourhood gossip.'

'That, I'm afraid, we can't take cognisance of, though no doubt his lordship will accept it as an explanation for your interest. But you are aware, I'm sure, that there have been cases – some of them as serious as this one – where the wrong man has been convicted on evidence of identification as sincere as that you have given.'

'I've read of such things, of course.'

'Have you ever heard of Adolf Beck?'

'The name seems vaguely familiar.'

'Then perhaps I may refresh your memory. He was charged, not once but twice, and convicted, not once but twice, of another man's crimes.' He broke off and turned to the judge. 'My lord, I should like to enter into evidence photographs of the two men concerned. It will be seen that the resemblance

182

between them is only superficial.'

'I'm afraid, Mr Maitland, that you have laid no foundation for such a request.'

'And I submit, my lord, that the foundation was laid when my client pleaded Not Guilty.'

'I don't think we can accept that. What do you think, Mr Halloran?'

'I agree with your lordship, the matter is not relevant.'

'You see, Mr Maitland?'

'My lord, I must protest. The question of identification is of vital interest to my client and cannot be called irrelevant.'

'No, Mr Maitland,' said the judge flatly.

Behind him Antony heard Geoffrey murmur something that sounded suspiciously like, I told you so. He allowed the silence to lengthen a little before he said, repeating himself, 'It is surprising how little likeness the photographs show between the two men.' And added quickly, before Halloran could raise another objection or the judge utter another rebuke, 'I apologize, my lord, I will withdraw the statement and merely ask the witness whether he is still quite sure of the identification he has made.'

'Quite sure,' said Cecil Alford. 'I should not have made it otherwise.'

After that there was Adela Alford, whose testimony echoed her husband's in every respect. It hardly seemed worth while to cross-examine, but as a matter of duty he did his best to shake her certainty. She lacked her husband's positive manner, but perhaps her insistence that she couldn't have been mistaken was all the more telling for that. For some reason when Maitland sat down Halloran glanced at his watch and decided to re-examine. There seemed to be no reason for this, everything was tied up nicely and tightly already, and when the court adjourned a little early, as the judge had promised, Antony turned to Geoffrey. 'What's he up to?' he asked.

For once in his life Geoffrey didn't start his reply with the words, 'If you'd only read your brief'. Instead he said, for all the world as if he had expected the question, 'He's only one witness left, his star witness I suppose you'd call her, Mrs Mary Barham. If she gives her evidence on Monday morning before we start our part of the proceedings, the jury won't have the whole weekend to forget what she has to say.'

'Yes, it was a stupid question,' said Maitland, though nothing in Horton's tone had implied as much. He looked from one of his companions to the other. 'Do you think we need to get together again over the weekend?' he asked.

'I don't see that it would do any good,' said Derek. 'Do you, Geoffrey?'

'Meaning, the case is hopeless?' said Antony challengingly.

'Meaning that you know exactly what you're going to do and you'll do it no matter what either of us say,' said Derek with unusual frankness. 'I should think you'd be glad of the chance to forget all about it for a couple of days.'

'If only I could.' His papers and books were piled together now and he turned to look for Willett, who proved to be hovering a few feet away. 'I shan't go back to chambers,' he said. 'Take these for me, there's a good chap.' Then he turned back to the others. 'I agree with you, there's no use our getting together again,' he said, in a tone that endeavoured to make light of the matter. 'But you might spare a little sympathy for me. Uncle Nick and Vera are coming to dinner tonight.'

III

For once he got home before his visitors had come upstairs. 'Was it a very bad day?' asked Jenny anxiously as soon as she saw him.

'Is it so obvious? I've known better,' he admitted. He was tired and moving stiffly, but both of them knew she wouldn't comment on that. 'I'll tell you about it when the others arrive, I don't want to have to go through it twice.'

'Of course not, but I'm not going to let you wait till they come to have a drink,' said Jenny firmly. 'Would you like something stronger than sherry, just this once?'

'No, I don't think so. Not before the bottle of wine I'm sure you've laid in, in the hope of mellowing Uncle Nick's mood,' said Antony. He went across to the chair opposite the one his uncle would presently take and sat down rather heavily. 'My dear and only love,' he said, 'what should I do without you?'

'Starve probably,' said Jenny literally. 'And pour your own drink, of course,' she added coming across the room and putting the glass down beside him. 'You're not as late as I expected,' she

184

went on. 'Has Mr Halloran finished putting on his case?'

'No, not yet. He spun out time with some quite unnecessary re-examination, so that he could put on the most important witness on Monday morning,' Antony explained. 'He's a cunning old so-and-so, but I don't really blame him. You know what juries are, they'll have forgotten everything they've heard over the weekend.'

At that point Sir Nicholas and Vera arrived, and were greeted and provided with drinks while Antony sipped his own thoughtfully. 'You'd better tell us the worst,' said Sir Nicholas as soon as they were all settled. 'If you proceeded on the lines you laid down for us I imagine you got pretty badly mangled.'

'That must be an expression you've caught from Vera,' said Antony smiling at his aunt. 'If you're not careful, Uncle Nick, she'll turn you into a human being with as many failings as the rest of us.'

Vera scowled at him, which he took at its face value – a warning, not disapproval. 'Matter of fact I said run over by a steam-roller,' she told him. 'Don't imagine Halloran would sit still and let you get away with anything.'

'He didn't,' said Antony. 'Nor old Conroy. If you want to hear the whole melancholy story – '

'From the beginning,' said his uncle. He paused to pick up his glass. 'Omitting no detail, however slight,' he said. The words might be light, but there was very little encouragement to be found in his expression.

'Here goes then.' It was not one of Sir Nicholas's evenings for listening passively to what he considered an account of somewhat reprehensible behaviour. His interruptions were frequent, and long before he had finished Maitland, tired as he was, got up out of his chair and began to move restlessly about the room. 'And that's really all,' he said at last, 'except that Halloran has managed to reserve his s-star witness for Monday morning.' He went to the window and pulled back the curtain; the square would be almost deserted now, but all he could see was his own reflection in the glass. 'I know you b-both think I'm m-mad,' he said at last. 'And perhaps Jenny does too, though she hasn't said so.' He dropped the curtain and turned back to face them again. 'Any c-comments?' he asked.

'Halloran is a formidable opponent,' said Sir Nicholas, with a mildness that surprised them all. 'I think you should have remembered that.'

'I did, sir, you may be sure. Nothing that happened today surprised me.'

'Your client has pleaded Not Guilty, and you have effectively closed the door on any possibility of qualifying that by claiming diminished responsibility,' said his uncle. He was speaking consideringly, but Antony knew him well enough to wait for the sting in the tail of his remarks. It came soon enough. 'You have further laid the foundation for accusing, on no grounds whatever except those of motive, a man who was quite definitely not in this country at the time of the murder. If you expect any applause for your actions I'm afraid you'll have to wait a very long time.'

'Uncle Nick' – there was a note almost of pleading in Maitland's voice – 'we've disagreed about the conduct of cases before, but I don't think ever quite so . . . so radically.'

'Should I congratulate you on your perspicacity? Good heavens, boy, you can't have thought I would approve. If you genuinely believe your client is sane –'

'I do, sir. As sane as I am. It isn't saying much, I suppose, as Halloran was careful to point out.'

'As I was saying before you interrupted me, if you genuinely think Simon Winthrop is sane, surely you could at least be content to explain that there were extenuating circumstances.'

'Be brought out anyway,' said Vera. 'Can't help that.'

'I don't want to help it,' Maitland protested. 'But don't you think he deserves a chance at least to clear his name?'

'You're thinking about that business up in Yorkshire,' said Sir Nicholas accusingly.

'What b-business, for h-heaven's sake?'

'Have you forgotten already? It was a very short time ago.' He eyed his nephew more closely. 'No, I see you haven't forgotten, but may I remind you that such things are very rare in domestic murders. It would be one of those coincidences you hate so much if you were dealing again with a hired killer. There is also the question of how Robert Camden is supposed to have found such a man?'

'They're not unknown in North America, I understand,' said Maitland mildly. He was trying very hard indeed to keep a rein on his temper.

'So that is what you're thinking? My dear boy, consider for a moment. You're postulating a deliberate attempt to blacken your client's name beforehand. Could this Robert Camden afford that kind of a fee, let alone find a man who resembled his cousin sufficiently to be mistaken for him on the night of the murder? Remember, they've never met.'

'I don't think I'm forgetting . . . anything,' said Antony, but there was a touch of doubt in his tone. 'Look here, Uncle Nick, couldn't we just take your opinion for granted and let it go at that? The identification business, I think, was a bit of pure luck for Camden. It made all that went before unnecessary, which is why the police have never been informed, but nobody could have foreseen the Alfords.'

'Very well, we'll leave the subject,' Sir Nicholas agreed. But in spite of that he hadn't quite finished what he had to say. 'It is only,' he added, 'that I've never known you before completely to disregard a client's interests.'

Yes, the sting in the tail was there all right. Nothing more was said on the subject that evening, but throughout the weekend that followed Maitland found his uncle's words quite impossible to forget.

Monday, the third day of the trial

I

When Mrs Mary Barham was ushered into the witness box the following Monday morning the first description that came into Maitland's mind was that she was a comfortable body. There was an air of – he sought for the word for a moment – of benevolence about her that he thought augured ill for his client if she persisted in her identification.

Halloran, of course, was feeling no pain at all. The jury were about to be reminded just how strong the prosecution's case was. He spoke to his witness rather, Antony thought, as though she were a Dresden figurine and might break if handled too roughly. The good lady herself showed no signs of nervousness, but as the questioning progressed Maitland realized only too clearly that she was hating every moment of it. But she was there to tell the truth, and tell it she would though the heavens fall.

She gave her name and the late Mr Wilmot's address, where she was still living, keeping an eye on things. She and her husband had looked after Mr Wilmot – though no rough work, mind you – for over twenty years, though she couldn't after so long remember the exact date they had gone to work for him. A fine old man, but lonely these last years. 'I shall soon be the only one left of my generation, Mrs Barham,' he'd said to her more than once, but he was a little impatient with younger people and hadn't seemed to want to make new friends. Simon – Mr Winthrop she should say – came to dinner regularly, however, which was how Mr Wilmot liked it. Certain days set aside for certain things, in this case always the first Sunday of the month. Halloran was letting her have her head, and Maitland saw no reason to intervene. The jury were entitled to as good a picture as they could get of the dead man's household and he had no wish to attract the judge's attention before he need.

188

But at last counsel for the prosecution decided that his witness had had enough latitude, that it was time to get down to the part of her evidence that was really important. 'I'm sorry to have to ask you this, madam, but will you cast your mind back to the night of Thomas Wilmot's murder and tell us exactly what you remember of it.'

'Yes, of course. When he was alone he liked to dine early, and I gave him his meal at seven o'clock. Afterwards he went back to the study where he always liked to sit, and I cleared away and filled the dishwasher – well not to say filled, with only the three of us, but put in the things that had been used – and then went to join Charlie, that's my husband, in our sitting-room at the back of the house.'

'Just one moment, Mrs Barham. I should like you to look at the weapon that was used to kill Mr Wilmot. Again, I'm sorry to distress you, but it is necessary for us to know whether you have seen it before.'

There was a brief pause while the dagger was produced.

'Nasty-looking thing, isn't it?' asked Mrs Barham conversationally. 'Yes, of course, I know it quite well. It lay on the table just inside the study door for quite six years now. I told Mr Wilmot he shouldn't keep such a heathen-looking thing about, but he said it reminded him of the days when his life had been fuller, and he wouldn't let me put it away.'

'So that the prisoner, as a regular visitor, would know quite well where it was?'

'If you mean Mr Winthrop, yes he would. Mr Wilmot might have used the drawing-room for special guests, but he preferred the study and always used it when Simon came.' She had carefully avoided looking towards the dock ever since she came into the court, but now she turned and looked directly at the man there. He met her gaze steadily. 'I'm sorry,' she said, 'but I have to tell the truth.'

'I think, Mr Halloran, you should explain to your witness that she must address the court, and not the prisoner,' said Mr Justice Conroy.

'Certainly, my lord.' But Halloran was not ill-pleased by this deviation from courtroom etiquette. 'You're fond of Mr Winthrop, are you not?' he asked the witness.

'If you're thinking it's not my place to be fond of the master's relations,' said Mrs Barham with spirit, 'I've known Simon since he was a boy.'

'Mr Halloran!' said Conroy, almost despairingly.

'I believe, my lord, that the answer to my question was in the affirmative,' said Halloran, 'That was what you meant, wasn't it, Mrs Barham, that you are fond of Mr Winthrop?'

'Yes, I am.' Maitland thought that she realized as well as everyone else present that the admission only made her evidence more damning.

'On the evening in question, the evening of March the first, you went into the hall and saw somebody leaving the house. Had you known Mr Wilmot had a visitor?'

'No, I hadn't.' She paused a moment as though getting up her courage for what must be said. 'I was surprised to see Simon because he was due for dinner the next day, but then I thought perhaps something had happened to prevent him from coming then so he'd called to explain.'

'You are quite positive that the man you saw leaving the house at nine o'clock that evening –'

'I couldn't speak definitely to the time but it was around then.'

'The real point, Mrs Barham, is, are you sure it was Mr Simon Winthrop that you saw.'

'Quite sure. I told you I've known him since he was a child.'

'Did he speak to you?'

'No, I only got a glimpse of him and he may not have seen me. He went out and shut the door.'

'What happened then?'

'I went into the study and found poor Mr Wilmot lying dead. I gave a scream as anyone would, loud enough for Charlie to hear and he came running, and it was he who called the doctor and the police.'

And that, in essence, was her story, except for the fact that Simon Winthrop had a key to the house in his possession, because his grandfather had an excellent collection of books on art and had given him permission to come in and refer to them any time he liked. 'Thank you, Mrs Barham, that is all I have to ask you,' said Halloran at last. 'But I'm afraid my learned friend who is appearing for the defence will have a good many questions for you.'

'Not so many, Mrs Barham,' said Maitland, rising. As she turned a little to face him he gave her his sudden smile, and for the first time that morning her expression lightened a little. It

190

was as though she was saying, 'You're his friend, isn't there anything you can do for him?' The question came to him so clearly that he almost answered aloud, 'I'll do my best', though that was a phrase he hated and very rarely used. 'You have told us,' he said gently, 'that Mr Winthrop had a key to the house, but the police state that the latch was up when they arrived, so that anyone could have walked in. Was that usual?'

'No it wasn't, but –'

'But, Mrs Barham?' He prompted when she hesitated.

'I've known Mr Wilmot to do that if he was expecting a guest of an evening. He was always considerate, and said we shouldn't be disturbed once dinner was over.'

'I see. So if someone he knew had phoned earlier in the day expressing the intention of calling on him –'

'My lord, this is no more than speculation,' Halloran protested.

'Yes, Mr Halloran, but I think in this case it would be interesting to hear the witness's reply.'

Mrs Barham took no notice of either of them, but continued to look straight at Counsel for the Defence. 'He always said we'd a right to some time to ourselves,' she told him. 'If that had happened no doubt he'd have fixed the door so that they could let themselves in, and never said a word to me. You see, the front door bell rings in the kitchen, he wouldn't hear it, so it would be no use telling me he'd answer it himself.'

'Thank you, that makes it very clear. So we come to the difficult question of identification. I'm sure you've thought about this very carefully –'

'It's gone over and over in my mind ever since that night.'

'Yes, I'm sorry. But perhaps you would tell us what made you so sure that it was my client you saw.'

For a moment she stared at him as though she didn't understand the question. 'To use your own words, Mrs Barham, you had no more than a glimpse of him,' Maitland reminded her after a while.

'That's right, but how could I make a mistake? Someone I knew so well.'

'Let's take his features one by one,' Maitland suggested. 'There aren't many men as fair as he is, but certainly there are some, even probably in your own neighbourhood.'

She was, unfortunately, an uncomfortably intelligent woman.

191

'I know that, sir, but the way it grows, in exactly the same shape as his poor grandfather's though Mr Wilmot had been a dark man in his day. And the shape of his head too . . . I'd like to say I was mistaken, but I can't.'

'Did you see his face?'

'Not his full face.'

'Like my learned friend, I don't like asking you to think about that evening,' Maitland told her, 'but if you could think for a moment and tell us exactly what you saw.'

She closed her eyes, as though to shut out the present and see only the past. 'He had the door half open,' she said, 'and his back was to me, but he turned his head a little, so perhaps he did hear me after all. He didn't turn all the way. I saw the shape of his head, the line of his cheek, the set of his shoulders, the way he moved as he slipped round the door. That's all I can tell you.'

Geoffrey might have been heard to mutter, and quite enough. Derek, in fact, did hear him, but Antony—as always when he was in court—was completely absorbed in his witness. 'What was he wearing?'

'A grey suit.'

'One that you had seen before?'

'Not that I remember, but there was nothing remarkable about it. He always took care to dress neatly when he came to see his grandfather. Mr Wilmot didn't like sloppiness.'

'Then there's only one more thing, Mrs Barham. You have told us how considerate your employer was, how he thought you and your husband were entitled to some time to yourselves in the evening. Why did you come into the hall at precisely that time, and then go to the study?' She stared at him for a long moment. 'Didn't anyone ask you that before?' he inquired, and smiled at her again.

'I suppose they thought it was quite natural, it being my home in a manner of speaking.'

'Yes, I suppose they did. But will you tell me now?'

'Yes, of course. It's a queer thing I hadn't thought of it from that day to this. I came because the bell rang.'

'The front door bell?'

'No, the one in the study. Mr Wilmot didn't often use it, but of course I thought he wanted something so I went to see what it was. And afterwards—I suppose it was the shock—I never thought how queer it was, because if he was dead how could he have rung the bell? And he wasn't lying anywhere near it, he couldn't have been trying to get help.'

'We're driven to the conclusion, then, that the visitor himself rang for you. Mr Winthrop would have known, but I think anyone could have guessed, that either you or your husband would answer immediately. It's almost as though the man who killed Mr Wilmot wanted him to be found without any delay.'

'I don't understand,' she said. 'I don't understand it at all.'

'Then I suggest, Mrs Barham, that you try to put all this out of your mind, don't distress yourself any further. Unless, of course, my friend has any further questions for you.'

Halloran was on his feet. 'No more questions,' he rumbled. 'Thank you, Mrs Barham, the usher will show you where you should sit.' He turned for a moment to his opponent, giving him a hard look, and then, more deferentially, addressed the judge. 'My lord, I realize that this matter has already been dealt with in what should have been a final way, but my learned friend's attitude forces me to ask again whether he intends to qualify his client's plea in any way.'

'Well, Mr Maitland?'

'If my learned friend will be more explicit, my lord, I shall try to answer him.'

'There have been references to unexpected behaviour on the part of the prisoner,' said Halloran, not waiting for the judge to speak again. 'Some stress has been laid on the fact that at times he shows signs of absent-mindedness, and now it is suggested that when he rang the bell to summon the dead man's housekeeper it was hardly a rational act.'

'Do you think it would have been?' asked Maitland amiably.

'What I think has nothing to do with the case.'

'No, I agree with you there. Like the flowers that bloom in the spring,' added counsel, who was only too apt to forget himself on occasion.

'Mr Maitland?'

'They had nothing to do with the case either, my lord,' said Antony apologetically. 'And my answer to my friend's question is still the same as it was on Friday. I think there is an explanation for Mrs Barham being summoned to the study at that particular time, though if my client had done so it would certainly have been irrational. But you see,' he added gently, 'I don't think he was anywhere near at the time.'

193

And there, though Halloran was obviously dissatisfied, the matter had to be left. Counsel for the prosecution had no further witnesses to call, and Maitland's opening address, brief though it was, carried them through to the adjournment for the luncheon recess.

THE CASE FOR THE DEFENCE
Monday, the third day of the trial

I

If Maitland had already succeeded in puzzling and surprising not only his opponent but the judge himself, his direct examination of his client only made matters worse. As soon as the preliminaries were over he said, 'I'm sure that the members of the jury will be tired by now of hearing either myself or my friend for the prosecution assuring the witness that we shall not keep him or her long, but I'm going to say it again to you, Mr Winthrop, and this time they will not be disappointed. I have two questions only. The first is, did you kill your grandfather, Thomas Wilmot?'

'No, I didn't.'

'Where were you at the time of his death?'

'I don't know. I've forgotten. I do get these blackouts sometimes.'

And that was that. Halloran assumed an 'I can't believe my ears' attitude, but rose readily enough to cross-examine. 'So you can offer the court no alibi, Mr Winthrop?'

'How can I, under the circumstances?'

'This convenient loss of memory, you say it has happened before.'

'On and off as long as I remember.'

'Since you were a small child?'

'I don't know for sure. I just don't know when it all started.'

'I'm afraid I don't understand that.'

'I don't remember my parents, but I've been told they died when I was seven. All I remember is living with Mr and Mrs Norman Patmore, who adopted me.'

'Since you were seven years old, at least, these incidents have been occurring?'

'Yes.'

'And nobody ever noticed?'

'I think now they did. You heard what Madeleine – Miss

195

Rexford – told you last week. If I could forget a date with her I could forget anything. Sometimes my mother – '

'You said just now you couldn't remember your parents.'

'Mrs Patmore. I've never thought of her and her husband in any other way.'

'You were going to tell us – ?'

'Sometimes when I was still a schoolboy she used to ask me where I'd been and I couldn't tell her because I didn't know.'

'But you never told her the truth?'

'I was ashamed to admit that I had these lapses of memory. It made me seem different from other people. I don't know why, but I couldn't face that.'

'Has it happened since your arrest?'

'Only once. I don't know if anyone saw me during that time, I don't think it was very long.'

'I see,' said Halloran, in a tone that meant he didn't. 'So no one can confirm what you're telling us?'

'I only found out myself the other day why it happened.'

Before he could go any further Maitland was on his feet. 'My lord, may I ask the court's indulgence,' he said. 'What my client can tell you would be hearsay only. When my learned friend has finished his cross-examination I shall be calling Dr Macintyre, a psychiatrist, perhaps not unknown to your lordship, who will be able to explain why it has been, if not completely natural at least not surprising, for my client to suffer from these lapses of memory. He will be followed by Mr and Mrs Norman Patmore, who can tell you at first hand, as Dr Macintyre cannot, exactly what happened when my client's parents died.'

'That's all very well, Mr Maitland.' Conroy's eye was severe. 'Do you still tell us that you're not preparing the ground for a plea of diminished responsibility?'

'No, my lord, I'm not. It is a matter on which my client cannot speak for himself, of his own knowledge. It was on my advice that he pleaded Not Guilty, and I firmly believe that that was the right thing for him to do, and without any qualification at all.'

'You speak very confidently Mr Maitland.' (Oh lord, I wish I were!) 'If you are going to suggest that the accused went to Mr Wilmot's house and found his grandfather already dead, may I remind you that the medical evidence is against you?'

'I am aware of that, my lord.' He was conscious of Derek

196

beside him, underlining something he had written; a possible point for an appeal perhaps, but he hadn't time to think about that now. 'Will your l-lordship accept my assurance, once and f-for all–' He broke off there, realizing suddenly that he was getting on to unnecessarily dangerous ground.

The judge looked at him hard for a moment. 'Very well, if Mr Halloran agrees we will proceed as you ask. Mr Halloran?'

'Provided, my lord, that I can finish my cross-examination on matters which come within the prisoner's own knowledge, and that I shall be at liberty to recall him to the witness stand later if that should seem necessary.'

'That is reasonable enough. Does it content you, Mr Maitland?'

'My learned friend is most generous,' said Maitland non-committally.

'Very well, Mr Halloran, you may proceed.'

'Then let us see, Mr Winthrop.' It wasn't the first time Antony had realized how formidable counsel for the prosecution could be when he wished, and at the moment he would have welcomed a more friendly atmosphere. He could see the sweat breaking out on Simon's forehead, and no wonder, poor chap. 'Before your arrest you were engaged to be married?'

'I was.'

'You didn't feel obliged to tell your fiancée about this alleged mental condition of yours?'

'I'm not mad.'

'You didn't feel she had a right to know?'

'I think she knew . . . almost as much about it as I did myself. She accepted me as I was.'

'And yet you delayed your marriage, according to what she told us, beyond what she would have wished.'

'Everything Madeleine told you was true.'

'But was the reason you gave for the delay also the truth?'

'Yes.'

'Because your financial position was unsatisfactory?'

'I think,' said Simon, 'that you know as much, or possibly more, about that than I do myself. The police took possession of all my records, and you heard what they made of them.'

'Confine yourself to answering counsel's questions, Mr Winthrop,' Mr Justice Conroy advised.

Simon glanced doubtfully from the judge to Maitland, but did

197

not attempt to reply. Halloran's voice recalled his attention. 'Would the full-time job you were contemplating have made all that difference?'

'A difference because I'd have been pulling my weight. We still shouldn't have been wealthy.'

'Did you know the terms of your grandfather's will?'

'Yes, he told me when I was twenty-one, and after that he talked about it often enough. He had this thing about man the provider. Perhaps,' he added, as though the thought had just struck him, 'that's where my own feeling that I should put off my marriage until I was in better shape financially came from.'

'An answer to everything, Mr Winthrop. Everything except the really important things. Do you really expect the court to believe that you don't know where you were while somebody – your double, presumably – was stabbing your grandfather to death?'

'I don't expect anything. How can I?'

'Your plea of Not Guilty. How can you be so sure that that is true?'

'Because the whole idea revolts me. Grandfather wasn't the sort of man you could love, but I respected him deeply and the idea of harming him . . . I couldn't have done that and not remembered it.'

'On that point at least I can agree with you. You've been here in court while Mr and Mrs Alford, and then this morning Mrs Barham, identified you positively as the man they had seen leaving your grandfather's house immediately after the murder. Are you saying they were all lying?'

'No, I'm sure they weren't. At least, I don't know the Alfords but I can't see why they should, and Mrs Barham . . . as she told you I've known her as long as I remember. She wouldn't have tried to hurt me unless she couldn't help it.'

'That is very generous of you, Mr Winthrop.' The sarcasm in Halloran's voice was very marked. 'And so you've no explanation to offer us, and there are points in your evidence that I am for the moment debarred from going into.'

'I didn't give much evidence, I couldn't. I only said I didn't kill my grandfather, and don't know where I was that evening.'

'I'm grateful for the reminder. You may stand down, Mr Winthrop, unless your own counsel has some further questions for you, but you'll remember my proviso. You may be called upon to undergo further cross-examination, and if you are I shall remind you at that time that you will still be under oath.'

Derek scribbled a note on the small pad he kept for the purpose and thrust it under his leader's nose. 'Chap talks too much,' it said baldly, and Maitland grinned at him absent-mindedly but made no reply. He was already concentrated on Dr Macintyre and wondering whether he'd been mistaken in calling him before the Patmores. It might have been better . . .

But whether he was right or wrong, it was too late to worry now. He'd used the doctor's evidence too often to be in doubt about the preliminaries. Between them they rattled off the impressive list of qualifications glibly enough, but not too quickly for the jury to take them in and be duly impressed.

'The first question I want to ask you, Doctor,' said Maitland when they had finished, 'does not directly concern the case, but out of kindness to my learned friend, who doesn't yet seem to be convinced of the truth of what I tell him, I should like you to assure the court of the basis on which I asked you to examine my client. It was not, as I'm sure you will confirm, that I had any doubts as to his sanity.'

'Wouldn't have done any good if you had,' said Macintyre at his most laconic. 'I should have told you the idea was sheer nonsense. These periodic fits of amnesia from which he suffers are perfectly normal in the circumstances. Which you left to me to explain to him,' he added with a touch of tartness.

'With your experience, Doctor, I thought the explanation would come better from you,' said Maitland smoothly, and watched the witness grin irrepressibly. 'I should explain, my lord, that the account of the traumatic experience which my client underwent as a child was given to me by his adoptive parents, and the defence will be calling both of them to confirm it. In these circumstances, I must ask you to hear what the doctor has to say, and not regard it strictly as hearsay evidence.'

'It sounds very much like hearsay to me,' said Conroy. 'However, if some confirmation is to be forthcoming . . . is this the point you have been trying to lay a foundation for, Mr Maitland?'

'It is, my lord. A complete explanation of why my client cannot remember the events of the night of his grandfather's death.'

'It may explain his forgetfulness,' said the judge rather tartly, 'but that in itself will not prove his innocence.'

'No, my lord, I realize that. You must remember that I have barely begun calling my witnesses.'

Conroy obviously didn't like the sound of that, but he picked up his pen again and said rather ungraciously, 'You may proceed.'

'If your lordship pleases. I think perhaps, Doctor, we had better begin with the matter I asked you to break to my client when you went to see him in prison.'

'If that's the way you want it. You told me what you knew of the accident that caused his parents' death when he was seven years old, and of which he was the only survivor.' Fortunately the doctor did not need any prompting, and even Halloran heard him out in silence.

'Thank you, that's very clear,' said Maitland when he had finished. 'Now, perhaps, Doctor, you could explain to us a little about amnesia.'

'Amnesia,' said the doctor, settling himself as comfortably as the confines of the witness box allowed and obviously preparing to enjoy himself, 'could well be expected after an experience such as this child of seven had undergone. It can be defined as a functional disturbance of memory, and at the time was no doubt diagnosed as being of the retrograde type. In no circumstances can the memory of events immediately preceding the experience be expected to return without some prompting, but it was quite possible that remembrance of his parents and his life with them would come back eventually. Even if it had done there would have been the possibility later of the subject suffering from headaches, attacks of giddiness, and possibly loss of memory, but as everything preceding the accident seems to have remained blotted out, I can only conclude that the later attacks of amnesia were of the hysterical variety. This must not be confused with hysteria in the sense that the word is generally used. Hysterical amnesia is a condition in which the patient retreats from certain memories, a defence mechanism against something it would be intolerable to call to mind. Is that sufficient for your purpose, Mr Maitland, or do you require any further explanation?'

'The information is very adequate, Doctor, but I'm afraid I've still one or two questions for you. When you told my client about the accident that killed his parents how did he react?'

'I was quite prepared for the information to bring on another attack,' said Macintyre, 'and quite determined that it should not be allowed to do so. I made him remember step by step until everything was out in the open between us. And then he did what was perhaps the best thing he could have done. He began to cry as though he were a child again.' He paused and glanced at the prisoner. 'I should be glad to know whether the attacks have returned since that time,' he said.

'From what Mr Winthrop told my friend under cross-examination I believe not,' Maitland told him. 'But you said just now, Doctor, that you expected your story to bring on another attack of amnesia if you weren't very careful about it. Do you think that is what has happened on the previous occasions when he has, as I believe I've heard you call it, retreated from reality?'

'Yes, I think so. A sudden realization that he could remember nothing of his early life for instance, or even a chance remark that reminded him that Mr and Mrs Patmore were not his real parents. He would be on the brink of remembering, and he couldn't face it, and so momentarily everything was wiped from his mind.'

'One moment, Doctor.' Maitland turned to the judge again. 'I have already, my lord, put into evidence a letter which was found in my client's desk by Mr Horton and myself after the police had completed their search. At the same time we found this newspaper clipping, which again I should like labelled as an exhibit. I should also like the opportunity of asking Chief Inspector Conway whether he saw it during the police search of my client's studio.'

'This is very irregular, Mr Maitland.'

'I agree with your lordship that the circumstances are unusual,' said Maitland, twisting Conroy's meaning a little.

'Very well, very well. The Chief Inspector is in court. Do you wish Dr Macintyre to stand down while he takes the witness box again?'

'A glance should be sufficient, if you will permit him to look at the exhibit.'

There was a moment's delay while Conway came forward. A moment later he was nodding. 'There were some newspapers on the floor by one of the armchairs,' he said, 'and I recall that this cutting was on top of them. But it seemed of no significance, so I left it where it was.'

'And very naturally,' said Maitland cordially. 'Thank you,

Chief Inspector, that is all I wanted from you. I should like to explain to the court that Mr Horton and I had no reason at that time to think the cutting of any significance. If the usher would kindly pass it to the witness . . . will you tell us what it concerns, Doctor? The headlines would suffice.'

'THREE DEAD IN BURNING CAR,' read Macintyre. 'There is also a rather graphic picture of a car, the remains of a car, that had crashed into a tree. This was found in Mr Winthrop's studio, you say?'

'Yes, Doctor. And what I want you to tell us is, could seeing this have been one of the sort of incidents that could have sent my client into a state of temporary amnesia?'

'I don't see how it could have failed to do so.' He turned to look at the man in the dock who was staring down at his hands clasped in his lap. 'Simon!' he said sharply, and Winthrop looked up. 'You are not going to forget again,' Dr Macintyre said slowly. 'You know what happened to your parents and you have accepted the fact. It was a long time ago and they couldn't have suffered for very long. You are not going to forget again.'

The judge was thumping his desk with his gavel. 'I will not have this court turned into a psychiatrist's consulting room,' he said. 'Dr Macintyre, there is a time and a place for everything.'

'I apologize, my lord,' Maitland put it quickly. 'I have just one more question for the witness before I throw him to the wolves.'

'I beg your pardon,' said Conroy incredulously.

'Before I finish my direct examination, my lord.'

'You are not by any chance referring to counsel for the prosecution as a wolf?'

'Nothing could be further from my thoughts, my lord. A manner of speaking, I regret the informality.'

'Very well then, ask your question. But I should advise you to be very careful.'

'It is just this, Doctor. You say that newspaper account is the sort of the thing you meant might have induced a fit of amnesia in my client?'

'I think it would undoubtedly have done so.'

'If he found it that evening, the evening his grandfather died, he'd have forgotten all about his appointment with Miss Rexford, and closed his mind completely to what had happened?'

'It is, of course, impossible to swear to that, but my own

opinion is that reading it would have had that result.'

'And the amnesia might have lasted for several hours?'

'With a shock like that, a description of an almost parallel case, very likely.'

'Very well, Doctor, I'm deeply indebted to you. But I'm sure Mr Halloran has his own set of questions.'

He was quite right about that, of course. Halloran attacked the evidence with everything he knew and by the time he had finished it was rather later than the usual hour for adjournment.

'Don't look so pleased with yourself,' Horton adjured his friend as they left the court together. 'We've given the court a possible explanation for our client's lack of an alibi, no more than that. And even if the attack of amnesia is accepted in full it doesn't preclude his having killed his grandfather.'

'I thought you'd come round to my way of thinking, Geoffrey.'

'I have, I think. I'm telling you how it will look to the jury. None of the witnesses to identification were shaken in the slightest degree, and Mrs Barham, the most important of them, is obviously sympathetic to Winthrop.'

'Don't be such a little ray of sunshine,' said Antony. 'I know the difficulties as well as you do, and I know what constitutes legal proof and what doesn't. But Macintyre came up to proof magnificently, and that, for the time being, is enough to be going on with.'

'Yes, I suppose so,' said Geoffrey rather grudgingly.

'I'm more concerned at the moment,' said Maitland thoughtfully, 'about what Uncle Nick will say when he hears Conroy complained that I was turning the court into a psychiatrist's consulting room.'

Geoffrey grinned. 'I should be more concerned, if I were you,' he said, 'as to what he will say when he hears that you referred to your learned opponent as a wolf, even by implication.'

II

On reflection it seemed best to make a clean breast of both those matters, rather than to wait for his uncle to see them in the newspapers in the morning. There could be no doubt at all, by now, that the case had caught the public fancy, and that

203

whatever could be reported at the present juncture would be written of at length.

Surprisingly, Sir Nicholas took both revelations with comparative calm, saying only, 'I think you've gone quite mad over this affair.'

Antony exchanged a puzzled glance with Vera and then looked back at his uncle. 'Something else is worrying you, sir?'

'Tomorrow you will be proceeding to blacken your client's character,' said Sir Nicholas.

'Not exactly, Uncle Nick. I shall be trying to demonstrate that someone else was doing so.'

'I wish you joy of the attempt,' said Sir Nicholas bitterly. 'What is concerning me at the moment is what you propose to do after that. Are you going to accuse Robert Camden straight out of having arranged the murder?'

'No, Uncle Nick, we've been into all this already, and I thought you knew me better than that. I hope some of my witnesses will do it for me.'

'You're going into your defence blindfold, without the slightest idea of what these witnesses of yours are going to say.'

'I thought it would be more effective that way. More convincing.'

'More convincing perhaps, but certainly a good deal more dangerous.'

'Well, at least, there's a chance that the jury will have some sympathy for Winthrop.'

'Possibly so, but are you sure that will be justified?' He paused, but his nephew made no reply. 'Are you sure, Antony?' he insisted.

'Oh God, Uncle Nick, don't you know I may be wrong?'

'And if you are you'll have made a fool of yourself, and let your client down into the bargain,' said Sir Nicholas, rubbing salt into the wound with a lavish hand. 'I don't like it, Antony, I don't like it at all.'

'Neither do I, Uncle Nick, but there's no turning back now. It's difficult to explain exactly; mostly I'm sure I'm right but then these doubts creep in.'

'Then you'd better go upstairs and forget all about it until the morning.' For a moment Maitland stared at his uncle unbelievingly, the remark was so completely out of character. And as he went rather wearily up the stairs the thought came to him that if

204

his uncle was too worried even to abuse him he must be very worried indeed.

He didn't find that idea any consolation at all.

Tuesday, the fourth day of the trial

I

When Norman Patmore stepped into the witness box the
following morning he was looking pale and shaken, but
reasonably calm. He paused deliberately to smile at the prisoner
before accepting the Bible and taking the oath, and when he
turned to face Maitland's questions, it was with an air of
resolution that seemed unclouded by doubt. Geoffrey must
indeed have made his explanations well.

'I should like to start, Mr Patmore,' counsel told him, as
soon as the preliminary questions had been asked and answered, 'with an account of how you came to adopt my client
when he was seven years old. A detailed account, if you please,
as this is a matter of some interest to the court.'

Norman launched at once into an explanation of his and his
wife's long friendship with Simon's parents, Rosalie and Peter
Winthrop, before their death in a car accident, and of the steps
that had to be taken before the adoption could go through.
'But the accident itself, Mr Patmore. Could you describe what
happened fully, and my client's part in it.'

'Yes, of course.'

'As fully as possible,' Maitland interrupted him before he
could go any further. 'I am anxious to spare Mrs Patmore from
questioning on this particular subject when her turn comes to
give evidence.'

'Thank you.' He paused a moment as though to collect his
thoughts, but his reply when it came was almost word for
word as he had given it originally to Maitland and Horton.
Antony thought that perhaps, though Simon had never spoken
of it and Norman Patmore and his wife had thought it better to
respect his reticence, they had often spoken together on the
subject, so that the description had become firmly fixed in his
mind.

When he had finished Antony asked only, 'Simon Winthrop came straight from the hospital to your home?'

'Yes, that was the obvious thing, and his grandfather, as I told you, had no objection. My wife was anxious to look after him.'

'And he never spoke of the accident?'

'It seemed obvious he had completely forgotten what had happened, and it was, naturally enough, not a thing of which we wished to remind him. He never spoke either of his parents or of his past life. My wife consulted our doctor—'

'Yes, Mr Patmore, that is a matter I must take up with her,' Maitland intervened quickly. 'The result of this consultation was, however, that you both decided not to question him or remind him in any way of his past life.'

'Yes, that is quite correct. He accepted us without question, and when we explained to him later that he was adopted, we said only that his parents had died. And, of course, we told him what good friends they had been of ours, and what fine people.'

'And as regards the rest of his family?'

'His aunt, Celia Camden, was at that time a resident of Nova Scotia. After the legal questions were settled it was my wife who corresponded with her, so I suppose you will wish to ask her those questions too instead of hearing of the matter from me at second hand.'

'Yes, Mr Patmore, that is exactly right. We come then to Thomas Wilmot, my client's grandfather.'

'That again, Mr Maitland, is a question that can better be answered by my wife. I may say, however, that we both were quite determined that Simon should never feel, as he grew older and perhaps his memory returned, that we had prevented him in any way from knowing his blood relations.'

'Thank you, that is very clear and I shall do as you suggest. We now come to the question of what you found when you went to take my client's paintings from his studio to a place where you thought they could be more safely stored.'

'We had the permission of the police, the investigating officer I believe he's called, who said they had finished their examination. But Simon's paintings are so much a part of him, it was natural we should want to keep them for him. There were quite a number, he was beginning to be known a little but

207

it is a slow business to get recognition in a field like that. We had carried them down to the car when I thought of the cupboard where he always kept his materials. There might be something there by chance, so I went back to look. There were three canvasses there, face to the wall. My wife, I should have said, came with me. I pulled them out and we were both quite appalled by what we saw. It is difficult to describe –'

'There is no need to worry about that, Mr Patmore. My lord, I should like at this point to introduce the three paintings as exhibits. They're unframed and quite light, and it will be easy, I think, for the usher to display them to the jury as well as to your lordship.'

'These are all signed *Simon Winthrop*,' said the judge looking over his spectacles at counsel when he had examined the pictures himself and the usher had moved on to the jury box.

'They are, my lord, but they are not by my client. I shall be calling evidence later –'

'Very well, Mr Maitland, very well. Are you telling us that the prisoner was storing these – I can only say these vile paintings – for a friend? If so, what relevance do they have to the matter in hand?'

'I must ask your lordship's indulgence. The relevance will be made clear as we go on.'

'Then you may proceed,' said Conroy rather grudgingly, 'if you have further questions for this witness that is.'

'I only wish to ask him, my lord, what he did after the discovery of the pictures.'

Norman Patmore had obviously been following this exchange closely, and now answered without any prompting. 'We took them home with us,' he said, 'but we were very bewildered and rather shaken by what we had seen.'

'Did you look in Mr Winthrop's bureau while you were in the studio?'

'No. The Chief Inspector had told us it had already been searched, and he very kindly gave me the few bills Simon had left so that I could pay them.'

'Did you notice, Mr Patmore, whether the bureau was dusty?'

'I didn't, I'm afraid.'

'You believed that my client had painted the pictures? The ones we have just seen.'

'What else could we think? It was so unlike him but . . . as I said, we were completely bewildered.'

'Yes, Mr Patmore, I can understand that. Now, we are both bound by the rules of hearsay evidence, so I can only ask you: did any further evidence of strange or unexpected behaviour on Mr Winthrop's part come to your knowledge?'

'Indeed it did.'

'Thank you, Mr Patmore, that is all, though I'm sure my learned friend will have some questions to put to you.'

Halloran was already on his feet, bristling with indignation, and making no attempt whatever to moderate his voice. 'My lord, we have heard this very affecting story of the prisoner's childhood, and we are being subjected to continual hints about strange behaviour on his part. Does my learned friend still maintain that he is not trying to persuade the jury that there is some trace of insanity here, or at the very least automatism or diminished responsibility?'

'Well, Mr Maitland?' asked the judge with a cold look in counsel's direction.

'I've no intention of m-making any of those pleas on my client's behalf, my lord. If I had I would have s-said so when my friend raised the matter before.'

'Then I think I must insist on knowing the relevance to the defence of these repeated references to strangeness.'

Here it came, the question that was bound to be asked sooner or later . . . and how he wished it had been later. 'I'm suggesting, my lord, that before Thomas Wilmot was murdered there were repeated attempts made to blacken my client's reputation. If your lordship wishes I can go further into the matter now, but I am sure it would be more satisfactory if the story were to unfold in its own way.'

Mr Justice Conroy sat quite silent for a moment looking at counsel. 'I suppose,' he said slowly, 'I must take your word for that, and for your assertion that your client's Not Guilty plea will not be modified in any way. You may sit down, Mr Maitland, and you may proceed with your cross-examination, Mr Halloran.'

'I have no intention,' Halloran boomed, 'of inquiring into this hearsay evidence which my friend so wisely avoided. But I think I have a right to ask the witness what effect these – these revelations had on his opinion of his adopted son.'

'I told you,' said Norman Patmore. 'At least, I told Mr Maitland. I was completely bewildered.'

'And when this evidence of further mysterious strangeness came to your notice –'

'I'm sorry to keep repeating the word, we were more bewildered than ever.'

'Forgive me for pressing the point, Mr Patmore, but we cannot leave it there. You had heard by this time of the evidence identifying the prisoner as the man seen leaving Mr Wilmot's house immediately after his death. Did you at no time think he must be guilty?'

'My lord!' said Maitland, scandalized, 'my friend has no right to ask what can only be an opinion from the witness.'

'I seem to remember, Mr Maitland, that you asked a very similar question of Miss Rexford last week. I am giving you a good deal of latitude in mounting this rather odd defence, and I think in the circumstances Mr Patmore may answer the question.'

Norman Patmore cast one appealing look in Maitland's direction. He had gone very white, whiter than he had been when he first entered the court if that were possible, and it was obvious that Geoffrey's instructions had been only too well heeded: tell the truth, but don't mention the theory you once held if you can avoid it. But there was no help for it. He turned back to counsel for the prosecution. 'We thought about an article we had read about multiple personality disorder,' he said, 'and because all these things were so unlike the Simon we knew we felt that must be the explanation.'

Ignoring the witness, ignoring for a moment courtroom etiquette, Halloran turned furiously to Counsel for the Defence. 'And I was to be denied the opportunity of having an expert witness to give his opinion of this phenomenon?' he demanded.

'There was no need.' Maitland's tone was mild, but he got to his feet to answer the question, and the slight stammer when he spoke again betrayed the fact to anyone who knew him that the mildness was no more than surface deep. 'Ask the w-witness whether he still b-believes that,' he challenged.

'Very well.' Belatedly Halloran added, 'I ask your lordship's pardon. May I proceed?'

'If you and Mr Maitland between you have decided which of you should put this question, certainly,' said Conroy.

'Then I ask you, Mr Patmore, do you still hold this theory of yours?'

'Only until I realized that there was an alternative.'

'The alternative being – ?'

'That Simon isn't guilty at all.'

'And when did you realize this? When you talked to Mr Maitland, I suppose?'

'Actually, it was Mr Horton who explained the matter to me.' Norman Patmore was composed again now. And he had need of his composure because Halloran did not let him go quickly, though he elicited no contradictions, nothing new at all.

When the cross-examination was over, but before the next witness had been called, Halloran again addressed the judge. 'My lord, in spite of my learned friend's denials this question of multiple personality disorder has been raised. I feel it is my right to call expert witnesses on the point, and to have the prisoner examined. May we adjourn so that I can arrange for this?'

'What have you to say to that, Mr Maitland?'

'That I'm sorry my friend finds himself unable to b-believe what I say. However, may I suggest to your lordship that if he is still not satisfied when I have completed the presentation of my case that will be the time to present the expert evidence he is calling for? To do so now would be to delay matters, and to waste the court's time unnecessarily.'

'That on the whole seems reasonable,' said Conroy. 'Do you agree, Mr Halloran? After all, we have already given permission for you to recall certain of the defence witnesses if you wish.'

'If your lordship pleases,' said Halloran, obviously not at all reconciled to the judge's verdict, and sat down again with a thump, leaving his learned opponent still on his feet.

'Before I call my next witness, my lord,' said Maitland, 'may I ask my learned friend for the prosecution to confine his cross-examination to the few points I shall raise with her. I do not wish to distress her by asking again for details of the accident that robbed my client of his parents, and I hope the court may feel that Mr Patmore's evidence was sufficient on this point.'

'Well, what do you say to that, Mr Halloran?'

211

It wasn't really fair, Halloran could hardly disagree without seeming an insensitive boor; on the other hand, Antony was as sure as he could be that no harm was being done to the prosecution's case. Norman Patmore had been a completely believable witness. In any case, Halloran agreed quite graciously, though the glance he gave his opponent was not altogether friendly.

'My learned friend need have no fear for the sensibilities of the witness,' he said. 'Even wolves, I believe, have their softer side.' Maitland grinned at that, but there was no flicker of a smile in return. Sooner or later he'd be called to account for that remark, but in the meantime he'd better delay no further in calling Mrs Sylvia Patmore.

She was more obviously nervous than her husband, though, like him, she was doing her best to hide it. She too took time to smile warmly at the man in the dock, who looked, his counsel thought, more shaken than he had done at any time during the trial, even during Madeleine Rexford's evidence . . . or his own. 'There are just a few things you can tell us, Mrs Patmore,' said Maitland, achieving pretty well a conversational tone which he hoped would be reassuring, 'to which your husband could not speak of his own knowledge. For instance – a very minor point – when you went together to Mr Winthrop's studio did you happen to notice whether his bureau was dusty?'

'What a strange question,' said Sylvia ingenuously. If Maitland had been looking he would have seen Bruce Halloran nod approvingly. 'As a matter of fact I did, because there was a film over everything; you know how it is in an empty room. But the bureau might have been freshly polished. We could only think that the police had been kind enough to do that after they'd searched it, trying to leave everything as they found it as much as they could.'

'Thank you.' If the image of Detective Chief Inspector Conway with a can of furniture polish and a dusting rag amused him, he gave no sign. 'Your husband has told us that soon after Simon came to live with you you consulted your doctor about the fact that he seemed to remember nothing of his former life, and that there were still occasions when he seemed unable to tell you where he'd been or what he'd been doing.'

'One moment, Mr Maitland,' Conroy broke in. 'I presume we shall be hearing from this doctor.'

'I'm afraid not, my lord. He died some time ago. I hope your lordship will have no objection to Mrs Patmore answering the question.'

'In the circumstances, she may answer.'

'Yes, I talked to him,' said Sylvia Patmore, before Antony could turn back to her. 'I wondered, you see, if we ought to take Simon to a psychiatrist, but Dr Morton said that he was suffering from retrograde amnesia – I remember the name because I looked it up afterwards in the encyclopaedia. He said it was quite normal in the circumstances, and there might be further attacks of loss of memory, or he might suffer from headaches (though he never complained of anything of the sort) and that over the years the situation would become normal. He also said that Simon would probably never remember the accident, and I was grateful for that, and so we just let things go on as they were. And he was happy with us, Mr Maitland, indeed he was. I was quite sure we were doing the right thing.'

'The diagnosis, when it was made, was a very natural one,' Maitland assured her. 'But you did feel, I believe, that though you came to regard Simon as your own son he should also keep up with his real relations.'

'That is so.'

'So you made sure he saw his grandfather, Mr Thomas Wilmot, regularly?'

'Yes, until he was old enough to go alone I used to take him to see Mr Wilmot every month. He was a very formal man, and we always went on the same day of the month, a Sunday, but only during the holidays, of course, after Simon went to boarding-school. I think at first the old man was a little ill-at-ease with children, but once he discovered Simon's interest in drawing and painting, which he had from a very early age, they got on famously together. As far as I know this continued until the time of Mr Wilmot's death, though the visits turned into dinner parties as Simon grew older.'

'And Mrs Camden, Simon's aunt?'

'I kept in touch with her for a long time. I thought some day they might come home –'

'They?'

'She and her husband and their son Robert. They emigrated

213

to Canada two years before Simon came to us, when Robert was eight years old. But as I was saying they might have come home some day and I didn't want them to feel completely strange with him. Or perhaps he'd have liked to have visited Canada and the same thing would have applied then. I used to write a letter at Christmas, and Celia would write back, or sometimes just send a card. But then about ten years ago there was a brief note saying that Bob – her husband – was dead, and after that the cards stopped coming. When that had happened for two or three years in succession I decided that perhaps she'd moved and didn't write again.'

'But you wrote to her at the time of Mrs Rosalie Winthrop's death?'

'Oh, of course I did. After all, they were sisters.'

'Did you describe what had happened?'

'Yes. It upset me, and I knew it would upset her, but I thought she had a right to know. I know I would have wanted to in her place. And she seemed really concerned for Simon, so I told her about his forgetfulness, and she said she was sure the doctor knew best and I was doing the right thing. Of course that's long ago, before Simon went to boarding-school.'

'Thank you very much, Mrs Patmore. I'm sorry to have troubled you. I don't know whether – '

But Halloran was already on his feet, his voice for once subdued to a reasonable degree. 'I have no questions for the witness, my lord,' he said. 'I should like to mention again that I consider the line the defence is taking is completely irrelevant, and I have no wish to add to the court's confusion by a further waste of time.'

Maitland made him a small, ironic bow, and, since the judge had obviously no intention of adjourning for lunch just yet, took the opportunity of calling his old acquaintance, Julian Verlaine, the art expert that Horton had consulted, to give the court his opinion that the paintings which had been introduced as exhibits were not by the same hand as those known to be by Simon Winthrop, of which a specimen was also introduced, though the signature was obviously intended to look the same. Whoever had executed them, however, had some knowledge of the art, though probably not a great deal of experience or training.

After that, to everyone's relief, the luncheon recess was called.

II

Maitland had anticipated no pleasure out of his next two witnesses, and true to his expectations he got none. Bertha Harvey herself was not averse to answering his questions, but Halloran was extremely unwilling to let him hear what she had to say. As Antonia Dryden was dead, however, and there could be no question of resurrecting her to give first-hand evidence, there was really no objection he could validly use, and after a while she was allowed to tell her tale in her own way.

Horace Dryden was another matter. He considered it in the worst of taste to drag the matter up at all, whatever the circumstances, and said so loudly and clearly for everyone to hear. But half way through his evidence he obviously realised that there was no mending matters, and here was a chance to get back perhaps at the man who had caused his daughter's death. Thereafter he answered the questions without hesitation. The inquest was described, the drug which had caused Antonia's death identified – Maitland had memorized the name, but promptly forgot it again as soon as this part of the witness's evidence was over – and so they came to the inquiries that Dryden himself had instigated into the matter.

These had been exhaustive, he said, covering every place that Antonia had ever mentioned in correspondence to him, or in conversation with Bertha Harvey. As no proof of her having been seen with the prisoner was forthcoming he had eventually and with reluctance given the matter up. A crime had been committed, and if he could have offered proof he would have gone to the police. As it was there was nothing anyone could do about it, and the fellow had gone scot free – until now, he added with a venomous glance in the direction of the dock.

Maitland sat down at the end of his questioning without regret, and again Halloran declined to cross-examine.

In spite of the lack of cross-examination this had all taken time and the afternoon was already well advanced when Mark Benson was called. Derek's hand continued to travel across the paper, taking the note, quite steadily. Antony remembered a case, and allowed himself to dwell on it for a moment, when

215

his junior had been very concerned indeed, but in a matter in which he had no personal interest it would take more than this to shake him.

What he was doing, Maitland realised suddenly, came very close to the hysterical amnesia that Dr Macintyre had described so graphically, and he hoped so convincingly, to the jury. He didn't want to think of the answers this witness might give to his questions; he didn't want to remember the oft-repeated truism, never ask a question to which you don't know the answer; he didn't want to listen to Geoffrey's uneasy movements behind him and realise that his friend was as nervous as he was, so he turned his thoughts carefully to something that had happened many years before. It was only a step from there to forgetfulness and he realized suddenly – this was perhaps part of the same thing – that the loss of certain memories for which he had sometimes wished so fervently wouldn't be a blessing at all but very much the opposite. The rough with the smooth, that was life, and for him at least there was no alternative to acceptance. He called his wandering thoughts sternly to order and settled down to observe his next witness, who was now in his place and repeating the oath in a firm voice.

Mark Benson was a man of middle height, with black hair that curled strongly, and a round face that looked as though it was made for laughter, though at the moment his expression was unnaturally solemn. He studied Maitland with frank curiosity as he answered his introductory questions, and immediately interrupted with one of his own. 'You're this man Simon Winthrop's counsel?' he asked.

'I am,' said Antony solemnly. For the first time he became conscious of a glimmer of hope that perhaps after all this afternoon wasn't going to be one long difficulty.

The witness had turned and was staring at the man in the dock as curiously as a moment before he had been studying his counsel. 'So that's Simon Winthrop,' he said.

'Mr Maitland.' The judge said, and coughed in an admonitory way.

'Yes, my lord?'

'You may not object to being cross-examined by your own witness, Mr Maitland, but I should remind you that you have called him – I presume – with some purpose in mind, and that any questioning should therefore be in the opposite direction.'

216

'Yes, my lord, of course. But in a way, Mr Benson has already answered what would have been my first question,' Maitland assured him.

'Then perhaps you will put it in a proper form,' said the judge coldly.

'If your lordship pleases. I should like you to look carefully at the accused, Mr Benson. Have you ever seen him before?'

Mark Benson took his time over answering, and obeyed the injunction to study Simon's face to the letter. 'I've a sort of feeling I may have seen him somewhere,' he said at last, 'though I never knew his name. In the King's Head, that would be it. He used to come there sometimes with a girl but we've never got into conversation.'

'But you knew his name. Before you heard about Thomas Wilmot's murder, I mean. I imagine there's been a good deal of talk in the pub you mentioned since then.'

'Yes, of course there has. I don't think I'm a vindictive man,' said Mark Benson – certainly he didn't look it – 'but in a way I wasn't sorry when he was arrested, even though I'd no reason to fear him by then.'

'To fear him, Mr Benson?'

'Yes, he was blackmailing me,' said the witness simply. 'And if you'll excuse me saying so I think it's damned odd that you're calling me. What I have to say about him won't incline anyone in his favour, I can tell you that.'

'Mr Maitland,' said Conroy with a sigh. 'You really must keep your witnesses in order.'

'If your lordship pleases,' said Maitland even more vaguely than that meaningless phrase is usually spoken. And then, smiling suddenly in Conroy's direction, 'You must admit, my lord, the witness is saving my learned friend for the prosecution a good deal of trouble. Their sentiments are only too clearly the same.'

'Perhaps they are,' said the judge non-committally. 'All the same I think you should explain to the witness that he should answer your questions as briefly as possible, and not add any comment of his own.'

'Your lordship's wish is my command,' said Antony, forgetting himself again. He turned to the witness, 'Do you understand, Mr Benson? We are all bound here by certain rules with which you may not be familiar.'

217

'I understood what he said all right,' said Benson, apparently not at all put out. 'Speak when you're spoken to. It's only that I've always thought when a lawyer was defending you he had to put on the best show he could, whatever he really thought about what you'd done.'

Maitland glanced quickly at the judge, who had closed his eyes as though what was going on was too painful to watch. 'Please, Mr Benson,' he said. 'You don't want to get me into trouble, do you? And as you will be remaining in court after your evidence has been concluded, perhaps in the long run your curiosity will be satisfied.'

'If you say so,' said Benson doubtfully. 'It all seems very odd to me, but I suppose you know your own business best. I admit I was fair flabbergasted when I got that *sub poena* thing, but here I am and I've taken an oath to tell the truth, so if you don't like what I have to say, it's your own fault.'

'Yes, I understand that and I'm obliged to you for the warning,' said Maitland, whose sense of humour, never very far below the surface, was threatening to get the better of him. 'My lord, may I ask the usher to show the witness the letter that Mr Horton and I found in my client's studio. Exhibit E, I think it was.'

'Certainly, Mr Maitland. I am glad to see that you're at last about to get down to what I suppose is the purpose of this witness being called.'

'Thank you, my lord.' If a question was implied in Conroy's last remark Antony chose to ignore it. 'Now, Mr Benson, you see this note. Do you recognize it?'

'Of course I do, I wrote it myself.'

'To my client?'

'It says so, doesn't it?'

'May I ask you how it came about that you owed him money?'

'I didn't owe him a thing! Look here,'—he swivelled round to face the judge, adding, 'my lord' by way of good measure—'is that a fair way of putting it? He was blackmailing me, that's not at all the same thing.'

'I can appreciate your indignation, Mr Benson,' the judge told him, 'but I should also be obliged if you would confine yourself to answering counsel's questions.'

'Well then, I didn't owe him money. What that note referred

to was the amount he extorted from me every month for the price of his silence,' said the witness, obviously relishing the phrase. 'And I don't mind telling you why I was paying him now that it's all over, because we're all men of the world. And you ladies too, of course,' he added glancing towards the jury box, where five of the twelve good men and true were women. 'Only women of the world doesn't sound quite right somehow and I don't want to offend you.'

'Perhaps,' said Maitland, 'if you could just tell us the reason—'

'That's what I'm trying to do, isn't it? Only I've got to go back a bit to explain. I was married, you see, and my wife Annie had cancer. She was dying, we both knew that, but sometimes the doctor said it'd be quick, and sometimes that it'd be slow, and the Lord above knows I didn't want to lose her, but a man has his needs, and there was a girl I used to go with . . . still do, for that matter. And there was a letter came to the office one day, signed by this Simon Winthrop, and saying he knew all about what was going on and would tell Annie if I didn't pay him. I wouldn't have hurt her for the world so I paid up as often as I could, only it was £100 a month he wanted and sometimes with the mortgage payments and all of that it just wasn't possible to send it to him. But then Annie died, not so long after I wrote that note, so I'd no reason to be afraid of him any more. I'm going to marry Maisie when a few months are up, so she said she didn't mind if our going together was made public. And that's really all there is to it, except that he made the sad time while Annie was so ill even more unhappy than it needed to be. But she never knew, poor girl. At least I spared her that.'

'Thank you, Mr Benson, I'm sure we all have the greatest sympathy for you in your loss and in the unhappy time that preceded it,' said Maitland. There was a sincerity about this man that appealed to him, as did Benson's clearly irrepressible nature, and that had knocked on the head all the humour with which for a moment he had regarded the situation. 'Do you mind telling us when you wrote this letter?'

'Must have been January, because of saying I'll make up the payment in February. Only I didn't need to, because it was at the end of January that Annie died.'

'Did you address it to Mr Winthrop at his address in Earls Court?'

'No, I never knew where he lived. Come to think of it I daresay he'd have been in the phone book, but I never bothered to look. I mean, there was no question of going to the police while Annie was alive, and afterwards there was Maisie to consider. I sent it to him at the G.P.O., which was what that first letter of his told me to do.'

'Your note was found in the desk in Mr Winthrop's studio. How do you suppose it got there?'

'That is hardly a matter, Mr Maitland,' the judge interposed, 'about which the witness can be expected to have any opinion.'

'No, my lord, but perhaps I may be permitted to speculate about the matter myself. The sequence of events was this: Mr Thomas Wilmot was murdered, almost immediately my client was arrested and the police very properly searched his studio for evidence. After that Mr and Mrs Patmore went there, and discovered what I believe your lordship referred to as the vile paintings, which Mr Verlaine has told us were not painted by Simon Winthrop. Later again, Mr Horton and I made a search, with the knowledge and consent of Chief Inspector Conway, and discovered Mr Benson's letter. It had not, the Chief Inspector testified, been in the bureau when the police searched it, and my client had been in custody during the whole of the intervening period. How then did it get there?'

'You will have ample time later to address the jury, Mr Maitland,' said Mr Justice Conroy frostily. 'And Mr Halloran will likewise have the opportunity of putting before them the various explanations which I'm sure are at this very moment hovering on the tip of his tongue. But this is neither the time nor the place for speculation. You have put your witness through an ordeal which I consider to have been quite unnecessary, and I sympathize with his bewilderment as to your reasons for wishing to blacken your client's character.' He raised his hand as Maitland seemed about to make some retort. 'Yes, I remember your assertion that it is all part of a plot against him, and if this is true nobody is denying you the opportunity of proving it. But at the moment, we are concerned with facts, not with your theories, however interesting they may be. So, though we are all grateful to Mr Benson for giving us this insight into what has been going on, I think – unless Mr Halloran has any questions for him – that you should now let him go.'

'I have no questions, my lord,' said Halloran, well enough satisfied. If the defence really wanted to dig their own grave he wasn't going to say a word to stop them.

So Maitland complied, having really no choice in the matter, and let his witness go. He called instead Martin Ridley, the owner of the house where Simon Winthrop's studio was situated, and therefore his landlord. A few questions elicited the fact of the flooding of the first-floor flat at a time when Mr Winthrop was away, the calling of a locksmith to get into his studio, and later the installation of a new lock. In view of what had happened he had felt it better to keep a key himself, though he had never had occasion to use it.

'Did you inform Mr Winthrop of this fact, Mr Ridley?'

'I don't really remember. I might have done, or again I might not.' He thought for a moment. 'No, I'm wrong about that, I must have told him because he certainly knew and was able to make use of it on one occasion.'

'How did that come about?'

'I had a phone call one day when he was out. He'd left his key behind, and asked me to put the extra one on the ledge above his door so that he could use it to get in when he came home.'

'Did he make that call himself? Did you recognize his voice?'

'No, I couldn't have done, it was made by a woman.'

'Did she give you her name?'

'No, just said she was calling for Mr Winthrop. Well, I wasn't surprised, he was a bit absent-minded, not only about the key, and we all know what artists are like.'

'Was the key returned to you?'

'Yes, about two days later. Someone had tied a tag on it, *Key to S.W.'s studio*, and dropped it in my letter box.

'It is quite possible, is it not, that someone other than my client had possession of the key all the time, that an extra one had been cut, and that therefore this other person had access to the studio?'

This time it was Halloran who intervened. 'My lord, my learned friend is again putting words into his witness's mouth.'

'The point is well taken, Mr Halloran. Mr Maitland, I really cannot permit you to continue in this fashion any longer. Have you any more questions for the witness?'

'No, my lord.'

'Or you, Mr Halloran?'

'I see no need, my lord. I do not question the witness's story, and as you yourself have said, speculation at this point will do no good.'

'Very well. Mr Ridley, you are excused.' Mr Justice Conroy glanced at his watch. 'The court is adjourned until ten o'clock tomorrow morning,' he said, 'and I should advise you, Mr Maitland, to take the opportunity to reflect a little on the conduct of your case.'

The reporters were scribbling frantically.

III

Maitland was delayed in getting home by a talk with his colleagues. They went to Horton's office because that was nearer than chambers, and Geoffrey was not acrimonious now but clearly worried. Maitland was in one of his vague moods, but after a while he roused himself to ask, 'Geoffrey, why did you really bring me in on this?'

'You seemed to be the best person to make some sense of what seemed to me then a preposterous suggestion on the Patmores' part.'

Antony was immediately alert. 'What seemed to you then,' he repeated, but the inflection in his voice made the words a question.

'I'm beginning to wonder . . . was that first idea really so absurd?'

'Multiple personality disorder.' Maitland sounded incredulous. 'I thought I'd gone a good way today towards showing the likelihood of a frame-up at least.'

'Yes, you did, but by the time Halloran's had his say . . . and there are still the identifications to get over.'

But Antony's concern was with one particular point. 'Not convincing enough for you?' he queried.

'I don't know,' Geoffrey confessed. 'I think Simon Winthrop's telling the truth as far as he sees it, that's why I said I wondered if the Patmores' original theory could possibly be true. Otherwise, there's a lot left to be explained away.'

'I've told you a hundred times –'

'Yes, .Antony, but Halloran will have an explanation for everything, as you would have yourself in his place. Winthrop painted the pictures himself . . . art experts aren't infallible, even your friend Verlaine. The accident that killed our client's parents is nothing to do with the case except as an attempt to gain sympathy for him; and Mrs Patmore's correspondence with Celia Camden is likewise, as the prosecution have pointed out rather frequently, irrelevant. Antonia Dryden was genuinely Winthrop's victim, the fact that they were never seen together proves nothing at all. And as for the blackmail Mark Benson paid, there's nothing to say it wasn't to Winthrop too.'

'What about the availability of the key to the studio?'

'There's nothing to say that telephone call wasn't made at Winthrop's instigation. I asked him just now before they whisked him away, but he says no. It may be just one of the things he's forgotten though.'

'And the letter that appeared after the police had searched the place, and the desk that had been wiped clean when everything else was dusty? Don't these things mean anything?'

'To err is human,' said Geoffrey. 'The best of men can overlook something, and that's what Halloran will say happened.'

Maitland looked at him in silence for a moment. 'There's still tomorrow,' he said.

'And how far is that going to get us? You do realize, don't you, that you've nowhere near enough groundwork laid to justify your making any sort of an accusation against Robert Camden? I'm right about that, don't you agree, Derek?'

'I'm afraid I do. It's a risky business under any circumstances, but with what we've got so far—' He broke off and shrugged.

'I realise there's nothing I can do unless I can get some sort of an admission out of him. And don't remind me that he's our own witness and I can't cross-examine him.' He paused in his turn and added rather bitterly, 'You're telling me we've lost the case already.'

'I'm trying to warn you—'

'To prepare myself for the worst.' Maitland laughed, but there was no amusement in the sound. 'I asked Simon Winthrop to trust me,' he said, getting to his feet, and went away without any of the usual salutations.

Tuesday evening. Most likely Uncle Nick and Vera would be already with Jenny, but he thought he would walk home just the same to try to get his thoughts in order. Which plan he carried out as far as walking was concerned, though without any conspicuous success in the thinking line, and sure enough found Gibbs hovering in his usual place at the back of the hall with the message that his guests were already with Mrs Maitland. Antony went up the stairs slowly, so tired that he thought fleetingly it would be nice to have the use of his right arm to help drag himself up from stair to stair. But his shoulder was hurting damnably already, and even if it weren't, there was no strength available for tricks like that. When he got inside his own front door his worst fears were realized. Jenny had been waiting for him, probably with the excuse that she was seeing to something in the kitchen, which meant that she had something she wanted to tell him at least, and in this case it was most probably a warning.

She came across quickly to his side and he noticed with compunction that her usual serenity had deserted her. 'Antony,' she started, and broke off as he bent his head to kiss her.

'What is it now, love?' He was getting out of his coat as he spoke.

'I just wanted to say, don't do anything to annoy Uncle Nick more than you can help.'

'In one of those moods, is he?' The attempt at lightness was a dismal failure.

Jenny took his left hand and began to pull him gently towards the living-room door, which she had left prudently closed. 'The worst kind,' she said, and on a less serious occasion he would have accused her of trying to imitate Meg in one of her more dramatic moods. 'You see,' said Jenny with her hand on the door knob, 'Vera was in court today.'

'Forewarned is forearmed,' said Antony tritely, and smiled at her as she pushed the door open.

On the face of it everything was as usual. Sir Nicholas in his usual chair, relaxed and at peace with the world, though that, as his nephew knew, was certainly on this occasion pure illusion. Vera, also in her usual place at the end of the sofa nearest her husband, turned her head to smile at him but she hadn't Uncle Nick's gift for play-acting and there was no mistaking her worried look. He crossed the room and took his stance on the hearthrug, leaving Jenny to provide him with a drink as he knew she would, and greeted his aunt with the slight formality which he still observed towards her, though only at the moment of meeting. 'Jenny tells me you were in court today,' he added. 'I'm sorry I didn't notice you, we might have had lunch together.'

'Would it have done any good?' asked Vera bluntly.

'If you mean, could you have argued me out of the course I was pursuing, I don't suppose it would,' Antony told her. 'But at least I expect you've told Uncle Nick and Jenny all about the day's events, so I shan't have to go through them all again.' Jenny arrived then with his sherry, and he drank a little before placing it on the mantelpiece beside the clock. He was wondering as he did so whether there was any chance at all that Uncle Nick would be content to leave matters as they were without further discussion.

It was perhaps as well that he had no real hope that this would happen. Sir Nicholas said, so quietly that it was perfectly obvious there were squalls ahead, 'You're quite right in thinking that we don't need any further factual account from you. I should however be interested to know your own view of the situation.'

'Conroy's fit to be tied,' said Maitland flippantly, and realized when his uncle made no comment on the colloquialism that matters were even worse than he had expected. 'As for Halloran, I don't know, Uncle Nick, but I've a nasty feeling he's beginning to doubt my motives.'

'I think he at least knows you too well for that,' said Sir Nicholas, at his iciest. 'But as for the foolishness of your actions –' He broke off as though at a loss for words.

'Won't do, Antony,' Vera finished for him.

'You've no need to tell me, I've been through it all with Geoffrey already at some length. It might interest you to know that he's veering back to the multiple personality nonsense. He thinks Winthrop is telling the truth as he sees it, and can't see any other explanation for all the things that have been happening.'

'He doesn't accept your explanation of the facts then?' asked Sir Nicholas.

'Not any longer, and even if he did he doesn't think we've a chance of proving it. And as I expect he's right about that there's really no more to be said on the subject, is there?'

'I don't quite understand.'

'He covered the evidence that has been given by the defence witnesses, and provided the answers Halloran was likely to make to every small admission I obtained, in case I'd overlooked them. What else could there be for us to discuss?'

'If I could induce you to take this matter seriously, Antony—' said his uncle again.

At that Maitland flung himself down in his chair, and put up his left hand for a moment to shield his eyes, a gesture of weakness so uncharacteristic that both Vera and Jenny were seriously alarmed, and Sir Nicholas abandoned his languid pose and sat up a little straighter. 'Tell me this at least,' he said, abandoning the accusation he had just made, 'what is it about this case that is upsetting you so much?'

'My concern for my client, I suppose, and for his family, which is how the Patmores consider themselves, and for the girl he is going to marry. They're all nice people, and to make it worse they all seem to trust me.'

'And so you feel responsible for them,' said Sir Nicholas, with the first lessening of the severity he had been displaying ever since his nephew came in.

'I suppose that's as good an explanation as any.' Jenny got up quietly and retrieved his glass from the mantelshelf.

He took it from her with a grateful look and drank again before he went on, a little encouraged by the slight softening in the older man's manner. 'Look here, Uncle Nick, if you're worried about me we've had it all out before. I may have advised my client badly but the worst that can happen is that the press will have a field day reporting the case. It won't be the first time, and the world hasn't ended yet.'

'I thought that myself,' Sir Nicholas admitted, 'though I can't say I view the possibility of bad publicity quite as lightheartedly as you seem to do. But that was before I heard, from you last night, and especially from Vera today, exactly what has been going on in court. There are some rather unpleasant possibilities.'

'You'd better tell me, sir.'

'I intend to. But first I must ask you to bear in mind what Superintendent Sykes told you, that the attitude of one member at least of the police force is unchanged from that which Chief Superintendent Briggs held of your activities, and that now the person entertaining these suspicions is of an even higher rank.'

'But we agreed—'

'As your strategy has unfolded I've had time to consider the matter,' Sir Nicholas told him. 'And there are two ways of looking at it. The one we have already discussed, that you may be considered not to have been acting in the best interests of your client through taking a mistaken view of the situation, in which case, I agree, I expect we shall all survive. But there is also the possibility that you, and I am sorry to say Geoffrey too, may be thought to have been tampering with the evidence.' He stopped, fixing his nephew with a baleful eye, daring him to interrupt. 'And if you say that because you haven't done any such thing nobody can prove you have, Antony, I shall be seriously annoyed.'

Maitland gulped, rather as though he was swallowing an unpleasant draught, and groped blindly for his glass again. 'I won't say it if you'd rather I didn't,' he said, 'but I do wish you'd explain.'

'If you were not, as usual, completely blind to your own interests you would have seen it for yourself already,' said Sir Nicholas. 'There is absolutely no proof that Winthrop didn't seduce Antonia Dryden, that he didn't blackmail Mark Benson, and as for the pictures in a different style from his . . . art experts are not infallible.'

'Geoffrey pointed all that out already.'

'I'm sure he did. And Geoffrey is in general a very sensible young man,' said Sir Nicholas judiciously. 'I'm sorry though that he allows himself on occasion to be carried away by some of your wilder ideas.'

'But, Uncle Nick, the key to the studio.'

'May have been needed for exactly the purpose stated. And if you are about to quote to me the letter from the blackmail victim which you and Geoffrey found in the studio . . . that's what I'm afraid of, Antony; it may be said you put it there.'

'I see,' said Maitland rather faintly. 'Is there more, sir?'

'Only that Vera tells me that on cross-examination Mr Norman Patmore admitted to a theory he and his wife had held at one time . . . that their adopted son was suffering from multiple personality disorder.'

'Geoffrey had told him not to mention that unless he was asked, but when Halloran got after him there was no way of getting out of it, as Vera also told you, I expect.'

'I think it may be held that that was an alternative plan, in case the first one didn't work out and your client was still considered guilty. It's the sort of thing that would stick in the minds of the jury, and a verdict of insanity might lead to your client being free again rather sooner than he would be in serving a life sentence.'

For a long moment the silence lengthened. At last Maitland said rather tentatively, 'I wouldn't have done a thing like this to Geoffrey for the world. And there's nothing I can do about it now except to proceed as planned. And pray, I suppose,' he added rather despondently.

'And pray certainly,' said Sir Nicholas. His tone was grim, 'How *do* you propose to proceed tomorrow?'

'There's just the landlord of the pub, at least his evidence can't do any harm. Can it, Uncle Nick?'

'From what you've told me I should think not. The question is will it do any good either.'

'Well, after him, Robert Camden. Even in direct examination I can ask him some pointed questions, but whether he'll be shaken enough to admit anything . . . I don't know what kind of a man he is, you see. And if that fails there's the girl who lives in Madeleine Rexford's flats, and whom Madeleine told about Simon's occasional fits of forgetfulness. She's denied everything, of course, but I think the information came from her, and, along with the knowledge of how Simon's parents died, and of his occasional strangeness of behaviour, which Robert Camden must have had from his mother, anyone might have got the idea that this weakness of his could be put to advantage. Halloran hates that word, "strangeness", and I can't say I like it myself, but I can't think of any other to use.'

'And when that is done you will outline your theory that someone has been deliberately trying to blacken Winthrop's character to the jury, naming no names.'

'Yes, Uncle Nick, unless –'

'Don't think you must count too much on succeeding,' Vera put in. 'If this man Robert Camden really plotted all this from a distance he's quite capable of looking after himself in court.'

'I expect you're right.' He looked from Vera to Sir Nicholas

228

with the ghost of a smile. 'Have either of you any more home truths for me?' he asked.

'I think not, I think we might try at least to think of something else,' his uncle told him. 'You've no alternative but to carry on as planned, and even though you've talked so much about Camden's responsibility for the murder, I know I can trust you not to make a direct accusation unless something unexpected happens to prove your point.'

Roger came in later, but the Hardings left when he did and Antony and Jenny were left alone together. 'It's not worth making up the fire,' said Antony, kicking what was left into a blaze. 'In fact, if the weather goes on like this we won't need one much longer.' He turned then and held out a hand invitingly, so that she came to stand close to him. 'I thought you told me, love, that Uncle Nick was about to greet me with thunderbolts.'

'Well, I didn't quite know,' said Jenny, 'but on the whole I wish he had. When he gets in one of those gentle moods you know he's worried and –'

'And then you're worried too. Don't be, love. There's just a chance we may bring it off, and whatever anyone may say they couldn't *prove* that either Geoffrey or I did anything wrong. I'm sure Uncle Nick realises that.'

'Of course he does. But once the accusation was made, even if you got off . . . a rumour would do it,' said Jenny.

'And it's happened once too often,' said Antony, with compunction, completing her thought.

'No, no, that isn't what I meant, Antony. Just . . . you see I thought this was a thing that would never happen again when Briggs left the force and everyone knew the charges he was trying to bring against you that last time were completely false.'

'He only faked them because over the years he'd begun to believe I was really doing that kind of thing and had to be stopped.'

'That isn't any excuse.'

'In a way I think it is. I mean, not really, but he'd become paranoid on the subject. This other chap, the Assistant Commissioner, isn't likely to do that.'

'How do you know, you've never met him.'

'There couldn't be two like Briggs,' Antony asserted.

229

'It may not matter, he may be able to–to hurt you without trying to frame you as Briggs did. That's what Uncle Nick and Vera think and I'm afraid they may be right.'

'My dearest love,' his good arm was round her shoulders, and his grip was tight enough to hurt, 'try not to worry until we know what we're worrying about.'

'We *do* know, Antony,' she insisted.

'I'm not so sure.' He released his hold on her and pulled her round to face him. 'I only know, Jenny love, that somehow I can never manage to do things just like anyone else. I've destroyed your peace of mind again and again, and I'm more sorry about that than I can say. Without me–'

'You've got to do what you think is right,' said Jenny. 'And without you . . . surely you know by now, Antony, that I'm with you all the way. Whatever happens I couldn't live with myself knowing I'd asked you to–to compromise.'

For a while he looked down at her without speaking, then he took her arm and began to urge her across the room. 'That being so, Jenny love, let's go to bed,' he said. 'No, leave the damned glasses alone. We can clear them up in the morning.'

Wednesday, the fifth day of the trial

There was no doubt about it there was a distinct air of expectation in the court the following morning. The press box was full to overflowing, and there were a good many more people in the public gallery, too. Until the entrance of the judge the hum of excited conversation was almost deafening.

Before Mr Justice Conroy took his place on the bench Halloran had swept in, greeting the defence team in passing with suspicious amiability, so that it was only too evident he was completely confident about the outcome of the trial. Returning his look as blandly as he could Maitland came to the conclusion that his uncle had been right. Halloran knew him too well to suspect him of any funny business other than being – as the older man had said to his face on so many occasions – rather too unconventional for his own good. But in view of the other things that had been said last night he didn't find too much consolation in this. If Sir Nicholas was right not only his client's but also Geoffrey's good name hung on his efforts today. About the possible outcome for himself it was better not to think, but it couldn't be denied that he was nervous, though he did his best to disguise the fact.

The landlord of the King's Head, Walter Kenmore, was a big burly man with a friendly manner that was undoubtedly a distinct asset to him in his work. He showed no signs of self-consciousness at finding himself under public scrutiny; on the whole he seemed inclined to treat the whole affair as a pleasant social occasion.

When he had taken the oath and his identity had been established Maitland turned for a moment to the judge. 'My lord, in view of some of the questions I shall have for this witness, may I again assure you and my learned friend, Mr Halloran, that I am not trying to lay grounds for an insanity plea

231

of any sort.'

'Very well, Mr Maitland,' said Mr Justice Conroy, 'we shall bear that in mind. You yourself should also remember, I think, that if you do not succeed in proving your claim that your client has been the victim of some sort of a plot against him Mr Halloran has the option of recalling him for cross-examination, which I should have no hesitation in agreeing to.'

'I remember that very well, my lord.' He turned back to the witness again. 'Mr Kenmore, you have told us that you are the owner of the King's Head inn.'

'That's right. A free house,' the witness amplified.

'And you run it yourself, and serve in the bar on most evenings.'

'That's right,' said Kenmore again. 'No way of seeing things go as they should unless you're there yourself to keep an eye on things.'

'Precisely.' Maitland's rather stiff manner came as a surprise to some of his legal brethren, though the onlookers of course saw nothing strange about it. He had, in fact, quite unconsciously, begun to imitate his uncle, who was one of the most effective counsel he knew. 'Now I should like you, Mr Kenmore, to take a good look at my client, the man in the dock, and tell me if you know him.'

'Of course I do, it's Mr Winthrop.'

'I'm afraid I was not being sufficiently exact. Naturally you know that Mr Simon Winthrop is on trial here today for the murder of Thomas Wilmot, and from the papers you received – the *sub poena* – you know that you are being called as a witness in his defence. If none of these things had been within the scope of your knowledge, would you still have recognized him?'

'If you're asking me if I've seen him before, yes, I have, many a time.' He took a moment to look round the court. 'There's nothing wrong in a man coming down to the local for a pint now and then,' he said, rather as though someone had attacked him on the point.

'Nothing wrong at all,' said Maitland soothingly. 'How long have you known Mr Winthrop?'

'I'd say about five years, though I can't say I've known his name all that time. He'd come in two or three times a week, something like that.'

'I should like you to tell the court in a little more detail exactly what you know about him.'

'Now there's something,' said Mr Kenmore and thought about it for a moment. 'When he first used to come in he was always alone, but lately, for perhaps a year now, he'd sometimes have a young lady with him. A friendly sort of chap, always a word and a joke to me and the lads, the barmen, Bill and Stan.'

'Do you recognize the young lady he used to come in with? Look round the court and tell me if you can see her.'

Again Walter Kenmore took his time, a deliberate man as well as a friendly one. 'Why, that's her over there,' he said, pointing to where Madeleine Rexford sat along with the other witnesses who had already given their evidence.

'Thank you. Would you stand up for a moment, Miss Rexford, so that there can be no mistake?' Madeleine complied, and the witness nodded vigorously.

'That's her,' he asserted.

'Thank you. There is no need for you to stand any longer, Miss Rexford. You have told us, Mr Kenmore, that my client's visits in this lady's company have only taken place during the past year.'

'That's right, and not every time he came in.'

'I believe we all understand that. Could you go back a little, to his earlier visits.'

'Well, I told you he'd always have a word, and most evenings he'd find someone among my other customers to talk to. That's why a lot of people come to the pub, companionship, you know.'

'Was that his invariable custom?'

'So that's it! I said to the wife when I got those papers telling me to be here, going for insanity, I said.'

'Mr Maitland, you really must keep your witness in order,' complained the judge. 'It seems I must be continually reminding you.'

'I'll do what I can, my lord,' said Antony, for the moment forgetting the role he had been cultivating. 'What his lordship means, Mr Kenmore, is that you should confine yourself to answering the questions, without adding any comments of your own.'

'Well, me lord, I can only say I'm sorry,' said the witness.

'Strange to me, you see, all this.'

Mr Justice Conroy inclined his head graciously. Maitland said, quickly enough to prevent his witness from saying anything else of an injudicious nature, 'You were telling us, Mr Kenmore?'

'You mean about the times when he seemed to be queer, like.' He turned again, and this time it was the people in the jury box he seemed to be addressing. 'And I'm not meaning what perhaps you think I'm meaning by that, the way words get twisted around these days. Just . . . odd. Not a bit like himself.' He really was incorrigible, and in spite of his worry Maitland felt his spirits rising. He had a weakness for the unconventional, about which he had received so many complaints concerning his own actions, and it was obviously going to be quite impossible to tame Mr Kenmore. An unruly lot, these witnesses of his.

'Yes,' he agreed. 'That's exactly what we do wish to hear.' The judge perhaps had also given up all hope of achieving his own high standard of courtroom etiquette, and this time made no remark.

'Well then, there were evenings when he'd come in and not seem to know us. I'd say "Good evening, Mr Winthrop", just like usual, and he'd look at me blankly as if he'd never heard the name before and say "Good evening" as polite as you please, but not call me by my name. And the same with Bill and Stan, always a perfect gent but no familiarity. And those evenings he'd take himself off and sit with his pint in the corner, not talking to anyone, not unless they addressed him first. He'd stay an hour, or perhaps a bit longer, and sometimes when he left it'd be just like he was when he came in and other times he seemed to be his usual self and it'd be, "Good night, Mr Kenmore", the same as always.'

'Did you ever mention these occasions to him? The occasions when he was . . . odd was your word, wasn't it?'

'Now what do you take me for? A chap can do as he likes in my place as long as he behaves himself, and as long as he pays his bill. If he feels like keeping himself to himself he's a perfect right to.'

'I take it, Mr Maitland, that the witness is answering your question in the negative,' said the judge, recovering himself. Evidently it had been too much to hope for, that his spirit had

234

been broken by all these talkative witnesses.

'I believe so, my lord. That's right, isn't it, Mr Kenmore? You're telling the court that you never spoke to Mr Winthrop about the occasions when he wasn't behaving as he usually did.'

'That's what I meant, that's what I said, I thought.'

'Then let us turn to the people who talked to him when he was in one of these strange moods. Were they all known to you?'

'All regulars, yes.'

'People you've known for some time?'

'Well, there was one – and that's funny when you think about it – a chap I didn't know till he started coming in about five, six months ago. When Mr Winthrop was in one of those moods I told you about he'd go and talk to him, but never on the times when he came in cheerful-like and greeted us all by name.'

'On the times when my client was normal did he seem to recognize this other man we're speaking of?'

'No, I never saw them greet each other. Struck me as odd, but then there's no end to the strange things people do, and no use worrying about it,' said Mr Kenmore philosophically.

'Will you please tell the court about the time the – shall we agree to call him the stranger? – about the time the stranger first spoke to Simon Winthrop.'

'Mr Winthrop, he'd taken his pint into the furthest corner as he would on those occasions.'

'Oh the occasions when he was in a withdrawn mood?'

'That's right. That's a good word for it. So after a while this other chap goes over and says something to him and then sits down. Mr Winthrop seems to cheer up as they talk and get quite animated, but when he left he was still odd, still didn't seem to recognize me.'

'And that wasn't the only time it happened?'

'No, there was one other time as well.'

'Then, Mr Kenmore, we come to the point that interests me most. Had the stranger ever asked you questions about my client?'

'There was a lot of talk about Mr Winthrop after his arrest. Lots of people had noticed what I've been telling you about.'

'I'm talking about the time before Mr Thomas Wilmot was murdered.'

'That's different.' Kenmore wrinkled his brow as though the last question required some serious thought, but his answer came readily enough. 'The first time he came in, this stranger, as you call him, and as good a name as any, being as he was an American by his way of talking, he took a good look all around, and then came and stood by the bar and chatted to me for a while. About all sorts of things, but then he did ask if I knew an artist called Simon Winthrop. He thought he might be one of my customers, as his studio wasn't too far away. He'd seen a painting of his somewhere, he said, and was interested in it. So I told him, of course, that Mr Winthrop came in two or three times a week, sometimes with his lady friend and sometimes alone.'

'Was that all that was said?'

'No, he asked whether Mr Winthrop was at all eccentric. I think that was the word. He said he'd met an artist once and you could never tell the mood he was in, up in the clouds or down in the dumps, might be either. So I told him about Mr Winthrop and what a nice gentleman he was, only sometimes odd in his ways.'

'Did you explain the way in which he was odd?'

'There wasn't any harm in that, was there? He'd see for himself if he came in regular.'

'No harm at all. Thank you very much, Mr Kenmore, that is all I have to ask you. No, don't step down for a moment. My friend – ?'

'One question only,' rumbled Halloran coming to his feet. 'I imagine, Mr Kenmore, that it was common knowledge among your customers that the prisoner is an artist.'

'That's right. That's why I didn't think it was odd when this stranger chap asked all those questions.'

'Thank you.' Halloran sat down again.

Maitland was still on his feet. 'If either you, my lord, or Mr Halloran feel it necessary to corroborate Mr Kenmore's evidence, the two barmen are here and can be called to confirm what he says.'

'For myself,' said Conroy, 'I see no reason to doubt what he has told us. Mr Halloran?'

'I see no reason either, my lord. To put it bluntly, none of this evidence seems important enough to require confirmation. Frankly – I am sure your lordship will agree with me – I feel there is some disrespect to the court in this charade being prolonged any longer than is necessary.'

'My sentiments exactly, Mr Halloran,' said the judge cordially. 'Have you any more witnesses, Mr Maitland?'

'Two, my lord.'

'Then get on with it, get on with it,' said the judge testily, and with rather less dignity than usual.

'The first is my client's cousin, Robert Camden.'

The ushers took up the cry, and a few moments later Robert Camden stepped into the court and was directed towards the witness box. Maitland studied him with unashamed interest while he took the oath. A little taller than the accused, and much thinner in the face, but with the same rather startling fairness. His years in Nova Scotia had left their mark, his accent was very pronounced, and Antony was conscious of the first stirring of excitement, and of a very faint hope that perhaps, after all . . .

'Mr Camden,' he said, when the oath-taking was finished, and the witness turned to him inquiringly.

He gave his name and present address and added gratuitously, 'I've been in England only a few weeks, since I left twenty-two years ago.'

'Do you know my client, your cousin Simon Winthrop?'

'I know that must be him there.' He jerked his head in the direction of the dock. 'I'm sorry about all this, of course, but I haven't seen him since he was five years old. When I came over he was already in prison.'

'Then, since you arrived to this country so recently and had never been here before since you were a child, you couldn't have known your grandfather either.'

'I was eight years old when my parents took me to Nova Scotia. I remember fairly well, and of course Mother talked of him often.'

'In the course of these talks did she mention the terms of Mr Wilmot's will?'

For the first time he thought he saw a flicker of uncertainty before the witness answered. 'Of course she did. She'd always said that Grandfather didn't approve of women having money of their own, but all the same I think she was a bit hurt when

237

he wrote and told her about it. But after a while I managed to persuade her to regard it as a sort of family joke, and of course I'd always have looked after her, even if she hadn't re-married. But that isn't what you want to know. I realise that's the only reason you called me, to confirm the fact that Simon and I were the main beneficiaries. Though from what I've read about British trials I can't quite understand why *you* should want that brought out.'

'Perhaps I'm interested in the fact that each of you knew you'd have to share with the other,' said Maitland in a conversational tone. From the corner of his eye he saw a slight movement from Halloran, and went on quickly before he could voice a protest. 'So you arrived here on the twenty-fifth of March, I understand, knowing nothing of your grand-father's death.'

'I'd been out of touch with Mother for a while. To tell you the truth, I wasn't finding it all that easy to get a job, and kept putting off writing to her until I had some better news.'

'That was why you came to England perhaps? Feeling you might find a better market for your talents here.'

'Such as they are,' said Camden modestly. 'But, yes, I did think I might stand a better chance and it was worth trying my luck at any rate.'

'What did you do about getting in touch with your relations here?'

'I didn't know anything about Simon, or where he lived, or what he was doing now, because Mother had stopped writing to the people who had adopted him some time ago.'

'There's always the telephone book,' Maitland murmured, as though in an aside.

'Yes, and of course I should have come to that only I did know Grandfather's address and I knew he could tell me . . . I thought he could tell me where Simon was living. So I went to his house, and his housekeeper told me what had happened and that Simon had been arrested. But she was upset and I didn't like to press her for the details, and I shouldn't have liked to ask Simon's people even if I could have remembered their name. So I thought the best thing was to ask Mrs Barham the name of Grandfather's solicitor, and I went to see him. I know Grandfather was an old man, but it was a shock, you know, and I couldn't just shrug it off without finding out exactly what had been done to him.'

'A very natural impulse,' Maitland said. Nobody could have objected to his tone, except perhaps to the fact that words were drawled and might have been intended as sarcasm.

Robert Camden stood a little straighter, and said rather sharply, 'It was all I could think of to do.'

'The police could have given you the details of the crime,' Antony suggested.

'I didn't want—'

'To get mixed up in anything unpleasant,' Antony concluded the sentence for him.

'If Mr Maitland is going to answer his own witness's questions,' said Halloran, getting up in as much of a hurry as he could manage, 'I really see no point in his having called Mr Camden at all.'

'That wasn't what I was going to say in any case.' There was no doubt about it, the chap had his wits about him and wasn't going to be caught out in a hurry. 'I haven't seen Simon since he was a kid and three years is a big difference when you're as young as that. But I found it hard to believe, I thought the police must be mistaken somehow. I wanted to hear the facts from an unbiased source.'

'I see I should apologize for interrupting you, Mr Camden.' Maitland's tone had acquired a smoothness not completely natural to him. 'And when you had heard the story—?'

'I was desperately sorry, of course, but there seemed to be no doubt about what had happened.'

'Mrs Patmore . . . Patmore is the name of Simon's parents, as you say you have forgotten it. Mrs Patmore has told us that when your aunt and uncle, Rosalie and Peter Winthrop, were killed she wrote to your mother complete details of the accident, and of what had happened to your cousin as the result of it.'

'That's a long time ago. I was ten years old and she just told me they were dead and Simon had gone to live with these other people.'

'You must have remembered your aunt and uncle in the same way that you remembered your grandfather. Yet when you grew older you didn't show the same concern for their fate and ask for more details?'

'Aunt Rosalie was Mother's sister. I didn't want to remind

her of the tragedy.'

'You knew then at least that they had died in some unpleasant way?'

'I knew it upset Mother to talk about it.'

'You know, of course, of your grandfather's fame as a portrait painter,' said Maitland, changing course abruptly. 'Have you inherited any of his talent?'

This time he did get a reaction. To Antony, ever imaginative, it was as though some wild creature had suddenly become aware of threatened danger. He could almost have put words to the question Robert Camden must be asking himself, 'How much does he know? How much can he prove?' Aloud the witness said, after a barely perceptible pause, 'I've done some sketching as a hobby, but I was told quite early in life that I wasn't good enough to make a living that way.'

'You took some lessons?'

'A few.'

'In anatomy perhaps?'

Halloran's voice was booming through the courtroom even before he was fully on his feet. 'My learned friend,' he said, 'is coming perilously close to cross-examining his own witness. May I ask him, my lord, if he is making some accusation against Mr Camden?'

'Are you, Mr Maitland?' asked the judge.

'No, my lord.'

'You would certainly seem to be implying –'

'At this point, my lord, I am neither accusing the witness, not implying that he has been guilty of any wrong-doing.' The next question would take him into deep water, and it might well prove to be more chilly than he liked. 'May I have your lordship's permission to ask Mr Camden to stand down for a moment while we recall Mr Walter Kenmore, the landlord of the King's Head?'

'I don't understand you, Mr Maitland, but I suppose if I refuse you will accuse me of obstructing justice.'

'I hold your lordship in far too much respect,' said Maitland solemnly. Conroy eyed him suspiciously for a moment, and then said, 'Very well,' in a chilly tone.

But once again the formalities were not to be observed. Walter Kenmore was on his feet pointing at the witness and speaking excitedly. 'That's him, me lord,' he said. 'That's the stranger as was asking me about Mr Winthrop. I told you he was an American, didn't I?'

'Mr Maitland!' said Conroy despairingly.

'Yes, my lord. Will you come forward, Mr Kenmore.' Robert Camden was still in the witness box, and looked incapable of movement. 'His lordship has given permission for this further evidence from you,' said Antony to the landlord, 'but I must remind you that the oath you took when you went into the witness box before is still in force.'

'Oath or no oath I'm telling the truth.'

'So long as that is clearly understood. Now, Mr Kenmore, we spoke together of a stranger who had talked at times with my client in your hostelry, and who had previously been . . . shall we say a little curious about him.'

Walter Kenmore used his seemingly favourite expression in reply. 'That's right.'

'Do you identify the man now in the witness box, Robert Camden, as the same man?'

'I'd know him anywhere.'

'You also recognised the way he speaks. He has been living for a long time in Canada, I should tell you, and is not an American, but many Englishmen mistake one accent for the other.'

'Well, it's different from us,' Kenmore insisted. 'But it's the same man, I knew it the moment he opened his mouth.'

'And all that you have told us about his meetings with Simon Winthrop took place before the twenty-fifth of March last?'

'Why, that's only a few weeks ago. This was before the murder, before Mr Winthrop was arrested; he couldn't have talked to him after that.'

'No, Mr Kenmore, thank you, I'm sure we all see your point. Perhaps you will take your place again.' He waited a moment until the landlord had done so, and then turned back to the judge. 'Have I your lordship's permission to continue my examination of Robert Camden?' he asked.

'You have, Mr Maitland,' said Conroy grimly. It was difficult at that moment to know exactly what was in his mind.

Maitland turned back to the man in the witness box. 'Well, Mr Camden?' he said.

'He's mistaken, that's all. I have been in the King's Head, and seen him there since I came over, but that was after Simon's arrest. He's just made a mistake that's all and I can prove it by my passport. It shows I came in on the twenty-fifth as I said, and there are no previous entries.'

'Your Canadian passport, Mr Camden?'

'Yes, of course. My parents took out citizenship after the five years were up, and mine along with theirs.' But he was rattled now, badly rattled, and Maitland's questions began to come a little faster, frankly pressing him, and praying that Halloran would not see fit to intervene again, even when the impropriety of his next remark dawned on Counsel for the Prosecution.

'For your information, Mr Camden, I shall be calling one witness only to follow you. A Miss Freda Parkinson.'

'Freda?' The question was out before Camden realized, and Maitland went on without giving him time to recover himself.

'I see you know the lady.'

'No, I . . . that is I've met her. But you can't believe a word she says, she hates me since we broke up.'

'That seems to imply more than just a casual meeting. When did you know Miss Parkinson? In Canada?' He was so intent on the witness now that it never occurred to him until later to feel surprised that neither Conroy nor Halloran made any attempt to stop him.

'Since I came here.' It almost seemed as if the words were choking him.

'A little over two weeks ago. I think I should congratulate you on being such a fast worker, Mr Camden.'

'I don't know what you mean.'

'You told us she hates you. That implies a certain amount of intimacy . . . don't you think?'

'It's lonely, being in a strange place. I expect I was eager for some companionship.' He paused, and then went on in a rush when the expected question didn't come. 'I tell you I can prove I wasn't here before the twenty-fifth of March. I haven't got my passport on me but—'

'Ah yes, that Canadian passport.'

'It's in my room at the hotel.'

'I'm sure it is, and I'm sure the entries in it will prove to be exactly as you say. But what you forgot to tell us, I think, is that, having been born in England, you would have no

242

difficulty in obtaining a British passport, and I think if we were to make inquiries of the proper authorities we should find that you had indeed done so.'

Wednesday, after the verdict

Inevitably Sir Nicholas and Vera were dining with the Maitlands again. It was really more convenient, because there was no chance there of Gibbs taking it into his head to insist on waiting on them, as he would certainly have done if he had known they wanted privacy. Besides Jenny, from long experience, was always ready for any emergency, and tonight she was so relieved and happy that she would willingly have fed the entire Brigade of Guards if she had been asked to do so, though there might, she said to herself when the thought occurred to her, have been some difficulty in getting them all round the dinner table.

Anyway, Maitland had phoned during the luncheon recess, and she had been able to set the wheels in motion almost in time to prevent any offence on the part of Sir Nicholas's housekeeper, who didn't like to prepare a good meal and see it wasted. Now, with the table laid and Jenny's casserole, augmented by this and that (which Sir Nicholas said sounded sinister) already in the oven, there was nothing more to be done but take it out when it was ready, and they were able to settle round the fire with their drinks and plenty of time to talk before dinner.

Vera, it turned out, had been in court again. 'Right at the back, couldn't possibly have seen me,' she said when Antony asked her. 'Heart in my mouth,' she admitted, 'but thought you did very well. Though how you got away with it, without the judge coming down on you again like a ton of bricks I can't imagine.'

'Perhaps he'd got tired of lecturing me, or perhaps he was just curious,' said Antony, relaxed enough this evening to have taken the chair opposite his uncle's, but still, as they all knew, suffering a little from reaction. 'It would be awfully nice,' he added coaxingly, 'if you were to tell Uncle Nick and Jenny all about it.'

'Just told Nicholas enough to reassure him,' said Vera, who seemed in a particularly elliptical mood that evening. 'Your story,' she added firmly.

Antony resigned himself, but took a moment to think before he started. Anything but a perfectly clear narrative would, he knew, draw adverse comment from his uncle, and it was bad enough having to go through the whole thing again without having to fight every inch of the way. As it was, he achieved his objective fairly well, and proceeded almost without interruption until he reached the point where he had suggested to Robert Camden that it would be quite easy to check with the passport office. 'At that point,' he said, as though he found the memory distasteful, 'the fellow went to pieces. It was an odd thing,' he added thoughtfully, 'that even when he was perfectly confident at the beginning he never denied anything that he realised could be proved.'

'There's one thing that puzzles me, Antony,' said Sir Nicholas. 'You said last night, very properly, that you would make no accusations against this man unless he gave himself away.'

'I didn't exactly—'

'I hesitate to contradict you, but you certainly seem to have gone a great deal farther than I expected.'

'Well, you see, sir, when we talked last night I hadn't heard all that the landlord of the King's Head had to say. He'd never mentioned an American accent before, nobody thought to ask him I suppose, but as soon as he did and then I heard Camden speak . . . nobody over here ever knows the difference, one North American accent or another, it's all the same to them.'

'That seems reasonable,' conceded his uncle. 'You were saying that the fellow went to pieces. What exactly did you mean by that?'

'At that point he just admitted he'd used the British passport about six months ago to come to England, and return to Toronto in time to come back again on the twenty-fifth of March. It was a good idea really, because I don't suppose anyone's meant to hold two, even though if you're English you never lose your nationality. Yes, Uncle Nick, I agree that was another bit of guesswork, but I don't see that it matters either way.'

'And when he had made this admission, what happened

next?' demanded Sir Nicholas.

'Old Conroy took the bit between his teeth,' said Antony.

A pained look crossed his uncle's face. Vera was the only person from whom he would tolerate slang without at least a silent protest. 'I suppose by that you mean that he took control of proceedings which showed every sign of getting out of hand,' he said frigidly. 'As is only too common, I know to my cost, when you are involved.'

'Yes,' Antony agreed, 'I meant exactly that. He ordered Camden out of the witness box, with strict instructions not to leave the court, and said with a rather nasty look in my direction that presently he would require some explanation from me, but that first he thought we should hear what the witness I'd referred to, Miss Freda Parkinson, had to say. So we called her, and she came up to proof beautifully. Well, no, that isn't exactly right, because when Geoffrey talked to her before she was anything but forthcoming.'

'Oath may have scared her. Does sometimes,' Vera suggested.

'So it does. Anyway, however it was she made it clear that Robert Camden had made an excuse to get to know her. She was very vague about dates, but seemed to think it might have been about five months ago. He was calling himself Robert Carleton, but she identified him readily enough. Their friendship had proceeded rapidly and she thought they had an understanding, but then suddenly he disappeared and the people at the place where he'd been living didn't know where he'd gone. She knew Madeleine, of course, and she'd met Simon, so Camden didn't even have the trouble of bringing the subject round in some devious way. She said to him on the second or third date that he was ever so like her friend's fiancé, and from there had gone on to give him every scrap of information Madeleine had ever let fall about his cousin, and that was that, except that she'd made the telephone call about the key, thinking it was part of a rather elaborate joke, and Halloran, I think, was too eager to hear what I had to say for myself to detain her, so I was left with my explanations to make under the disapproving eye of the judge.'

'I know you hate explanations, Antony,' said Jenny, 'but Uncle Nick and I are just as curious as you say Mr Halloran was.'

'I know, love, and I'm going to tell you, but don't be surprised, Vera, if what I say now varies a little from what I said in court. A few things that Robert Camden came out with later are mixed up in it.'

'Shan't interrupt,' Vera promised, 'though I can't, of course, speak for Nicholas.'

'I know you can't,' said Antony, 'Nobody could, especially as I've no intention of trying to put things particularly formally.' He paused for comment, but his uncle was silent. 'I think that some time or another Robert Camden was told by his mother exactly what had happened to his aunt and uncle and cousin Simon, and at the same time, or later, heard something of Mrs Patmore's comments on her adopted son's health. He could get information from any library about the possible results of such an experience, though I daresay it didn't occur to him to do so until the idea of getting the whole of his grandfather's estate for himself began to form in his mind. That may not have been until after he left the Montreal firm because he didn't like living in the province of Québec, and then found difficulty in getting another job, or he may have talked about it with his step-father, who was a doctor. It would have been quite a natural thing to do. However it was, he was unmarried, he had savings (we confirmed this later, Uncle Nick, I'm not just making it up) so the trip to London was a distinct possibility. Any telephone book would give him his cousin's address, it wouldn't be difficult after that to discover a good deal about his habits, the fact that he frequented the King's Head, for instance, and that he was engaged to Madeleine Rexford. Mark Benson didn't mention it in court, Vera, but you may remember Kenmore said he often brought a girl to the pub with him, so that it's quite possible there was some gossip about that too, which gave Camden the idea of blackmailing him and using Simon's name.'

'Must be what happened, I should think,' Vera agreed.

'But that was later. First Camden picked up Freda Parkinson, on the off chance that she knew Madeleine, and it turned out that she did and that she was a chatter-box only too willing to talk about anything and everything. Then he talked to Walter Kenmore at the King's Head, and what he was told confirmed what he'd come to believe about Winthrop's occasional amnesia. So one day he took his courage in his hands and went up to

247

talk to Simon. After all, if he'd been his normal self that day no harm would have been done. Again I'm going to quote him, he said he even went so far as to introduce himself as a cousin from Canada, and Simon seemed pleased to see him but obviously didn't know who he was or even that he had any relations. After that he learned to recognize for himself when Simon was normal and when he was in a state of amnesia. But before that, I imagine, he began to put his plan into operation.'

'You said once you didn't think he had any idea of mixing people up with the suggestion that Mr Winthrop might be suffering from multiple personality disorder,' Sir Nicholas reminded him.

'No, Uncle Nick, I don't think that came into it at all. I think he wanted two things, no, three. First, that the murder should be committed when he was demonstrably out of the country. Secondly, that it must be done on an evening when Simon had no alibi. Thirdly, that so many disreputable facts would come to light as to make even Simon's nearest and dearest doubt him, and that, along with his very strong motive, would almost force the police to suspect him. I don't know how Camden intended to bring these so-called facts before them, perhaps by means of anonymous letters, perhaps by anonymous telephone calls. It doesn't matter now. He was seen that night by three people, and all of them quite innocently identified Simon Winthrop as the man they had seen. As for all the other things that came to light, it was almost accidental that they did and caused a great deal of confusion. I daresay he kicked himself for having evolved such a complicated plot when after all it turned out to be so easy. Three positive identifications along with the motive was enough to damn any man. All he had to do was sit back and wait, and keep well out of Freda Parkinson's way, and never go to the King's Head again.'

'To take your three points,' said Sir Nicholas thoughtfully. 'He dealt with the first by the trick with the passports, and with the second by leaving that newspaper cutting in his cousin's studio, using the key which Miss Parkinson had arranged to make available to him. I suppose he had a duplicate cut.'

'Yes, Uncle Nick, he did. And of course he didn't know if the trick would work, but if it didn't he could always try again.

248

I said he'd got used to how his cousin looked when he'd retreated from reality, as Dr Macintyre would put it, and when he saw him leave the house that evening he was pretty sure he was in a state of amnesia. He said later he'd followed him for a little, to make sure he didn't go to see Madeleine, for instance, or to the King's Head, or anywhere else where he might have been known. But when he was pretty sure Simon was just walking around aimlessly he went straight to his grandfather's house, let himself in, and killed him.'

'You're missing quite a lot out there, Antony. He had no key to his grandfather's house . . . or had he obtained that one also by subterfuge?'

'No, you'll remember the police found the door unlatched. I think he phoned his grandfather, introduced himself, and asked if he might go round to see him. This was probably not long before the actual visit, which would account for Mr Wilmot not saying anything about it to his housekeeper. Instead he put the latch up, to save her the trouble of having to answer the bell, and waited for this new grandson of his to turn up.'

'Camden couldn't have relied on that.'

'He said he had a story ready, something about not wanting the Patmores to know he was in England because Mrs Patmore and his mother had fallen out. But he didn't need to use it, Mr Wilmot told him the door would be open and he should walk straight in.'

'And the dagger that was used? From what you say Camden couldn't have counted on finding it so near to hand.'

'I don't think that's a difficulty, sir. He may have gone prepared, and then thought it better to make use of something that was already there, something that couldn't possibly be traced to him.'

'One more discrepancy—'

'Only one?'

'Only one that I can think of at the moment, because I take it I am right in thinking that it was through the step-father you mentioned that Camden obtained the knowledge that enabled him to arrange Antonia Dryden's abortion. It concerns your third point really. He had planted all his clues, you say, to blacken his cousin's character, but decided not to use them when the flood of identifications made them unnecessary. Yet he took the chance of going back to the studio to plant that note from Mark Benson.'

'I think that was a bit of mistiming, he didn't want to risk drawing attention to himself by any of this anonymous letter business, but he thought the police might as well find the note and the paintings – which really were rather devilish, Uncle Nick – for themselves. As it happened they'd already made their search when he left the note, and dusting the desk in case he'd left any fingerprints was a real mistake, though unless someone was already suspicious I don't suppose they'd have either noticed or commented on it.'

'That only leaves the identifications then.'

'Uncle Nick, when it came to the point that was the easiest thing of all. Everyone knows the stories of mistakes that have happened in that line. The Alfords identified Simon Winthrop in good faith, the only man with that exact degree of fairness in the identification parade they were shown. You can't blame the police, I'm sure they did their best to produce reasonable facsimiles, but it isn't easy. Mr and Mrs Alford had never seen Robert Camden, and though seen side by side they're by no means identical, there's enough of a likeness between the cousins to have confused them.'

'And Mrs Barham?'

'You remember she said she'd only got a glimpse of the man leaving the house. I pressed her to tell us exactly how she identified him as Simon, and she mentioned his hair, shape of his head, the set of his shoulders, the way he moved. In all these ways, when you come right down to it, there's a remarkable resemblance between the two cousins. She couldn't be expected to notice the slight difference in height, and as she never saw the man leaving the house full face she couldn't be expected to notice either that Robert's face is thinner. If you remember she said she only saw a little of his cheek. I think if Conroy had asked her she wouldn't have been able to say even now for sure which of them it was she'd seen, but it never came to that.' He paused, glancing from one to the other of his listeners, and Jenny rose and fetched the decanter to refill their glasses. 'Thanks, Jenny love,' said her husband when she reached his side, and looked up at her for a moment as though the sight of her might give him strength for what he was going to say. 'I don't much like thinking about it,' he confessed, 'it wasn't a pretty scene. Robert Camden just went to pieces . . .

did I say that before? And when you can only help one person by condemning another – '

'Simon Winthrop was your responsibility, not his cousin,' Sir Nicholas reminded him.

'Yes, Uncle Nick, I know. And now I've unburdened myself I should forget the whole thing, is that it?'

'Except that there's one thing I still don't understand,' said Jenny. She replaced the decanter and came back to the circle round the fire. 'Mrs Barham was answering the bell when she went into the hall and then into the study and found Mr Wilmot dead. What on earth possessed this Camden man to ring it, did he want to be seen, did he expect her to mistake him for his cousin?'

'No, that was just a bit of luck for him. Temporary luck, if you like to put it that way. He wanted his grandfather's body to be discovered immediately, so that there'd be a good chance of the doctor fixing the time of death pretty exactly, as in fact he was able to do. The thing was you see, love, he knew Simon had lost his memory but he couldn't have known how long that state would last. He might recover at any moment, and if he'd gone somewhere where he'd be recognized it would have spoiled the whole thing. Camden wanted the whole of his grandfather's money, remember, not just half.'

'Yes, I see. And now, I suppose, it will be the other way round. But Uncle Nick's right, Antony, anything's better than that an innocent man should go to prison. Or to a lunatic asylum, which might very well have happened.'

'I know, love, but – ' He broke off and sat looking at her, and for a while there was a dead silence in the room. Jenny returned his look serenely and after a while he smiled at her. 'I gave you a bad time,' he said, 'but I expect as usual you've forgiven me.'

'You gave your aunt and me what you call a bad time,' said Sir Nicholas before Jenny could replay. 'That, I suppose, is not worth mentioning.'

'I'm sorry,' said Maitland meekly. His eyes were dancing now as though, for the moment at least, his misgivings had departed.

'I take it then,' said his uncle, 'that there is nothing more to fear on the lines of our discussion last night.'

'Nothing at all, Uncle Nick. Camden admitted planting the

251

letter and the newspaper cutting. It went against the grain, but old Conroy even congratulated me when it was all over for what he called rather pompously my zealous pursuit of the truth.'

'You surprise me,' said Sir Nicholas dryly.

'Perhaps his spirit was broken, after all,' said Maitland irrepressibly.

'I doubt it. And Halloran?'

'He was his usual generous self to an opponent. As a matter of fact he used that same phrase, that I'd given him a bad time, which coming from him I didn't quite understand.'

'I expect he was afraid you'd taken leave of your senses,' his uncle told him. 'Well, Antony, I hope you realise that you and this unfortunate client of yours –'

'Not so unfortunate after all, Uncle Nick. The judge directed the jury to acquit him without even leaving the box.'

'That I could have deduced for myself, even if Vera hadn't already told me.' It was never really wise to interrupt Sir Nicholas, and quite useless when he was determined on having his own say. 'As I was remarking, you have both had a very fortunate escape, which, on your part at least, was completely undeserved. You should never have taken such a chance.'

'It worked, Uncle Nick,' Maitland pointed out mildly. 'You're only annoyed because you didn't think of that passport dodge yourself.'

'I do not claim your own familiarity with the criminal mind,' said Sir Nicholas, in his most dampening tone. 'Have you given any thought to Winthrop's future?'

'Mrs Patmore kidnapped him and took him home with her.'

'I meant, as I think you know, as regards his mental stability.'

'Dr Macintyre will look after that. No, Uncle Nick,' he added, forestalling Sir Nicholas's obvious intention of commenting on this statement. 'I haven't changed my opinion, I still think psychiatry is for the birds.' (His uncle moaned faintly, but refrained from any more explicit criticism.) 'But when it comes to common sense I think Macintyre has got Simon's measure, *and* his confidence, which is perhaps more important. If you'd seen them in court –'

'From the description that has been given me, I can only say, thank heaven I did not,' said Sir Nicholas devoutly.

'Take it you foresee a happy ending there,' Vera put in quickly.

'Yes, I do.' He paused to smile again at Jenny. 'It really will be all right,' he assured her.

'In that case,' said Sir Nicholas, 'there is nothing more I can say.'

Maitland exchanged a despairing glance with the others. In this at least, as they all realized, Sir Nicholas was very far from accurate. And indeed it was only a quarter of an hour later, when he at last ran out of remarks on his nephew's foolhardiness, that Jenny was able to escape to the kitchen and avoid any further inspired remarks on the subject by bringing her casserole to the table. For some obscure reason, though legal shop was permitted at Saturday lunchtime it was strictly forbidden at dinner, a veto which Sir Nicholas very rarely allowed to be disregarded.

To everyone's relief this was not one of those occasions.